KID CALVERT

The Complete Series

Kid CALVERT

THE COMPLETE SERIES
by CLINT DOUGLAS & PHIL RICHARDS

INTRODUCTION BY
WILL MURRAY

COVER BY

TOM LOVELL

ALTUS PRESS

2015

EDITED AND DESIGNED BY

Matthew Moring

PUBLISHING HISTORY

"Introduction" appears here for the first time. Copyright © 2015 Will Murray. All rights reserved.

"Owl-Hoot Horde" originally appeared in the November 1934 issue of *Western Aces* magazine (Vol. 1, No. 1).

"Horde of Hated Men" originally appeared in the February 1935 issue of *Western Aces* magazine (Vol. 1, No. 4).

"Hell's Recruit" originally appeared in the March 1935 issue of *Western Aces* magazine (Vol. 2, No. 1).

"Señorita Death" originally appeared in the April 1935 issue of *Western Aces* magazine (Vol. 2 No. 2).

"The Hell-Born Clan" originally appeared in the August 1935 issue of *Western Aces* magazine (Vol. 3, No. 2).

The cover artwork originally appeared in the March 1936 issue of *Star Western* magazine (Vol. 8, No. 2). Copyright © 1936 by Popular Publications, Inc. Copyright renewed © 1963 and assigned to Steeger Properties, LLC. All rights reserved.

THANKS TO

Chad Calkins, Joel Frieman, Will Murray and Ray Riethmeier

CONTENTS

T HE SHORT saga of Kid Calvert is the tale of a pulp
Western hero who had his magazine shot out from under
him before he could saddle up.

What we know about the origins of this fighting fugitive in
the mold of Billy the Kid can be found in an obscure writer's
magazine called *Writer's Review*.

From its October, 1934 issue's Major Markets column, we
have this:

> Magazine Publishers, at 67 West 44th St. New York, pub-
> lishers of *Western Trails, Ten Detective Aces, Sky Birds*, and *Fly-
> ing Aces*, are also in the western magazine bandwagon, soon to
> bring out a new western with a lead feature by a house name
> and a few scattered shorts by any writer who can click with
> rip-roaring stuff. Lawrence A. Keating is doing the feature,
> but not under his own name. John A. Saxon turned down the
> opportunity. He said he'd write as Saxon or not at all.

Western pulps were booming in '34. Martin Goodman had
launched *The Masked Rider Western*, while Street & Smith's *Pete
Rice* had been going for a year by this point.

Yet no Western hero pulp ever emerged from A.A. Wyn's
Magazine Publishers, later known as Ace. In fact, he issued no
hero pulps at all, leaving that market to his wife, Rose, whose
Periodical House was responsible for *Secret Agent "X"* and the
short-lived *Captain Hazzard*.

However, Wyn did release *Western Aces* with a November,

1934 cover date. But it was an attempt to duplicate the success of Popular Publications' *Dime Western Magazine,* which pioneered the mature pulp western tale, and was not a showcase for a single action character. *Western Aces* ran short stories and novelettes, not novels.

So what happened? Evidently, Magazine Publishers gears up to publish their new Western hero pulp and for some reason, they develop a sudden case of cold feet.

A clue might be found in the Major Markets column in the December, 1934 issue:

> Three months ago everybody and his uncle was shouting "Detectives are down, the western story is the thing."
> For a while westerns outsold detective pulps, with a half dozen new western magazines started overnight. But suddenly the taste has reverted to its old love—and westerns are second.

One of those new Western titles was Popular Publications' *Mavericks,* which featured a posse of Robin Hood-inspired owl-hoots. Thomas Mount wrote the series as Kent Thorn. Begun just a few months before, Popular was folding it around the time Wyn was poised to launch his new book. It could be that the cancellation of *Mavericks* alone was the cause of Wyn's cold feet.

So what happened to Lawrence A. Keating's Western hero?

The thing about putting together a pulp puzzle is not the pieces you have, but the pieces you don't even suspect exist.

There was one giant piece of the puzzle I didn't have. And that was a copy of *Western Aces* #1, November, 1934.

I spotted a huge clue after I looked into that magazine. On the cover was emblazoned the rawhide name of Clint Douglas, which I recognized as an Ace house name of long standing. You don't need psychic powers to know that a house name could mean a house-name series, so a hard look at *Western Aces* was in order.

Digging further, I learned that *Western Aces* #1 featured a 31-page "novel" (which actually constitutes a novelette) called "Owl-Hoot Horde," featuring a buckaroo called Kid Calvert. It was buried in the middle of the book, between stories by R. Craig Christensen, Ralph Condon, Garrison K. Rumford writing as Kingsley Moses, and Les Rivers, who was really Clyde A. Warden.

Kid Calvert was the 22-year-old son of Gunner Calvert, boss of a wild bunch of semi-outlaws known far and wide as the Calvert Horde. When his father is killed, Kid Calvert takes over his father's band, which includes the likes of Giant Anderson, Nate Willstock, Dandy McLain, Grama Sinton, Arizona Al and many others. The setting appears to be either Utah or Nevada. The Kid—no first name is given—rides a black stallion dubbed Star.

Interesting complications ensue when Sheriff Mart Reynolds is murdered and the Calvert Horde is falsely blamed. For under an assumed name, Kid Calvert falls in love with the sheriff's daughter, Terry, not knowing her true paternity. When the truth comes out, Terry has taken to wearing her father's star as sheriff-elect and is looking to gun down or hang high the fugitive Kid. The two heartbroken lovers realize that they are now sworn enemies.

Notice the general resemblance to Popular's short-lived *Mavericks*. Sure sounds to me like Kid Calvert was Wyn's attempt to jump on a bandwagon whose wheels were going bust just as he was hitching up his team.

The editor promised more Kid Calvert yarns in future issues. That made it a series. Yet the Kid was conspicuously absent from the next two issues. I asked around and discovered the February, 1935 issue featured another Kid Calvert tale called "Horde of Doomed Men." Here the byline was not Clint Douglas, but Phil Richards, a name I didn't recognize, and presumed to be yet another Ace house name.

It turned out that Richards was a real writer, full name Phil

Macleod Richards. Under house names like Nelse Anderson and Frank J. Litchfield, he was writing for *Wild West Weekly* about this time.

Little is known of Richards, but thanks for Mort Weisinger, we have this:

"Two other pulp writers, Albert Richard Wetjen, who also sells many of his stories to the large national weeklies, and Philip Richards, write by touch system in the dark. Why Richards likes to write in the dark I do not know, but Mr. Wetjen once explained that he started writing while living alone in a shack near Salem, Ore. He worked outdoors every day and his only illumination in the place was a smoky oil-lamp. His imagination seems to function best, he says, in semidarkness."

Since this anecdote dates to 1934, we have to assume that Richards' Kid Calvert yarns were composed in similar circumstances!

With a new writer in the saddle, Kid Calvert settled down to appearing every month until the April issue. Each story was cover-featured as a new "Kid Calvert" novel, indicating he was a star. But once L.L. Foreman's Preacher Devlin stories began running monthly, the Kid fell out of favor. After skipping May through July, a final Kid Calvert installment, "The Hell-Born Clan," ran in the August issue. After five bullet-torn installments, that appears to close the books on the ill-starred Kid Calvert. Preacher Devlin, on the other hand, ran clear into the late 1940s, after jumping over to Street & Smith's *Western Story Magazine.*

As for the backstory, what seems to have happened was this: On the verge of releasing his new Western single-hero pulp, publisher Aaron Wyn (a former Wyoming cow-poke known to intimates as Art) changed his mind before going to press. I can't believe he was about to release a *Kid Calvert Western Magazine,* but you never know. It's not a terrible name for a hero responsible for carrying of his own title, it just doesn't sing. Then again, *Pete Rice* doesn't sound like much, and he ran for three solid years. Maybe he planned to call it *Owl-Hoots* or something else similar to *Mavericks*.

Whatever the original title, Wyn replates the cover, renaming it *Western Aces*, has the lead novel cut by anywhere from a third to a half, and loads up the rest of the book with more mature *Dime Western*-style oaters.

Author Lawrence A. Keating, his money horse shot out from under him, abandons the drygulched series, a year later landing upright in the saddle of a new stallion named Flash Steele, a roving Arizona Ranger, which he rides happily for two rollicking years in the pages of Teck's *Wild West Novels and Complete Magazine*. Wyn recruits Phil Richards to continue Kid Calvert, who doesn't catch on with readers, and is soon abandoned.

Coincidentally or not, a month later, Flash Steele debuts in "The Trigger Boss," in the September, 1935 *Wild West Stories and Complete Magazine*, the month after Kid Calvert hits the sunset trail for the last time.

I should mention that stylistically, the first Kid Calvert yarn smacks of Keating's style. It's not as juvenile as Flash Steele, but pet stylistic phrases like lobos and likening mounted cowboys to Cossacks do show up in "Owl-Hoot Horde." The story also opens up in the Panther Mountains—the same setting as the Flash Steele story, "Colt Showdown," which features a villain named Gunner Logan. Obviously, Keating was a lazy cow-poke when it came to coining character names, not to mention places.

So there you have it: the story of a hero pulp that never got properly off the ground and the lone writer who launched not one, but two Western series worth knowing about. And a new reason for pulp collectors to take a second look at both *Wild West Stories* and *Western Aces*.

The one thing I'd really like to know is this: Why did the byline change on the Kid Calvert stories? It was obviously a house-owned series. What possible reason was there to drop a cowboy byline like Clint Douglas for mild-sounding Phil Richards?

I will leave that for others to speculate over. But in the pages that follow are the complete exploits of Kid Calvert and his hard-riding horde, all previously uncollected, and gathered together for the first time.

OWL-HOOT HORDE

The Kid was brought up in Gunner Calvert's Horde. He knew these long-riders as his father's friends, his own friends. And they taught him the miracles of rope and gun. But the Kid didn't know the other side of the owl-hoot trail—the relentless hatred of the law, and its followers. He was to learn that hatred—learn it from one he loved. For a girl had sworn an oath to get the Calverts.

I

THE SUN was gone behind the ragged peaks of the Panther Mountains but the brown carpet of the valley below still lay dimly visible in twilight to the owl-hoot band that lurked on the timbered hill.

Nineteen there were in all; nineteen chosen and led by old Gunner Calvert, as sagacious a veteran of back trails as ever carried oiled Colts in thonged holsters. Keen-eyed and experienced, superbly mounted, ill-dressed but well armed, they comprised the nondescript crew whose exploits and daring had made them notorious from Peace River in Canada to the Rio, muddy and twisting under the wide blue skies of the south.

Calvert's Horde, enemies called these beyond-the-law defenders of true justice—men of all ages and temperaments from the two hundred and forty-pound Swede known as the Giant to pint-size Dandy McLain, the flowery-vested gambler. But the Horde had friends, too, in shabby shacks and on small ranches throughout the West. Friends who murmured prayers for their safe keeping though often other folk reviled them.

Gunner and his men had need of prayers this night.

Under mountain ash branches heavy with clumps of yellow berries the men looked to their equipment. One adjusted a cinch, another a headstall strap, and a third shifted cartridges to handier front loops in his belt. There was a guarded hum of talk as they mingled and worked—no mention of the action that perhaps lay ahead, but jocular badinage about poker and

Terry swung her gun
to cover Kid Calvert.

appetites and laziness. Yet under surface raillery there was tension. The likelihood was strong that by midnight or early tomorrow some of their number would be resting in unmarked, unvisited, uncared-for graves.

Apart from the men, standing on a knoll, Gunner Calvert was alone. His spade chin and tight, narrow mouth were painted luminous by the light of the moon fast rising out of the east. The upper part of his face was shadowed under the floppy brim of a sweat-stained sombrero. Calvert gazed on the Diamond-X Ranch below, and ran his piercing eyes up the ribbon of road that went to the cowtown of Deadline. Then to the left where, a mile away, massed steers milled restlessly in the charge of a lone cowpuncher.

There was no sign yet of the law. Mayhap Sheriff Mart Reynolds would not undertake the devil's own work men plotted for him in the town of Deadline?

At sound of some one climbing to his side, Gunner turned. Tall, Kid Calvert had the strong features of his father without the spraying wrinkles of age. They were fifty and twenty-two, both straight, firm-lipped, slender, and muscle-hard. The Kid had an excited, eager way about him as he came.

"Stoner's comin'! He's comin' with the law—Sheriff Reynolds and a crowd, every man loaded for bear! They're headin' for Ed Ryan's spread, so it sure means a fight now. And we'll fight!" the Kid breathed, his eyes aglow. "We'll stop those hellions, crush 'em, wipe 'em into grease! And we'll do it quick!"

CALVERT RESPONDED nothing at once. There was sudden heaviness in his heart and tiny muscles in his face went tighter. It was the worst then, an open clash at last with the law in this county in which he had always avoided any clash, for a reason. He peered into the eager face of his son. "Kid, yuh sure? Yuh know Mart Reynolds is headin' for Ryan's spread?"

"Giant come in with it. There's no mistake, Dad. Mike Stoner is out to nail Ryan's hide to his barn door, to ruin him. For two days he's belly-ached for the sheriff to serve that court levy, the judgment for damages. And Reynolds is goin' to do it tonight.

"It means takin' all Ryan has and askin' more. He's just small fry to a steer grabber like Stoner. Ryan ain't got the ghost of a chance without us. But with us—" He left off. His hand closed over the cool gun-butt on his thigh and iron biceps under his sleeves twitched with the power that was in them. Cossack reckless, the Kid zested for the tussle over the small rancher's property—and perhaps his life as well, and the lives of Ryan's wife and child.

Then he realized Gunner was not sharing his impetuous anticipation, and scowled questioningly. It was something in his father's mien and his silence as they stood face to face in the twilight, overlooking the valley.

"What's the matter? The boys are set. We can't waste time if we're still to get down there ahead of 'em!"

Still the older man did not move. His heart felt heavier. He was thinking what this meant—more than the Kid could realize in his youthful lust for the excitement of a fight. It was a grim, deadly, bitter business to try balking the law, and Gunner Calvert knew that. He had learned over the outtrail years. And tonight especially he hated balking Sheriff Mart Reynolds.

He lifted a hand to his son's shoulder as a man gentles a stallion pawing with eagerness for a mad race over bunchy sage. "Well, it's come, then, and all out o' greed. Mike Stoner's greed to make his place bigger and richer, to grab and grab. And Mart Reynolds in it. They blinded him, damn them! Yuh ever see

Justice carved over a court house door? With scales in her hand and a bandage over her eyes? In a way of speakin', son, Mart Reynolds is blindfolded now just like that. Stoner managed it, with Reynolds' deputy. Yeah, with their rotten judgment for damages from court!"

His bitterness rang responsive chords inside the Kid. He swallowed and scowled, and moved with lingering impatience to be gone.

"Yes, it started over water. Stoner and his crowd have gobbled other spreads, Dad, workin' any way they can, mortgages, grabbin' steers at roundup, hirin' men away. Bothered Ryan until he blazed up and shot a Stoner waddie. Then war. Ed blocks the creek and Stoner hires a slick lawyer and goes to a judge whose note he holds. I know all that, Dad. But what do you mean about Sheriff Reynolds?"

Gunner passed a hand over his forehead, then glanced wearily at his son. His eyes measured the Kid from scuffed boot toes to the dented crown of his hat. What he saw was all man, and Calvert felt pride warm his veins. But he was troubled because the Kid did not comprehend all that the rolling years had taught him.

"STONER'S ALL skunk like yuh say," he began slowly. "No, I never worried about a sheriff before, but son, Reynolds is different. There never was a minute in Reynolds' life he meant to be anythin' but just. You and I and the gang are wanted, and I hate the law for the way crooks use it to wreck honest men. The way it backs gents like Mike Stoner against small fry like Ed Ryan. Well, Mart Reynolds and me ride different trails but maybe we're aimin' for the same night-camp after all. Reynolds never was the kind to crush the weak 'cause the strong wanted him to. Somebody roped him into this job. Stoner, I reckon. Deputy Quill, and talk around town about doin' his duty. Reynolds finally had to act and no more buts.

"I've side-stepped clashin' with Reynolds up to now. But," he waved vaguely with his hand, "I reckon it's come. I promised

Ryan I'd take care of him and I never yet went back on my word. But I'm sorry to go up against Reynolds, because he's always done his own thinkin'.... Look there!" Gunner exclaimed, pointing.

Faintly seen in the darkening night a cloud of dust rolled down the road from Deadline toward the one-story chinked log home of the Ryans squatting in the valley below. Twenty-five horsemen there were, possibly more.

Both Calverts watched intently. They saw the straggling knot divide. One group of men swept toward the range dip, heading where the Diamond X steers were held bunched a mile beyond. The second group turned up the rutty lane to the house and surrounded it.

A low whistle floated through the grove of mountain ash with the effect of a bugle call to arms. While Gunner Calvert and the Kid stumbled hurriedly for their horses there was a series of muffled grunts among the trees. Riders appeared, silent, grim-jawed, ready for the struggle.

"Kid!" The old man forked his big roan and heeled it toward his son. "Don't let the boys kill where it ain't necessary. Yore job tonight is to see Ryan safe, and his wife and his girl. Yuh handle the house. When yuh get clear, come an' make shore we're doin' all right with the stock. If things don't work out, we meet in the gully yonder, at the two pines."

The other nodded. He turned in his saddle. "Come on, boys."

Seven of the waiting band detached themselves to spur in his wake. Gunner Calvert led the remainder. They went down the slope of the hill separately and with ever-widening space between. Winding among the solemn, sleeping trees they rode with reckless haste for the flat land.

There was a shot. Then another. As he swept through a brief clearing Kid Calvert saw two quick-answering tongues of flame from the windows of the ranch-house.

The shots rang through the night with staccato, snarling barks. There came a swift rattle of them, then a lull broken only by the throaty roar of a Winchester. The seven men pressed close behind Kid Calvert and they swept out onto flat range. They streaked for the house in single file, like Cossacks riding to reckless death.

GUNNER CALVERT led his ten men northward toward the steers. They were lost to the Kid in the vague silver light of the rising moon. Glancing around he found the great bulk of the Giant astride a massive sorrel almost nose-at-flank to Star. Behind trailed the others, their horses drumming a rattly tattoo on the hard loam. The Giant always trailed young Calvert that close. He was like a bulky shadow wherever the Kid would permit him to follow.

The Kid's carbine came high and he fired into the air. It was a signal the others saw and heard. Yells burst from their throats. They wheeled and rushed the crouching men who formed an inner circle around the Diamond X headquarters, crawling nearer while indoors, Ryan dashed frantically from window to window in futile effort to hold back the emissaries of the law.

Abruptly firing turned on the new attackers. *Wham! Crash!* Some one yelled, "Calvert's Horde!"

There was a scream that rose above the thunder of hoofs, and then raucous oaths. A man pitched full length and lay still. Kid Calvert's teeth clenched. For above the hammer head of his racing stallion he saw fire burst out, a long tongue of it, from the roof of the cookshed of Ryan's cabin. Stoner or one of his tools had set fire to the place.

Some one rose blackly in Calvert's path. His stallion reared in fright. There was a growled, malevolent curse, then the roar of a forty-five. The Kid was sliding off the broad flanks of his horse; he landed on his feet clutching the carbine. But the hurtling lead clipped his sombrero and wrenched it back from a sweaty forehead, part of its brim shot away. Next instant the Kid lunged like a greased streak as another shot snarled at him.

He stepped in a hole and lost balance. His carbine spilled,

but the bullet whizzed overhead and he was unhurt. A Colt leaped into his right hand and he charged again.

He wanted to avoid a killing. But the other did not. The lawman's gun thundered a third time and the Kid twisted with the tug of the bullet ploughing his shirt. Then the Kid closed in.

They melted into one black figure, panting, jabbing, swaying. Calvert had the posseman's gun wrist in a locked grip of iron. The weapon there blazed skyward. Then came a snap of bone, a shriek of fury and of pain, and the Kid stepped clear of the falling body. As he moved, his six-gun swept down. It pounded a glancing blow off the skull, and the man was insensible.

Calvert flashed an encompassing glance around. The ranch-house cracked redly, its flames fighting higher and higher into the evening sky. Twenty yards to his right the great brute strength of the Giant easily overpowered a fellow in leather chaps and cast him aside like a broken match stick. Growls rumbled from the vast chest of Swede Anderson as he rushed nearer the house.

Back a mile and more, there was the growl of heavier shooting. Steers on the run made the ground tremble; and in that split-second halt to learn how the battle went, Kid Calvert knew the herd was beginning a mad stampede.

That was right. Gunner had a hiding place for the steers.

His face tightened. He saw a woman topple screaming out a side window of the ranch-house. She sprang to her feet, leaned on the sill and drew back with a child in her arms, a child of seven with flaxen hair over its face, wild-eyed numb with fear. Then the Kid spied a bow-legged hombre twist around the corner of the building. He bawled a hoarse shout. The woman turned to stagger in flight with her burden. Coming after, the man raised his arm, and gun-steel shone.

ANGER GRIPPED Kid Calvert. He slammed out two shots. The bow-legged hombre stumbled and slapped his face on the ground, and lay still.

Out of the window the woman and child had come, pelted a man—Ed Ryan, owner of the Diamond X. His hair was singed off. His eyes staring with the bulge of a man half insane. Wisps of smoke curled from his charred shirt and trousers. He had glimpsed the attempted killing of his wife but he could not have helped, just pitching into lung-sought night air.

He saw Kid Calvert and lurched drunkenly toward him. On both sides and beyond the house the posse crowd were beaten. Calvert's Horde had lost Sonora Charlie. But they had the law masqueraders on the run here.

"Ryan!" the Kid panted, grabbing the man's shoulder. He dragged him the few feet to the woman who had stumbled and lay sobbing hysterically as she held her child close. "Ryan, *get what I say!*"

He lifted his wife, took the child in his arms, and stood gulping fresh air into his smoke-stinging lungs.

"Get into the hills. Head south for Prairie Flats. Wait there. It may be a week. Two weeks, a month! Wait for a package at General Delivery. There'll be one for you, Ryan! It'll be proceeds from yore beef. *All* the proceeds—so yuh can start over!"

The man's jaw dropped. He scarcely grasped it.

"Proceeds from yore beef—General Delivery, Prairie Flats—a week to a month! Don't talk about it. Don't show the money when yuh get in. But yuh will, Ryan. You hear me? Yuh'll get it!"

He thrust two fingers between his lips for a scream-like whistle. Calvert stepped to the woman huddling against her husband and again repeated his instructions. She nodded, trembling. As it seemed to sink into her consciousness, what his words meant, she stretched her hand out to him and leaned.

"Who?" she quavered thankfully. "Who are—you?"

"Nobody much. We're men the law wants to cut down. Men that want yuh to get a square deal. Giant!" he yelled as the big Swede trotted up leading two horses. "Help 'em aboard. Easy!"

Anderson halted and stooped. He swept the woman off her

feet and with the ease of a man lifting a stick, placed her in the saddle of the first horse. The Giant next took up the whining, crying child. There was a soft expression on the face of the Swede, a look of such tenderness as is given only to strong men. Then he turned to Ryan and helped him mount the second horse.

"Adios!" Calvert cried, as they wheeled and went off.

The fighting broke out anew as the enemy gathered routed forces. The Kid saw there was yet work a-plenty on his hands and that he might still lose out on part of his mission.

A black horse with ears laid flat forged out of moonlight, streaking across the range. Its rider tightened the reins and the horse's legs went stiff as poles. Giant Anderson was first to the man before Calvert could reach him to hear the message. Giant and the fellow exchanged short, crisp words. The Swede stiffened and fell back as if struck. The Kid ran up just then.

"They drygulched us, Kid! There was another crowd up the cut! Yuh got to pull out, and damned *pronto.* That's orders. Yuh got—"

"Pull out!" Kid snarled the words incredulously. "Pull out, hell! Our crowd never pulls out, Lefty. Gunner never gave such an order in all his life! Come on, boys, we—"

The man grabbed his arm. "Yuh—yuh got to! And fast, Kid—yuh got to! Let it all go. Everybody ride for the hills. The sheriff's been kilt!"

He broke off. The face that came close to his was etched with mingled fury and suspicion. The Kid despised him with the suddenness of a gunshot. Then he whirled on his heel without further argument, flinging the hand off. "Giant, get over there! Those lobos want more of it. No Calvert men ever pulled out yet. I tell you we can win. We *got* to win! Our work ain't finished here!"

The big Swede leaned and reached. His fingers closed over the Kid's belt at the small of his back and with a mighty yank Anderson snapped Calvert into his arms. There was a brief struggle, but the younger man was a toy in those massive paws. "No! Listen, Kid, it's—" He stopped. "Gunner's hurt, then. He wants yuh. He's—old Gunner's hurt, Kid, and wants yuh."

2

DEADLINE'S NEW SHERIFF

THEY WERE only five to leave the ashes of the ranch-house although eight had come. Looming black in the night they roweled their horses in the race down the valley. Spring Creek swam toward them and they plunged in. With the cold water a little deeper than knee-high on the horses, they splashed through and were up the sandy bank opposite. In the lead on Star, black as pitch but for the five-pointed splash of white on his ribs, the Kid led Giant Anderson, Nate Will-stock, and Arizona Al to the rescue of the eleven of Calvert's Horde named to run off Diamond X steers.

He knew they had failed, but he wasn't thinking of it now. It was impossible, Calvert cried mutely in his brain—impossible, about old Gunner. He was not believing it yet for there must be a mistake. There had to be a mistake.

There was not a steer at the former feeding place but they came on three trotting nervously about as if the herd had been scattered to the four winds. Suddenly the Kid saw gun flashes among trees at the first dumpling hills. He swerved the stallion. Giant Anderson had seen, too, and blew anxious curses in his cheeks. Willstock and Arizona reloaded hot guns as they followed.

Crimson daubed the hill, tonguing higher as if the fighters ran as they shot. The Kid feared the remnant of the bold eleven were near capture by overwhelming odds. The posse force was hot after as they retreated with the burden of their hurt leader.

Calvert called a sharp order. The men scattered. The Kid climbed Star, his horse, among the trees.

"We're the law! Drop yore guns!"

At that unexpected command the Kid was out of leather in a flash and charging the man who uttered it. The fellow was raising his gun on Willstock. The Kid's charge bore him backward and he glimpsed on his antagonist's chest a metallic star. It was Reynolds' deputy, Pete Quill. Quill shot, but wildly. The Kid landed a haymaker. All around him guns flamed. It was no good to prolong this.

"Clear out!" he yelled. *"Drift!"*

The rescued and rescuers got to their horses while the possemen shot and cursed and stumbled for them through the trees and shrubs. Afoot, they were left behind.

The men drew around the Kid, and pressed on with Lefty guiding. Silence, save for the creak of leather, panting of men, and the hoof-thuds of their horses climbing. Until at last a challenge rang out Calvert could answer. They were on the high ground site from which the Horde had descended tonight to clash with Stoner and Sheriff Reynolds.

Disheveled, sweaty, wounded, members of the gang stood near a guarded fire that cast an eerie crimson-yellow light on a form huddled under a blanket. The three who had brought Gunner here gave no reception save looks. No one spoke. All watched the Kid as he turned from his horse and stood stock still. The Kid's stomach went cold. His father, old Gunner, the invincible, lay on the ground. At first the Kid could not grasp it.

THE SILENCE was ominous, charged. Kid Calvert's feet dragged like lead weights around the fire. He dropped on his knees, unable to talk because of the lump that ached in his throat. Beside him stood Giant Anderson. The Giant's eyes, now incredibly tender, flicked once to the Kid, then dropped.

The Kid forced words out. "It's me, Dad. You comfortable? You'll be all right."

But the taut silence of the men—the waxen hue of his father's face—iced the Kid. And the glow of the Gunner's eyes, and the quivering of bloodless lips as if he were striving to talk. There was a red blotch on his shirt. Another wound soaked his shoulder. His pant-leg, when the Kid chanced to touch it, was sticky with blood.

"Lean down, son."

Kid Calvert bent closer. Something reeled in his brain. He had never thought of living without Gunner. Gunner was a fixed thing in his life, a sturdy post to tie to. But now that post was down.

"Kid—I ain't got long. An' I got a lot that oughta be said." Gunner's voice was strong on one word, thin on the next. It jarred the Kid to the pit of his stomach.

"Day in an' day out we've been hunted like sheep-killin' coyotes. I—ain't been the old man to you I'd—like to've been. But you know how I was run into the hills. About yore—mother. An' the little place we had."

"I know," said the Kid softly.

"So I couldn't bring you up no other way but like I did. Crooked law put us on the owl-hoot. Most all of our crowd, too, an' kept us there.... Not Mart Reynolds' brand o' law—for Reynolds is square. Only he was wrong tonight. He maybe couldn't see it."

Giant Anderson knuckled one eye as if something was in it.

Gunner went on in that jerky croak. "The Calvert Horde, as we've been branded, ain't done all the things folks say. Stories grow an' change to a lot worse. We never killed men unless we had to, never killed anyone tryin' to do the right thing. So long as I was leadin' the boys we've tried for real justice."

He lay resting a moment. The Kid was about to speak but a movement of his father's hand clenched in his own stopped him. Gunner then spoke again, his words barely audible.

"Kid—when a man gets to the end of his string he does a heap of thinkin'. I'm even thinkin', Kid, that—maybe I've been ridin' the wrong trail. But I've done what I figgered was right.

A man must always do—what *he* figgers is right. A man has gotta think—for himself. An' you, Kid, must figger—"

The Kid said quietly, "They don't make 'em better than you, Dad."

Old Gunner pressed the Kid's hand. "Always act so yuh can hold yore head high, Kid. Do what yuh can for weaker folks that need help—like Ryan. Take care o' Ryan. It was my job—"

"I will take care of Ryan, Dad."

Giant Anderson sniffled like he had a bad cold. A lonely tear struggled down Giant's cheek, seemed to have trouble going over that range-weathered face.

"An' Kid—" whispered Gunner—"watch sharp two-three men in our crowd. They ain't got the same ideas the rest have. They'll take—handlin', son. Whoever's leader—unless yuh disband—will have to watch sharp—"

Gunner Calvert slumped limply on the arm of his son. Giant knelt with a choked cry. There was a shuffling of booted feet behind Calvert. Gently he laid his father on the ground, and scarcely breathing for the awe that engulfed him, leaned slowly back.

Gunner Calvert was dead.

THROUGH THE GATE of the bleak, barbed wire-enclosed cemetery came a procession of buckboards, spring wagons, and creaking carriages. Ranchers and merchants in stiffly uncomfortable Sunday best sat soberly beside their wives dressed in black and wearing lacy poke-bonnets. Reaching the main road, fully half of the vehicles turned toward open range, for now there had to be resumption of the day's work. The remainder headed slowly toward Deadline two miles away.

In the cemetery the undertaker jerked off his celluloid collar and hung it on the wire. With two helpers he began shoveling crunchy loam into four open graves; one, the last resting place of Sheriff Mart Reynolds.

In the first two-seater carriage a brown-haired girl rode alone. Teresa Reynolds, only child of the slain lawman, was dry-eyed now the funeral was over. She knew her stern, un-compromising father would want her dry-eyed and thinking out what lay ahead. Terry was the last of the Reynolds line. She had no one, except half-deaf Aunt Ella Broderick whom she called "Mother." They would live on in the white cottage a block behind the main thoroughfare of the cowtown. There was no place else to go. It was going to be lonely—in the white cottage.

Terry brushed a hand over her forehead. Wearily she took off her hat and laid it on the seat beside her. The sun blazed on her thick mass of wavy brown hair and lighted her tanned, slightly pale face that was etched with strong feature-resemblance of her father.

Mart Reynolds' girl clenched her fists on the reins of the horse plodding through the dust. Resentment blazed in her. Intense longing to make some one *pay!*

Why did he have to be killed? He was a good sheriff. Honest. Afraid of nothing alive. And they had been such pals—as great pals as though she were a man instead of a girl.

Calvert's Horde had done this thing. And had slain three others of the posse and cowboy crew from Mike Stoner's Double Circle. Two now under the care of Doc Slaby might die.

Down the wide street of the town she drove to the livery stable, and stopped. Terry climbed from the buggy unimpeded by her black filmy dress, as easily as a man would climb out.

At the boulder-and-cement jail across the street a crowd of men stood talking. Their horses waited at the hitch-rail. Terry saw ruddy-faced Mike Stoner alight from a funeral carriage and join the crowd. The men talked on while they looked to their rifles and carbines.

That building had been her father's headquarters for twelve years since Terry was seven. She found herself walking across the street with a look of inquiry on her grave, handsome face.

"Is there—more trouble?"

The men looked at each other. Several shifted weight. Mike Stoner stepped forward.

"That bunch of killers didn't do what they tried last night—but they did too much harm. Me and the boys decided not to waste time. We're plumb anxious to fill some graves with them skunks, Terry."

As she studied the men, Deputy Sheriff Quill spoke up. "Mart Reynolds is shore goin' to be missed a lot. An' there's no bringin' Mart Reynolds back, either. But we'd all feel better if we could hoist some o' them gun-slingers to cottonwoods!"

"That's right!" Bud Breen said vigorously. "If we don't square for Mart, we're nothin' but cowards."

"Yeah, and the country's liable to go hawg-wild unless we drive out that gang o' murderers right *pronto!*"

TERRY REYNOLDS listened, twisting her hat in her hands. "Dad told me once that he knew why Gunner Calvert took to the hills," she heard herself say.

"He did, Terry? Why?"

Another voice boomed in with, "Jus' natcherlly crooked, that's why!"

Terry shook her head slowly. "No. That's not what dad told me. He said that some lawman killed Gunner Calvert's wife in a quarrel over range. Gunner Calvert killed the lawman, and had to take to the hills."

Stoner butted in. "An' now we'll bring in Gunner Calvert an' nail his hide to the hoosegow!"

The men moved for their horses.

She watched them, thrilled by this proof of the high esteem in which her father had been held. For it was no light matter to hunt the Calvert Horde.

Suddenly Terry ran into the street and clutched the bridle of Deputy Pete Quill's piebald. "Wait!" she called out.

The crowd stared at her. Face flushed with excitement, she said quickly, "Wait for me! Just five minutes, won't you, Pete?"

"Huh? What do you mean—wait?"

"I—I'm going, too! It's *my* father you want to—to avenge, isn't it?"

"But, Terry—" protested Quill—"gosh, yuh can't!"

"I'm Mart Reynolds' girl—and that means that I can shoot as well as any of you. Do you think I'm afraid? Haven't I been with dad at— What about the time on the 66 Box when you, Pete, and dad, and I took in those two rustlers? Was I any hindrance?"

Quill scratched his cheek. He shot a look at Mike Stoner. "She shore nabbed one jasper that time, and—"

"You can't leave me behind! Wait until I get home and change," Terry pleaded, fingering her skirt with disdain. "It will only take a minute. Pete, you saddle a horse and get my rifle." She started away but stopped to look questioningly at Mike Stoner as he dismounted.

Mike wore a ghost of a smile. "Are yuh willin', boys? Mart Reynolds' girl goes along?"

There was a brief hesitation. Then: "Well, shore."

"Yeah, why not?"

"Terry ain't the faintin' kind of woman. Old Mart taught her plenty. An' say, gents—" The speaker called several of the older men to one side. He talked earnestly to them. Some nodded. Others of the crowd joined them. The man then turned to a group of the leading ranchers of the district, and talked low-voiced to them. They nodded solemnly. Then the man walked over to the puzzled Terry, laid his hand fondly on her shoulder.

"There's been some talk about who's to be the new sheriff here. Pete Quill's the man, most everybody figgers. Pete's all to the good, but we gents—" he waved an arm expansively to include the crowd—"have other ideas."

Pete Quill started to protest. Stoner gripped his arm, whispered hoarsely, "Keep quiet, Pete."

The man who had appointed himself townspeaker, went on, "We gents knew Mart Reynolds right well. He was as fine a man as ever wore a sheriff's star. We're all Mart's friends. An' right here an' now we've held a special election to appoint Terry

Reynolds—Mart's girl—to the office o' honorary sheriff! At votin' time we-all can confirm this election!"

A mighty cheer went up from the crowd.

Pete Quill, red-faced, swung off his horse, clenched his fists. Mike Stoner grabbed him roughly.

"Lissen, you numbskull! Things are playin' our way. Keep that trap o' yours closed." Then Mike Stoner walked over to Terry, grasped her hand, saying in a loud voice, "I'm the first to congratulate the new sheriff—the new Sheriff Reynolds!"

Another cheer went up, louder than before.

Stoner raised his fist. "Wait'll the Calvert Horde hears of this! Wait'll they hear that we've put up another Reynolds to run 'em down!"

3

CALVERT THE SON

AT TIMBER-LINE on one of the snow-crested peaks of the Panther Mountains a man dragged a last boulder to the little heap atop a new grave. He straightened and took the broken-brimmed sombrero from his head. A wistful breeze rumpled the Kid's hair down over his high forehead as he paid silent tribute to the mound that enclosed the body of Old Gunner.

At last, turning, he strode to the horse tied to a tree limb. The animal watched him with mute sorrowful eyes and when the Kid led it toward the grave, hobbled painfully, dragging a useless right leg caked with blood.

The roan had been found early this morning. Calvert swallowed hard as he drew a six-gun from his low-cut holster. He pressed its muzzle to the forehead of the animal, looked away, and fired. Gunner's faithful friend pitched to earth with a thud.

Its forehoofs lay on the stones that marked the resting place of a famous outlaw.

That was all the ceremony Gunner had wanted. The Kid remembered his instructions from a moody talk a year ago during his father's convalescence from a minor gunshot wound. Calvert jerked the sombrero lower over his eyes, picked up the cartridge belt he had removed from the body, and went slowly to Star waiting a distance away.

As he rode down the mountain heading for the headquarters camp a sense of hate waved through him, deeper, colder, and infinitely more bitter than he had ever known. His knuckles shone white as moonstones. It was wrong—wrong that a man like his father should find final resting in that unknown grave.

The Kid led his horse to a newly repaired corral and turned the animal in. He unsaddled and lifted the leather onto the top bar. As he came out he noticed three men in earnest conversation out of earshot of the big, sprawling, flat log shack that was the gang's headquarters hidden cleverly away in mountain timber.

Bronk Beckly's back was against the round of the corral. But the Kid heard part of what he said: "We got a chance to get in on the big *dinero* if we work it right. Listen, Wells Fargo ships dust from Deadline every Friday. It comes to the bank Thursday about noon and stays overnight. I tell yuh, things ain't goin' to be like they was while Gunner—"

One of his companions spied the Kid and interrupted in a low tone. Beckly turned for a glance. He nodded, grinning to Calvert, but his face changed as he turned away. The others followed the Kid with covert eyes, all standing in silence.

He walked to the open rear door of the log shed that was large enough to contain living facilities for twenty men. Peel Rogers, monarch of all he surveyed with one glass and one genuine eye, watched him with a welcoming grin. There was an unending contest between Peel and the Kid—the one to guard his eatables, the other to snatch them before meal-time. But Peel saw that Calvert was in no mood for the game now.

"YOU AIN'T et nothin' all day yet. Wait up, Kid."

"No. Nothing for me, Peel."

He started through the kitchen but Rogers stopped him. "Here!" He thrust a heavily laden plate at Kid Calvert. "Eat it. Yuh figure a man can think on an empty stummick? Yore paw's dead and gone, Kid. Now it's up to you, and yore job won't be no cinch. Yuh goin' to finish the Ed Ryan affair?"

Their eyes held. "Of course, Peel."

"Yeah, I knew yuh would. Well but if yuh don't eat how can yuh live to do it? A man's most important organ outside his heart," Peel notified with flour-smeared forefinger wagging, "is his stummick. You can get along with yore legs an' arms. A man don't really need to hear stuff, and like at night he can't see nothin' anyhow but he gets along, don't he? But yore stummick's next important to yore heart. Yuh gotta have it workin' right. It's where everything comes from, like thoughts, ideas, appetite, muscle, belly-ache even. Everything!

"And Kid," he went on, "there's some brewin' around here that won't turn out beer. Yuh usually steal my best grub," he charged, suddenly cross to hide his true emotion. "Today you eat this and be darn glad I'll turn out grub 'tween meals. Git out, now. Git out, git out!"

Calvert smiled wanly, took the food, and entered a larger room in the center of which stood a long bare board table. Bunks lined the walls. In them several men lolled, or sat on their edges dressing last night's wounds. Others thumbed grimy cards, and still others mended clothing, their faces screwed painfully as they wielded needle and thread.

When the Kid had finished and was rolling a brown-paper quirley Giant Anderson lounged nearer and sat down. Latigo Malone, a man missing a finger and thumb on his right hand and with a curving knife scar along his jawbone, followed Anderson.

"The boys been augurin' about what's gonna happen now," Malone said in his whispery voice.

Calvert blew a lazy blue smoke ring. He sat back inhaling. "I don't know, Latigo. It isn't for me to say."

"We ought to talk it over, though," Dandy McLain urged.

"That Deadline crowd, Stoner in special, will be gunnin' for us," Grama Sinton pointed out. "Shouldn't wonder if they'd 'lected that deputy to be sheriff now, and had men out huntin' to finish us. We didn't make no hit with Stoner last night, Kid."

Beckly entered, his two confidants behind him, and sat on a bunk. The man's smoky eyes, slanted at the outer corners, always held a surly, menacing glint. He brushed a hand over his three-day stubble of beard and spat into a sawdust-filled cigar box. "That deputy'll want to make his new sheriff job shore. What we oughta do is raid the dam' town before they raid us.

"Kill off five or six o' them yella bellies that tried to put us all under sod last night," he growled on. "Yeah, and it'd pay, too! There's plenty gold dust in the bank right now, waitin' for the Denver train tomorrow. We'd make maybe five, seven thousand apiece and at the same time show them rats the Calvert gang don't stand no—"

"You mean a robbery for cash we don't need? And killings just for blood?" the Kid interrupted.

"You betcha I mean it! Why, all them stores and saloons in town got money. They oughta be worth a few thousand! What if there is only fourteen of us now? We could sweep in so they'd think it was a hundred. Take the hull burg, and when we get through, set fire to it! That would show how we like Gunner gettin' lead in his belly! What do yuh say, boys? I'll show yuh how to work it! Are yuh with me?"

HE LOOKED eagerly around the circle of faces. Malone wore an expression of grim satisfaction at thought of a fat share of the loot.

"I'm with yuh, Bronk!" he whispered.

"It'd serve 'em right for what they done," the Giant vowed. His chest rose and fell and his breath whistled in his big nostrils. Slow to arouse, Anderson exhibited every emotion, revealed every thought. He rose, his massive fists clenched. "Yah!" he boomed suddenly. "I kill three—four! I break 'em with my hands," he boasted, showing his long, thick fingers opening and closing. "I kill for Gunner, because they killed him! I, the Giant, will tear the guts out of that new sheriff!"

"Sit down! Shut up!"

The Giant started. A look of hurt disappointment crossed his face as he stared at Kid Calvert. Grunting in his barrel-like chest, Anderson dropped, obedient as a dog, but exhibiting the hurt of that sharp command.

Every man watched Calvert. He exhaled smoke deliberately as his eyes went from face to face. "There'll be no burnin' of Deadline. Nine out of ten folks there haven't done a thing against us. There won't be any bank-bustin' or any lootin', either. That ain't the way we do things, boys!"

Beckly's jaw jutted forth. "Who says so? Gunner's dead. Who made you boss?"

Kid looked at him. "You're right, Bronk. We got no leader now, nobody to give orders. We all can do as we want." He rose and stretched. "But me, I got work. I'm meanin' to finish it."

"What do yuh mean, Kid?" McLain asked.

"I mean the Ryan Diamond X job. The law backed Mike Stoner on a crooked deal, and we agreed we didn't aim to stand for it."

"Yeah," Malone growled, "but we didn't get the steers!"

"That's what I'm aimin' to do, though—get 'em. And when I've sold 'em, send Ryan the cash. I gave my word. I'm meanin' to carry things through."

"Yuh can't get them steers!" Beckly sneered. "Yuh can't do it!"

" 'Course not, Kid!" chimed in Willstock. "Stoner's got twice as many men as we are, drivin' 'em back near Ryan's place. Anyhow, as many as they can round up. There was plenty scatterin'. It'll take a week o' combin' the hills to get the hull lot."

Calvert nodded, making no other reply.

Beckly rose and hitched his trousers. "Yeah, that's all right if yuh want it. But we did what we could for Ryan, and is it our fault if things didn't pan out? Didn't we lose five men tryin'?

"Me," he stated deliberately, "I'm sick of passin' up all kinds of chances for *dinero*. Gunner always crabbed when I mentioned it, but what's wrong with a guy gettin' money? We ain't church deacons, are we? There ain't a sheriff in five hundred miles wouldn't shoot first and look second at us. If towns and big ranchers want me dead, I'm gonna get it while the gettin's good. And if anybody wants to be a milk-leg for nothin'—that's their lookout!"

Again, silence. The men looked at each other. "Bronk's right, ain't he?" Malone argued. "Let's trim that town and move on. Either we kill or they kill. Who's with Bronk an' me?"

"WAIT!" CALVERT held up his hand. "Boys, I say again, every man should make his own decision. But we never did murder for the sight of blood and it's no time to start now. We never did rob for—"

"Dry up on the preachin'! Who asked you?" flared Beckly.

Calvert straightened, a look of controlled anger on his face. His eyes were like shiny pinpoints of steel. "I'm not used to that kind of talk, Bronk. You can cut it out!"

The other returned a derisive laugh. "I always knew yuh'd show a yeller streak once yore old man wasn't handy to nurse yuh and tuck yuh in! Yeah, and he was always crawfishin', too. Tough, he was—until it came to really pullin' a job. Then—"

"Beckly, that's enough from you!"

Bronk cocked his head. "Yuh little squirt, for two bits I'd blow yore head off! Why, I'll talk about yore old man all I want! He was a cheap, four-flushin', tinhorn—"

Calvert sprang at him. But Beckly anticipated it and dodged aside. The Kid halted, whirled, and drove a stinging right for the man's jaw. But it struck Bronk's guard, shoving his hand into his face.

Twenty pounds superior in weight, he lunged at Calvert. It

was the Kid now who dodged and lifted an uppercut that struck with a low crunch on the point of the man's jaw.

Beckly teetered on his heels. He staggered and barely saved a fall. An instant he wavered dazedly, spitting out a lower tooth and blood after it. Then with a growl he streaked a hand to his thigh.

They were eighteen or more feet apart. The others had leaped to their feet to stand with sagging jaws and bulging eyes, yet careful to stand out of the line of fire. The tensity of expected murder was in the air as Calvert, on the balls of his feet, also drew.

Dandy McLain it was who had trained him how to aim the instant the muzzle had cleared leather. Nate Willstock, fastest of all of them here today, and old Gunner himself, had taught the Kid to carry his weapon in an oiled, low-cut holster. And he was fast, faster than the eye could follow. So fast that the drive of his arm and the pull of his gun, then its crashing report, seemed all of a piece and of one movement.

Bronk Beckly's forty-five thundered too late. His bullet crashed into a ceiling beam. He was falling, his face turned yellow. A cry of pain and insensate rage burst from the man's lips. Rolling on the floor he seized his right wrist with his left hand. The blue six-gun had risen in a crazy parabola from his grasp to spill into Anderson's bunk twelve feet away.

The smoke of the two explosions mushroomed lazily upward. Dandy McLain, first to move, rushed to Beckly. His boot toe shot out and the fellow's second Colt went scraping across the rough floor.

"Yuh fool! He'll kill yuh next time! Yuh dumb fool!"

Malone hesitated, wiped a hand over his lips awedly, then went to help Bronk to his feet. Calvert ejected the shell from his gun, stuffed in a fresh cartridge, and holstered the weapon without ever taking his eyes off the rage-trembling man.

"Boys," he said coldly, "those who feel like Beckly does had better go with him. Clear out. The rest of us can break up."

"Huh?" Grama Sinton exclaimed. "Bust up? What for?"

"Ain't you Gunner's son?" protested McLain, coming nearer him. "What more do we want, boys?"

"I go with the Kid!" Anderson thundered.

"Yeah," Willstock snapped incisively, "me, too!"

Arizona Al's eyes were quizzical as they roved from Malone and Beckly to the little group before the front doorway of the cabin. Al shuffled over, dragging a shirt with needle and thread attached to a half-mended place. "Hell! I had plenty raw deals in my time. I ain't got any love for no law. But I like the way Gunner done things and I'm stickin' with the Kid as long as he does 'em the same."

They watched closely for his reaction. A frown tugged at Calvert's brows. At last he nodded, and spoke almost curtly. "All right, boys. If you really feel that way I'll do my best."

He walked toward Bronk Beckly and Latigo Malone. Beckly had recovered his guns and the Kid watched him with hawklike vigilance.

"Clear out, both of you. Get out of the county. If I see you around here, Bronk, I'll kill you. Reckon that's plain?"

4

STRANGE MEETING

THE KID had taken particular pains to find a mount with a brand registered forty miles from Deadline, and he had paid a fancy price for a middling roan cowhorse. He was dressed today in striped blue overall trousers well worn and not too fresh from their last washing. He carried a carbine in the boot under his saddle, one walnut-butted forty-five in a new yellow holster, and wore a cheap, rather new sombrero.

It was Mike Stoner he had come to see, although Giant Anderson had argued and pleaded with him not to do it. "Yo're puttin' yore head right in the bear's mouth, Kid! Listen, Stoner might recognize yuh from the fight. He'll kill yuh! Or he'll spot yuh an' say nothin' until he traps yuh with the law, and then where's our helpin' Ed Ryan goin' to come in? Don't go workin' for Stoner, Kid. Don't do it!"

But Calvert was here on Ryan's Diamond X....

Mike Stoner with the ruddy face that turned apoplectic blue when he was angry, was a man with massive shoulders and a stomach that grew rounder from continual stuffing at the table. He rode, walked, and talked with an air of truculent authority. Stoner had all his riders cowed but growling behind his back. He relished his own overbearing pose and tried it out on the meek-looking cowpuncher who drifted along Spring Creek early that afternoon as Stoner tallied recovered Diamond X cattle thrown together for the sheriff's sale that would benefit him nine thousand dollars.

"What do you want?" Mike snapped as the stranger stopped his horse.

Calvert looked scared. He managed to force out, "A—uh, ridin' job, mister. I'm a good hand."

He dropped his eyes while the boss of the Double Circle looked him over. "Admit it, eh? Well, I ain't needin' anybody." His eyes sharpened. "Yuh look— Say!" He dropped a hand to his hip. "One o' that lobo Calvert gang, darn it! I saw yuh! I'd know that face in the dark! Yuh crawlin' snake, I'll—"

"No! You made a mistake! I—"The Kid gulped, his eyes wide. "I—I ain't done nothin', mister, honest! I'm from over Hondo way. Just needin' a job, that's all. But if yuh think—"He gulped. "Maybe I better be ridin', should I?"

There was a twenty second wait of tensity. Stoner looked undecided. Calvert feared if gunplay did come that his new, stiff holster was going to impede him.

Neither man looked, but three steers trotted up while they glared at each other, three steers with a puncher hazing them a few yards behind. He was a man with a large square face, mild eyes, and shaggy blond hair down his neck.

"What's wrong, boss?" Giant Anderson asked Stoner. Then his gaze was on the Kid. There was in his eyes the plainly written message, "I told yuh not to come here!"

Unexpectedly Stoner laughed. He turned his back, bit the point of the stub pencil, and tallied the three steers. Anderson addressed Kid Calvert with a friendly, "Howdy."

"KNOW HIM?" Stoner snapped.

"A little."

"Well, where's he from? What is he, bone-lazy, or a worker?"

"From over to Hondo, I reckon. I saw him there in a saloon. Said he was on the Spade W. Don't think he's lazy, boss."

Stoner looked knowing. "Yeah, the Spade W is over that way. Swede," he said more reasonably. "You a rimrock man? Yuh dally or tie?"

"I'm better where it's sort o' flat," Anderson admitted. "I tie, boss."

"I dally, mister," Calvert ventured. "I can ride rimrocks. I got the hoss for it, too."

There was a short second examination. "Some gunners run off these steers t'other night. They're scattered to hell-an'-gone—wild bunch anyhow. Old Ryan didn't do much but let 'em grow, and he was lucky. I got to throw all Diamond X stuff together an' get it to town," Stoner explained truculently. "What's yore name?"

"Dawson. Stan Dawson."

"Yo're hired, I guess, and yuh come back tonight with beef out o' them rimrocks yonder or don't come back. I got no time for fellas can't earn their salt."

Kid and Anderson exchanged looks no more friendly than any casual acquaintances might exchange. "How much?" Calvert asked.

"Forty and. Git on yore way! If I wasn't worried that bunch

o' murderin' hellions might try to rush off Double Circle stock I'd have my own men here." He turned his horse to ride away. "Come on, yuh big Swede. I need you."

The Giant winked before he rode off after Stoner. He had a subtle way of ingratiating himself so that Stoner fancied him already. He was carrying out Calvert's orders excellently so far.

Whistling, the Kid swung his roan to a lope for the red and gray rocks that rose sheer at the northwest rim of the valley, where Stoner had pointed as he hired. The Kid did not relish riding rimrocks on an untried horse, for it was dangerous. But he could work dally or tie. He was better with the dally. Gunner Calvert had stayed two winters in the southernmost Sierras and had always run a little beef. A Mexican knife killer named Santos had taught the Kid during his mid-teens to compete with the best. He rode on whistling, trying not to think how much he missed Gunner.

There followed three hours of hard, gruelling work. The roan was none too adept at sudden stops on dry, bare rock, nor at adjusting its weight on a precipice edge while a half-wild steer alternately tugged at the rope and charged. But Calvert kept doggedly on, holing up a half-dozen cattle in a draw where there was plenty of grass. He would drive them all below in a bunch.

Calvert had about decided to end the afternoon's work when his sweaty mount stopped dead, ignoring the lift of the reins. It trembled violently in sudden terror.

Came a panic-stricken shrill of a horse in pain. Then a series of snarls as from some animal, and the clatter of steel.

There was a shot. A terrific struggle set up from somewhere among juniper shrubs and humpy pines off to the Kid's left. His own horse uttered a neigh of terror and started full tilt away from the sound.

CALVERT BROUGHT the horse to its haunches and slid out of leather. With his heels braced he clung to the head-stall strap, holding the fear-ridden horse while he tried to hear what it was that spooked the horse. His face set as a guess flashed to his mind. He heard a human cry and another shot.

The Kid dragged his thoroughly frightened cowhorse to a tree and lashed rein ends over a thick branch. He had the carbine out of its boot and was trotting toward the sound, his dark eyes cruising this way and that lest inadvertently he step into the midst of wild battle.

He did blunder into it, almost in time to take a bullet through his head. A six-gun smoked. The slug whizzed over Calvert's shoulder, making him duck with involuntary reaction. He caught a glimpse of a light-stepping figure cringing against a trunk. Brown hair half covered the pale face. A girl.

Calvert loosed a gasp. Threshing madly a matter of five yards away was a brown horse almost torn to ribbons by the bloody fangs of a puma. They rolled over and over. A steel trap dragging from a rear leg of the cat rattled and banged on the stone littered ground.

Calvert rushed nearer. But he was not as quick as the girl. She passed him, her mouth open as she panted, her face chalky. She had the six-gun gripped in her hand, smoking from its last shot. The cat was on top now.

"Stay back!" the Kid yelled. The girl was in the way of his shot.

Just as the horse flopped with a thud that shook the ground under their feet she fired at the hard-eyed skull of the puma. Her bullet took effect, but it only further infuriated that wounded beast.

Of a sudden it let go the horse. There was a ring of steel on stones. The trap and its thick chain clattered as the tawny puma sprang without crouching.

She had time to sweep an arm over her face in horror. Calvert's carbine roared. He pumped quick as a flash and put another bullet into that hard slanting skull.

But he was too late to save her from harm. The momentum of the puma carried it at her with claws outstretched hungrily, though the beast was dead before it struck. There was another thud, the smack of a furry body against flesh. The girl snapped backward. The cat lay half on her, still quivering an instant before its body rippled in a final convulsive spasm.

Calvert dropped his carbine. He leaned, and seizing the tail of the beast, hauled with all his strength. A moan broke from the insensible girl. The Kid went on tugging to get the several hundred pound beast off her.

It was done. He was short of breath; his denim shirt was dark with sweat. Calvert hated to go closer to look at the girl, hated the awful mess of her slender body that probably awaited him....

HE FORCED himself on both knees. She lay with her head thrown far back and her hair tossed over dusty plants. Her face was like a plaster mask, her lips pale blue and her white, even teeth parted as if a scream had frozen in her mouth half uttered.

The girl looked seriously hurt, though she lived. The puma's spring over nine feet, dead when it struck her, had given it a pawsweep that was ferocious. One leg of her dark woolen riding trousers was ripped at the knee and white flesh was laid open gushing blood. Calvert was anxious whether her knee was torn off. He could not tell for the blood.

That was her only wound, though it looked ugly enough. He dug out a pair of fresh bandanas he always carried in a rear pocket and began swiftly to staunch the blood by binding them tightly. Deeper crimson oozed through them at once, and he started to his feet worried.

The Kid ran back for his horse. His swift calculations told him that it was only three miles as the crow flies down to the valley floor. But it would be seven miles or more the way he would have to go. It was twilight, and Western twilight is brief. Stoner and his men most likely were gone back to the ruins of Ed Ryan's house to camp near the well. That was a long way.

Calvert halted, staring around him in dismay. But he knew

he had made no mistake. He stopped and picked up a four-inch scrap of leather rein. The cowhorse had broken loose, bolted.

Jarred by the discovery, he trotted back to the spot where the girl lay. They had to get to water. If he could find the proper herbs he knew how to make a poultice that would draw out the poison of the puma's dirty claws. They could not reach help afoot, so it would have to be some such resource. It was up to Calvert alone to save that girl's life.

From his experience in these foothills he remembered a caved-in shack perhaps a half or three-quarters of a mile distant. It had been thrown up by some trapper out for wolf and coyote pelts at a bounty from the cattlemen of the section. There was water near that shack and where there was water there should be herbs.

The girl still lay unconscious, breathing jerkily, and bleeding. Calvert picked up his carbine and clenched it under his arm. He shoved the girl's six-gun into his belt. Tenderly he lifted her light weight in his arms and set off toward the shack.

The insensible weight began to tell on him when he at last saw the hulk of the cabin a little to his right. Gently he laid his limp burden on the ground outside the shack. Its roof sagged in drunkenly and a wall had bowed out at the pressure; but there was some shelter available even in that wrecked place. Calvert managed to scrape the warped slab door inward. He heard a pack rat scuttle to its hole as he poked about for matches. His hand slid over cold stones of a fireplace. Then a bunk that had sagged at one end since a leg caved at the gnawing of squirrels.

There were no matches and the Kid had used all of his own. The Kid straightened. He heard some one talking unintelligibly. In the night silence it startled him so that instinctively he dropped a hand to his gun. Then understanding broke over him like a cold shower. It was the girl babbling incoherently her terror of those spike-like claws. She was delirious.

HE WORKED with feverish energy to prop a stick of firewood under the bunk. Fumbling inside to make sure it was smooth, he cursed himself because he had no blanket or coat or so much as a slicker by way of a mattress. Calvert hurried out of the shack and tore small branches from the nearest pines. He made a rough bed of them, none too soft but pleasantly odorous.

He carried the girl inside and laid her gently in the bunk. Her eyes were wide and terrified as she gibbered on in a way that almost made him sick. Calvert tore himself away though she clutched out both hands in nameless fear.

The Kid halted on the threshold to think. He got a length of hard stick and made a bow with a rawhide string carried to tie his holster to his thigh. With his knife he sharpened another stick and twined it in the rawhide. Then he built a bed of tinder-dry twigs in the crude rock fireplace, relying wholly on an alert sense of touch in the pitch darkness. Over in the corner the girl mumbled crazily, tossing and pitching about.

At last the Kid was ready, and using a rotted slab of wood from the caved-in roof, he began awkwardly to whipsaw the pointed stick within the circle of his thumb and forefinger. The rawhide bow made it whirl and a spark leaped out.

He fumbled the first. But at last Calvert had a fire climbing eagerly that drew off the damp chill of evening and served to light the cabin with eerie, dancing tongues. He rushed outside again with a pine knot torch for his search among the ferns that grew near the spring. Finding what he wanted, he dipped a broken stone jug brought from the cabin, and carried back two quarts of cold water to bathe her wounds.

The girl raved deeper in delirium. She kept rolling so that he had to hold her while he worked. Far off on the rimrocks a coyote wailed dismally. The Kid drew coals out of the fire and placed the refilled jug to heat. He inspected the girl's leg, shaking his head. It had an ugly look. The bleeding had almost stopped but the claw wounds looked to be festering. They would require fresh poultices at intervals all night.

Suppose she—died? The Kid had never seen a woman die and the thought that she might become cold, a corpse like Gunner—

For the first time in his life, Kid Calvert knew fear.

5

ON OPPOSITE SIDES

THE MORNING wore on in sunlit brilliance. Near the murmuring spring a smudge of pine branches and damp leaves raised a dark gray plume of smoke high in the air. Calvert squatted on his heels smoking a brown-paper quirley down to its last quarter inch. He rose, ground its coals under heel, and stepped inside the tumble-down trapper's shack.

She lay propped up as he had raised her to sip quail broth an hour ago. The girl's cheeks were slightly flushed and her eyes unnaturally bright with lingering fever. But she looked better, though a little wan. She smiled at him in her friendly way.

"Nobody yet?"

"No. Yuh'd think that smoke would attract somebody. If it doesn't in another hour or two I better start on down."

The suggestion brought disappointment flashing across her face. "I suppose that would be the thing. It's not being alone I mind. But you'd have an awful hard walk on those high heels. It's miles down."

Calvert swung a leg onto the corner of the worm-eaten slab table. "You feel better, though, don't yuh? Looks like the fever is almost gone. How is your knee?"

"I can't tell much because of those splints you bound on. I think I might bend it a little. It doesn't feel so awful. I'm not hurt as badly as it must have looked when you brought me here. And stayed up all night with me. I surely appreciate it, Dawson."

He met the brown eyes briefly. "How'd you happen to get mixed with that puma anyhow, uh—"

"Terry. I live in Deadline with Mother Broderick. My father is dead—lately." She studied her slim fingers a moment.

"I was with a posse hunting the Calvert gang. My horse went lame, so I decided to go to Stoner's Double Circle for another. I guess that trap must have been set by Ed Ryan, who lived in that ranch-house that burned? My horse stepped on it, and things began to happen. I was thrown. When I got up—" She shook her head as if to drive the scene from her eyes.

"Yeah. Cats won't attack anybody most times. But I s'pose he figured you'd come to finish him, and he'd rather finish you first." The Kid laced his fingers over his knee. He looked at her out of the corners of his eyes. "Yuh say you were hunting the Calvert gang? Seems funny a girl should be doin' that."

"Perhaps it does to you. But the whole country ought to be hunting them right now. And until the lot of them are either dead or in jail!"

His brows raised. "That bad? I heard once that they weren't so hell-awful. They're wanted several places, of course. Reckon they're sorta hard on folks that have lots of *dinero,* but they ain't so hard on the poor folks."

Terry thought about that. "You know, Dawson," she said finally, "my dad told me something like that. But it's kinda hard to believe. Do you know what Calvert's Horde did the other night?"

Kid looked at the scuffed toe of his boot. "What did they do the other night?"

"Plenty. Mike Stoner got a court judgment for damages, and he came out to the Diamond X with officers to levy on Ryan's property. Ryan wouldn't let Pete Quill—he's deputy sheriff—close enough to talk. He fired on the men. Well, Pete had his orders from Mart—" she cleared her throat—"the sheriff. Pete was ordered to take Ryan, and he started to do it. Meanwhile Mart and Stoner and some men went out to get Ryan's stock.

"Then Calvert's gang came in two bands, one at Pete Quill, the other trying to stampede the steers. They stampeded them all right. But they didn't run them away. Four of our men were killed. And Ryan's house burned to the ground. Suppose his wife or little girl had been killed? They—"

"Yuh mean Calvert's crowd fired the house?"

The girl sat straighter in her bunk. "Of course they did! They saw a chance to steal four hundred beef. I tell you, Dawson," Terry burst out angrily, "I would like to wrap my hands around Gunner Calvert's throat for what he did that night!"

KIDS FINGERS clenched tighter over his knees. A muscle twitched in his cheek, and his eyes fixed on Terry's flushed face. He drew a deep breath. "Heard tell that Gunner Calvert ain't livin' any more for you to put yore little hands around his throat."

"You mean he's dead?" cried Terry, her feelings carried off by her grief. "I'm glad!"

Kid flinched. "You—talk sort of bloodthirsty, ma'am."

Terry sank back on the bunk, her thoughts in a jumble. Her sheriff father had always had a sort of respect for Gunner Calvert. And Gunner Calvert had never operated in Sheriff Reynolds' locality. But now Mart Reynolds was in his grave—put there by Calvert's Horde. Terry said slowly:

"With Gunner Calvert dead—maybe the gang will break up. But I'm not so sure. I hear there's a son of the old man. He's probably worse than Gunner—a wild, young killer."

Kid said nothing as he drew makings from his shirt pocket and twisted another smoke. He went to the fireplace and picked up a flaming stick, touched it to his cigarette, and inhaled deeply. When he returned to the slab table he wore a forced grin.

"I figgered maybe the Calverts were like that puma, sort of. Trapped. A lot of men get in hot water like that cat did. A fight or some misstep and they have to run for it. They're hunted—until they get caught and shot down. They mean all right, or anyhow, they did before it all started. The other animals just don't care much for the way they do things, and there's more of the law kind of animals."

"Sentiment!"

They bored each other with challenging eyes. Suddenly both yielded to laughter. Smoke mixed with the Kid's words when he said:

"Yuh better rest, Terry. Try to get some shut-eye. Too much talk won't help yuh none."

Terry lay back and closed her eyes. Minutes passed. When she heard his light step she did not open her eyes. Terry felt his hand touch her forehead as he leaned over the sideboard of the rough bunk.

Even then she did not look at him, because something urged her not to halt what he was going to do. And because she felt a queer thrill steal into her heart at the sureness of his touch.

His hand withdrew. She opened her eyes to discover the Kid's lean face quite close as he still bent motionless. He was studying her the way she had surprised him studying her at dawn when she awakened out of her heavy slumber. Then, Dawson had stood straight with a guilty flush creeping up his cheeks. But now he nodded his head slowly.

"You're—shore pretty, aren't you?"

He turned his back to go slowly toward the door. She could think of nothing to say, no way to make him return though Terry wanted him to stay.

At the threshold he twisted at the waist and shot the stub of his cigarette into the fire. Over his shoulder he said:

"I mean it, Terry."

HORSES WERE coming through the woods across the small clearing around the spring. Calvert was conscious of apprehension born of years of hiding at any sudden approach. He overcame the impulse to slink behind the cabin, and merely waited. Three riders broke into view, coming on rapidly until they were quite close.

One was red-faced Mike Stoner looking more truculent than he had yesterday. Another was a lantern-jawed man whose cheek bulged with a quid of tobacco. The third was a cowboy Calvert had seen from a distance working Diamond X stock.

They dismounted quickly.

"Where is she?" Stoner demanded.

"In there." The Kid thumbed over his shoulder. His eyes held Stoner's steadily. "You saw the smoke, then?"

Pete Quill nodded. As he strode nearer the Kid to pass him into the shack Calvert's skin crawled on his spine. The law always caused that when it came near.

"Where in hell do yuh get the guts to run off with Terry and hold her all night?" Stoner stormed. "Yuh skinny range rat, I had my suspicions of yuh right off, and I see now they was right!"

"Hold on, Mike," Pete Quill protested. "Don't jump at no conclusions. Terry!" he called. Then he stepped inside the shack and the Kid heard the girl answer with a glad cry.

Stoner bored the Kid with a threatening look as he, too, entered the tumble-down cabin. His voice was more pleasant to the girl. Uneasy but deciding to remain where he was, Calvert looked at the rannihan they had brought along. The fellow grinned.

"Talk about a search! Stoner and Quill ain't thought of nothin' else since Pete and the boys come in last night and found Terry missin'." He gnawed the black end from a plug of tobacco. "Don't reckon you was runnin' off with her at all."

"Hardly. We didn't meet until twilight yesterday. A puma draggin' a trap almost got stepped on by her hoss, which was lame. There was quite a fracas. She got a bad gash from the cat's claws. My hoss ran away and she wasn't able to walk. So we stayed here. She was out of her head part of the night, and she's still weak."

"Uh-huh. Yore roan come along this mornin'. Stoner was shore worked up. And Quill—he's kind of sweet on Terry, though it never got him anywhere. 'Course Quill keeps it quiet.

He's sort of fond of doin' what Mike says, and thinkin' like Mike thinks. Which means—"

He chopped off his words significantly. The Kid turned to see Stoner emerge from the shack. The lawman stood in the doorway watching.

"Dawson, it might be like yuh say, and maybe it isn't, too. But I don't like yore looks. Yuh get that?" The rancher planted himself in front of the Kid, feet apart, fists jabbed on hips. "I still got a hunch you maybe ain't what yuh say. And I won't stand for no tamperin' with my affairs."

"I haven't tampered. I wanted a job—"

"Yo're still wantin'!" Stoner snapped. He jerked his head. "Climb out o' here. Go down to Agnew on the Double Circle and give him this note." He was scribbling on a pad as he talked. "Yuh got a day's wages comin'. Use it to *vamos*. And remember, if I see yuh hangin' around this county I'll have yuh run in for bein' one o' that damn Calvert gang. I don't want yore mug around no more. Savvy?"

The Kid's crestfallen expression reached Pete Quill, who stepped over the threshold of the cabin.

"Hold on," he protested.

Quill came to Calvert. "Those herbs you put on maybe saved her from the poison and dirt of that cat's claws. Uh—I'm glad you took good care of her." He offered his hand and Calvert took it. "Thanks," Pete Quill said. "We're all fond o' Terry. That's why Mike is a little worked up."

"He better clear out!" Stoner insisted angrily.

The Kid's look was one of inquiry. Reluctance came into Quill's face as he nodded. "Yeah. I guess you better, at that. Strangers ain't wanted in this county right now."

Calvert dropped his hand and turned away.

"Give him a hoss to get to the ranch, Bo." Stoner pivoted on his heel and reentered the cabin.

"So long," Quill offered as he turned to follow.

"So long," the Kid said.

He trailed Bo to the knot of rein-staked horses. It was going to be more difficult to care for Ed Ryan than he had thought. And it seemed he was not even to be allowed to say good-by to Terry, whom, most likely, he would not be seeing again.

6

BRONK BECKLY'S PLAY

FROM AGNEW at the Double Circle ranch, the Kid learned that the reassembled Diamond X steers were to be driven to Deadline on the morrow. From there they were to be shipped to market, the proceeds to go to Mike Stoner. The Kid returned to the outlaw headquarters in the hills.

He was thinking that the beef would not fetch as much money as the amount of Stoner's court damages. Ryan would owe a deficiency judgment. It was one way of keeping a luckless man perpetually in the debt of powerful Mike Stoner, so that Ryan never would dare return to the county.

In the morning there was a conference. Dandy McLain, the flowery-vested gambler, had arrived in Deadline by train and masqueraded briefly as an itinerant cattle buyer. "The stuff is supposed to pull out tonight after Number Eight, the limited, goes through. There'll be a special stock train. Feller name of Clark is handlin' the deal. Stoner figures he's practically got the money banked right now."

"It'd be easier to grab the cash than the train," Willstock pointed out.

The Kid looked inquiringly at Dandy.

"I dunno when he pays it over. Clark argued with the feller in the bank about a draft, but it seemed they didn't want to cash it for him. On account of the steers bein' a county proposition now it ain't likely to be a cash deal at all."

"Well," Calvert decided after some thought, "we have got to

play safe. We'll want Pete Quill out of town tonight. He's in Cass Reynolds' shoes now. If the actin' sheriff is out of town there won't be so much fuss when we do what we're going to. Nate, did you pick up any acquaintances?"

Willstock inclined his head smilingly. "I'm old pals with one o' Stoner's men. He's one of these fellers would sell out his grandmother for a ten dollar reward. He thinks I'm for the state cattle association, wantin' track of the Calvert gang and workin' alone because I don't think much o' the lawmen around here. What you want done, Kid?"

"I want you to send that man in town a-flyin' about seven o'clock tonight. Have him all worked up about findin' our gang, and make out that it would be a cinch for Quill to nab us. Fix it so's the crowd you're expectin' to capture is in some different direction," he grinned back. "While your friend comes for Quill, you ride in town to be handy at the shipping pens."

"I'll do it. This hombre'll smell reward and think I'm lettin' him in on a swell thing." Willstock chuckled at the thought.

Calvert turned to McLain. "The Giant is still with the beef, and he'll stay there. You get in town and hang around, Dandy. Don't let Grama Sinton lap up too much redeye so he isn't any use when he's needed. The rest of you boys can ride in as soon as it's dark enough and keep out of sight until things start. Well, reckon that's all."

The conference broke up. Calvert spent the morning grooming Star and repairing a worn cinch. At noon he went alone to the boulder-strewn grave on Smoky Mountain to discover that Quill's or some other party had found the grave and had buried the brown horse Gunner had prized so highly.

LATE IN the afternoon, riding his Spade W cowpony, the Kid reached Deadline. He still was dressed in the nondescript puncher outfit of Stan Dawson. Passing the once-white cattle pens some two blocks before the beginning of the town, he saw Giant Anderson and two other men lolling on top rails, smoking and talking. The stock train had just rolled in and lay like a sleepy snake on the siding, its locomotive sighing wearily.

Mike Stoner was not in view, evidently being gone to the Double Circle to attend his regular routine of duties.

The Kid rode into the alley behind the south line of clapboard store buildings. He dismounted in front of an empty three-wall shed and tied his horse inside, leaving the animal saddled. Then he strolled to the sidewalk and leaned against the false front of the hardware store for a look up and down.

It was five o'clock. Deadline looked in a daze as usual. A pair of ranch wagons stood in front of the feed barn and there was a handful of cowponies waiting with flattened ears and drooping heads at saloon hitch rails.

Calvert sauntered down to the Longhorn Bar. As he thrust the swinging doors aside he heard the clack of chips, and found five men in silent concentration on a stud game. The Kid's cheek quirked in a grin. Dandy McLain had a fat stack of blues and reds at his left hand. He grumbled the loudest when another player scooped the pot, but had nothing to say as his own winnings mounted.

The men looked at Calvert, nodded amiably, but paid him no heed. McLain's stare was as casual as the looks of the others. The Kid ordered a drink and stood toying with it lazily. After a while two new customers stomped into the place. The face of one was flushed with drink and he sang in a raucous tenor. The other man looked sober, to Calvert's relief. He was Grama Sinton.

The Kid minded his own business with a five-day-old Salt Lake newspaper until the talk veered to the Calvert Horde. Then he joined the two men and the bartender with an occasional remark, gradually striking up an acquaintance.

"String 'em up—thash what they oughta do!" Sinton's friend declared loudly, pounding his fist on the bar. "String up them Calvert fellash. Don't even need trial—washe money. Thasso, Dawson?"

"Seems like they ought to get the same trial anybody else would get," the Kid returned thoughtfully.

"Shoot 'em down!" Sinton declared. "String 'em up or shoot 'em down—whichever's handy. That's what *I* say. The lobos!"

"Sure thing, boys," the bartender agreed earnestly. "Kill 'em the quickest, handiest way. Get rid of 'em like you would vermin. And I bet Pete Quill will do it, too, unless them fellers *vamos*ed already."

Calvert caught McLain's eye but gave no sign. Presently the drunk was snoring at a wall table and the Kid and Sinton, like two strangers ripening a chance acquaintance, were discussing an item in the newspaper. As the ancient clock on the back bar showed six the Kid paid his score to leave the saloon. He had found opportunity to warn Sinton against any more drink. There must be no befuddled brains in the Horde tonight.

CALVERT STEPPED through the batwing doors with the thought in mind of seeking a restaurant for a meal. He glimpsed the tall figure of Terry just passing the Longhorn. Hurriedly he retreated with the saloon.

But she had seen him. "Oh, Stan! Stan Dawson!"

The Kid hesitated, frowning. Not that he liked avoiding another meeting with Terry Broderick as he supposed her, but there was important business on hand shortly and he wanted to be free to attend it. More than that, Calvert had thought over his acquaintance with the brown-haired girl. He realized that as a man marked to be shot on recognition, it was hardly fair to cultivate Terry's friendship.

He hated lying to her. And every minute he was with her as Stan Dawson was another lie. Calvert rubbed his chin indecisively. She was such an ardent champion of the law. If ever she learned the truth about him Terry would despise him for this masquerade. There was a barrier between them, grown out of their opposite training over many years.

And he knew now that he could not be satisfied with a casual friendship with her. Calvert had admitted that to himself as he pondered the whole thing. There was something magnetic about Terry that excited him deep down inside.

All this flashed through his mind in a fraction of a second as he stood within the batwing doors of the saloon. The bartender looked at Calvert curiously. "That gal callin' you, wasn't she?"

The Kid opened the doors and emerged the second time. She stood with thumbs hooked in her gun-belt, gazing at him.

"Well, stranger!" Terry Reynolds greeted cheerily. "Is that where you've been hiding since yesterday?"

He moved down the plank platform to her side. He felt his face burning under his tan.

"Uh—no," he answered hesitantly. Of a sudden they both smiled, at ease now. "But I've been—around. You got over yore clawin' all right?"

"I'm not supposed to ride for a few days. But Doctor Slaby says he'd like to know just half what you know about herbs. He says if it hadn't been for your treatment, and keeping cold cloths on my forehead while I was delirious—"

"Glad yo're feelin' good again," the Kid broke in, plainly embarrassed.

"You shrinking violet! Yes, I walk up and down the street for exercise. But, Stan, have you had supper?"

"No. I was just headin' for that café yonder."

Terry Reynolds tucked her arm through his in a comradely way that made him utterly helpless. "Then come right along with me. Mother Broderick has everything ready and there's always pot-luck for one more."

"No, gosh! I—I hadn't ought to!"

She halted, staring at him provocatively. "But you will, won't you? Fine!" Terry laughed, and dragged him on down the walk. "I want to show Mother the man who saved my life. She doesn't think I'd look very good all torn to ribbons by a puma. In fact, she said I'd look messy. She expects you must be a wonder. I told her—

"I mean," Terry shifted, reddening, "you may as well eat with us. It's quiet, just the two of us, since dad's gone."

The Kid longed to say something consoling about that. "I bet it is. I reckon yore dad must've been all man, Terry."

THEY MOVED a hundred feet in silence. The genuine pleasure he felt in her company made Calvert tell himself that it was all right. There was plenty of time. He could say something about a business engagement at seven-thirty and break away to attend that matter of Ed Ryan's steers.

There was no lack of lively talk between them, nor was it long before their friendly quarrel over the Calvert gang was renewed by the impudent Terry. "You still think it's a fine thing to be a thief and a killer?" she demanded. "Stan, I half believe you are one *muy malo* hombre yourself!"

He halted at the short flight of steps to the cottage door. "Terry," Calvert blurted out suddenly, "I—I am! You think—"

She went off in a gale of derisive laughter. It made his face whiten, made him stand irresolute while the pain of his deception knifed through him. The Kid took her hand from his arm and turned as if to leave. "Terry, I—I can't eat with yuh after all. It's doggone nice of yuh to ask—"

"Of course you can, silly! I believe you're afraid of Mother. Isn't that it? You're not afraid of me, are you, Stan?"

He stared down at his calloused hand. "Shore not. I—like you, Terry. That's the whole darn trouble. You don't savvy—"

"Here she is now. You have to shout at mother: she's a little less deaf than a hitching post."

He was introduced to a keen-eyed, bent old lady who at once demanded to know whether Calvert had suffered any ill effects from his tussle with the wildcat. And while the talk ran on between the three of them, the Kid realized with a heavy sensation in his stomach that he had missed making his confession. That he was liking Terry a good deal more with every passing minute—much as he tried to steel himself against her.

The savory, well-cooked supper over, Terry led him to the

parlor of the cottage while Mother Broderick promised to leave the dishes for the girl. The old lady bade Calvert a cordial good-by as she tied the strings of her sunbonnet to go down the street for a visit.

Time flew on wings of silver.

There was a thud of boots on the steps outside and Pete Quill burst through the front screen door. "Terry!" he exclaimed. "What do yuh think? We got track o' them lobos for shore! Oh," he said shortly, recognizing Calvert. The deputy looked somewhat hostile.

"You did, Pete? You mean," she breathed eagerly, "you've learned where they are? Oh, Pete! To think I can't go! My leg's too stiff. I couldn't—"

"Now, don't git worked up. I'm awful glad yuh can't 'cause your might get shot. But I tell yuh, Terry, I believe this here's the time we'll nab 'em! That Johnson on the Double Circle— he's been friendly with a detective for the state cattle association. Feller's been workin' here on the sly, can yuh beat it? He rode hell-for-leather to Johnson an' tells him to rush in and fetch me. So I thought yuh'd want to know, Terry. I got to git now. So long!" He opened the door and was gone.

SHE STOOD staring after him with eyes that glowed with excitement. The Kid watched her intently, saw how the color burned in her cheeks. He stepped to the girl and captured her hands in his.

"Does it mean so much to yuh? Are yuh so awful anxious to see the—the Calvert gang nabbed?"

Terry Reynolds made no answer for a moment while she calmed herself. "I'm sorry I'm so bloodthirsty. It's just that I can't help wanting revenge. They've done so much, Stan! Not only here, but over several states. I've seen accounts of robberies they've committed when they shot people wantonly, burned ranches, and—

"Oh, but let's forget it. Come, Stan, we'll talk of pleasanter things. I don't want you to think all I think about is the Calverts."

They did manage to change the subject but the Kid could not shake off the sense of despair that gripped him. He wondered if all Deadline, all of the county, felt as violently about it as this girl did? Good Mother Broderick, for instance: did the old lady also hate his name, with every ounce of hate of which she was capable?

They were interrupted again but in a less explosive manner, by a short fat man dressed in city clothes who knocked at the door. Terry admitted and introduced him as Mr. Clark. The little man thrust a fat hand into his inside coat pocket and drew out a sheet of paper which he handed the girl.

"You just sign that, miss, and I'll hand yuh the money. It's for them Ryan steers. Quill not bein' in town, I reckon you can take the cash as well as the next."

Calvert was puzzled that Terry Broderick should accept payment for the Diamond X cattle. Why did Clark seek her out? Watching the girl write her name at the bottom of the paper, he could make nothing of it. Maybe she was just an intermediary, selected because of the prominence her father had had in Deadline. The Kid made a mental note to inquire more particularly about her father, when he had died, and what position he had occupied in the cowtown.

Clark took his paper, handing in exchange a sheaf of money in twenty and hundred dollar bills. "Nine thousand, two hundred even. It's quite a parcel o' cash, miss, to have around the house with a bunch of outlaws roamin' the neighborhood. But I hear the deppity's goin' to bring 'em in at last. And yore young man there," Clark grinned. "He looks like good protection for a pretty girl."

The man took himself away. Calvert saw Terry place the wad of bills carelessly on the shelf over the fireplace. She had started across the room to take her seat beside him on the old-fashioned haircloth soft when—

"Easy, folks! Shove up yore hands! Quick!"

SNARLED HARSHLY from an open window in the east

wall of the parlor, the command froze them both. Terry Reynolds' hand swept to her throat. Calvert jerked almost off the sofa, then crouched tensely motionless at the threat of two six-guns.

"That's right, lady, reach! Hurry it, Kid!"

Slowly and reluctantly while rage blazed in his throat, Calvert did lift his palms ear-high.

The speaker stood behind his pal with the guns. The low-pulled anthill hat and the bandana mask disguised that Colt wielder effectively. But the kid knew those eyes. And he knew that voice.

There was a light scuffing of boots as the leader of the pair came up the steps and creaked open the screen door. The next instant he had stepped to the mantel and gripped the thick wad of paper money in his left hand. His right held a blue forty-five. He began to back cautiously for the door.

"Not bad, not bad! Yuh ought to've seen the light, Kid. Nine thousand goin' to waste right under yore nose! Or was yuh plannin' to take it after yuh kissed the gal nightie night? Naw, you got fancy ideas—too fancy, if yuh ask me. Bad as yore old man! Wal, I tell yuh, I'm goin' to plant yuh here so yuh'll be found out—dead. Say yore prayers *pronto*, Kid! I'll give yuh three to do it, and I'm sayin' *One! Two! Thr—*"

7

THE WALL BETWEEN

THE KID plunged at Terry standing statuelike in front of him. His charge lurched her across the room to the floor.

Crash! Wham! Bam!

Calvert's gun flamed almost simultaneously with the three leveled guns of the holdups. He had snatched the Colt from his holster while he made his desperate dive at Terry. He had shot twice before Latigo Malone at the window creased his back and knocked him into a heavy rocking chair. The light blotted and a shower of glass fell on Calvert.

He rose on hands and knees dazedly. A body lay near him. Outside, supposing both men dead, Malone cursed as he shoved a leg over the window sill to enter for the money. He spied the looming form of Calvert. Two shots blared in a deafening exchange.

There was a cut-off grunt. The Kid watched shoulders and head fall back from the sill and the booted foot flip high as its short spur raked the wood. Then a thud, and silence.

The parlor was choked with acrid, swirling powder smoke. Calvert stood in a crouch, scarcely breathing. He relaxed slightly and went in a single long stride to the form of the girl. But as he put his hand gently on her shoulder she propped herself with one hand.

"Wh-what happened? Oh!" Terry quavered. "Stan! Are you hurt? Oh, *Stan!*"

She toppled in his arms. Struck forcibly with comprehension of how much he meant to her to bring that tone, he tried to swallow the heavy lump in his throat. He heard shouts of anxious inquiry and running steps coming closer. He lifted the girl to her feet and pulled her against his chest while he crushed his lips on hers, hard, hard as he could!

"Terry! What the devil's happened? Hey, you—"

Man and girl broke apart. She turned unsteadily toward the door. "It's—all right. Come in. Who is it? Wait. There's some one lying right in your path. Wait till I strike a light."

Calvert took a match from his shirt pocket and rubbed it once along the sole of his boot. In the yellow mounting flame he glimpsed her face with its strange mixture of emotion. Her eyes glowed radiant. Panting, she hurried to the next room to return at once with a lamp. Calvert touched his match to its wick.

Mike Stoner stood with a gun in each fist. His eyes traveled from the girl to Calvert, then to the motionless body on the floor. They rose again, accusingly, to Calvert.

"Damn you! I told yuh to clear out o' the county! So yo're tough, huh? I'll—"

"Mike!" Terry cried.

It stopped him an instant. But the malevolence etched deeper on his face, jealousy and suspicion combined with wrath at the thing that had happened here. He hesitated, for once yielding to a will other than his own. "I betcha he's one of them Calverts! Heard the shots. He pulled a gun but it was just a fake!"

He broke off abruptly and stooped to rip off the hat and bandana and pick up the broken wad of paper bills.

"This here is the steer cash Clark paid over, eh?"

"Y-yes," Terry said. She looked shakily at the Kid. "Stan, that was brave of you! I—I'm proud," Terry said, her voice trembling. "But look—you're hit! There's blood on your shirt!"

"Skimmed me is all." Ignoring Stoner coldly, he went over to the corpse and knelt for a closer look. It was Bronk Beckly. Beckly had indeed gone in for easy money—nine thousand dollars of it. But his career had been brief.

CLARK PUFFED into the house, " 'Nother feller dead— jest outside the window," he breathed jerkily. "Dead as a fried chicken! You—you got the money safe, huh?"

"Yes. Everything's all right." Calvert reloaded his gun absently and dropped it into his holster. He glanced at the clock on the mantel. "Terry, I'm sorry, but I got to go. I plumb forgot an important business talk I got on with a man. He'll be waiting—"

"But you can't, Stan. Wait. I'll get water and bandages—"

She ran from the room. At that instant Calvert heard the rumble of Number Eight, the long all-Pullman westbound passenger as it clicked over the switches several blocks away. While he listened it was gone, plowing endless threads of steel toward trestled Panther Mountain canyons. Then short, sharp blasts of the cattle train locomotive whistle floated over the sleepy town.

"Ready to go, I reckon," Clark observed.

The Kid stepped toward the door. Just then Terry hurried back with a basin of water, salve, and clean cloths. She placed them on the table and started to dip a fresh rag to use for a sponge.

"I—really got to go, Terry. Yuh see—"

Shots floated in the night, the bass roar of a Winchester and the bark of Colts.

Mike Stoner roared, "It's the Calverts! Clark—Dawson! Come on! They're stealin' my train!"

He pounded out the door without another glance to see if they followed. Clark frowned, moved, stopped—then with a muttered ejaculation sped in front of the Kid and pitched out of the cottage.

Calvert's eyes glued on the questioning eyes of the girl. With an effort he roused himself, for now of a certainty it was farewell. "Never mind the bandagin', Terry. I got to go." He turned on his heel and put a hand to the screen. "Thanks for the chance to know yuh—even for a little while. So long, Terry!"

She cried something and rushed onto the stoop, but he was running back to the alley, lost in moon-made shadows at the side of the white cottage. Kid Calvert's breast felt crowded but he dared not permit himself to think. Nor was there time. For the band was there and had started things moving. But some rider of Stoner's had interfered. So that now it would be a test whether Giant Anderson and the other members of the gang were going to be able to run off that train before citizens of Deadline gathered in too great numbers.

The Kid thought of the cattle-cash Stoner probably had on him now. He could have seized it either surreptitiously before anyone came into the parlor after that shooting, or by force from Stoner. Somehow he hadn't brought himself to do either. Thieving money in Terry's home just was impossible

Calvert halted. He felt of his back to learn how bad the wound was. Awkwardly he mopped inside his shirt with a clean bandana. He resumed his dog-trot toward the west. There were shots coming sporadically from the railroad siding. Over to his right, horses and men rushed down Deadline's main street. Shouts, demands for help, oaths directed at the Calvert Horde floated to him. But the alley was deserted. The Kid ran on for his horse. Then it was a matter of wrecking the telegraph instrument to prevent warnings being flashed to nearby towns.

He did not greatly care if he missed the train. And he figured that Giant Anderson, McLain, Sinton, Willstock, and the others could handle the loaded special all right. They knew where to halt it, and Calvert could go there to meet them.

He got his horse from the three-walled shed. Astride, the Kid headed for the low hump of the telegraph office that rose at the center of a brief cinder platform beside the rails of the steam road. The office was lighted but the door stood open. He guessed the operator had rushed out to learn the cause of that shooting.

Calvert left this horse and strode in—cautiously. Yes, the place was deserted. He looked around for some club to smash the instrument.

He heard a step. The Kid whirled. He had his gun out in a flash and he all but fired before he realized that it was not a man on the threshold.

"Terry!"

SHE HAD a look of wide amazement as she came in. "Why, Stan!" She moved purposefully toward the telegraph key. "Stan—it's the Calverts! They're running off the stock train! I've got to—"

Shots broke in on her words, told that it was a real battle there at the siding. Then they heard the convulsive clattering jerk of the stock cars.

Terry moved closer to the telegraph instrument. "I've got—"

The Kid holstered his gun as he stepped over to her and took both her hands. "Terry, I have something to do here. And there's something I have to tell you. I tried to tell you before, but I hadn't the sand. It's about me. It's going to mean—"

"Wait, Stan," she said, freeing herself from his grasp. "I can't stop for anything now." She struck a match, lighted the lamp. Her back was to the Kid. He saw that now she was wearing a man's vest over her shirt. And he saw her reach out to grasp the telegraph key. He asked quickly:

"What are you doing, Terry?"

Without looking around, she said, "Telegraph down the line. If Calvert's Horde gets away with the train, I can trap them at—"

"Terry! Take yore hand from that key!" The Kid's voice was low, husky.

The girl threw a startled glance over her shoulder. Her fingers now grasped the key. The Kid leaped over, grabbed her hand, swung her around close to him. With his free hand, he swung his gun barrel down on the telegraph key, wrecking it.

"Stan!" cried Terry. "This means— Oh, you're one of—"

It was then that the Kid saw the front of Terry's vest as she stepped away from him.

"What's this star? You— Why!" he stammered. "It's a sher-iff's!"

"Of course it is! I'm honorary sheriff here. Since father got killed I—"

"Got killed?" he cut in hoarsely. Of a sudden Calvert shook her with brutal insistence. "Who was he—your father?"

"S-Stan! Don't! He was—" she panted, wrenching away— "Mart Reynolds!"

The Kid backed as if struck across the face with a whip. He was a statue in the yellow lamplight of the railroad station office. A dry, wrenched sound came from his throat. For an endless moment, he stood still—with a lifeless stillness.

"Terry—Reynolds! *Reynolds!* I thought yuh were Terry Broderick! Yuh called her mother. Yuh said—"The world reeled drunkenly in Kid Calvert's heart and there was pressure at his brain that threatened to burst it.

A Winchester slammed a quarter-mile away. They ignored the thinning barrage of shots and yells that meant the cattle train was rolling faster, faster to the west down the steel trail of Number Eight.

Terry gasped, "You're one of the Horde! You wrecked that key!"

He nodded, choked another bulging lump in his throat. "My name is Calvert. I'm son to Gunner Calvert." He brushed a hand over his eyes in great weariness. "Can yuh just savvy a thing like that? I ain't Stan Dawson and never was. Why, I'm the leader now, leader of the Calvert Horde you hate so much!"

His voice rose with defiant pride. "I'm against yuh, Terry Reynolds. There's a big, high, steel wall between us, and it'll always be there! I'm the only Calvert left for yuh to hate. I'm Calvert of the Calvert Horde yuh wouldn't even wipe yore feet on, Terry—yes, and those are my men right now, tearin' that train load o' Diamond X beef away from yore side, from yore law-pryin' hellions yuh like so damned much!"

He choked back the torrent of words that still welled up for utterance. Choked them back to peer more intently into the white oval of her face, blanched by the shock of this thing.

A desolate, stricken moan came from her pale lips. It knifed the Kid to his very heart. Swaying, the girl fell away. He thrust out his hands ready to catch her, but dropped them. She stumbled across the office to the wall, where she leaned sobbing brokenly.

He followed. Then, unexpected as a clap of thunder the daughter of Mart Reynolds struck a hand to her waist. It came up with a weapon. There was a glint of lamplight on steel and with a cry of undying hate from the coral lips curved wide above and below her straight white teeth.

CALVERT LUNGED out, caught her wrist in a grip of iron. He snapped the Colt from her grasp. "No yuh don't! You ain't killin' me! You'd cry yore life away if you did that, Terry. I reckon yuh would!"

Her struggle was futile against his man's strength. He forced his lips hungrily searching for hers, forced them over the smooth warm chin with the little dimple in it, and up her cheek. He found her lips at last, warmly moist. And crushed his own down on them.

Calvert broke away panting. He went past her out the door to his horse and while the girl started after in amazement and the confusion of emotions that battled for dominance, Calvert was back. He swept her inside the office again.

He had to seize her as she began to fight him with the spirit of an angered wild colt being broken. Another instant and Calvert shook the hemp lass-rope free. Grimly while she cried out and fought and kicked he bound her arms to her sides, but not so tightly that she would be hurt.

Calvert laid her on the dusty floor, very gently. He had her ankles lashed in a twinkling. "Terry, yuh'll be found in a couple of minutes. I—I hate to do this! You must know I hate it by what I did a minute ago. Kissed you…. I meant that, too. And I'll always mean it. Only, the world's against us, Terry!"

He paused for a last look, and a shadow crossed his face. With heavy heart Calvert passed through the telegraph office door to his horse. He climbed into the saddle wearily. Rowels clapped to his mount, lunging it forward. They shot past the platform end, over an open space, and on past the cattle pens on the left, shot recklessly and with the speed of a rough-riding Cossack bent on the kill.

Some one halloed to the Kid. He paid no heed. His eyes saw the faint pinpoints of green and red that marked the caboose of the steer train. His men had got away, then. A pair stood over the engineer and fireman, he knew, in the swaying locomotive cab. And those captives made her roll—cursing and threatening the six-guns that rode the iron horse with them tonight. In the caboose there would be others of the Horde, gun-ready and grim to the brakie and conductor while the special high-balled for the mountains that crouched like wraith sentinels against the western sky.

The Kid rode past the straggling remnants of defense of the law crowd. They thought him a townsman and yelled to him to turn back. They would be heading for the telegraph office soon, he knew. But Calvert pressed on a mile, three miles, with the coolness of night washing his hot face and the girl he had loved and lost back there helpless amidst the wreckage of the telegrapher's key.

Where Spring Creek snaked its murmuring way under the rails two forms poked suddenly into his path. Calvert reined in.

"Kid?"

"It's him, Dandy!" the Giant sighed with relief. They strode closer, peering up at him. "We was scared yuh'd got nabbed, Kid, and maybe was fit for buryin' by now. Or they had yuh put away somewhere. We looked in the jail and the saloon and all over. Yuh all right?"

"I'm all right, boys. Get on your hosses."

They looked at each other, hesitated, then did as ordered. McLain splashed through the creek at the side of Calvert while Giant Anderson followed close behind, his horse nose-to-flank to the Kid's as he always rode.

Things went off pretty good. We didn't lose anybody. Got 'em sort of leanin' over, Kid," Dandy chuckled. "Now it's a cinch! Just unload out there at the end o' the mile trestle, haze the beef over to Mountain Hole, and deal with that feller that always handles our stuff. It went off like a rocket, swell! Didn't it, Swede?"

"Yeah. Shore did!" The Giant agreed with enthusiasm.

Dandy saw the silent man at his side twist for a long look back toward Deadline. Their horses loped over the dark range and the scent of dew-freshened sage was sweet in the nostrils of beasts and men. At last McLain had to know.

"Well, Kid, aren't yuh glad the way things went?"

He turned his head startledly. "Went? Oh! Shore. Good work, boys—fine. Two more days and a package'll be mailed to Ed Ryan at Prairie Flats. Ryan and his wife and his kid. They'll get their money now. It's what we started out to fix and I reckon we're fixin' it. Ed Ryan'll be all right. He can start over some place.

"Ryan's lucky," said the Kid with a depth of feeling that the others missed. "Shore is lucky." He snapped his head up, looked over the men—his men—Calvert's Horde. Then he said quietly, "Dad can rest easy now, boys. The Ryan job is done."

HORDE OF HATED MEN

Kid Calvert's hated Horde was in the saddle. Gun-devils they were, riding on a mission of death. For one of their band, little "Dandy" McLain, had broken the stern code of the Horde. Dandy had murdered. Hordemen could kill— but never murder. The code of the Horde was relentless. Dandy must die by the hands of his best friends. But not only Calvert's Horde was riding to get Dandy. Another band was swooping down on Beaver Creek—the law! And at their head rode a girl sheriff, the Horde's bitterest enemy—and the girl whom Kid Calvert loved.

I

THE HORDE was riding. Calvert's Horde. Calvert's wild bunch of unbroken, untamed human mustangs, the roughest string that ever bucked injustice and crooked law. Out of the smoking dust billowing from drumming hoofs plunged wanted men, killers, bait for the gallows—desperate, fate-badgered citizens of the lawless trails. They were riding to stop hangman's hemp from strangling a comrade, riding hell-for-leather into the shrieking fury of Satan's quarter section. And maybe they were too late.

At the head of the long-riders streaked a blur of gray speed— Star, the steel-dust stallion that had borne "Kid" Calvert away from the pounding threat of many a death-dealing posse. The Kid himself, waspish of waist, with shoulders like the walking beam of a river steamboat, bent low over the silky mane of the stallion.

He twisted in the saddle. "Scratch them crowbaits, gents," he yelled. "Don't spare 'em. Think o' Dandy. Mebbe right this second them lynchin' hombres are trompin' the life out o' him. Mebbe he's swingin' already. Swingin', men!"

Grief clouded the Kid's thoughts. Baptized in gunfire, seasoned by powder smoke, and dedicated to a lifelong fight for the underdog, the Kid had been thrown into the leadership of the Horde by tragic circumstance.

He was the arbiter of the Horde's code—a code as harsh as life had been to these Coltmen. By the code, a man could kill,

but he could not murder. Yet "Dandy" McLain, the flowery-vested little gambler, had murdered. That was the soul-searing word which had come to the Horde's hideout, which was driving these forsaken men in a mad race to Beaver Creek. Dandy McLain had murdered. And he had to die.

He had to die! A shudder shook the Kid's powerful frame; a frame as durable as ox bone bound in whang leather. Since the time that life had fled through the bullet holes in the body of his father, old "Gunner" Calvert, the Kid had felt toward Dandy McLain much as a son feels toward his dad. Between them existed the bond—fashioned of respect, admiration, and understanding—which holds strong men together.

Yet if the Horde rescued Dandy McLain from the lynch

If the Kid grabbed for
the Colt, maybe Terry
would be killed.

mob, the Kid would be forced to the heart-shriveling task of pronouncing death sentence over the little gambler. The code demanded it. Dandy would be given a gentleman's chance—the chance to blast out his own life. Failing, he would have to face a firing squad of his comrades. And to the Kid would fall the duty of signaling for the execution, or firing the mercy shot. The Kid would have to kill the man whom he admired above all others.

Calvert's Horde plunged across a sage and alkali flat, weaved through the chaparral of a slope, and struck into the timber of the altitudes. Grouse whirred out of the brush, went drumming before the terrifying thunder of hoofs. Jack rabbits zigzagged for safety. A deer left a water hole in graceful flight.

The Horde was nearing Beaver Creek. Always the Kid's steel-dust kept in the lead. The long, easy stride of the close-coupled, deep-barreled stallion had often left posse mounts far in the rear.

Eleven men rode with Kid Calvert, men whom the law would shoot down like hydrophobia coyotes, men who forever had to fog the owl-hoot trail, hunted and reviled. The Kid knew that only their loyalty to him, to the Horde, to the memory of old Gunner Calvert, saved them from joining the murderers' legion.

The constant defense of the downtrodden submerged their hate. But they were men without hope. Ever-present hovered the danger that the spark of bitterness would flame up that hate. They bordered the line that separated those who killed in the cause of justice from those who took life wantonly, treacherously. It was said that Dandy McLain had crossed that line.

"I can't believe it," muttered "Giant" Anderson, the man mountain riding close behind the Kid. "Dandy wouldn't kill a jasper that didn't deserve it. Dandy's so square, he'd almost let a cougar take a bite outa him afore he'd blast the brute."

Anderson toted two hundred and forty pounds of gristly strength on his massive frame, and the only surplus he carried was a surplus of courage and kindness.

A boyish, simple son of the open range, Giant was always fussing over a motherless fawn, a lost bear cub or a cougar kitten he had rescued. He had herded in scores of tattered kids riding the chuck-line to starvation, had built them up on beans and steak, and then had looped them jobs. Yet life had scarred Giant a-plenty. If ever the wounds to his spirit were rasped, a savage killer was apt to spread terror across the land.

"Dandy ain't a killin' hombre," said Nate Willstock, veteran of the outtrails, who long had gripped lawless guns. "Dandy's an artist. He ain't gold-minded a-tall. To him, winning means more than winnings."

A strange, somber gent this Willstock with the wintry eyes and the barbed wit, a brooding gunslick who lived only to deal sudden justice to the unjust. Often he had admitted that he stood on the line, that save for the Horde, long ago he would have gone down, wearing a murderer's boots.

"If Danny murdered them gold-diggin' gents," said "Grama" Sinton, the meek and low-voiced one, "then kindness should bring a feller to the gallows an' a drygulcher oughta get a medal of honor fer every hombre he plugs in the back."

A man with a gentle smile and brown eyes as soft and glowing as a calf's, Sinton depended on his loyalty to the Horde to check his sudden, unreasoning rages.

LIFE HAD handled them all as ruthlessly as Dandy McLain handled a wolfish tinhorn gambler. They stood on the line, every man of them, yet if they pulled Dandy from the lynch mob, they would have to take his life. They would have to kill a pard who had crossed the line. The wicked irony was like a canker eating into their hearts.

The Horde pounded up a rock-studded slope, raced along a sandy hogback, dipped into a brush-choked draw, and then struck a slant that led to a skyscraping ridge. On the other side lay Beaver Creek, where yellow colors glittering in the gravel had flung men into a wild stampede, and overnight had sprouted a mushroom town across the valley's floor. The creek yielded rich pannings.

That was why little Dandy McLain had trekked in. Some one was bound to haul in the dust at night for which men mucked and slaved all day. Dandy was as smooth a cardsharp as ever cold-decked a greedy, mouthy tinhorn. He was a master of the "spread," the trick of picking wanted pasteboards out of the discard. He could slither them from the bottom of the deck even while keen, suspicious eyes watched. Men didn't cheat Dandy. Cheap tricksters and strutting sports had tried endlessly to ring in marked decks, but Dandy could read face-down cards like a blindman reads raised printing.

Dandy McLain was a lawbreaker and a cheat. He cheated for humanity. His huge winnings didn't linger in his pockets. A little finery to please his dude's nature, an extra sack of grain for his mount, a few plugs of chaw and a jug of cactus firewater for "Peel" Rogers, the cook, and the rest of the loot went to the needy.

Now they said Dandy was a murderer. Lynch fever burned in Beaver Creek. The Kid visioned Dandy dragged from the jail and strung up. Were they too late? Had the ugly noose done its work?

The sweating, foam-flecked horses pulled to the top of the ridge. On the rim the owl-hooters drew rein, and gazed down onto a broad valley where the town of Beaver Creek sprawled nakedly over the rolling expanse.

A groan escaped the Kid. He felt as though his heart were pumping lead into his veins. On the northern edge of town stood a gray building of rock with barred windows. Around it swarmed a wild, yelling, gesticulating man-pack. The owl-hooters saw the door flung open, saw a small man shoved out to the lynch-crazed mob. Dandy McLain. Dandy, whose crooked cards had brought peace, happiness, health to a vast army of the poor and oppressed.

Fists descended on the little gambler. The Kid's mouth went dry as a gun barrel glinted, as a knife flashed. Before the Horde could ride in, little Dandy would be a crimsoned mass of pulped and mangled flesh.

Red anger swept Calvert's Horde. Giant Anderson ground his teeth and spurred his horse. Nate Willstock's eyes grew as bleak as a Montana blizzard. Old Peel Rogers swallowed a quid of cut-plug and clawed for a black-walnut gun butt.

The Kid reined around. "Draw in, men!" he rapped fiercely. "I'm thinkin' the same way—about them jaspers. But hold a tight rein. Cuttin' them down won't save Dandy, an' yuh know the Horde's stand on murder."

"Gawd!" breathed Giant, clenching shoulder-of-mutton fists. "Dandy's down. They're kickin' him. They—they're stompin' him!"

THE KID brushed a hand across his face. He fought against the mad desire to burn powder. The miners of Beaver Creek had become grandsons of the devil. They were demented with hate, shrieking and milling in an orgy of raw, savage justice.

Knots of muscle bunched on the Kid's jaw. His eyes were sunken and burning from the turmoil that raged within him. He clamped down on his self-control. Let him break the leash, and blood would splash the gold of Beaver Creek. The town would become a shambles. One word from the slim long-rider on the ridge—and scores would die.

"Easy does it," he said quietly. "We'll do what we can. If Dandy ain't gone, we'll save him—somehow, some way. Fan out now. Ride in solo. Easy, *sabe*—easy. Don't let 'em get hep we're here. If I give the signal, bunch up. We'll try something. But no wallowin' in blood."

That was all. The Kid had spoken—and he was the law. Those cold-eyed killer men rode into Beaver Creek, rode in singly, unnoticed, fighting to mask blazing emotions. By the time they reached the town square, Dandy McLain had been revived and dragged to a cottonwood tree.

Already a rope was dangling, a noose gaping for its victim. Men were howling, jeering. In the pit of the mob, Dandy McLain sat astride a snorting, quivering sorrel. Dandy alone in Beaver Creek was calm. Clothes torn, fancy vest in shreds, face clawed and bruised, the battered little gambler was smiling coldly, contemptuously.

The significance of that scornful twist to the lips was like a knife thrust in the Kid's heart. Was that cold contempt a silent admission of guilt?

Dandy McLain called to the crowd for silence. The response was a wild outburst of hate. Then a seamed and labor-gnarled prospector bellowed for attention. The din ceased like the sudden lapse of a storm.

"Give the skunk his say," he boomed. "It's fittin' an' proper that a jasper should spill his last words. Go ahead, McLain. Wag yore tongue. Tell us yo're sorry yuh killed Pocket Peters and Hardrock Benson. Tell us yo're glad. Tell us yuh wish

Beaver Creek had jest one heart an' yuh a gun to puncture it. Tell us anything. It's the fittin' thing fer a dyin' man to do."

"Thank you, Lem Dorgan," said Dandy easily. "Comin' from a thumb-handed card fumbler who bowed to me seven nights straight, that's right high-minded talk. Waal, pards, I ain't denyin' an' I ain't apologizin'. I put Peters and Benson out of their misery. Did it jest as yuh figured. Scratched them with my gold rowel watch charm, dipped in rattlesnake p'ison. They've cashed in their chips, an' now you figure I'm headed for the discard heap. Uh uh, pards. I'm in a jack-pot, but I'm holdin' the high cards."

Life seemed to drain out of the Kid. He had admired Dandy so, had admired him for his artist's skill with the cards, for his nimble brain, his humanity, his reckless daring. Now—the end was near.

"Come on, come on," yelled a miner. "Get it over with. The sheriff is liable to fog in. I ain't one to fight agin' a skirt. If Terry Reynolds hits town—me, I'm slopin'."

A pang far more agonizing than the stinging bite of a slicing knife stabbed through Kid Calvert. Terry Reynolds. Daughter of the lawman whose posse had killed the Kid's father. Terry's father was gone, too—dropped by lawless guns in that terrific battle months ago. The girl was carrying on. The Kid experienced a fleeting moment of warmth. Such a little thing—a wisp of beauty and trail-toughened spunk. She could ride like the wind and clip a candle wick at twenty paces.

She was the honorary sheriff of Washakie County. Back in Deadline, the county seat, a furious political war was raging. Teresa Reynolds stood as the candidate of the town's solid element, on a platform planked with the promise to ride the Calvert Horde out of existence.

"But you're not going to string me up, gents," Dandy McLain was saying. The gambler nodded at a grizzled prospector. "You, Hank O'Day. The sign's on yuh. Two-three days, an' they plant yuh in boot-hill. Mebbe less. Yo're marked for the streak of death. Hello, Link Wilson. Yuh've sloshed out yore rum-eaten belly with tequila for about the last time. The streak's goin' to turn yore bloated carcass into buzzard bait."

Link Wilson's booze-flushed face washed out to putty-gray. He drained a whisky flask at a gulp.

"You, Bill," Dandy went on. "The streak ain't overlookin' yuh. Horned in on the party, eh, Singlejack?" the gambler spoke to a labor-humped miner. "Reckon yuh forgot that I tossed back my winnings when I heard 'bout that sick kid in El Paso. Waal, with me in hell, yuh'll be as safe as a steer in a slaughter-house pen!"

Dandy's funereal voice rolled out a prophecy of doom to a score of men. Tied, beaten, with a hangman's noose dangling near his head, Dandy McLain was the master of that fear-inspired mob.

On the fringe of the swarm, saddened men slumped in their saddles. The Horde had known Dandy McLain for a prince and a tophand gent. But the Coltmen had heard, and they were speechless. The world was whirling for the Kid. The others stared as though just run through with cold steel.

"Go on, yuh yellow skunks!" Dandy McLain flung at the mob. "String me high! Then gawk at my strangled corpse—an' think of the death that's waitin' for yuh!"

2

TERRY RIDES IN

THE KID wished that Dandy had been killed in one of the Horde's battles against injustice. Better had the little fellow gone out in a halo of powder smoke, clutching hot, pounding guns that roared in defense of the underdog. Now treachery smudged the name of Dandy McLain.

"Mebbe this feller's drawin' the long bow," spoke the miner

Lem Dorgan, "but he shore spieled a line that's gonna keep a lot of us awake nights. Hangin' him won't fetch back Pocket an' Hardrock, an' I ain't hankerin' to git branded by that streak o' death. He's probably got a pack o' wild uns ready to scratch us into hell. Ef we take him back to the 'gow, we stand a chance of whuppin' the truth out of him. So—"

A ripple of assent answered Dorgan. Dandy McLain laughed, hurled contempt and defiance into the teeth of the mob. No countering jeer ripped out. Beaver Creek was subdued, sobered, frightened. A path split through the man-pack, and Dorgan grabbed the reins of Dandy's sorrel.

Crushed by his pard's viciousness, the Kid nodded slightly to Giant Anderson, and reined away from the spreading mob. The Horde trailed, and presently the owl-hooters bunched behind a rambling frame stable off the main street.

The Kid raised his hands helplessly. "Yuh heard," he said bitterly. "Dandy's gone over. It could happen to any of us. Hate's liable to trigger our Colts. Law guns have shore shot up my life—took my mother—burned down dad. Scarred me—not jest on the outside, gents. Sometimes I—well, we got to bust Dandy out o' jail. I've got a plan—"

The Kid's voice trailed off. Men stared at the ground. Men studied saddle pommels, fumbled in building smokes, spilled the makings.

"Dandy would like it better if we left him there, son," muttered the wintry-eyed Willstock. "He's through. In our hands, he wouldn't hear no howlin', but politeness doesn't stop a man's innards from flip-floppin' when he's facin' a firin' squad. The Horde's got a tough code, Kid. A tough code."

"I'd stick my foot in a rattler den fer Dandy," rumbled Giant Anderson fervently. "When yuh've been sharin' beans an' whiffin' gunsmoke together as long as me an' Dandy, yuh don't talk 'bout codes."

The Kid traced his finger around a silver concha on his batwing chaps. He didn't say anything. He couldn't say anything. He felt as though a fire had hollowed him out. His mouth and throat were parched from burning grief.

Men cleared their throats. Men started to speak and stopped as words ran together. Sadness and uncertainty fogged their brains. Giant Anderson, who preferred plug tobacco to a smoke, rolled three cigarettes in the space of an awkward, silent minute, took a few puffs and threw them down.

The Kid muttered savagely, and then he called for the show-down. "Yuh know how I feel personal," he said huskily. "I'm jest a gun-branded yearlin'. Need an old head back o' me. Dandy was readin' face-down cards afore I busted out with my first squawl. Thinkin' his way out of a thousand scrapes didn't take the edge off his brain. I look up to Dandy sorta like—well, dad's gone an'— If the decision is left to me, I've got the answer."

The Kid's jaw clamped, his lips pressed into a scar. Men waited, expectant, anxious.

"We'll get Dandy," the Kid said in a low voice. "We'll try, anyway—like all hell. If we get him, we'll fog to the hideout. Then—" the Kid gnawed his lip so fiercely that blood trickled down his chin—"the Horde is finished. We scatter, gents. Scatter. Plenty o' range. We can spread out an' run solo."

The announcement hit them as a dousing of ice water would affect a sleeping man. They weren't the kind who were easily surprised, but the Kid had slugged them with their guard down. Peel Rogers uttered a wail.

"By dogies, the shock was too much fer yuh, son!" he exclaimed. "Bust up the Horde! I'll be a sun-fishin' chipmunk! Drink the Rio Grande dry! Burrow through the Mogollones with a spoon. Do something easy like that. Bust hell, but not the Horde, 'cause the Horde jest ain't a bustin' outfit."

Fright showed on their faces. Fright! The end of the Horde meant their end. They were strong men, but the Horde was their backbone. It was the reins that guided them, the whip that checked them.

The Kid challenged the gaze of every man in the Horde. "I

can read yore thoughts. Men, what yo're thinkin' is mild compared to my feelings. The Horde has been splashed with dad's
blood. The Horde was his dream. Calvert's Horde. What it
stands for is what dad always fought for, a law higher than
what's on the books—the law of humanity."

His eyes burned into the men with an intensity of feeling
that threw a spell over them. "I'm thinkin' about that law, an'
I'm thinkin' about the code. If the Horde isn't stronger than any
of its members, then—" The Kid made a helpless gesture.
"Dandy is my friend. *Is*—men. Yet he's violated the code. I'm
willin' to answer to a greater law. But without the code, the
Horde is just a pack of gunslicks on the dodge. It can't go on.
That's all, gents. We ride."

KID CALVERT was a yearling, but he was the son of a
gunman, and he had the flash and persuasion that held men.
He gave a few directions and they split, most of them heading
south of town, while the Kid reined with Anderson, Willstock,
Sinton, and the cook toward the jail.

Save for sunning hound dogs and hitched mounts, the
wheel-rutted, hoof-pocked main street was deserted. In the
false-fronted saloons men shouldered one another along the
shining mahogany bars, sloshing liquor over the heat of lynch
fever.

Riding up a back street, the owl-hooters dismounted behind
the jail. Peel Rogers stayed with the horses. The others sauntered out singly. Every one knew of the Horde; few knew the
men in it. Somebody might recognize them—a chance they
took whenever they rode into a settlement.

The Kid sidled up to a knot of men in front of the jail. Two
of the miners had been warned of death, condemned by Dandy.
Clean-cut young fellows, already muscle-bound from swinging
picks and singlejacks. Fifty years ahead of them, good years,
unless— What had happened to Dandy? He'd always had more
balance than the rest, more reason for bitterness, and less of it.

"Any word, men?" the Kid asked, blending in. "That McLain

hombre looked plenty poker face to me. Looked like he could sop up one hell of a poundin' without waggin' his tongue. Yuh jaspers scheduled for boot-hill oughta saddle up an' drift for healthy range."

"I'm ready to fade," answered a condemned man. "But I've got a hunch Deputy Fenston will make him jaw-whack the facts. The lawman's got a prize fighter from New Orleans up there. Sunrise Sorrell, too—blood brother of a Yaqui tribe. What that gent don't know about torture, yuh kin paint on the toenail of a gnat. Couple of champ floor-fighters up there from the Twisted Horn Saloon. If they don't jar loose the names of McLain's outfit o' killers, I'm goin' to git a sudden interest in Montana."

No one noticed that the Kid's gray eyes glinted like burnished gun-metal. He got the information he wanted, information that struck him like the slash of cold steel. The Kid believed in law. But law mocked justice when it brought in bruisers, torturers to slug and burn a prisoner.

A harsh outburst came from the jail. The Kid winced. He shot a warning glance at his men. Giant Anderson's eyes slitted and he ran his tongue over his tightening lips. His face a slate-gray mask holding two burning coals, Grama Sinton caressed the worn, shiny holster of his six-gun. A savage roar broke from the second story of the jail. A hollow thud suggested the bruising impact of bone against flesh. No cry of pain or protest, though.

Those butchers could flay little Dandy until his hide dripped, could scorch the soles off his feet until the torturers themselves turned green from the smell of cooking flesh. And the only sound they'd get out of Dandy would be a harsh grating of his teeth as he ground off the enamel.

Filling his hand, Peel Rogers—always dynamite with a short fuse—was lining out for the jail. The Kid's scalp twitched. Dread froze the marrow in his bones. He couldn't call out, didn't dare draw attention. The others were on the way. There was no stopping them. The miners saw them go, didn't catch the significance.

The Kid stiffened with trembling apprehension. The racket upstairs grew in barbarous intensity. Then it ceased, and the silence was evil, maddening. The Kid's shaky hand dragged across his sweat-bathed face. His heart trip-hammered against his breast-bone.

He heard coming from the cell: "He's yore buzzard, Sunrise. Show him yore tricks. We can't make him talk, but we can make him howl."

The sheriff had turned the job over to Sunrise Sorrell, the Yaqui blood brother, the torturer. A thin spiral of smoke curled from the cell window, and the Kid felt sure he was losing his mind.

"Where are them jaspers goin'?" demanded a miner. "Seems like they're almighty interested in—"

A thunderous blast of gunfire smashed the murmuring quiet of the town. The Kid's heart leaped exultantly. Hell had torn loose from its hinges at the south end of town. Colts were bucking law and order down there, growing hot in renegade hands. Men shouted, cursed; horses squealed, snorted. Screams more terrifying than the night calls of prowling cougars shrilled across the town.

Then the devil's overtone of horror spread above the nerve-shattering din. The snap and crackle of flames licking eagerly at dry wood. A building was ablaze, folding up under the gutting onslaught of a roaring inferno. Two, three. Smoke fogged the atmosphere. Fiery tentacles reached through the billowing clouds.

A fear-laden cry blared out: "The Horde! Calvert's Horde!"

THE SALOONS disgorged men turned cold sober by the cry. Beaver Creek suddenly bristled with six-guns. The miners sprinted from the front of the jail. The Kid was alone. The town forgot Dandy McLain, forgot the dead and the doomed, the insidious streak of death. The town was riding against Calvert's Horde, riding against a wild bunch that trampled authority.

The Kid bounded for the jail, got ahead of his men. New fear assailed him. He had ordered an attack—a sham attack. He had instructed his men to fire empty shacks, to page the citizenry with heavy gun talk. The ruse had worked—but maybe too well.

Men were running along the jail corridor. The Kid drew his bandana over his face, motioned his pards to hug the wall. Out of the jail catapulted Deputy Sheriff Fenston, a scowling hulk of fury. He saw the masked Kid and clawed for his six-gun.

The Colt leaped from the leather in a draw that practice and necessity had smoothed to the flashing speed of burning powder. The Kid's square-cut fist was on the way in a sweeping drive to the jaw. The .45 spouted and bucked in the lawman's hand. But the gun exploded after the Kid had set off the dynamite in his punch.

Deputy Fenston dropped like a front-footed bronc, his Colt smoking and a cloud of dust puffing up where the bullet had burrowed.

Another man plunged from the door, aware that disaster awaited him, but unable to check his rush. His face was a war-torn map of unnumbered brawls. One of the Twisted Horn bouncers, this gent, a brute whose character probably was as twisted as the horn that hung above the saloon's batwing doors. His hand flipped hipward; went down, didn't come up. For once he was on the receiving end of the bounce.

Giant Anderson settled for him. The blow started about three feet behind Giant, with the big fellow's knuckles trailing in the dust. That hambone fist all but smoked through the air, a walloping, wagon-tongue right that collided with the point of a lantern jaw. When the saloon bruiser stopped spinning, he collapsed ten feet away, relieved of his senses.

The Kid was in the corridor. A cry of terror came through the gloom. Flame gashed the murk. A tug at his left sleeve made the Kid press frantically against the wall. Another fiery lance stabbed out. A bullet seared the flesh of his shoulder, seared like a white-hot branding iron. The biting pain cleaved his tongue to the roof of his mouth. Calvert fired wide of the blazing streak.

"Yo're through!" he yelled savagely. "Another shot, an' yuh'll have more holes than a sponge. If yuh want to dirty up the jail with yore blood—let 'er go, hombre!"

Talk—but the kind of talk that got results. The Kid was red-headed over those shots. They might draw help. And he was icily aware of what they would have done to him had they connected solidly. The man in the gloom had Kid Calvert just where he wanted him, but he didn't know it. The Kid couldn't shoot the man, couldn't shoot a gent defending the law. But his tough manner was more convincing than his wild shot.

"Don't drill us!" came a fear-choked plea.

Guns clattered on the slab-rock floor.

The human barrier between Dandy McLain and the Horde was down. Four men shuffled into the light—the jailer, the prize fighter, the white Yaqui, the second saloon bouncer—and they were reaching high.

The Kid looked them over. Defenders of the law, eh? Compared to the clean-cut, sharp-eyed men of the Horde, these whisky-nosed specimens looked like the faces generally seen on the "Wanted" bulletins of the law. Except for the old jailer, who kept his neck stiff and his jaw tight, they were the human counterparts of whipped curs.

Sinton and Willstock frisked them for hideout guns.

"We want no truck with yuh," the Kid told them gruffly. "Start clumpin' for town, an' don't look back. If yo're honin' for a ruckus, yuh'll find Calvert's Horde right obligin'."

The four were wise men to whom a word was sufficient. Giant Anderson had the jailer's keys. Peel Rogers, who had rushed around, hoping for the chance to make his gun snarl, returned to the horses. While the Kid kept his eyes on the four who were busy putting distance between themselves and the jail, the Hordemen went after Dandy.

GIANT HAD the little gambler out of the cell by the time the Kid reached the second floor. The muscles of the Kid's stomach contracted in pity and dread when he saw Dandy. The little fellow of few scruples and many charities looked as though he had been thrown into a cougar's lair. The cruel ordeal had drawn deeply on his physical resources, but his cut and bruised head was up, his split lips bleeding from a broad grin.

"Howdy, Kid," Dandy greeted in his breezy manner. "Many thanks for my life. Yuh fellers shore was high cards to me. I thought I was never goin' to hear the chips click again. The maulin' of that lynch mob wasn't a patch to the goin'-over them law Johnnies was slippin' me."

The Kid was tongue-tied by Dandy's jovial manner. Had the gambler forgotten those murders, forgotten the code? Here was a man whose poker draw could get him far more than another outlaw's gun draw. Yet the owl-hooter had taken life wrongfully—and he was feeling jocular.

Suddenly the Kid started. The drum of hoofs reached his ears. He swung around, ran to the cell window. Riders were streaking down the main street toward the burning shacks. The gunfire south of town had dwindled. The Horde had stayed just long enough to draw Beaver Creek into a hot pursuit. Shots still rang out, but distance muffled them. The newcomers were heading toward those shots. On a rider's vest, the Kid glimpsed the glint of metal. A lawman. The Kid's temples throbbed. He felt sure that Terry Reynolds was riding with the posse.

Anxiety and eagerness sent a tremor through the Kid. "The law! Get Dandy out o' here. The back way. Fog fer the hideout. Backtrack plenty. Backtrack so even a wolf can't trail yuh. I'm stickin'."

The men hurried from the jail, while the Kid crouched at the window, gripping his Colt and ready to make a gun bluff. Now that he was alone, he began to feel the pain in his bullet-creased shoulder. His shirt was drenched crimson, his arm stiffening. The lawmen vanished into the line of buildings. Presently hoofs thudded again. The Kid smiled grimly. His owl-hooters would soon be on the dim trails. His men would lose any posse in the canyon-slashed country beyond.

Holstering his gun, the Kid went down the front stairs. He hadn't seen Terry Reynolds in the posse from Deadline, but the girl might have been hidden from his view by other riders. The Kid intended to follow. No harm would come to her because of the Horde. He'd see to that. He crept down the stairs with the caution that had been born on the owl-hoot trail. He moved toward the office with the soft pad of a stalking panther.

Suddenly he sensed eyes watching him. He grew rigid. A horse whinnied outside. It wasn't his steel-dust. He slapped at his holster, whirled around, whirled to stare into the black mouth of a leveled .45. The gun startled him far less than the person behind it.

"Terry!" he cried, eager light flashing in his eyes which suddenly clouded with deep hurt. His pulse quickened with delight, even while anguish stabbed at his heart.

Always would emotion tear at his spirit when he saw her. Futility engulfed him. Circumstance had raised an impenetrable barrier between these two. They were close, but still as far apart as though they stood on separate planets. He felt as helpless as a lone dogie on a storm-blasted prairie.

Her beauty took his breath. It'd take the sweep of a grizzly's paw to sink him. But a look in those eyes which held the darkness and mystery of midnight, and the world reeled. His knees went weak. He was a man before men, but a child before this girl who had the freshness of a fawn, the grace of a deer. He looked at those teeth, glistening like dew at the flush of dawn, as a jeweler would gaze in admiration at matched pearls. Beneath her sun bronze lay a lovely tint that made him think that peach blossoms had brushed their beauty into her cheeks.

"I knew you were here," she spoke in a low, vibrant voice

tinged with reproach and regret—and resonant with feeling. "I rode in to save Washakie County the disgrace of a lynching. Those gunshots told me I was too late. Then I saw your horse, and I knew I wasn't too late to catch the biggest force for evil in the state. You—Kid Calvert! I sent my posse on. None of my men is going to fall before your guns. I can handle you, Kid Calvert. Since your father's death, the Horde is built around you. With you taken care of, we can easily round up your pack of murderers."

The girl, too, was suffering from warring emotions. In her eyes was the glow that only a lover sees; in her voice the grim note that a captured outlaw hears. The Kid warmed to that look and chilled to that tone. Rather would he have had a beetle-browed killer focus a gun muzzle on him than this slip of a girl. He knew how to handle killers.

He stared at the sheriff's badge on her dark blue jacket. She was dainty, feminine, but the holster hung against her corduroy split skirt had belonged to a gunman, her father—Sheriff Mart Reynolds. Her calfskin half-boots were solidly planted on the floor. Terry Reynolds meant business.

"Terry, I—" The Kid broke off lamely. There was nothing for him to say, nor was this the time for talk. Terry was safe. That was the big item. But now he had to get back to the hideout grounds.

He wouldn't hurt Terry Reynolds even to save himself from the gallows, but he had to get away. He thought of walking from her with his back turned. There were few booze-soaked killers inhuman enough to shoot a man in the back. Certainly Terry wouldn't. But she might bring a gun barrel down on his head, take him back to Deadline senseless. An idea brought a gleam to his eyes.

"Terry, I—" he began again. Then he staggered, clutched at his crimson-drenched shoulder. His eyes rolled; the lids flickered. His knees buckled. He pawed at the air. His last glimpse was of Terry's oval face going white under its bronze, her gun lowering.

The Kid collapsed, lay still.

"Stan! Stan!" she cried, using the name she had known him by before she learned that he was the leader of Calvert's Horde. She knelt beside him, put a warm, trembling hand on his forehead. "Oh, Stan boy—" and there were tears in her voice— "you're hurt—hurt."

3

THE DEVIL'S DIGGINGS

THOUGH THE KID lay like a corpse, never had he been so alive. The touch of her hand sent a tingling through him that was genuine agony, like the piercing of a million needle points. He had done this trick for the Horde's sake, to give himself a chance for the getaway. But now that he had the chance, he couldn't stop the pretense.

Her spontaneous display of anxiety made him feel like a brute; mean, despicable, unworthy. He had faked a faint to catch her off guard. But her amazing reaction startled him, caught him unprepared.

Deep shame surged through him when she got a jug of water from the office, bathed his forehead and cradled him in her arms as she washed his wound. The fragrance of her hair, the murmur of her voice, the delicious closeness of her, soothed him until he felt transported from a world in which he had known little but pain and hardship.

He believed he would go mad from the magic of her touch; felt that ecstasy would consume him. Life had given him a great capacity for misery, small room for happiness. His exquisite, torturing joy took greater toll than would have a savage clash with a barroom brawler.

She held him close, and the warmth of her closeness sent his rapture into wild crescendo. This rider of the outtrails, this veteran of the owl-hoot, this grim, bullet-scarred youngster, to whom the biting pungency of powder smoke was as commonplace as the aroma of ground coffee to a storekeeper, was starved for tenderness, love famished, hungry for the gentleness that this girl wanted to give him.

He knew that she thought the barrier was down for a while, that his need of help changed them from the hunter and the hunted into a girl and a man who loved deeply. He knew, too, that she would shrink in horror, loathing him, if she learned that he knew her true feelings.

The vision of a small ranch and this girl riding happily at his side through life tormented him until he shook his head violently to jar out the picture that suddenly smothered his ecstasy with despair and hopelessness. Terry gasped. The Kid realized that he had to move swiftly.

He had to get away, and he didn't intend to betray his pretense. As much as to save her from overwhelming embarrassment, he wanted to fend off any chance of her hating him. He knew of her love, and the knowledge thrilled him, gave him a memory to cherish, to bolster up his spirit when fate was cutting loose haymakers from all angles. But if her intense hatred for what he represented ever shifted to him, he felt that life would suddenly hold no more value than a lead bullet.

"Huh!" he grunted, sitting up and feigning bewilderment. "Where—" He looked dazedly at the girl. "What— Terry, Terry, what are you doing here? Oh!"

The girl was going for her gun. He grabbed her hand before it reached the black butt, and snatched the Colt from the holster. He was back in harness again. This was routine business—disarming people.

"Sorry, but hands made to hold brooms and babies ain't for jugglin' smoke poles," he spoke with a hardness that he didn't feel. His face was set, but his eyes glowed. "I'll take the stingers out of this hornets' nest, an' leave the gun uptrail a few miles."

The Kid bowed to Terry and rushed from the jail, taking her gun. He left behind a bewildered girl, who also had been through an emotional experience, one that had caused the rôle of sheriff to fall away. She was still under the spell of those tender moments. Possibly there were guns in the jail office, but she didn't run for them. The Kid's last glimpse of her, she was still standing like one in a trance.

If he'd had his choice, his leave-taking would have been entirely different. But hoofbeats had brought up the practical side, made him aware that his tender thoughts were in danger of being strangled by hangman's rope. Riders were heading for the jail. They saw the owl-hooter. A wild shot punctuated the command to halt. But the Kid had a habit of ignoring commands. He forked Star without touching the stirrup, and shortly he was over the ridge into broken country.

The Kid gave the mount its head, and the powerful steel-dust held a pace through the rugged hills that would have killed an ordinary horse. He saw nothing of the sweeping grandeur of this vast wilderness. Desolation rode with him. In his eyes the world was as bleak as a crater in the moon.

Star's hoofs beat a rhythm that symbolized the approach of doom for Dandy McLain. How could the Kid return to the Horde? He believed in the code, but he was doubting his right to enforce it. Yet the Horde would start to crumple the day the code was ignored.

Shadows were deepening into dusk when he reached the hideout.

A mile below the holing-up grounds a sentry rode out of the underbrush. "Great work, Kid," he greeted jovially. "I shore figured we was never goin' to see Dandy again. The boys are celebratin' with a little jamboree up yonder."

The Kid nodded curtly. His astonishment at the sentry's good nature changed to bewilderment when he rode into the pine-grown basin atop a ridge, where the Horde lived in old wood-choppers' cabins. Peel Rogers was just cracking the neck off a bottle—not the first one obviously. He slopped the liquor into a tincup, and hailed the Kid with a toast.

"Here's to high-blood pressure, pard. Light down an' embalm yoreself with the triple-distilled essence of sassafras roots. The elixir of life. One guzzle, an' a jack rabbit would hamstring a wolf."

IN THE past, with the exception of old Peel, the Hordemen seldom had given the bottle a play. Too often did their lives depend on split-seconds and steel nerves. John Barleycorn had never improved a man's speed or his aim. But now most of the men in the hideout showed that they had tilted flasks.

On his wheezy, battered concertina, Giant Anderson pumped out a tune that was as mournful as a wolf calling to the frozen moon.

Grama Sinton was showing the crowd tricks of fancy roping that had taken top money in rodeos from the Milk River to the Gila. Even Nate Willstock, the humorless, had thawed out until he was as noisy as a cowboy getting rid of a month's wages.

The hilarity spoke of the fondness these men had for Dandy McLain. A chill went through the Kid at the sight of the little gambler, patched and bandaged, and rigged in new finery. The gambler displayed his wizardry with the cards, spreading them along his arm to the shoulder in perfect formation, or twisting the deck in amazing gyrations.

The Kid didn't answer Dandy's full-hearted greeting. Out of the corner of his eye, he saw the gambler staring in hurt puzzlement. A deep bitterness assailed the youngster. As much as he had always admired and respected Dandy, he couldn't ride with a murderer. The Horde or Dandy was doomed.

The Kid had profound sympathy, almost pity, for these gunslicks. They were simple men, hard fibered and soft hearted. Daily they risked their lives, giving all, taking nothing.

The Kid couldn't blast this harmless jamboree with a showdown. And yet to postpone it seemed unfair to Dandy. The Kid could overlook countless faults. It was his own imperfections that made him Kid Calvert. But he couldn't overlook treachery.

He was unsaddling when Dandy strode up, riffling a pack of cards and looking anxious and hurt. "Gosh, son, what's the trouble? Yuh look like a jasper who's coppered his bet on a winnin' play. No holdout on yore tinhorn pard. Deal what's on yore mind, an' I'll take 'em as they fall—deuces, treys, or high cards."

The Kid didn't answer. He threw his saddle across a saw-buck. After Star had taken a roll, the Kid led the steel-dust to water, then curried him, while the mount nosed into a double measure of grain. Dandy didn't speak for a long while, but he followed the Kid. The little cardsharp knew when to talk and when to keep a short tongue. Not until the Kid had washed up, and was wandering moodily through the brush did Dandy break the silence.

"All right, son. Stop holdin' yore cards so close to yore vest. Yuh ain't actin' like old Gunner's boy. What's got yuh upset?"

The Kid eyed the golden rowel watch charm hanging from a nugget chain on Dandy's flowery vest. "Jest thinkin' of Pocket Peters an' Hardrock Benson, that's all. Wonderin' what sort o' gents they were."

"Hm-m-m. I thought so. The best, son. They'd been scratchin' the landscape for nigh on a half century, an' they was jest gettin' their first feel of wealth at Beaver Creek. I played stud with them two-three times. We finished even on the chips, son. Which means I liked them."

"Then yuh—"

"Of course not. I was framed. That spiel to the lynch mob was because hell began to loom up too conspicuously, an' it was too nice a day for a hangin'. If I had brayed my innocence, they'd 'a' given me no more chance than a greenhorn ag'in' a short-card player. I didn't murder Peters or Benson, but a gent always sounds convincin' when he says he's guilty. So I baited them lynch hombres plenty. Got 'em listenin' with my fake confession. Got 'em worryin' with my bluff about the streak o' death. After that, I spent my time gettin' slammed around in the hoosegow, an' hopin' yuh fellers would fog in."

DANDY SHUFFLED the cards, twisting them into a circular fan. "A pack o' hellions raided Beaver Creek last night. I was throwin' plenty lead at the buzzards when some one clunked me from behind. When I come to, Deputy Fenston an' a bunch o' miners was standin' over me. An' they was plumb unconcerned about my health. Them pick swingers was for disjointin' my neck right then, but Fenston drug me off to the lockup, with two murders rung up ag'in' me."

Dandy paused and shook his head grimly. A reminiscent look clouded his eyes. The Kid's face brightened. He felt as relieved as though he himself had been rescued from a lynch mob.

"Somebody framed me neat," went on the gambler. "Three-four pokes of dust was pulled out o' my coat. Stuff that'd belonged to the dead uns. The spurs of this here rowel"—Dandy tapped his watch charm—"had been dipped in rattlesnake venom. Bottle of rattler poison planted on me, too. Shore was an open-an'-shut case ag'in' me. Peters an' Benson had red welts around their necks. Flesh was split. 'Peared like my gold rowel had done it. They'd cashed in from snake poisonin', all right. Some skulker cold-decked me purty."

The Kid was inarticulate with feeling. "Gawd!" he breathed fervently. "Gawd!" There was an awkward silence while he groped for words. "Yuh—yuh ought to hoss whup me for—for thinkin' yuh was—"

The Kid felt so good that it was hard to keep from slugging at something just to unlimber from the frightful strain. They stared at each other awkwardly. They were painfully conscious of the strong bond between them.

They headed back to the bull-moose frolicking. The Kid was so boundlessly happy that he didn't have a thought in his head, nor a care. A quartet had formed to drown out the wails of Giant's concertina. A group was huddled around a race between two cockroaches selected from the flour barrel.

The Horde was punishing the bottle. It was a gala occasion and a wild night. The Kid and Dandy blended into the orey-eyed hilarity, but they left their share of the drinking to Peel. When they found the old chuck wrangler in the cook house making a chilli-pepper pie, they dragged him off to his bunk and bedded him down.

By now the Kid's thoughts had returned to Beaver Creek. "I'm wonderin' about that streak of death," he told Dandy, when they left Peel to his snoring. "It don't add up right that those fellers were killed jest for what they had already panned. An' why that streak o' death? Why couldn't the killer have knifed 'em in the back?"

Dandy rubbed his chin. "Doesn't seem like good business to kill a jasper for one or two sacks of dust, when the dirty son could rob him from time to time, an' have the feller workin' for him."

The Kid built a quirley over that idea. "I've got a hunch there's goin' to be more killings. That streak o' death. It's a heck of a lot more mysterious than a knife in the back. Some gent is tryin' to spook up Beaver Creek. Kill a few miners, get the rest jammed full of fear, an' soon them placer men'll be humpin' for distant parts."

More tragedy was scheduled for Beaver Creek. The Kid worried about the prospectors, and that worry preyed on him until he had the intense urge to saddle up and fog for Beaver Creek. But he and Star needed rest. The Kid turned in early; but he piled out early, too. Long before Peel Rogers awoke to a headache patterned for a range bull and a taste as though a gopher had crawled in his mouth and died, the Kid was on the trail.

HE HIT Beaver Creek while the sun was still climbing. Leaving Star hidden in a brush-covered gulch, the Kid wandered into the diggings. Scores of tents lined each side of the creek which was sheltered by aspens, cottonwoods, a few pines. Hundreds of miners squatted over gold pans. Men were cutting timbers. Hammers and saws added to the bustling activity. Shacks were going up; sluice boxes were being constructed.

Every foot of the creek for miles above and below discovery was staked out. Scores of late-comers were hopefully trying to pan colors beyond the paydirt area. Even some were working on No Gold Creek where the only glitters came from the scales of trout. A small army trudged up and down Beaver Creek trying to wheedle jobs from the fortunate ones.

The Kid watched waddies from the cattle spreads take a month's cowpunching wages out of the gravel with every panning. This sudden wealth meant trouble. In the envious, grumbling crowd that wandered along the creek were many who doubtlessly were planning to exchange gray lead for yellow gold. Down at the mushroom town, saloons and honkatonks were going up as swiftly as carpenters could pound in the nails. Tinhorns and percentage dames were swarming in.

The men who slaved for the gold would have the shortest tenure on it. Peddlers and sutlers were charging boomtown prices for fire-sale goods. While the Kid watched McGrane, who had staked out the discovery claim, shovel into his sluice boxes gravel that yielded sixteen-dollar nuggets, a little fellow drove up in a rickety buckboard. On the side of the buggy ran the sign:

TIN-PAN TUTTLE
Everything for the Camp
From Needles to Dutch Ovens

Out of the buckboard climbed a wizened, half-pint man with a gimp leg. Tin-pan Tuttle had a pinched, wan, pathetic little face. Supporting himself with a cane and tugging along a peddler's sack, he hobbled up to McGrane. The Kid watched a gold-camp transaction, and saw that Tin-pan Tuttle had staked one of the richest claims in Beaver Creek by setting up a trader's business.

He sold McGrane hardware that wouldn't have cost twenty-five dollars in a Deadline general store. The miner offered to pay for the merchandise with one goldpan of gravel scooped from the claim. Tuttle snapped up the proposition, and when the panning was weighed, the peddler had a hundred and sixty dollars in yellow dust.

The Kid spent the afternoon sauntering from claim to claim, fascinated by the spectacle of men scratching sudden wealth from the creek bed. Yet despite the generosity of nature, a pall hung over the mining camp. Men worked under strain, squatting at their toil with sawed-off shotguns in reach. Men grew more uneasy with every panning. Armed guards patrolled many claims. Often a brandished scatter-gun warned the Kid away from a stretch of the creek.

An undercurrent of terror flowed with the stream. Suspicion glared in every miner's eye. Death shadowed the diggings. Men toiled hard, but furtively, like crooks looting bank vaults.

The Kid was wary, careful that he wasn't recognized. He saw no one he knew; but it was a certainty that men were here who had hunted the Calvert Horde, men who had seen the Kid's picture on "Wanted" bulletins.

By now the sun was splashing glory over the western peaks. Goldpans were at rest and camp fires were blazing. The aroma of bubbling coffee and the mouth-watering smell of sizzling bacon started the Kid toward town.

He didn't get far.

Suddenly a frenzied, choked scream of maddening agony shrilled out from a tent near the Kid. Before the echoes died, a miner bounded from the creek, arms upflung, racing like a fear-driven creature of the wild. He plunged into the tent and out again.

"The streak!" he bawled in shivering terror. "The streak's got him, got my pard, got ol' Link Wilson. Gawd! The—the streak!"

Men poured from tents. Men kicked over pots of grub. Men left fortunes in gleaming gold lying where even a deacon would be tempted. But the crooks as well as the workers were under the spell of fear.

The Kid got to the tent. A slit in the canvas at the rear showed how the murderer had escaped. The victim was dragged into the open. Puffy, booze-soaked Link Wilson was one of the lynchers who had heard Dandy's pronouncement of doom. The twisted, bloated, dough-colored face showed that Wilson had died horribly. And that angry welt was there. Around the neck. The streak of death!

Terror and fury swept the mob. The grisly corpse drove reason from the miners. Madness clutched Beaver Creek. Men grew hideous with fear and desire to destroy the sinister scourge.

Then a savage cry sent the flesh crawling along the Kid's spine. He suddenly felt as lost as a lamb in a vulture's nest. A slack-jawed youngster with froth on his lips and madness in his eyes was pointing at him. The Kid was split-seconds from being stomped and ground into the dirt, a mangled thing that even the buzzards would scorn.

"There he is!" shrieked the gopher-toothed youngster. "There's the killer! Get him quick. Get Kid Calvert!"

4

SIX-GUN ELECTIONEERING

THE KID was in the center of that raging mob. There was not a chance in the world of fighting his way out. Before he could draw, a dozen men would hurl themselves upon him. A Colt wouldn't check that avalanche of hate and madness.

The swiftest brain in that howling, milling throng was the Kid's. Even as the youngster was pointing at him, the Kid was cutting a long chance from the herd of ideas that stampeded through his head. He whirled on a boot heel and pointed directly behind him.

"That's him! Yuh picked the right hombre, button," he shouted. "Close in on him, men! That younker with the snakeskin hat band and the long knife scar on his cheek. Looks innocent, but he's Kid Calvert—Calvert of the Horde. There he goes. Yuh'll lose him. He'll trick yuh."

Except for the Kid, there wasn't a clear thinker in the diggings now. The sheep-brained mob surged forward, hunting for the fellow the Kid had described. The slack-jawed youngster was piping a protest, but his thin voice was lost in the deafening roar.

Weaving through the shifting man-pack, the Kid slipped into a tent. There he waited, back muscles bunched and fists cocked. The miner who stepped into this tent now would think dynamite had exploded on his chin.

Night settled quickly. It was as dark as crude oil when the Kid sliced the back canvas wall and sidled through the slit. Wild confusion overran the gold camp. Men were rushing about like sheep scattering before the attack of wolves. Men peered into the Kid's face, but they were hunting for a long knife scar and a snakeskin hat band.

They were still searching when the Kid hit the outtrail, with Star pointed toward the hideout. The Kid wasn't forsaking the miners of Beaver Creek. He was going back to war against the mysterious killer who marked his victims with the brand of his treachery. Already the Kid had built a plan and selected his bait.

Knowing he was on the trail to oats and corn, Star took the bit in his teeth and swept along benches and hogbacks like a gray cloud. It was short of midnight when the sweat-lathered steel-dust pulled up over the rim of the home ridge and dipped into the basin that sheltered the Horde. The owl-hooters were asleep, but the Kid routed out Dandy McLain and told him of the killing at Beaver Creek.

"Bad," muttered the gambler, "bad. Washakie County is shore

buckin' agin' the devil's stacked deck. Deadline is set on a powder keg, too, son. Plenty trouble shapin' up there. Reckon the Horde'll have to ride ag'in. Reckon we'll have to tangle gunsmoke with the Stoner outfit."

The Kid stiffened with a jerk. "Huh! What sort o' hell is that pack of back-shooters stokin' up now? I thought a hoss piled Mike Stoner, an' he was laid up with a busted shank."

His face grew hard. The grim lines, the hate-slitted eyes, and the knots of muscle ridging along his jaw added ten years to his appearance. Mike Stoner was the big noise in Deadline, a cattle king whose punchers swung hungry loops, whose cows had twins. Mike Stoner had clawed into wealth over the bleached bones of nesters, the blotched brands of rustled stock. He drew revenue from shady *cantinas* and gambling hells. With lead hornets and gold eagles, he controlled the votes in Washakie County.

The Kid went white at the thought of Mike Stoner. It was the war against Stoner oppression that had taken Gunner Calvert from the Kid, that had left Terry Reynolds an orphan.

"Tomorrow's election day in Deadline," said Dandy. "We got word that the Stoner pack will be at the polls. Gents who figure on votin' for Terry Reynolds are going to get invited to change their minds plumb sudden. An' if they don't—"

"Busted jaws an' cracked skulls, eh?"

"Stoner won't stop at that," said Dandy. "He wants Pete Quill in the sheriff's office. Quill's his tool. With him sheriff, Washakie County would be the headquarters for every gunslick in the state. Stoner runs Deadline now. If Quill's elected, Stoner'll build up power that'll soon have the hull state under his heel."

The Kid didn't say anything for a while. He walked slowly toward the bunkhouse, rolling a quirley and sealing it with his tongue. Suddenly he flicked the brown-paper cylinder into the darkness.

"No time for a smoke. I got to fork my bunk an' do some tall slopin' through snooze land. Reckon a man needs plumb rested nerves for politics."

The Kid had the gift of falling asleep the instant he sprawled out, so a few hours in the bunk refreshed him more than another man would be with his full quota. Darkness still cloaked the land when the Kid rode out of the hills toward the Double Circle Ranch. Stoner's spread. Founded with blood money, subsidized with graft, expanded with rustled herds.

A single light was gleaming from the Double Circle ranch-house when the Kid left Star ground anchored in a cedar brake. Making sure that a dog wasn't prowling about to announce his arrival, the Kid crept up to the building. From the moment he'd learned that Dandy McLain was innocent of the Beaver Creek murders, the Kid had believed that Mike Stoner had something to do with the gold-camp tragedies.

Yet a man with a broken leg couldn't very well direct a campaign of terror. Not Mike Stoner, at least. His gunhawks weren't the sort to take orders from a bed-ridden man. They'd sell out to anyone who'd raise the ante with liquor, promises, and hard coin.

The Kid peered through a window into a lighted room. A man was propped up in bed, reading. The bulge of the blankets suggested a massive frame. The shoulders were broad and full. The square ruddy face, harsh and glowering even in repose, left no doubt. Mike Stoner—the man who fattened on crooked law.

His leg was in a cast and raised in a wooden trough suspended by ropes from the ceiling. He shifted his position and winced. Stoner wouldn't be putting on an act now. The Kid saw the name on the cover of the book. Shakespeare.

"Never knowed that buffalo was interested in high-grade readin' matter," mused the Kid. "He shore must be gettin' ready to slouch down in the governor's chair."

DAWN WAS breaking when the Kid reached the edge of town. His men had gathered at a crumbling adobe. A clear-eyed bunch, those owl-hooters. There was no fat on their brains, no mold on their personalities. Their clothes were slicked and their guns were oiled.

The Kid saw voting booths at the drug store in the center of Deadline, others at a harness shop near the southern end of town. Deadline was just beginning to stir when the Kid rode back to his men.

"Yuh know what to do," he said. "We can't vote, but we can see that others get a chance to make their own choice. We might have to persuade some jaspers not to cast two ballots or to stuff the boxes."

By the time the polls opened, the town was thronged with punchers primed for a holiday jamboree. The Horde sloped in unnoticed. A few of the owl-hooters stayed in the saddle, to cover their pards if a ruckus broke out. The others paired off and mingled with the crowd. The Kid and Peel Rogers were together. Dandy McLain alone was missing. He and the Kid had decided on that. The gambler hadn't been cleared of those gold-camp murders.

A boisterous man-pack milled in the streets. Miners, lumberjacks, cowpunchers, desert rats, mule skinners, stage drivers, barflies, nesters, preachers—every one with a vote, and his post-office box, at Deadline, piled into town. The Kid saw scores of men he had seen squatting over goldpans at Beaver Creek. There went Hank O'Day, a gent Dandy had singled out back at the gold town for a sudden trip to boot-hill. Hank wasn't taking chances. He had three bodyguards—flint-eyed gents with notched guns in oiled, low-slung holsters.

Tin-pan Tuttle, the two-bit peddler with the mother-lode business, was in town, hobbling down the street on his cane, still looking hungry and abused. Lem Dorgan was around, too. Lem, the labor-twisted prospector who had led Dandy through the lynch mob back to jail. Lem was toting a sawed-off shotgun and two Colts. Singlejack Smith, also warned by Dandy, staggered down the street, reeking of tequila and *marijuana.*

The Kid spotted a lot of slinking, smirking, strutting gents around the polls. Bruisers, gunslicks, blademen, Stoner's crew. They were strangers, pilgrims, scum on the dodge, stopping on Stoner's payroll for a while. Soon they would be fogging the death's-end trails again. They wouldn't know any of the Horde.

Pete Quill, the candidate, was orey-eyed. The Kid saw him reel out of the Broken Spur Saloon and almost pitch headfirst into a water barrel. He was a good man behind a brace of guns, but a natural *segundo*. Quill was the kind who wilted under responsibility. The election was getting him down. A couple of strong-arm men from the Broken Spur rushed Quill out of sight.

The Kid nudged Peel Rogers and pointed to a man stagger-ing toward the polls. "Take care of that drunk, chuckie. He's blooied on Stoner liquor. He's got a vote, but it's no good till he stops seein' double."

"I'm votin' fer Pete Quill," yelled the soak. "Goo' ol' Petey boy. Don't wan' no skirt makin' thish a nine-o'clock town."

Old Peel tried to be friendly, tried to lead him from the drug store gently. The drunk swung an uncorked flask, spraying whisky over himself. Peel dodged and moved close, planting a short, inside uppercut on the drunk's jaw; a neat little jolt with just enough kick. Then he dragged the man up an alley.

Down at the harness shop, the Kid saw two slit-eyed men escorting a protesting miner off the main street.

"I'm tellin' yuh I'm votin' fer Terry Reynolds!" exclaimed the miner. "She'll clean yuh hellions out o' Washakie County an' make it spick-an'-span fer an honest man. She'll mop up thet Calvert Horde, an' shoot skunks like that McLain killer to the gallows. Go ahaid. Lay it to me. Knock me cold, bring me to, an' knock me cold ag'in. When yuh git plumb tuckered out, I'll vote fer Terry Reynolds an' decent law!"

The renegades saw the Kid sauntering up the alley. Saw him grinning, saw his thumbs stuck in the arm holes of his vest. One of the tough gents was puffing a big cigar. He didn't savvy the Kid's grin. He winked at him and started rubbing the cigar's lighted end on the old veteran's chest. Then he noted that the Kid's grin lacked mirth, that the eyes were like obsidian.

"Get goin', mister, or—"

The Stoner man didn't finish. He clawed for his six-gun. The Kid glided in. His hands went up. He grabbed the bruisers each by the scruff of the neck and banged their skulls together. He banged hard, and then let them drop.

"Best be gettin' along to the polls, vet," he spoke quietly to the miner. "Brand yore ballot with yore own iron."

THE KID saw that the bruiser gents were breathing, and left them to their slumbers. The miner was still spluttering his gratitude when the Kid disappeared in the mob. Reports came in. Giant Anderson had all but torn a bullet head off the lumpy shoulders of a tough who was making voters miserable around the drug store.

Grama Sinton came out of a fracas with a six-inch slice across his back. But for every inch of that slice, he had knocked a tooth out of the blademan. Some one had pistol slugged Peel Rogers, and the cook had been out for an hour. He was still in a fog, talking in Spanish, his native Gaelic, and the Cantonese dialect learned long ago from a chink cook.

Nate Willstock shot three fingers off the gunhand of a man whose threat was quicker than his draw. The Kid's guns cleared holsters twice, but his foes backed down when those Colts seemed to leap from the leather. There was plenty of work for all the Hordemen. Citizens crowded the polls, voting as they wished.

At noon a throng bunched up in front of the town hall. From the steps Terry Reynolds addressed the voters. The Kid was in the mob. He was nursing his knuckles which had collided with the blue-stubbled jaw of a *mestizo*, who had been showing a shopkeeper how to vote by twisting his arm. The Kid had brushed up against a lot of rough stuff in the last few hours, but his toughness dissolved at the sight of Terry.

"My friends," she said to the throng, "I feel a deep humility, appearing before you as a candidate for the sheriff's office—for a man's office. I don't applaud women who do as I'm doing. I avoid them. But I will argue that women are capable, strong. Martha Slade lost her husband. In ten years she built the Rafter S from a homestead into a cattle kingdom. Jean Lake built up the Lake General Store from a peddler's sack to one of the most prosperous businesses in Deadline."

The crowd was growing. It stood silent, attentive. Terry's silvery, full-throated voice and her quiet, humble manner were more effective than a spellbinder's flourishes. The Kid's eyes were shining. He was like a devout person worshipping before a shrine.

"Women are capable," Terry went on, "but they don't belong in sheriffs' offices. They have no more business heading posses than they have smoking black cigars and sitting up all night playing stud and drinking white mule. I don't want to be a sheriff.

"I want to be a home-maker. I'm more interested in dress catalogues than in stockmen's magazines. The moon means more to me than a light that will reveal a killer's trail at night. I like to make frocks for little girls, and I like to wash the grubby, busy hands of little boys. I'd be more at home in a spick-and-span kitchen than in a smoke-filled sheriff's office. I get more pleasure out of baking a good apple pie than in hitting a bull's-eye three out of five."

THE CROWD was puzzled, troubled. Voters felt that they were being let down, felt that, with half the town's ballots already in the boxes, the people's candidate was welshing. Even the Kid grew cold with disappointment.

"Citizens, I don't want to be sheriff—for myself," said Terry. "But I do want to be sheriff—above all things in the world—for a principle that is stronger, of far greater importance, than I."

The girl paused. For a moment her face clouded, and a faraway look came in her eyes. "My father died for that principle—died for his relentless stand that law must be stern, just, unyielding. Law must be impartial. Any child knows that. And any child in Deadline knows that Washakie County soon may be ruled by crooked law—law that will oppress the many so that a few may gorge on wealth. To prevent this, I want to be sheriff."

The crowd responded with a whoop.

"I want to be sheriff to rid Washakie County of a dreadful scourge—Calvert's Horde. I believe in humanity, in giving every man a chance. But the renegades in Calvert's Horde are not men. They are scorpions in man guise. They are inhuman creatures mastered by hate. When they are caught, I promise Deadline a wholesale hanging. Citizens, I pledge my life to ridding the country of Calvert's Horde!"

The crowd's boisterous appreciation was cut short by a flesh-creeping howl that spread fear across the town and chilled holiday spirits to trembling awe.

"The streak!" came the horror-filled cry. "The streak of death. It got Singlejack this time. Singlejack Smith!"

A roaring, wild-eyed mob was pushing through the batwing doors of the Broken Spur Saloon. The Kid pried his way through the jamming throng. Singlejack Smith was stretched out on a table. His eyes had the glaze and the fixed stare of death. His face was blue.

"It's the Horde's doings!" some one shouted. "The Horde's in town. Every man on the look-out for the Horde an' that McLain hombre!"

The Kid went cold. That gent didn't know just how much hell might pop from his harebrained outburst. Let some one recognize a Hordeman, let Deadline open up on the Calvert owl-hooters, and the town would be reduced to a sickening shambles.

The Kid got out of the saloon, and sent the word for his men to gather. Riding out singly, they bunched at the adobe on the fringe of the town.

"We're washed up for the day, gents," the Kid told them. "One of us is liable to be spotted. There ain't no point in us makin' a perfect holiday for Deadline by gettin' our necks busted. I shore went for Terry's spiel, but she dampened my festive spirit with that little sally about a wholesale hangin'. We was needed at the polls this morning. But the death of Single-jack Smith will ride Terry into office on a landslide of votes."

The Kid was right. A nester brought the word that night to the hideout that Terry Reynolds was swept into office on a three-to-one vote. The Kid was boundlessly happy and vastly concerned. He realized that the zeal the girl would throw into a campaign to round up the Horde might prevent him from fighting against the killer of Beaver Creek. The Kid had to do something about Terry Reynolds and her zeal.

5

NO GOLD CREEK

IT WAS night. Kid Calvert sat on a chair made of cowhide thonged to a piñon-pole frame, and explained away the fears of old Annie Deak and age-bent Matt, her husband. Nesters. The Kid had found them slowly starving, existing on berries and fish.

"She's sech a sweet gal," said Annie, who was wrinkled like a squaw. "It don't seem right, holdin' her agin' her will."

"Shore, shore," answered the Kid. "I know how yuh feel, Mrs. Deak. Looks like a lowdown, ornery trick. But it worked, an' yuh got to go through with it. Three-four days, a week at the outside, an' yuh can let 'er go. Then yuh an' Matt get the *dinero* to buy back that little spread yuh lost down in Arizona. One week's work, then ease an' comfort the rest of yore lives."

"I reckon we'd be nigh daid ef yuh hadn't come along," said old Matt Deak, drawing worriedly on an old corncob. "We'll go through with it, but I hate havin' Miss Terry think I'd wallop Annie. Annie an' me will be together fifty years, come Michaelmas. Gosh—me wallop Annie—"

The Kid laughed kindly. He'd picked the right couple. The scheme had gone through without a hitch. He had sent a nester boy to the sheriff's office with the word that his father was drunk and beating his mother. The bait had led a beautiful girl into a trap.

In the other room of the Deak cabin, imprisoned by a locked door and windows too small to allow escape, was the new sheriff of Washakie County. Terry Reynolds, the Kid's captive.

This kindly old couple would watch her, while the Kid worked unhampered at Beaver Creek. The plan had worked smoothly. The girl had asked one of her deputies to accompany her to the homestead. But the gent had an accident while saddling up in the barn. Terry had thought her lawman had been kicked by his horse.

Figuring that Terry wouldn't ride alone, the Kid stationed Giant Anderson in town to take care of the girl's escort. Giant had leveled the gent with one mule's-kick smash of a hambone fist. With her deputy out of commission, Terry had gone into the hills by herself.

At the cabin, the Kid had blown out the light and snatched her Colt. Without being seen, he had rushed her into the other room. It had been a neat maneuver, and the only hurt was to her dignity.

For a while Terry had to be kept out of the way. The kidnaping probably would save many lives, for the Kid wouldn't be able to work at Beaver Creek with her combing the country for the Horde. He knew he was in the right, yet he felt mean, ashamed.

He gave the Deaks their final instructions, thrust a fat roll of bills in old Matt's paw, and left the cabin. He should have gone on without seeing Terry. He knew it meant misery to face her scorn. But the wild pounding in his heart drove him to her window.

"Terry," he spoke softly, "I'm sorry, I had to— Terry, please understand. Please—don't—th-think—"The words seemed to coagulate in his mouth.

She appeared at the small window, the moonlight revealing the delicate contour of her face. Her manner was cool but her eyes were burning. Hate wasn't expressed in the line of her lips, in the flash of her eyes. The Kid could face hate—even hers. But her look was one of amusement, of pity sandwiched between tolerance and contempt. The Kid suddenly felt sheepish, like a small boy caught stealing jam.

The girl who liked housework and home-making could be hard. "You've given me a good tip, young man. I'll have my staff say, 'Pardon our fists' when they slip the strong-arm routine to our guests who aren't talkative. I'll say, 'Forgive us if the rope is too rough' when I have the Horde lined up in the jail yard for its necktie party. Keep on apologizing, child. I'm always anxious to learn new wrinkles."

The Kid knew that the longer he stayed, the more would his feelings be flogged by her scorn. The longer he stayed, the more he would blunder. But he stayed and blundered.

"Terry—I wish yuh could understand," he blurted. "The rest don't matter. But you— The Horde isn't what you think. We're outside the law—but we were driven out. There isn't a man in the crowd who hasn't the same cloud-scrapin' ideals that yore dad had, that yuh have. Lawdy, do yuh think we'd be livin' like a bunch of sheepherders, if we even had the clutchin' habits of an ordinary shopkeeper? Why, we got a gamblin' man who could 'a' been a millionaire three times over. But all he's got are a few fancy duds that any cow-poke could buy. Terry, believe me—please—"

"I suppose you're right," said the girl, with mockery in her voice. "Undoubtedly the Horde is a club of sad-eyed, misunderstood men. I suppose right now your Dandy McLain is sobbing like a lost child over those foul killings he performed at Beaver Creek."

THE KID wanted to blurt out that Dandy was innocent. He had the impulse to name a thousand acts of mercy that justified the Horde's existence. His thoughts were eloquent, but his tongue was tied. He could manage nothing save lame utterances. Talking against a barrier of misunderstanding was like trying to be heard on the other side of a mountain.

"Terry—I'm going," said the Kid in a halting, uncertain voice. "I reckon there isn't any use explainin' why I'm holdin' yuh."

Terry's laugh was metallic. "Why would an outlaw kidnap a sheriff?" she put the question. "A primary class of school children could answer that. While you hold me, the Horde probably will rip Deadline apart. Once I thought there was a chance for you. I know better now. You're a copperhead. You strike without warning."

The Kid brushed a hand across his drawn face. He suddenly felt very old, as though he had lived for a thousand years and had been flogged every day of every year.

"Good-by, Terry," he murmured, with a catch in his voice that he wouldn't admit to himself was a sob. "I've been kicked by hosses, an' slugged, an' knifed, an' shot, an' burnt—but all that was jest a lot o' playful sparrin' compared to the clubbin' I'm gettin' from love. I reckon the least thing in the world I know about is love. An' I reckon, too, that love is the strongest thing that's in me—exceptin' mebbe the principle that dad died for."

Star had trotted up to the Kid and was nuzzling him on the neck. "Mebbe love always hurts. I dunno. Mebbe lovin' some one—even if she hates yuh—is the only thing that matters. I dunno 'bout that, either. But I do know that the sight of yuh comes near makin' my heart bust open, because I'm so happy an' miserable at the same time. An' it'd be ten-to-one easier for me to face the gallows an' a howlin' mob than it is to face yore hate. I reckon I've talked too much already, an' I reckon what I say is jest so many words to yuh, anyway. But there's jest one more thing—an' some day yuh can hang me for it, if yuh want. Terry—I love you."

The girl broke into brittle laughter. The Kid swung into the saddle. Her laughter was more crushing than a judge's sentence of death. He cast a last, heart-rending look at the window. He stiffened. The life surged back into him. She was laughing—as harshly as a honkatonk dame that's fleeced a greenhorn. But the moon caught a glistening on her cheeks. And as he reined away, he thought he heard muffled sobs.

The Kid rode with an uncertainty that numbed him. Miles away, he stopped at another nester's cabin. When he left there, the identity of Kid Calvert was lost in the tattered trappings of a carefree peon who smelled of tequila and looked heavy-lidded from *marijuana*. Star was left behind, grazing in a horse pasture. In the steel-dust's place was a sway-backed, box-ankled sorrel crowbait that showed every rib beneath a mangy coat. Behind the Kid trailed a flea-bitten, sad-eyed burro drooping under a heavy pack.

Coffee-colored stain on his face and hands, and black dye on his hair made the Kid look like a Mexican. He was decked out in shabby finery. His high-crowned sombrero had moth-eaten tassels. A tight-fitting velveteen jacket had faded to a bilious green. His bell-bottomed trousers were threadbare.

A few miles from Beaver Creek, a horseman rode out of the shadows. The Kid's hand started for his gun. Then he saw it was Nate Willstock.

"Perfect!" appraised Willstock, when he had inspected the Kid in the moonlight. "Yuh look like yuh've been eatin' chilli an' tortillas for twenty years. Everything's set, Kid. We did as yuh said. Lifted an ounce o' dust from every claim on the Beaver. The hull Horde was workin' at it. A stretch of No Gold Creek is marked off and the gravel's salted with slathers of the yeller stuff. Man, what a stampede yo're goin' to start!"

"That's great," said the Kid. "Yuh tell the men to be in an' around the camps all the time. Never know when a showdown will come. Mebbe the idea won't work. But if that killer spots me pannin' a fortune outa the creek bottom, he'll be around to add me to his string of victims."

The Kid rode on, alone. The Horde had robbed an ounce of gold from each of the claims. That was a tax—payment for the work the Kid hoped to carry through. Ridding Beaver Creek of the streak of death.

IT WAS dawn when the Kid rode into the gold camp. A half-empty bottle of tequila was dangling from a strip of rawhide tied to his saddle horn. He had swabbed out his mouth with the fiery liquor, had sloshed some of it down his jacket front. He swayed drunkenly in the saddle. A long quirley was glued to his lower lip. Ashes spilled over his shirt.

He twanged a battered guitar and sang a lilting Mexican love song in the melodious voice that peons often have, but with a drunken slur to the words. He looked like a peon who didn't care if hell busted loose as long as he had a sack of beans, a string of chillis, and enough makings for the ever-present cigarette.

The camp paid little attention to him until he headed up No Gold Creek. Then miners left their claims to watch the tequila-soaked peon stake out territory on the poverty-stricken branch of the Beaver. Experts had been over No Gold Creek. A gent couldn't even pan mica out of that dull gravel. Soon that Mexican would be dragging from camp to camp, trying to rope himself a cook's job. Suckers strode in to watch another sucker at work.

The Kid set up a tattered tent, hung a bunch of dried peppers over the flap, and then proceeded to stretch out on the bank of No Gold Creek and take a siesta. Hours later, he built a fire, cooked a tin can of beans, and made some leaden-looking tortillas.

Then he got out his goldpan—a ten-cent wash basin, and began to make history in Washakie County. He scooped the pan full of gravel and lazily began shaking it. Scores of miners and camp hangers-on peered from the woods, waiting for a laugh.

They waited long. Never had they seen a man work more leisurely. The Kid shook the basin a while. Then he sprawled out and puffed a quirley, contemplating the unfinished task with supreme distaste. With a display of extreme reluctance, he returned to the work. Another miner would have completed ten pannings in the time it took him to paw the gravel from the basin. The bottom of the pan glistened. His hands were steady with indifference as he slowly filled a tobacco sack to busting with luscious gold.

Saddling the crowbait, he rode into the land office at Beaver Creek where his discovery was recorded. The yield of his first panning weighed five ounces, and that yield sent a thousand wild-eyed men in a mad stampede to No Gold Creek. A thousand men would labor and fight for nothing. The Kid watched with regret, because so much aching toil would go unrewarded; and with delight, because he felt this futile sweat would build his scheme toward success.

Hidden under his simple peon disguise, the Kid posed as a dutiful son of *mañana*. He returned to his claim, where he hired two miners to pan the gravel, while he lazed on the creek bank and listened to them grunt.

Up and down No Gold Creek men shook out pan after pan to nothing but the dullness of sand and gravel. The rumor went forth that the peon had struck the outcropping of a mother lode. That sent a swarm of men digging and blasting through the woods, little knowing that the Kid's claim had been salted— with pounds of stolen dust and nuggets.

The Horde had relied on an old method of salting a claim— using shotguns to blast the precious specks and lumps into the ground.

That afternoon tricksters, land-grabbers, money sharks—all the sure-thing gentry that prey on boomtowns and gold strikes—swarmed around the Kid like pesky flies around a sleepy burro. The Kid played the part of a crazy spic who had tipped up the horn of plenty and thought that good fortune would flow on forever.

He tossed a nugget at every hard-luck story, and cocked a brown attentive ear to each wildcat proposition devised to reduce him to beggary. He made promises as fluently as a politician.

The traders descended on the Kid, and he dealt with them as lavishly as with the swindlers. One look at the grinning peon crooning over a tequila bottle—which happened to contain nine-tenths water—and the meanest, most abject peddler jacked his prices up to the skies and then sadly discovered that he had been a piker. Tin-pan Tuttle, limping along with his cane, was looking his hungriest. He knew all the tricks of the trader, but he needed none of them to sell to the brainless spic. The Kid ordered everything that Tin-pan suggested.

Toward sundown, the Kid raised his hand as Tuttle, his eyes glowing, was inserting carbon paper under a fresh sales blank. Already his scrawl filled three sheets. The total had passed a thousand dollars—and for all it meant to the Kid's pocket, it could have passed a million. He had no intention of paying for the goods, just as he had no intention of using them.

"Enough, *amigo mio*," he said grandly. "All day I geeve to business. My neck ees stiff weeth the nodding; my tongue theeck from saying *'Si, si señor'* to ever' hombre who want me to mak' heem *rico*. I am ver-ry tired. I go to the Tweested Horn *cantina*, an' get ver-ry dronk, I theenk."

TIN-PAN TUTTLE rubbed his hands. "Yes, Don Federico," he addressed his patron by the name the Kid had assumed. Turtle's thoughts lingered on the main issue of his life—profits. "A night of pleasure will not be amiss for one who has had sech a difficult day. I have brought along a scarlet sash an' a purple jacket. Fit garments for a night of mirth an' hilarity. Had 'em in stock. An' I got some delightful perfumery. Some hair oil, too, by jiggers."

"Amigo, amigo," broke in the Kid, putting his hands on the little trader's shoulders. "You theenk of ever'theeng. Don Federico de Flores y Romanez go to the *cantina* like a peon! Certainly not, *señor!* And you weel drive me to town, yes?"

Tin-pan Tuttle was delighted with the chance. Possibly he could fill that fourth sales blank.

Dressed in cheap elegance and reeking with sickening perfume, the Kid swung up beside Tuttle on the buckboard, and the trader started to town with the Mex who had bounded from peon to *caballero* over one pan of gravel.

The buggy rattled along. Tuttle cleared his throat and began the lead-off to the sale of a wood stove. The Kid softly sang a Spanish love ballad, but he nodded to everything Tuttle said.

A large, ugly fly buzzed around the horse, causing it annoyance. It lighted between the animal's ears, and the horse whinnied, tossing its head violently.

"Drat them hossflies," muttered Tuttle, raising his long rawhide whip. "They're always pesterin' Bess."

He swung the whip. It snapped like the crack of a rifle. The rawhide tip picked the fly from the horse's head and flung it away, crushed and lifeless.

"Beautiful—beautiful!" exclaimed the Kid. "For that you win thees leetle nugget." And the Kid handed Tin-pan Tuttle a chunk of gold worth fifteen dollars. "What the hell! Don Federico de Flores y Romanez—that ees me. Some day I go back to Mexico—an' when I go, I tak' millions—millions."

Soon the Kid swept into the Twisted Horn, flourishing three gold-filled tobacco sacks and vowing that the whole world was his brother. Five minutes later, the saloon was packed. The Kid leaped upon a table, struck a grandiose attitude and made an expansive gesture.

"Tonight, *amigos,* the dreenk eet ees on Don Federico de Flores y Romanez. Dreenk to your sorrow that the creek ees so stingy to you, so generous to Don Federico. Thees morning you laugh at me. Tonight, *amigos,* you laugh weeth me, no?"

This was the crazy spic's big night. Men slapped him on the back, then crooked their elbows at his expense. The Kid was swaying when he pushed through the batwing doors. In an hour he was staggering and talking with a thick tongue. He lifted a glass of whisky with anyone who spoke to him. But he drank nothing. He used the trick of swinging on to the next group of men, leaving behind a filled glass that he had only touched to his lips.

Toward midnight he flopped down at a table in a corner and began to make snoring noises. Having emptied his sacks, he was ignored. But never had he been so alert.

Nate Willstock reeled into a chair near him, cradled his head with his arms on the table, and talked out of the side of his mouth.

"Stoner men are in town, son," he spoke in a low, tense voice. "We've found out that the claims of them murdered gents are being worked by gunslicks Stoner imported from Idaho. Yo're takin' an awful risk tonight, son. This pack figures yo're a no-account spiggoty who has no right to yore good luck. There's gents here who'd do a drygulchin' job for the price of a drunk."

"I know, I know," returned the Kid in a guarded voice. "I'm takin' the chance. Tell the men to shy clear of the claim. Don't want that killer scared off, if he's got ideas concernin' me. Keep the boys up, though. Something might happen. I'm not sleepin' tonight."

Shortly afterwards the Kid staggered out a side entrance unnoticed by the crowd. He kept up his drunken rôle back to his tent on No Gold Creek. He was wondering about his scheme.

If Pocket Peters, Hardrock Benson, and others had been murdered by the streak of death for gold claims which gave only fair yields, it seemed logical that the murderer would attack Federico de Flores y Romanez—the Kid—who some thought had struck close to a mother lode and untold wealth. The gold strike and the masquerade were planned solely to draw an attack on the Kid.

He felt certain that Mike Stoner was behind the murders, but he was as puzzled as he was sure. He stuck to the belief that an injured man couldn't direct from a bed the sort of hellions Stoner employed.

The Kid meant to stay awake. But even an iron man has a limit to his resistance and the Kid had been up all of the night before. He sat on his blankets for a while. Then he sprawled out to stretch for a few moments—and he was lost.

Suddenly he snapped up, intensely alert. He had no idea how long he had slept—maybe hours, maybe minutes. He sprang erect. Hoofs were pounding along the bank of the creek toward his tent. The noise had awakened him, but it wasn't the noise that tensed his body.

Some one was in the tent. He didn't know how he knew. He heard no sound, not even of breathing. Yet a person was standing near. That strange sixth sense—gift of the lawless trails—warned him of danger.

Was this the killer? The thought made the flesh creep along his spine. His mouth went dry. His heart hammered as he visioned Link Wilson, bloated and blue, lying outside his tent. He saw the body of Singlejack Smith on the table in the Broken Spur. The Kid grabbed for his Colt.

"Who's there?"

Something swished through the air. The question had given the stranger his location. The Kid dodged. He heard a curse close by. From outside ripped a snarl, a harsh oath. Then came the scream of a woman—a scream that made the Kid's heart skip a beat. Terry's voice! A shot blasted the night. The girl screamed again.

She cried: "Stan! Stan!" The name Terry had called the Kid— in a moment of tenderness that he'd always cherish.

6

THE STREAK OF DEATH

AGAIN THAT swish, that blood-curdling swish that was the herald of a horrible death. The Kid's jaws were clamped. All his viciousness was bunching in his back muscles. He was in close—close enough to hear a man's breathing. Guided by that faint sound, he swerved sidewise and lashed out. His fist connected with paralyzing force. A clear, sense-destroying shot to the jaw. With savage satisfaction he felt his arm recoil in its socket at the impact.

His foe dropped like a sack of grain. No groan, no sound but the hollow plop of a body on soft ground. The Kid uttered an exultant cry. At last! Here was the damned rat whose treachery had nearly swung Dandy McLain on the limb of injustice. The Kid bent over his victim. He fumbled through his clothes for a match, found none. He ripped out an oath, but his voice died on a piercing cry that came from a distance.

Terry! God—what was he doing? Pleasing his curiosity while Terry needed help. This sleeping dog wouldn't bark for a long while. When the Kid hit 'em like that, they needed hot whisky and cold water to bring 'em around. Again the cry. Stan! Stan! And he was standing like something chipped out of rock.

He bounded from the tent. A new dread assailed him. Terrific gunfire crashed the night's stillness. Where No Gold Creek met the Beaver, he could see winking powder flames. Had the Horde been spotted? He shook the thought from his head. The owl-hooters were men whose hearts danced to the song of the six-gun. But the girl— How could he reach her? Not on the crowbait. He could run faster. Darkness had swallowed Terry and her foe.

A rider was streaking upstream toward him. And that gent right pronto was going to ride along on his own shanks. The

Kid ran toward him, gun ready, and a threat framed for utterance.

The horseman plunged into a shaft of moonlight. "Dandy!" exclaimed the Kid jubilantly. "Quick, man. Give me that critter. Terry's up yonder. Terry, yuh understand? She's in trouble. She called for me. For me, Dandy!"

"It's the showdown, son!" yelled Dandy, leaping from the saddle. "Stoner's pack." Scarcely had he hit the ground than the Kid was vaulting up. "Stoner's skunks are sackin' hell out of Beaver Creek. Posin' as the Horde. Our men are whammin' it to them—but the miners are crackin' down on us, too."

"Give them Stoners what they're askin' for!" rapped the Kid. "They're mounted, ain't they? The miners are afoot. Tell our gents to empty a saddle every time they spot a Stoner. Blast 'em so they'll do their next dirty work as cinders in hell. An', Dandy—in the tent. A jasper who's had an accident. Yuh know. Take care of him—but not gently. Don't let him out of yore sight."

The Kid jabbed Dandy's mount with slick heels and the horse responded with a violent lunge. The creek was like an overturned hive, swarming with miners streaming from their tents. As the Kid raced along the stream, he blared a warning.

"Hit for the Beaver, men. It's the Stoner crowd—the worst pack o' hellions that ever shot a man between the shoulder blades. It's yore fight. Give 'em the jump—an' they'll run yuh out, steal yore mines, leave yore bones to bleach in the sun!"

The Kid knew he was shouting facts. This was the climax of a campaign of terror. Stoner wanted the wealth of Beaver Creek for himself. He had tried to drive out the miners with the work of the man-devil whom the Kid had laid low.

The Kid's shouts sent an avalanche of fury against the raiders. The Kid swept on. Dandy's horse was fresh and willing. But ahead the beat of hoofs had ceased. Terror clawed the Kid. He expected an ambush, expected to find the girl dead. He cried out her name. Guns were snarling below him, but ahead all he heard was the voice of the wilderness.

The Kid rode on. He felt that the hoofs pounding through the silence were trampling the beauty out of his life. He called again and again. Suddenly he heard a savage oath that made him blaze with anger, yet sent a surge of boundless joy through him. The oath signified that Terry was in trouble, but it signified, too, that she was alive to be in trouble. Her captor had uttered the outburst.

"Leggo, yuh little she-devil!" snarled the man. "Quit bitin' me. I'll slug yuh. Ough! Quit it, yuh damn cougar-woman!"

The girl was putting up a fight. The Kid reined toward a moon-bathed canyon to the west. A bullet whined overhead. He stiffened, clenched his fists. He was a clear target. But he couldn't make gun-talk, couldn't take a chance on hitting the girl.

"Stan! Stan! Stay away. You'll be killed." Exultation made his heart thump. The girl was calling, and her voice was laden with fear—fear for him. "Mike Stoner's got me. And he's waiting to pick you out of the saddle!"

Flame stabbed the darkness. Lead whistled close. Mike Stoner! How did Stoner get here? Was the man riding with a broken leg? The Kid was sure that the person he'd seen at the Double Circle was Mike Stoner—and that man *had* been hurt. No doubt of it. What then? Had hate and greed mastered the man's pain, driven him out to marshal his hirelings against Beaver Creek?

The Kid wondered about the girl, too. He had rather expected that she would escape from the Deaks. But how had she known that he was the crazy spic of No Gold Creek?

His thoughts were cut into by the snarl of another bullet. The bullet missed him, but it left an idea. He reined his mount straight up the canyon toward Stoner and the girl. He could see them in the shadows. Dismounted. Mike Stoner was holding Terry as a shield. Rage choked the Kid.

He was not more than a hundred yards away now, riding squarely into the muzzle of a killer's gun. It was a desperate chance, but Terry was worth a million desperate chances. He started the mount zigzagging like a cowpony after a steer. Stoner's gun exploded again, and the Kid felt the sear of a bullet along his side. He clamped his jaws and rode on.

"That's five," he muttered, and yelled out: "Try again, Stoner. I can be hit."

Stoner thought so, too. Holding the girl before him with a powerful arm, he took deliberate aim. The Kid kicked his feet from the stirrups. He was sliding out of the leather when the gun thundered. A bullet shrieked close to his neck, so close that he could feel its hot breath.

"Six," he muttered. "Terry—Terry, has Stoner another gun? Quick! Has he?"

"No!" cried the girl, her voice rising with exultation. "No. Come on. His gun is empty. He can't reload in time."

MIKE STONER was swearing like a mule skinner. He clutched the girl in a torturing grizzly hug, and worked furiously to jam fresh loads into his Colt. His eyes were burning with insane hate. The Kid came on.

Stoner fumbled in his haste, dropped shells. He uttered a bellow like a wounded bull and slammed the gun at the Kid, who dodged neatly and came in with a smashing hook to the face that made Stoner release the girl.

"I'll tear yuh apart!" snarled the man, recovering and charging.

"I'm tearable," gritted the Kid, side-stepping and driving a blow to Stoner's bulging stomach that sank wrist-deep.

Stoner tried to wrap his grizzly arms around the Kid, who slipped away and peppered the lantern jaw at long range. He threw staggering force into his punches. A smashing drive opened a gash over Stoner's eye. Blood blinded him. The Kid stepped in with a chin-lifting uppercut, and while Stoner rocked on his heels, the owl-hooter knocked out three of the man's teeth, shredding his lips. A pulverizing right mushroomed Stoner's nose.

Not once did Stoner get in a clean blow. He saw that he was on the way out, and he made a terrific lunge for the Kid, catching him around the waist, butting him with his head, and grabbing for the Kid's gun. He got it clear of the holster and broke away, stepping back.

A gnawing dread all but buckled the Kid's knees. Stoner was gripping the gun butt. His finger was curling on the trigger. If the Kid grabbed for the Colt, maybe Terry would be killed.

He saw his one chance. Up shot his knee. The gun roared, bucked in Stoner's hand, but the bullet whined into the graying sky. The Kid's knee had given Stoner a terrific jolt on the elbow. The jolt wrenched the gun from his grasp, sent it spinning.

Stoner whimpered. The Kid piled into him with his square-cut fists hammering brain-shattering destruction. Stoner sagged. He pleaded for mercy through the blood that bubbled from his lips. But the Kid had but one thought—and that was to ruin this man. Possibly he would have killed Stoner had not a voice pierced his fury.

"Enough, Stan. I've got him covered."

The Kid stepped back from the battered hulk. Terry held a gun—the Colt he'd knocked from Stoner's grasp. His eyes flashed. Not so good. She was as lovely as a spray of jasmine, and he thought the world of her; but with a gun in her hand, she was the law. He leaped aside and grabbed the weapon.

Terry wasn't thinking of sheriffing. Danger had drawn them together, had made her forget the barrier. The sight of the slim Kid slashing and hacking that grizzly of a man had thrown her under a spell. Her eyes glowed. She was just Terry. She was just a girl standing beside the man she thought was the axis around which the world revolved.

They headed back to the gold camp. Their prisoner begged for his life, but his quavering pleas struck ears attuned only to the words of a lover. Life had rushed ahead of the calendar with these two. But now for a short while they spanned back over years they never would live. They were kids again.

The girl explained that she had escaped the Deaks by playing to their soft hearts. She had trailed the Kid to Beaver Creek, learned the story of the wild spic of No Gold Creek—felt sure of the spic's identity. Mike Stoner had seen her in Beaver Creek and chased her. His intentions had been, she'd learned in the canyon, to hold her as a hostage. She'd raced up No Gold Creek, hoping to find the Kid.

The quiet that had settled over the gold camp worried the Kid. How had the Horde fared? Captured? Killed? Was he riding into a trap? The sun was tipping the eastern ridges when they reined along the Beaver. A huge crowd had gathered. Some one hailed the Kid. Dandy! If the little gambler had his freedom with those miners there, then the Horde was still gripping gun butts.

"We settled 'em, son!" yelled Dandy. "We're plenty shot up, but we're all breathin' an' wishin' we could lay back our ears in Peel's chuck. Got the Stoner mob, kit an' caboodle. The hull camp is starin' at our smoke-poles."

The miners ranged along the opposite side of the stream, uncertain about a number of things, but showing no desire to buck the Horde's line of guns. The owl-hooters were mounted. Bullet-ripped and drenched with crimson, but feeling plumb salty after a tonic of gunsmoke. Three stiffs lay on the ground. Stoner men. Ten more hard-faced gunslicks were tied up and ready for delivery.

"Gents," the Kid addressed the miners, "allow me to introduce Mike Stoner, the hombre behind the streak of death."

Stoner had changed his key. He was off the high notes, now that they had proved useless; and he was rumbling in a bass voice again.

"Yuh haven't got a thing on me," he rasped. "Put me in jail. See how long I stay. My lawyer will get a change of venue, and I won't even come to trial—for anything."

The Kid nodded. "Mebbe. Find that jasper in my tent, Dandy?" he asked.

"Shore," answered Dandy. "The little feller is still as cold as a fish. Got him over beside them rocks, plumb uninterested in our little spats and sputterings."

DANDY DRAGGED his man into view. Tin-pan Tuttle!

The Kid gave a start at the sight of the little peddler. Even though he'd had a hunch about Tuttle. The trader had always been close by when some one was murdered. And the way Tuttle had manipulated a whip on that horsefly had made the Kid wonder.

Giant Anderson and Grama Sinton revived the little murderer. Tin-pan Tuttle opened his eyes, blinked, saw the crowd, and shrieked. He didn't have to be told anything.

"Gawd!" he cried in a broken voice. "Gawd have mercy on me! I don't want to die. I'm a good man—a good man. I jest wanted to be a little peddler, addin' up my receipts every night. I ain't the harmin' kind by nature. But I'm weak, Gawd, I'm weak."

It was a prayer and the utterance gave him strength.

"You know what's ahead of yuh, Tuttle," spoke the Kid in an ordinary voice. "Yo're talkin' like a man. Keep on. Yo're up against something yuh can't buck."

"Yes," muttered Tin-pan Tuttle, "yes, I know. I'm goin to hang." His jaw quivered at the word, but he bit back a sob, and pointed at Mike Stoner. "That's the man," he said quietly. "He forced me into this. I should have been strong enough to fight him. I faced a ten-year jail sentence. I was afraid of that. Which is why I'm goin' to hang."

He began to talk rapidly, and it was evident that confession relieved him, as though he was throwing off some noxious.

"I embezzled money from a bank in Denver," said Tuttle. "Stoner learned about it. He bent me to his will, forced me to kill. An' now I'm goin' to die. I guess I'm ready. But Mike Stoner has to die, too. It was his idea—the whip in my cane."

Dandy brought forth the peddler's cane. It sheaved a rawhide whip which wound on a small reel in the knob. The rawhide was cut in sharp ridges and coated with rattlesnake venom. Tuttle had snapped the whip around his victim's neck. The cutting was done as he had pulled it away.

"Well, gentlemen," the Kid addressed the crowd, "I reckon yuh savvy that once yuh come near hangin' the wrong jasper. Dandy McLain."

A buggy was rattling along the bank. Men saw the driver and gasped. His leg was in a plaster of Paris cast, and suspended from the buggy top by stripped blankets.

"Mike Stoner!" some one shouted. "Two Mike Stoners! What the—"

"Billy-be-damned if I'm one Mike Stoner or two Mike Stoners!" exclaimed the resonant, cultured voice of the newcomer. "I'm J. Worthington Carew. An actor, gentlemen. A Shakespearean actor. My Othello is considered authentic, but you wouldn't understand out here."

In a flash the Kid understood what had puzzled him, even before Carew explained that Stoner had hired him as a tutor in English, but really because of the resemblance. Obviously Stoner had been the cause of Carew breaking his leg. With the word out that Stoner was disabled, and the actor in bed to prove it, the killer had been able to work with a free rein.

"I heard Stoner talking to one of his henchmen tonight," Carew was saying, "and I learned I was a party to treachery. That's why I'm here. That's— Hey—look out for the girl."

Carew had been the focal point of attention. That had given Stoner his last chance, and he was making a desperate play for life. He lunged for Terry Reynolds, grabbing her arm and yanking her out of the saddle. He could use her as a passport to freedom.

A shot rang out. A grim smile played on the lips of a little man with a flowery vest. Mike Stoner brushed his hand across his face, clutched feebly at his chest where a blotch was widening, shook his fist at the crowd, and departed from life. Dandy McLain calmly blew smoke from the barrel of his Colt.

"Terry! Terry!" cried the Kid.

The girl had landed on her side in the dirt. Swiftly the Kid picked her up, carried her into a tent.

"I'm all right," she murmured.

"I know it!" the Kid spoke nervously. "I know it. But it was my only chance. Terry—I don't deserve—this—"

The Kid held her tightly, pressing his lips hard against hers. For a moment she pushed away from him defensively, and then—she clung. The closeness of her slender body sent a wild ecstasy through him. It couldn't last. Such mad happiness wasn't for him.

Soon, with the help of deputized miners, she would be taking the Stoner killers back to Deadline, while the guns of the Horde covered her departure.

Suddenly Terry wrenched from his embrace. "You had no right—" she cried. "I—I lost my head. I forgot that you are Kid Calvert, an outlaw, a—a killer. Oh, I wish I could believe differently. But I've sworn to do it. I must—I must rid the country of the Horde."

The spell was broken. She was the sheriff again, the relentless enemy of the owl-hoot clan. Her gaze shifted to the Kid's holster, and suddenly her hand darted for his gun. But her eyes had warned him. It wouldn't have helped her if she got his Colt, for the Horde was outside. But he jumped away, shaking his head grimly.

She stared at him. There was hurt in her eyes, but fury in her face. Then she flung from the tent, leaving the Kid engulfed in loneliness. She was gone, and all that remained was the warm memory of her kiss, of that maddening second that she had clung to him. He clenched his fists and closed his eyes. Was he foredoomed to misery and defeat? Would always the barrier exist between them?

HELL'S RECRUIT

Eagle Hawn, ace bank robber, swore he'd never tell the secret of his million-dollar cache. Terry Reynolds, girl sheriff of Deadline, trapped Hawn. And the law went to work on him. Down from the north of Deadline swooped young Kid Calvert and his gunhawk Horde. They, too, wanted Hawn's secret. Out of the crimson-drenched hills below the Line rode the loot-hungry Morales. And his kill-crazy bandido crew outnumbered both the law and Calvert's Horde. Eagle Hawn diced with love, hate, and death—while hell welcomed its newest recruit.

I

EAGLE HAWN

THE CELL was splattered like a butcher's chopping block. Men snarled like wolves closing in on a kill. They snarled in hate, but they swore in admiration, for the prisoner was taking a manhandling that would have lowered a shopkeeper into his coffin. The prisoner was sopping up that merciless punishment with a fixed smile on his puffed and bleeding lips, and without a sound of protest.

Four men were working on "Eagle" Hawn. Four men were sweating and puffing at the brutal business, but they weren't getting results. Another man, the age of Hawn, young, clear-eyed and as fresh and spirited as a range colt, watched the slaughter with mounting disgust.

"Kid" Calvert—Calvert of the Horde—was a blood brother of violence. He was the leader of the Horde—a clan of owl-hoot gents who had been driven onto the death's-end trails by crooked law and injustice.

They were harsh, embittered men, those gunhawks, held together by the code of the Horde, a code that pledged them to the cause of the underdog. Fate had blasted their illusions, had steeped them in hate.

The Kid was not the sort to look upon a hellion with the eye of sympathy, and Hawn was a hellion who had ridden a trail of misery and ruin. Yet the Kid felt his flesh creep at the savagery. His eyes filled with pity. He muttered and shook his head at the man's stamina.

The Kid wanted to stop this nightmare of brutality. Yet justice restrained him. Eagle Hawn was staggering like a day-old calf. His face had been smashed until it looked like raw beef. His eyes were swollen, his cheeks gashed.

Crimson drooled from his mouth, trickled from his ears, spouted from his nose. He was a wreck, an animated mass of pulped flesh. Yet he smiled, and somehow that smile got across the idea that Hawn wasn't licked.

The Kid kept starting forward, fists cocked, to sledge into these hate-inflamed sluggers. They were burly townsfolk drafted by Deputy Root. They rode the saddle of the law the Kid so often bucked. And Eagle Hawn was a citizen of the lawless trails, a brother of the owl-hoot.

"He's Kid Calvert—the killer!" Terry cried.

No—not brother. Half-brother. The difference lay in the codes by which they lived. Eagle Hawn was not a killer. Seldom was he known to pack shooting irons. Yet his nimble fingers and highly tuned ear had caused banks to close, had turned stores into rat's nests, had driven small ranchers to the wall.

That was why the Kid couldn't stop this mangling, flesh-ripping third degree. The Kid had killed. Men had dropped before his smoking guns, but the Kid had never dealt pain and disaster save to those who deserved it. He was an outlaw, because cruel circumstance had made him so. He would remain an outlaw, because the barrier of misunderstanding would never crumble. But the Kid who violated book law, daily and deliberately, answered humbly to the higher law of humanity.

Eagle Hawn had violated that law by looting banks of the golden eagles that had earned him his nickname. Twice he had rifled the Cattlemen's Bank in Deadline. Too wily to be caught at his work, he had tangled with the law on a night he had dropped into town for pleasure.

The prisoner's bank operations had made him wealthy. Everyone knew that. But no one knew where he cached his plunder. In that cache was centered the hopes of hundreds who were victims of Hawn's skill and daring. That was why Deputy Root was using all the tricks of persuasion to make Hawn talk. That was why Kid Calvert couldn't interfere.

Deputy Root was a bull of a man, who once had killed an owl-hoot gent with a single smash of his hairy fist. An importation from Montana, he was as hard as flint, incorruptible, as relentless as a mousing cat.

Now he swore helplessly. Three times nature had rebelled, and they had revived Eagle Hawn with fiery liquor. Each time Root had pleaded with Hawn. Root had no sentiment for owl-hooters, though he all but weeped as he begged the prisoner to open up. He tried to bribe Hawn with the promise of leniency.

His booming threats would have shriveled most men's vitals. He fashioned a hangman's knot and clubbed Hawn with it, promising a swift trial and a swifter dispatch through a gallows' drop. Hawn smiled cold defiance.

They couldn't hang the smooth blackguard. Men went into eternity for lesser crimes. But Hawn's death would seal the secret of his plunder cache.

Dropping his fists, Deputy Root stared in awe at Hawn. The lawman's huge frame trembled. Finally he grinned at his own helpless rage. In his eyes the Kid saw a gleam that suggested a grudging admiration for the prisoner. The officer swore savagely and shook his head. It was an indirect admission that the battered, defiant outlaw had him beat.

SCOWLING, ROOT paced up and down the cell. His body was strangely tense as he peered out the barred window.

He looked at Hawn again, growled, and kicked at the bunk. On a small, rough-hewn table lay a worn deck of cards—Hawn's property. He called it his good-luck pack. Few gamblers would let him use the cards, for the backs were decorated with a peculiar Aztec design, which aroused suspicion that Hawn could read them face down.

Deep in thought, Root picked up the cards, shuffled them, and began laying out a row for solitaire. "I can't lambast the truth out o' the critter," he muttered, "but there's some way o' learnin' where that *dinero* is buried."

The bank robber had come out of his punch fog. His poise made the bruisers gawk. Leaning against the cell wall, he gazed at the lawman, his look half sardonic, half amused. Mechanically Root was filling out the suits in the deck, while he mumbled.

"Keep your mind on the game, lawman," said Hawn, grinning contemptuously. "You don't win by playing a spade on your diamonds."

Rage rumbled in Root's throat. He threw the cards on the table and whirled. "Ain't yuh got a lick o' decency, Hawn? Come on, jaw-whack a little information. Where's that *dinero?* Hell, man, yore thievin' has driven folks to suicide."

Hawn shook his head. The Kid found himself staring in wonderment. Physical punishment couldn't break Hawn's will. He had quick come-back powers. He looked like a wreck, but his legs were steady, his eyes clear. He sauntered to the table, began gathering up the cards.

"You've got me wrong, Root," he said coldly. "I'm an artist, not a killer. I follow this work because the eagles on the gold-pieces screech for me to come and get them. I rob banks because they were made for me to break into, but I don't drive people to suicide."

His manner was insolent and contemptuous. Root couldn't stand his superior air. The deputy uttered a roar and lunged for Hawn, lashing out with all his crushing power. The bank robber dropped the cards, tried to cover. But Root got through to the jaw, and Hawn went spinning. The others closed in.

They didn't reach the prisoner. The rough stuff had failed. The Kid couldn't let this brutality go on. He got between Hawn and his tormentors. Side-stepping a blind bull rush, the Kid grabbed a bruiser by the arm and hurled him against the opposite wall. He tripped the second strong-arm gent, and blocked Root's deadly onslaught.

Astonishment checked Root. He stared bewilderedly. Anger carved harsh lines in the Kid's face, tightened his mouth to a gash. His eyes were cold, challenging. His fighting stance warned the others away. Those tremendous shoulders suggested bone-shattering strength. The slim, tapering build indicated cougarish speed.

The Kid had volunteered to help get the truth out of the safecracker, and Root had invited him to come along, after sizing up his muscular build. Now the deputy began to splutter. The Kid cut him short.

"Yuh've flopped," he said sharply. "Now let me handle this jasper."

Root scowled at the Kid. "What do yuh think yuh can do?"

The Kid motioned for him to keep still, and faced the bank robber. "Hawn, yuh look all man to me. I know there's no use handlin' yuh like a booze-soaked border rat. Mebbe yuh don't know the misery an' hell yore thievin' has caused."

Hawn sneered. "Don' try the sob stuff on me, mister. I rob the rich. The skunks I relieve of *dinero* would knife their best friends to pile up the simoleons. I'm jest a little more open about my business."

The Kid frowned. "That's yore idea, is it? Only rob the rich, huh? A while back yuh busted in the bank at Wolf Paw. The bank closed, an' a little old lady lost her life's savings. The Widow Barnes, she is. Folks found her starvin' to death. She had a nice little nest egg. Now she's on charity, keepin' alive on scraps people dole out."

"Yeah? The Widow Barnes, huh?" said Hawn. "Hm-m-m. Where's the old dame live? I'll fix 'er up with wood an' victuals. Send her some fancy duds, too."

The Kid gritted his teeth, growled. This gent was full of answers. But the Kid hadn't played his ace yet. And that ace was "Blade" Morales, a mad spic whose band of kill-crazy peons rode terror through the land. Morales was heading in—after Hawn. The Kid knew that once before the *bandido* had caught the bank robber.

"Made up yore mind to keep mum, huh?" said the Kid harshly. "Well, there's one man who'll make yuh wag yore tongue. He won't handle yuh so gentle, Hawn. Morales is headin' in. He wants yuh, mister. He wants all that *dinero* yuh've been collectin'."

HAWN GAVE a sudden start. The look of a hunted animal came into his eyes. He swallowed hard, shrank back. Then he gazed shrewdly at the Kid. He smiled in disbelief. Once more his expression grew contemptuous.

"Come again, mister. I don't fall for that trick. Morales is—" He stopped. Fear returned to his eyes. The deputy was nodding.

"That's right, Hawn," said Root. "Morales is comin'." He scowled at the Kid. "How the hell did yuh learn that?"

"Never mind," said the Kid coldly.

He wasn't telling about the hermit men scattered through the hills. Befriended by the Horde, these gents of solitude— prospectors, wood-choppers, trappers—often brought news to the owl-hooters from long distances. From them the Kid had learned about Morales.

The Kid whirled Hawn. He pulled up the bank robber's shirt, exposing his bare back. Men gasped, blinked their eyes, and gasped again. On Hawn's back was a great welted criss-cross of angry red scars where once the flesh had been cooked.

"Morales' little job," said the Kid grimly. "Hawn wouldn't talk for the spic, so he got branded. Not with a runnin' iron, men. A white-hot axle made these marks!"

Root turned gray at the sight of those hideous scars. He swore and sprang to the window. "God, if Morales gets here before—" His teeth were grinding. His eyes were wild. "Hawn, listen to reason! If Morales gets yuh, he'll hack yuh to pieces to make yuh talk."

A shudder went the length of Hawn's lithe frame. The name of Morales was enough to inspire fear in any man. The spic had begun his career as a cobbler's apprentice. He had knifed his employer and robbed his savings, using the money to gather a small band of tattered laborers. For years Morales had been shuttling back and forth over the border, sacking villages. He rode a fear trail that the law seldom dared to cross.

"Hell's fire!" exclaimed Root. "This town is turnin' into a headquarters for drygulchers. First that murderin' pack in the hills—that Calvert Horde. An' now Morales!"

The deputy didn't see the glare that the Kid shot him. Calvert's Horde would be forever maligned and reviled, and yet it was the strongest agency for peace and protection in the county.

There was a greenish tinge to Hawn's bruised face. The mention of Morales drained him of arrogance. He licked his split lips. He ran a trembling hand through his hair.

"I've got to act quick." Root was talking to himself. "I've got to loop me an idea before the girl comes back."

The Kid tensed, eyed the deputy strangely.

Hawn came forward and clutched the deputy's arm. He was fighting for control, but his face was haggard. "Root, you got to get me out of here. I won't sell out to the law. I'll never tell where I've got my cache. But you can't let that greaser get me. Morales has me licked. I admit it. He tried everything to make me yammer. An' when I wouldn't talk, he branded me, left me on the desert to die."

Hawn gritted his teeth. "I can't go through it again, Root. If Morales gets me this time, I'm finished. But even if Morales takes me apart piece by piece, he'll learn exactly nothing."

The men had been so absorbed in Hawn's talk, that they

hadn't heard the footsteps in the corridor. Suddenly a girl's voice swung them around. The Kid felt as though his blood was freezing. Terry! Terry had returned, and the sound of her voice numbed him. He pulled down his hat, lowered his head, sidled into the corner. His heart hammered. Cold sweat bathed his body. He knew he was trapped.

Terry Reynolds, sheriff of Washakie County, was the Horde's greatest foe and a person beloved by every slit-eyed gunslick in it. The Kid worshipped the girl. And now, with Morales riding in, she was in danger.

When Blade Morales cut loose with his hell guns, everything in front of him went down. If the girl fell before the peon's smoking sixes, the Kid would live thereafter for the sole purpose of dealing vengeance. With Terry gone, life for the Kid would be smothered by everlasting night.

The girl stepped into the cell. She seemed just a wisp of daintiness, but the steady gaze of her midnight eyes, the angle of her spunky jaw hinted of the steel that was in her nature. Washakie County had swept her into the sheriff's office with an avalanche of votes. But she held the office because of principle and not for preference.

She had vowed to carry on the work of her father, the old sheriff who had lost his life defending the law in Washakie County, who had fallen in the same battle that had robbed the Kid of his outlaw father, "Gunner" Calvert. When the girl had taken the oath of office, she had sworn to round up Calvert's Horde with hangman's rope.

Despite his danger, the Kid was overwhelmed by fascination. She was truly beautiful, with golden hair and loveliness in the delicate contour of her oval face. She was sturdy. She had the stamina of a frontierswoman. Yet she had a deer's grace, and to the Kid she seemed all clinging softness. He had known the maddening caress of those red lips. He had experienced the ecstasy of her warm embrace. And he had faced her withering woman's scorn, too.

The girl had eyes only for the battered prisoner. Those eyes flashed angrily. Her slender body quivered. Rage heightened the color under her bronze, mirrored hidden fires in her eyes. Her loveliness reached its peak under the stress of emotion. The Kid's heart hammered.

So often was he on the lonely outtrails, so often was he buffeted in angry storms of hate and violence, that the sight of Terry Reynolds nearly made him swoon with a torturing blend of pain and happiness.

"Mr. Root," the girl cried, "you've deliberately gone against my orders. That poor man! Five against one. How could you be so cruel? We're trying to stamp out brutality in Washakie County. We're not fostering it. Five against—"

Her eyes swept the group, and stopped on the Kid. For a moment incredulity tied her tongue. The Kid tried desperately to hide in the shadows. He crowded against the wall. His chin dug into his chest. He heard Terry gasp. Her foot scuffed the floor. Her hand slapped to the businesslike holster.

"Kid Calvert!" she cried. "Root! Get him! He's Kid Calvert— the killer!"

2

DECOY

THEY SWUNG around, went for their guns. The Kid's hand didn't move until their guns were half from the leather. Then there was a pop as his fingers hit the holster, and in a split-second he was behind a black bore that threatened to spout hell.

Deputy Root swore. His three bruisers shrank back. Fear put them out of the deal. Root showed that he had the impulse to bull into the Kid, but that menacing Colt persuaded him to let discretion govern his actions.

Suddenly Eagle Hawn lunged. He threw himself at the girl. As he catapulted across the floor, he swooped up his pack of playing cards. The girl was no tenderfoot on the draw, but indecision and surprise had made her fumble. Now as she whipped the .45 from the holster, it was to have Hawn snake out a long arm and snatch it from her grasp.

Then the bank robber sprang from the cell. The Kid was glad he was gone. Now the safecracker could get into the hills, away from the menace of Blade Morales.

The men in the cell raised their hands. They didn't know that the Kid was pulling a gun bluff. He would fight. He would burn powder, but he wouldn't shoot any of them.

"Yo're right reasonable, gents," the Kid spoke harshly. "I sure ain't a jasper to crowd when I got the business end of a hogleg focused on anyone. Now lift those Colts gently, an' toss 'em through the window."

Very carefully each hooked the trigger guard with the index finger of his closed gunhand, and flipped his Colt through the bars. The Kid grunted approval. Root was clenching and unclenching his hands, but he wasn't stepping forward. The Kid crab-walked toward the door. Suddenly he grabbed the girl by the arm and whisked her out of the cell. He turned the key in the lock, withdrew it.

The girl's eyes were filled with fury and hurt. The Kid interpreted the expression as one of loathing. A great sadness descended upon him. He holstered his gun and urged her along. His head was light, dizzy, and he thought that a leaden weight lay where his heart should be.

He loved this girl more than life. She was very close, yet as far beyond his reach as the moon. A mountain of misunderstanding towered between them. The Kid's ideals and principles soared as high as hers, but his were smudged by outlawry and rebel deeds.

He knew that the girl wanted to believe in him, had tried to see his side; but always circumstances had blocked the way to understanding. She was hating him now. The Kid felt sure of it. He got a sliver of consolation out of the thought that her hate actually was love melted in the fires of fury.

They were halfway down the corridor before the Kid could speak. "Terry, you must believe me," he pleaded. "I came here to help Root with Eagle Hawn. I didn't mean to let him get away."

The girl's lips curled in an ironical smile. "Always ready with an explanation, aren't you?"

Her tone stung him like a whip. Knots of muscle stood out on the Kid's jaw. Silently he cursed himself for being a weakling and the kind of a fool who would try to crumble a stone wall with his fists. He was a rider of the owl-hoot. If he stayed on the lawless trails, he could avoid much of the misery that now plagued his spirit. It is when a man is able to compare that he is unhappy with his lot.

The Kid's love for Terry had given him but a few flashes of happiness in a never-ending darkness of pain. She was not for him. He had to forget her. That should be easy for a man who lived so dangerously, who seldom had time to think of himself.

Then he looked at her again, and his resolution was swept away. Her face was set, her mouth tight. But mist filled her dark eyes. She had dropped the rôle of sheriff. She was just a little girl in the throes of deep emotion, valiantly fighting back the tears.

The Kid felt a great surge of tenderness. He knew then that he would never forget her, knew that it was for him to face her scorn and fury, asking nothing but the chance to help her, to give her the protection that only a gunslick from the owl-hoot could provide.

Suddenly he came upon a great revelation. It wasn't being loved that mattered. He realized how that life, which had cheated him of so much, had given him man's most vital heritage—some one who needed him. Never mind the barrier.

Terry truly needed him. Her black eyes admitted what her

lips would deny. What chance had a girl, backed by a few deputies whose fists were speedier than their brains, against the brutality that stalked across this raw frontier land? She had a courage that transcended the bravery of strong men. But life had equipped her for the home, not for the wild manhunt trails.

The Kid saw clearly now. The Horde was her guardian, the Kid her protector. He vowed that always would he be somewhere near. He knew now that being loved or hated didn't matter—as long as a man obeyed the dictates of his conscience. The important thing was loving; the important thing was for a man to realize that he was needed.

"TERRY!" THE KID'S voice was vibrant with the emotion that swelled his heart. Scarcely aware of the act, he reached out to draw her close. His thoughts had mellowed him. His thoughts had strengthened him with the knowledge that he could take any rebuke or lash of scorn with head high.

The spell had caught the girl. She swayed toward him, her eyes closed, her jaw quivering. But the touch of his hand broke the magic of that moment when love had risen above all the complexities of their lives. Her body tensed. She sprang back. Again fury was her master.

"I hate you!" she cried. "You came to free Eagle Hawn. You came to oppose my fight to keep law and order. You threatened my deputy. You would have killed innocent men. Yet you plead for understanding. Yes, I understand. I understand that you are a killer. If I get away from you this time, Kid Calvert, I promise to fight you and the Horde until the last of your hateful band is gone!"

The time had been when those words would have ripped into the Kid's soul. They would have shriveled his spirit, driven him onto the lonely trails feeling as though his life was an endless shame.

Now he merely shook his head and smiled at her. That smile, too, was misunderstood. She thought he was flaunting his contempt. She edged near him and her hand flashed for his gun.

The Kid grabbed her wrist and tightened his grip until she released her hold on the butt. He was still mellow, and he smiled again.

"You smug hellion!" the girl spoke angrily. "You know there is nothing I can do. But if I had a gun—if I had a gun, Kid Calvert, you'd surrender or I'd use lead to save the county the cost of hanging you."

They had reached the front door of the jail. The Kid's magnificent steel-dust stallion was ground-anchored outside. Clean limbed and deep barreled, Star was the Kid's inseparable companion on the owl-hoot.

He handed her the key to the cell upstairs. "Yuh'd better get those jaspers out before they begin wreckin' the furniture, Terry. Yuh don't need to worry about Eagle Hawn. He's a plumb up-standin' ranny, but I agree he hasn't any right buryin' gold where it can't draw interest. I'll bring him back, Terry—me an' the Horde. An' we'll try to bring the *dinero* along, too."

"I don't doubt that," the girl answered scornfully. "You'll get the money—not the folks who really own it."

"Terry, if the Horde was as bad as yuh think, we could control votes, get a whack of the profits out of every business, run all the saloons, honkatonks, an' gamblin' hells, an' ramrod the whole state.

"Why, girl, there's hardly a gunhawk from border to border who hasn't tried to get into the Horde. But we want no truck with thieves an' drygulchers. We steal an' we kill, but the hombres who suffer from us sure deserve their sufferin'."

Suddenly a fear-laden cry blared across the town.

"Morales is ridin' in!"

The Kid swung around. Hoofs were drumming in from the west. A cloud of dust streaked across the flats. He lowered into a fighting crouch, hand on gun.

Out of the smoking dust loomed a band of sombreroed riders led by a squatty, shapeless mass of evil forking a beautiful, spirited black mount. Even from the distance the Kid could see the splendor of the man's garb. The most dashing *caballero* in all Mexico would have been proud to wear such finery. But on the squat, bulky Blade Morales the costly fabrics interwoven with gold braid were wrinkled and sodden.

The *bandido* was entering town with a bewildering crash of gunfire. Down on the main street citizens were scurrying for cover.

Blade Morales reined his fiery bronc, and headed straight for the jail, his cutthroat crew thundering along in his dust. The Kid's face grew harsh. He knew what would happen if the peon found that Hawn had escaped. The lid of hell would pop off in Deadline. Morales would turn into a gun-blazing, knife-slinging maniac.

T H E B A N K robber was a rich prize for Blade Morales. When the savage peon, who should have been born with fangs and cloven hoofs, learned that the safecracker was gone, he would lay the blame to Terry Reynolds. The men in the second-story cell would be slaughtered. If Morales didn't kill the girl, he would carry her away.

The Kid was cold with the terrifying prospect, but his heart leaped exultantly as he realized that again Terry had need for him. The Kid couldn't stand off that pack of slavering killers. A gun challenge would make them kill crazy. He saw the one chance of saving Deadline from a massacre.

He grasped the girl's arm. "Terry—quick! Get a gun from the office. I'll fog out o' here. Yuh run from the jail, yellin' an' firin' at me. Shout the name o' Hawn. Savvy? That breed pig will think I'm Hawn. He'll think Hawn is escaping. He'll take after me, an'—"

The girl's eyes sparkled. She needed only a word. The Kid moved back into the gloom of the corridor. That howling crew of drunken spics was within Colt range. The Kid kept licking dry lips. A feverish light burned in his eyes. His hand wasn't as steady as usual. There was a chance that he would be caught between a cross-fire.

The girl had rushed into the office. She was back again, clutching a long-barreled, frontier-model Colt. The Kid's pulses were pounding. His vitals knotted up. He sagged against the wall, and horror twisted his face. Terry was leveling the six-gun at him!

Anger flushed her face. Her eyes flashed with triumph. She stepped toward the Kid, jaw grimly set. Long had she waited for this chance. Outside, hoofs pounded closer. The spics were yelling. She bit her lip. Doubt crept over her features. Her eyes shifted from the Kid to the door. Indecision furrowed her brow, and that indecision dissipated her anger. Suddenly she uttered a gasp. Alarm filled her eyes. The gun lowered.

"What am I doing?" she cried in self-reproach. "I'm insane—insane. Go—Stan! It is a risk, a desperate risk. It's not for me. But those men upstairs—and the folks in Deadline. There'll be a massacre if Morales thinks I tricked him, thinks I hid Eagle Hawn. Go, Stan boy. My heart is—is—with—"

The last word was lost as she brushed her lips against his cheek. The Kid was delirious with happiness. She had called him Stan, the name she had known him by, before she had learned that he was Calvert of the Horde. She had caressed him. In a flashing second the Kid experienced the essence of joy that is spread through many days of an ordinary man's life.

He wanted to hold her, wanted to press his lips hungrily against hers. But the thunder of hoofs sent him lunging for the door. He triggered his gun. From the corridor sounded a deafening blast.

The Kid leaped high in the air, forking his alert steel-dust mount without touching the stirrup. He gathered up the reins, nudged Star's flanks. The mount responded with a plunge and lengthened into a high lope.

The spics were howling like drunken Apaches. The girl rushed out the door, the sunlight glinting on her star. She fired after the Kid.

"Hawn! Hawn!" she yelled. "You can't get away. I'll kill you—kill you!" Again and again she shouted the bank robber's name.

A frenzied outburst of spic oaths roared from the Morales crowd. They were ripping their horses' flanks. The squat *bandido* was brandishing a six-gun and cursing his men on.

"It is Hawn!" he roared in Spanish. "Ride the gringo down. Kill his horse, maim him; but I must have him alive."

3

THE HATED HORDE

THE KID heard a whine close to the stallion's flank. His scalp twitched. Those howling spics were trying to cut down his mount. A slug nipped the Kid's right boot. Shrieking through the air on an angle, a steel-jacketed bullet from a rifle sliced Star across the withers.

The mount squealed and went into the air. Dread kinked the Kid's muscles. Star would lose his footing when he landed, and the Kid would be sprawled in the sage. There were no trees or boulders to offer shelter. He would have to make a stand. One hell-roaring moment, and those spics would bullet-cut the legs from under him. It would be his evil luck not to die.

The Kid felt that his blood was clotting in his veins as the stallion hit the ground. The snorting steel-dust stumbled, started to somersault. Sure that he had made his last ride, the Kid was ready to throw his feet from the stirrups. He would land upright and give those spics a glimpse of hell before they finished him.

"Steady, boy!" the Kid spoke softly.

The words were lost in the racket, but the stallion heard the Kid's voice. It bore the note of encouragement that the frenzied mount needed. Star responded with a shrill whinny, and then the Kid knew that he had underestimated the steel-dust.

Morales was bellowing orders for his gunhogs to spread out. Then the peon began getting his words twisted. For the man on the steel-dust was still out of reach. Star had saved himself from spilling by crow-hopping. A few stiff-legged jumps restored the mount to an even stride, and now the stallion was bounding across the flats.

The spics cut loose. A bullet plucked at the Kid's sleeve. He uttered a low snarl and twisted in the saddle. He rocketed a slug in the center of that pack. A spic stiffened suddenly and toppled from the saddle. A flying hoof almost tore the man's head off.

The Kid winced. Another hoof crushed the skull. The bandits rode over their fallen brother, leaving a mangled corpse sprawled in the alkali. Often had the Kid looked upon death, but he had never grown callous to the sight of it.

The Kid bent low along Star's neck. The mount had taken the bit in his teeth, and the gap between was rapidly widening. Morales' men had ceased firing. Their mounts were taking cruel punishment.

Reaching the hills, the Kid tightened rein. On a pine-fringed crest, he drew Star to a halt and waited until the spics rode within bullet range. Then his gun hammered. He didn't fire to empty saddles, but to bait them into a fury that would keep them in pursuit.

Wild shouts answered his gun thunder. Powder smoke swirled up around the Kid's face. A hard smile split his tightened lips. He would rather be thrown to a pack of hunger-crazed wolves than to have that crew ride him down. He jammed fresh loads into his gun, and sent Star down a rock-studded draw.

The going was slow through a boulder-strewn ravine. Morales and his hirelings were in bullet range for several tense, lead-screaming miles. When the Kid struck benchland, he burned leather on a straightaway until death no longer whined close. After that, he paused often to entice Morales on, but he didn't offer the spics any more target practice.

He led them on a chase through the canyon-slashed country until the band was cut in half by wind-blown horses that had fallen. Star was brush-scarred and lathered, but the mount still showed eagerness.

Shadows were deepening when the Kid quit the game and lost the remnants of that killer pack in the rugged, tumbling land. The Kid had played with Morales deliberately to wear the Mexican out. By the time the bandit got back to Deadline, he'd be too weary to cut loose on the town.

Darkness lay over the land when the Kid reached the Horde's hideout in a pine-grown basin atop a ridge. Before he made the last climb, he was stopped by a sentry.

"Shore glad to see yuh comin' in whole, Kid," the battle-scarred veteran said. "We got word Morales was on your trail. The boys are mighty worried. Giant an' Grama sloped for Deadline with some of the boys, in case word came that Morales had got yuh."

IF THE men of Calvert's Horde had the greed of the ordinary, respectable citizens who hated them so, they could amass fortunes. Yet they lived in wood-choppers' cabins. Their fare was as simple as chuck-wagon grub. They washed and mended their own clothes. A little straw in their bunks served to relieve the hardness of the piñon poles beneath.

The moment the Kid rode into the basin, the owl-hooters bounded from the cabins. The Kid dismounted, and immediately one of them led Star away to be fed and watered and curried.

"Lawdy, son, yuh shore had this old tinhorn seein' nothin' but the ace o' spades in the pack. I've been half nuts, thinkin' yuh'd crowded yore luck too far."

The speaker was an undersized man wearing a flowery vest. He had the appearance of a dude. His suit was of black broad-cloth, and had the formal cut of an undertaker's clothes. A golden rowel, suspended from a nugget chain, decorated his fancy vest.

"Dandy" McLain's one extravagance was his apparel. A professional gambler clever enough to cold-deck the wiliest cardsharp, Dandy would seldom sit in a game unless he looked as though he had stepped out of a mail-order catalogue.

"Yuh ain't shot up any, are yuh, Kid?" asked Nate Willstock, a wintry-eyed veteran of the outtrails. He studied the Kid anxiously. Nate Willstock's spirit had frozen years ago, when crooked law had driven him onto the owl-hoot. Yet his eyes thawed a little as he looked at the Kid.

"By dogies!" yelled "Peel" Rogers from the cook house. "Flank down on that chin music an' come an' git it. The lad's all right. By coots, he oughta git plumb indignant, havin' a bunch o' grandmothers mooin' around him. The spic that kin handle the Kid ain't never lifted a frijole or crammed a tortilla down his brown gullet. Come on, Kid. I built yuh a Johnny-in-the-sack that'll make yuh lay back yore ears an' neigh."

"We're ridin', boys," the Kid announced later, while he was wolfing Peel's tasty grub. "Morales will be in Deadline, feelin' proddy. I tried to wear down the dirty son, so he'd be too fagged to raid the town, but if tequila takes hold o' him— I'm worried about Terry. Some of the notches on Morales' guns are for women, gents!"

Nate Willstock jumped up and knocked over his chair. "I'm saddlin'. It'd be jest like little Terry to go after Morales. I reckon I'm plumb short on sentiment, but that girl hasn't a father, an'—an'—" Willstock clumped out of the cook house.

"Gawd, if anything happened to Terry—" Dandy dropped his fork and shoved back from the table. "I'm drawin' chips in this game. How about a showdown with that greasy spic?"

"Yuh know better than that, Dandy," said the Kid. "Yuh know what a showdown in Deadline means. Plenty o' law-abidin' jaspers who came to town for a little elbow bendin' would be headed feet first toward boot-hill before mornin'. We can't take a chance of innocent rannies gettin' in the way."

The Horde rode out of the hills. Into Deadline the owl-hooters fogged, into the weather-warped cowtown where the Calvert name was a curse. They sloped in to protect men who hated them, who wanted to see the Horde snapped out of existence in a wholesale necktie party.

The Kid was a bundle of hot nerves tightened like a bow-string. He mopped sweat from his forehead, although the night was cool. As jumpy as a spooky horse, he often jerked rigid for no reason save that he was on edge. His mouth was dry, his hands cold.

He couldn't break his tenseness, because his mind was on his men. He had seen the look in their eyes, the hard smiles, the frequent caress of gun butts. The Kid clamped his jaws. They had nodded to his caution, but they were hoping that trouble would crowd them.

Could the Kid hold his men in check? Not if Colts flamed in spic hands. Abuse from honest folks didn't make them blink an eye. Citizens could revile them without end. To the towns-men the Calvert wild bunch showed the patience of an old dog with a puppy. But not with Morales. If Morales began filling the atmosphere with gunsmoke—

The law gave the Kid grave concern. Would Terry be in town? Her rare moments of tenderness for the Kid didn't lessen her determination to destroy the Horde. She had picked hell in half-boots for a deputy. Let Root learn that the Horde was in town, and he'd throw a cordon of gun-handy gents around Deadline that a fox couldn't get through.

THE RACKET in the Broken Spur Saloon made the Kid feel as though he had an icicle for a spine. Morales was in there. Morales was slinging gold around and slapping gents on the back. The spic's drunken guffaws rose above the din. The hitchracks were lined with tethered mounts. Plenty of men were forgetting tonight that the spiggoty had shot down women and children, had left towns charred and smoldering.

The Kid knew that when Morales was around, laughter was apt to turn suddenly to snarls. Morales was having a jovial spell.

But he was as uncertain as a cat. He would claw even while he purred.

In the alley alongside the Broken Spur, the owl-hooters ground anchored their broncs. They bunched in the darkness.

"Drift in solo, gents," the Kid advised. "We're here to prevent trouble, not to start it. Side-step Morales if he's honin' for a ruckus. Humor him. Handle him like a child."

The Kid pushed through the batwing doors first. Through the tobacco fog, he saw Morales staggering from one group to another, a grinning orey-eyed idiot sopping up cringing flattery.

With the prospect of gain, many citizens were willing to blind themselves to the spic's true character. A dozen fawning men tagged after him. A puncher stared in open-mouthed awe. That pleased the peon, who tossed the cow-poke a small buckskin sack that clinked. Some of the gents who hung too close to Morales, scraping for his favor, got shoved in the face. Now and then the spic's viciousness broke through, and men shivered.

It was easy to see why this ex-cobbler's apprentice could surround himself with killers who would ride at his command into any sort of danger. The bully had an intensity which gave him the magnetism that drew men. His amazing vitality kept him going at top speed. There was no dozing while he was around.

The Broken Spur was crowded. Men jammed shoulder to shoulder at the bar. The tables were filled. The bartenders were drenched and puffing. In the dancing annex, where burly gents galloped about with percentage dames, a spic orchestra was scraping and blowing.

Not all of the citizens were kotowing to the spic. In the mob was a sprinkling of clear-eyed gents. The town's loafers and rowdies did the cheering. The law-abiding men frowned, but were afraid to make a play. Yet they maintained their self-respect by cautiously dumping Morales' liquor in the spittoons.

A man came toward the Kid, a Hordeman who looked as

mild and gentle as a deacon. He had soft brown eyes and a smile that suggested kindliness. "Grama" Sinton was mild and gentle—until he was crossed. Then hell flamed in his heart.

The Kid and Grama elbowed through the drunken pack to the side wall where they could talk unnoticed.

"I've been thinkin' yuh was buzzard bait, lad," said Grama. "Shore did. Me an' Giant tried to sound out some of Morales' spics. No *sabe*. Giant is at that table in the corner."

The Kid sauntered up to Giant Anderson, a massive-shouldered gunslick with two hundred and forty pounds of fighting strength distributed over his huge frame. Nothing of the Coltman in Giant's appearance. He had a boyish cast to his face.

Though a veteran of the dim trails, he looked more like a slow-moving, well-fed farmer from the corn belt. But the only softness that Giant Anderson carried was in his heart. He had the speed of a striking rattler and the fury of a wounded grizzly when there was fighting to do.

His broad, frank face brightened. "Lawdy, pard, I'm well-nigh bugs. Every time I looked at that grinnin' spic idjit, I saw yuh stretched in a canyon with a bullet in yore head. I've been expectin' Morales to make some slip that would tell me he had killed yuh. Then I was goin' to yank out his windpipe."

"MEBBE YUH'LL still get the chance, Giant," said the Kid, "because it looks like that hombre is buildin' himself up to start something. But we're not lookin' for trouble. I hope Morales drinks himself under the table."

Not much chance of that. Booze swelled the spic's conceit, but it didn't buckle his knees. The Kid's eye roved over the jostling man-pack. His Hordemen were scattered about the room, alert, waiting. Morales' blademen were circulating through the boisterous mob.

What had happened to Deputy Root? Fear didn't keep the lawman away. Maybe he was gathering a posse to nab the gunhogs when the spics reeled out of the Broken Spur.

An hour slipped by, an hour that saw many men dragged to the alley, dead drunk. Morales was still calling for drinks, and he was paying. That was a joke. The spic was making the cash drawer ring. But if the whim struck him, he would take the gold and everything that the owner had in the safe. And the number of men he killed wouldn't matter to him. It was the whim that mattered. Often men died or got suddenly rich, according to his mood.

"Dreenk, you greengo dogs!" yelled Morales, sweeping a pudgy hand over the crowd. He had just called for another round, and the bartenders were losing fat hustling the orders. "Tonight Morales love you, ever' rotten son of you. *Si!* I love you like a brother, you white rats. *Madre de Dios!* You are all my cheeldren. I—Morales—am the *bueno padre.* Dreenk, you damn peegs!"

Morales was on the verge of tears. He was gripping hands and embracing drunks. A barfly thought he saw a chance to make a stake. The Kid had seen this loafer cringing and whining around Morales. The lout annoyed the *bandido,* who had pushed him away many times. Now the barfly stepped in and circled his arm about the spic's shoulders.

Morales ground his teeth. His booze-puffed face twisted. Madness glittered in his tiny eyes. His squat, sloppy body quivered. He wriggled free of the barfly's arm, and uncorked a haymaker that drove the drunk into the mob.

The Kid started forward. He had been expecting something like this. If that barfly went for his gun— Morales was striding toward the drunk, boot raised, gunhand lifting. The Kid shot a glance to Giant Anderson. Peel and Grama were heading in behind Morales. Dandy McLain was springing onto a table. The hilarity died. Drunks were sobering, edging for the exits.

Morales' blademen were closing in. Blood would run as freely as the booze—if Morales' gun spouted hell. The spic's boot started down. The Colt was clearing leather.

Then Morales guffawed. He shrugged. He dropped his gun

into the leather, beckoned to the crowd to surge up to the bar.
The tension was broken. Gents laughed hysterically. The bartenders emerged from hiding places. Glasses clinked.

"Eet ees not right that we should have the shooting when
the law, he ees not een town," said Morales. "I play *bueno* treeck
on *Segundo* Root. A messenger come weeth the word that
trouble, she break out in Wolf Paw. And *Señor* Root ride queeck
to Wolf Paw. Ha! Root, he do not know that Morales send that
messenger."

"Think yo're purty damn good, don't yuh, chilli con carne?
Yuh think thar ain't nothin' in the world like Morales. Yuh got
'em all buffaloed, 'ceptin' me. My name is Tucker, savvy? An' thar
never was a Tucker what let a spic do anything but clean his
boots."

It was the barfly talking. Rather, it was the booze getting the
best of the soak. His eyes were glazed from the punch. He
wobbled toward the *bandido*, groping for his six-gun. He didn't
know what he was doing. The Kid tried to get to him, but others
stood in the way.

"Huh?" grunted Morales. He swung on the barfly Tucker.
His gun left the holster in a smooth draw. Tucker's eyes bulged
with horror. The sight of that black muzzle sobered him. He
cried out for mercy, raised his hands, sank toward the floor.

The gun snarled. The slug caught Tucker in the forehead. He
was instantly dead, but Morales still glared with murderous
intensity, his gun sweeping the crowd.

The Kid pushed forward. "Yo're spoilin' yore party, Morales,"
he yelled. The only way to handle this spic now was to humor
him. "Yuh've been showin' us the best time we ever had. The
night's young—"

"And so are you, *amigo*," purred Morales. "But you weel never
be older. I do not lak keeds to tell me what I mus' do."

The spic's gun focused on the Kid. There was no chance of
drawing against Morales. None of the Hordemen was in position to get a shot at the *bandido*. Dandy McLain had jumped

from the table too soon. The Kid ran his tongue over his lips, measured his chance of kicking the gun from the spic's hand. He couldn't reach the greaser.

He was sure it was the end. He felt no fear; only a grim desire not to die. There was a chance. If Morales didn't kill him with his first bullet— The Kid's hand was moving toward his gun butt. The spic's finger was tightening on the trigger.

4

THE SEARCH

THERE WAS a stir in the tensed crowd. The batwing doors were swinging. One of Morales' gunhogs shouted his name. The *bandido* relaxed his trigger finger, though his eyes were fixed on the Kid, whose hand paused close to his holster. A spic pushed through the mob, buzzed something in Morales' ear, something that brought a gleam to the evil little eyes.

The *bandido* muttered a name that made the Kid stiffen. Quill—Pete Quill, former deputy in Deadline, the tool of crooked interests, who had opposed Terry Reynolds in the last election. Quill had just entered the barroom. Quill was doing business with Blade Morales.

The spic showed the daring that had helped to build his reputation. He turned his back on the Kid, and pried quickly through the crowd. It was the kind of a gesture with which the *bandido* often awed the mob. He might have shot before he turned away, but sudden impulse governed him always.

The Kid felt a boundless sense of relief. Jumping on to a table, he saw Morales swagger through the swinging doors. With him went his swarm of gunhogs and a burly, red-faced man with his mouth shaped into a perpetual sneer. The Kid clenched his fists. Quill had been a lawman; now he was trafficking with the most savage raider in the country.

Dandy McLain eeled through the jabbering throng. The Kid jumped from the table. "I got a snatch o' the talk," said the little gambler. "Quill's been out scoutin' for Morales. Quill's learned that the jasper Morales chased wasn't Hawn. Musta found out from somebody in the jail that yuh led the spics on a blind chase."

"But what made those scuts pile out o' here?" asked the Kid.

"Because Quill saw Hawn in Deadline. An' Morales is throwin' a line o' spics around the town. No one's gettin' out or in."

The Kid's mouth tightened. "We got to beat Morales to it, Dandy. We got to nab Hawn." He stopped, scowled. "Does Quill know we're in town?"

"Didn't hear him say," replied the gambler. "But Morales is all-fired het up. His face purpled when Quill told about yuh. If Morales catches yuh, son— God, it'd be easier if yuh fell into a den of rattlers. A hell of a lot easier."

The Kid's eyes slitted. "Yeah, I know. His idea o' fun is feedin' a gent to red ants. Cuts off a man's eyelids, an' stakes him face up in the sun to go blind crazy. Yeah. But that's not goin' to stop me from huntin' for Hawn."

Peel Rogers and Grama Sinton were standing near the entrance, waiting. Giant Anderson was coming up. They started for the swing-doors.

"There's some reason why Hawn is stickin' around town, Dandy," the Kid said. "Why? Hell, he could be forty miles away. That Hawn jasper is all man—an' a gambler. Poker or banks— he's always ready to take a chance. H'm-m-m. I'd like to see him buckin' yore game some time, Dandy. Yuh've heard of his lucky cards. Hawn's never lost a game with them."

Dandy grinned. "Reckon we better find him, son. I shore hanker to bust that winnin' streak."

Outside, the Hordemen sauntered into the darkness, one by one. Already Morales and his spics had disappeared. Some of the sober gents from the barroom were packing Tucker's body to the undertaker's. Most of the men in the Broken Spur were too orey-eyed to realize that trouble was on a short fuse. Scarcely had the Horde gathered in the darkness than the racket in the saloon broke out again.

"Gents, I want this town combed down to the last rat-hole adobe for Eagle Hawn," the Kid told the owl-hooters. "Travel in pairs. If yo're spotted by Morales' men, use yore fists, do anything but shoot. Deadline's settin' on a powder keg now, an' one gunshot is liable to touch it off."

"Eagle Hawn musta gone nuts, stickin' in town," said Grama.

"Mebbe," replied the Kid. "But I'm figurin' that he's cookin' up a little deal. Hawn doesn't hit a town unless there's good pickings. What brought him to Deadline?"

Peel Rogers slapped his thigh. "By coots, that's it! The Lobo River dam. There's nigh onto five hundred men in that construction camp."

"Exactly," went on the Kid. "An' the payroll came in today. Five hundred gents averagin' five bucks a day means around seventy thousand simoleons for the monthly pay-off. An' the money's in the Cattlemen's Bank. Well, yuh see why we have to nab Hawn pronto."

Presently the Hordemen were scouring the town. The Kid climbed the drainpipe to the roof of the three-story Deadline Hotel.

There he had a view of the town and the surrounding flats. Dandy had got his information right. Beyond the skirts of the town, horsemen were walking their mounts back and forth. Not a chance of a man getting through that cordon. The spics were far enough from the houses so a sniper couldn't pick them off. The Kid searched for Morales, but nowhere along that killer circle did he see the chunky *bandido*.

TO THE northwest, where the hills were closest, the Kid saw the white of tents on the first ridge, marking the camp of the construction company. The dam was nearly finished. Already thousands of tons of water were stored up behind the gigantic bulwark. Along the base of the hills ran the deep cut of Lobo River, which had dwindled to a shallow creek since the building of the dam.

Tomorrow the construction gangs would be paid off. That made the Kid feel certain that Eagle Hawn would try to crack into the bank's vaults tonight. It would be his last chance.

The Kid lowered himself to the ground. He strode down the plank sidewalk. On the opposite side of the street an armed guard had been thrown around the bank. Seven men. Each carried a brace of Colts, a sawed-off shotgun, and cartridge-filled bandoliers criss-crossed from the shoulders. They were men like Deputy Root, bulldogs of the law. The creak of a board, the rasp of a lock would start them shooting.

The Kid's face set. "God!" he muttered. "Hawn will try anything. But he can't make it! They'll tear him to pieces with those scatter-guns."

The Kid clenched his fists. He started toward the Mexican settlement, where Giant and Dandy were searching. The Horde had to get Hawn before he tackled the bank, before scatter-guns could turn him into a blood-drenched sieve.

A few blocks away, the Kid found the two Hordemen prowling around crumbling adobes. They heard his approach, but couldn't see him. Dandy swung around, leveled a six-gun. The Kid uttered a low owl-hoot.

Dandy gasped. His gun lowered. "Hell, son, yuh should 'a' kept in the light. I almost mistook yuh for a spic."

"No sign of Hawn, eh?" asked the Kid.

"He's around, all right," said Giant.

" 'Bout two-three hours ago, he had chuck an' a wash-up at the Alvarez adobe down the street. You know Alvarez. We saved his brother from a lynch-law hangin' last year. Alvarez recognized Hawn, but he knowed yuh let him out o' jail, an' he figured the Horde wanted Hawn to get away."

The Kid shook his head. "Confound that Hawn. He doesn't know what hell he's firin' up."

Leaving the two, the Kid went to another section of town. There the searching Hordemen had met citizens who'd seen a man answering to Hawn's description. One gent claimed he had seen Hawn less than an hour before, heading toward the north end of town. But a search through that district didn't produce the bank robber.

The Kid started south. Save for the noise in the Broken Spur, Deadline was like a ghost town. The few citizens who were abroad kept to the middle of the street. Save for the few street lamps and the lights gleaming from the saloons and *cantinas*, Deadline was cast in gloom, for all of the residences were darkened against the prospect of attracting Morales.

Heading down a side street, the Kid almost collided with a man emerging from an alley. The gent recoiled, went for his gun. The Kid laughed, to put the stranger at his ease. He hadn't seen his face, but he saw that the man was an American.

"It's all right, pardner," said the Kid. "I'm not Morales."

"Kid Calvert!" yelled the man. His gun flashed from the leather. His Stetson fell off as he leaped back.

Pete Quill! The Kid recognized the voice before he saw the ex-deputy's beefy face. The Kid's hand slapped down on his gun butt. He didn't draw. He couldn't have got the gun clear before Quill fired—and he didn't want any shots paging Blade Morales.

The Kid's left hand whipped out as Quill's gun raised. He clutched a hairy wrist. Quill winced.

"Fire that gun," rasped the Kid, "an' I'll tear yore arm from the socket. Yuh mangy lobo—sellin' out to that spic cur. By God, yuh'll hang, Quill."

The ex-deputy was snarling. He smashed the Kid between the eyes. The Kid's senses reeled. He rammed a right against Quill's nose that crunched the bone and brought a crimson spurt. The Kid had such a tight grip on Quill's gunhand that the Morales man couldn't work his trigger finger.

The Kid started to circle his arm around his foe's head. He'd clamp on a lock that'd make this beef-face think he'd caught his head under a boulder.

"I—won't—hang," gasped Quill, struggling furiously. The ex-deputy brought up his knee viciously. "I'll kill yuh, Calvert. That'll make me—the—big—noise in Deadline." The Kid had worked him against an adobe wall and was pressing him hard.

Quill hadn't lost his arrogance. "Next election—I'll cop all the votes for sheriff." The Kid ground his teeth and got Quill's head in the bend of his elbow. The man still leered. "Terry will be out—an' I'll run the town."

THE MENTION of Terry threw the Kid into a killer's rage. This booze-soaked polecat talking about ousting Terry. The Kid exerted all his power. His headlock threatened to crush Quill's skull. Quill bawled in pain. The gun-hog couldn't operate his knees in foul tactics, because the Kid had one leg grapevined around Quill's. The Kid couldn't wrench the gun from the skulker, but his grip never relaxed. Quill's gunhand was cold as death, his trigger finger stiff.

His manner changed. "Let me go, Calvert," he pleaded. "I'll make a deal with yuh. We're pards of the owl-hoot. Shore! Leggo, Kid. I'll—I'll cut yuh in on the Hawn swag."

"Drop that gun," gritted the Kid. "Yuh ain't cuttin' in on nothin' but a heap o' tough luck."

The Kid gave a terrific snap to his arm that circled Quill's head. The man groaned. His legs gave way. The Kid held him up, added agonizing pressure. Quill wasn't out. Suddenly he gave a violent jerk, got free, and sank his teeth into the Kid's shoulder. His jaws clamped tight.

The teeth went through the Kid's shirt, cut into the flesh. Pain shot through him, sapping his strength. His grip on Quill's wrist loosened. Instantly the man's finger curled on the trigger. Six shots roared. Bullets whined skyward.

The Kid wrenched free, snarling, trembling with fury. He lunged. The beef-face retreated, flailing his gun barrel. Then he blared out a bull-throated bellow.

"Morales! Morales! The Horde's in. The Horde! The Horde! I've got Calvert—Kid Calvert. Oh-h-h, Morales!"

Quill's thunderous voice echoed from the hills. That rumbling outburst carried throughout the town, carried to the spic cordon out on the flats. There was a moment of deathly silence. Lashing out with battering-ram punches, the Kid swung into Quill, lurched at his foe with murderous intensity, while another roaring voice threw back an answer, and guns began to blast.

Even as the Kid dodged the downswing of Quill's gun, and slammed a haymaker to the man's middle, the voice of Morales ripped out from the distance, shouting orders in Spanish. Quill threw his gun at the Kid. It struck his shoulder, spun him.

Quill uttered a triumphant yell, shouted to Morales again, and bulled in. That was what Calvert wanted. He had to hurry. Hoofs were drumming. The spics were tearing into town, spraying lead. Already he heard guns blasting in Deadline. The Horde was ranging its forces. The Horde was showing those spics what it was like to face guns that spouted flaming hell.

The Kid dug his boot heels into the dirt and launched a two-fisted attack that tore at Quill's vitals. He rocked him about the head, dazed him with sense-shattering jolts to the jaw. Quill was in a fog. His wits had been scattered. He tried to trade punches, but the Kid was a maniac in close, and his shots to the ribs caved Quill.

The Kid heard running footsteps. Men were drawing near. He didn't know whether they were Hordemen, citizens, gunhogs. He redoubled his fury, banging in blows that made his arms recoil in the sockets at the impact. Quill was sinking. He flashed a knife, lunged drunkenly.

The blade slashed the Kid along the ribs, drew blood. The knife raised for the death stroke. The Kid crashed a left-right to Quill's underslung jaw. The wicked sliver of steel went sailing. Quill reeled, clawed at the air. Words bubbled in the crimson that gushed from his mouth. His legs failed him. He collapsed.

Men rushed up the side street. The Kid whipped around, hand streaking hipward. Then he uttered an exclamation of relief. Dandy and Giant! Their guns were smoking, their eyes wild.

"Yuh all right, son?" yelled Dandy. "Come on, then. The Horde's buckin' a stacked deck, an' the game's gettin' hot."

The three raced for the main street, where guns were thundering. All lights were out, even those in the saloons. Not a sound came from the Broken Spur.

In the moonlight, the Kid saw the peaks of sombreros rising above the water barrels which lined the street. Two dead horses lay beside the hitchrack in front of the Broken Spur. A spic was sprawled in the dust.

FROM THE darkness Morales bellowed orders. That was the gent the Kid wanted. Morales was on the other side of the street. The Hordemen were taking care of themselves. Both sides were firing from cover. If the Kid could get across the street— There wasn't a chance of making a run.

Dandy and Giant were standing beside him, ready to go into action. He motioned for them to wait. Down the side street, the Kid had seen a Conestoga wagon. He went after it, lashed up the shafts, and rolled it near the intersection.

"When I climb in this," he told his pards, "give it a shove that'll send it across the street. I'm headin' for Morales. Thud hell into those spics while I'm on the way."

The Kid lay flat in the wagon. The sides covered his body. He held a gun in each hand, ready to make one blazing stand, if the spics swarmed around him. The Hordemen were doubtful, but they didn't argue. They gave the wagon a violent shove. The wheels spun. Instantly the owl-hooters poured a withering fusillade across the street where spics hid behind streaming water barrels.

Lead showered the Conestoga wagon, ripped into the stout oaken sides, rattled against the wheel spokes. Bullets shaved across the Kid's shoulder blades. Oak splinters stabbed his neck.

Suddenly a wheel hit a stone. The wagon careened, crashed into a water barrel. A wild shout came from the spics. The Kid was trapped. Dandy McLain uttered a wail. A chill ran up the Kid's spine.

"Don't yuh come across, Dandy!" he yelled. "Hold him back, Giant."

"Hold hell! I'm comin' myself!"

The Kid's tongue cleaved to the roof of his mouth. He felt an icy prickle along his spine. He was through. Only a matter of time before bullets pierced the oaken sides, riddled him. He was gone, yet his men intended to run to his aid. The Horde would be slaughtered.

He stifled the impulse to jump up and gun a few of the dogs before he dropped. The spic behind the water barrel was blasting away at the bottom of the wagon. The Kid could feel the bullets thumping the wood about the middle of his stomach. A couple of rounds would put a hole through the board.

He ground his teeth, tensed his muscles. Dandy and Giant hadn't rushed out yet. If they saw him go down, they wouldn't expose themselves. They'd fight from cover then. The Kid was ready. He would jump up. It was suicide, but a quick way out. And he'd save his pards.

A thunderous roar crashed above the racket of snarling guns. It was a booming, ear-splitting blast that shattered windows, that threw men flat. The deafening explosion echoed through the hills. There was another terrific detonation—and another. The firing in town suddenly ceased.

The noise of blazing guns was replaced by another roar that sent a chill through men.

"The dam!" shrilled a voice on the edge of town. "The dam's been dynamited. The water's busted through. It's pouring down. The town will be flooded. Run, everybody! Run for yore lives!"

5

HAWN'S DECISION

THERE WAS a short space of dead silence, save for the roar of rushing, cascading water. Then Morales bellowed to his gunhogs. There was fear in his tone. He yelled for his spics to ride. His interest in Deadline was gone. The water would be flooding in. Let the citizens drown like rats. Morales had no love of water except as a chaser.

Before he had finished shouting, hoofs were pounding. The spic who had been drilling a hole through the wagon board, left his shelter and scurried into the darkness.

The Broken Spur was disgorging its patrons through doors and windows. Townsfolk were rushing from their homes. The roar from the dam grew until all noise was swallowed in it. Men were forking mounts and heading toward the water avalanching out of the hills.

In Mex Town frenzied peons were jabbering as they frantically gathered a few belongings. Men were hitching up teams and hustling their women and children into wagons and buggies. Deadline was in confusion as the inhabitants madly hastened to desert it.

Blade Morales was gone, forgotten. The only calm ones were the Hordemen. They gathered in the deserted Broken Spur, in a back room, closing the door against the racket outside.

"We best be foggin'," suggested a Hordeman. "I was in a flood onct. It ain't nothin' to be in. I was swimmin' along as nice as yuh please, when—biffo—a log clunked me on the nob, an' I drank a gallon o' yaller water before a feller fished me onto a housetop."

The Kid laughed. "Yuh won't get yore feet wet this time, Jake. The flats will be dampened some, but the dry bed of Lobo River will catch most of the water an' shoot it down its course. Folks hereabouts know that as well as I do. Reckon people jest went hog-wild with panic. But they'll come to their senses soon—but not soon enough, if I've got the right hunch. Gents, I want yuh to stick right here. I'm makin' a little pasear down the street. Yuh'll spoil my play if yuh follow."

Leaving the perplexed owl-hooters, the Kid went out the rear door and hurried through the gloom of a back street. He cut into an alley and paused in the shadows of a harness shop opposite the Cattlemen's Bank. The bank guards had been swept along in the rush.

The roar from the dynamited dam had diminished. None of the water reached Deadline. The Kid waited. The main street was deserted. The bank was silent, dark. He peered up and down the street. Shouts sounded from the dam, where men were working. Wagon wheels rattled down toward Deadline. Citizens were returning. But it was for a lone man that the Kid kept this vigil.

Fifteen, twenty minutes passed. The Kid became fidgety. He gnawed at his lip. His expression grew sour. He muttered, and began thinking of Terry, worrying. Where had the girl been during all this turmoil? Why hadn't Terry formed a posse? Why hadn't she directed concerted action against the spies? The Kid accused himself of laxity. He should have gone to Terry's home first, should have made certain that she was safe.

He snapped rigid. A faint glow appeared in the Cattlemen's Bank. The Kid's eyes flashed. He yanked a gun, raced across the street. Again the bank was dark.

Cautiously the Kid turned the knob of the stout oaken door. It was unlocked. He pushed the door inward, edged through. A dog wouldn't have heard his stealthy approach, but the man working the dial on the vault leaped to his feet and pointed a gun at the Kid. Draft coming through the opened door had warned him.

"Up with them, hombre," rasped the voice of Eagle Hawn. "Reach high or yuh'll be a candidate for a pine box."

"I'll call yore bluff, Hawn," spoke the Kid easily. "Yuh ain't a killin' jasper. That's why yuh've been caught so much, why yuh've tangled so often with the law. Yuh'd rather be arrested for robbery than hunted down for murder."

The Kid advanced swiftly, striding through a door in the heavy wire network. Eagle Hawn was exposed now, peering strangely at the intruder. He raised his small lamp.

"Say—are you—Kid Calvert?" he asked excitedly.

"I answer to that name when I'm among the right folks," replied the Kid. "Might as well pocket that toy pistol. An' believe me, Eagle, I ain't bluffin' with this smoke wagon. I won't kill yuh. Yo're too valuable a man to kill. But try anything tough—an' I'll sure put a hole in yuh somewhere. Comin' along like a gent?"

"Well, I'll be damned!" exclaimed Hawn. "You hoorawing me, Kid? Sure, I'll come like a gent. Why, I'm proud to walk with you. Wait a jiffy. I've got to rattle these tumblers. You might lend a hand toting away the money bags. That's the trouble with this profession. Lugging away goldpieces is very, very irksome, especially when a posse is on your trail."

"Yuh can neglect yore irksome duty this time, Eagle," said the Kid. "I don't think the boys in the hills would appreciate yore efforts, even though yuh gave them more work blowin' up their dam."

"Nicely timed, wasn't it?" replied Hawn, his eyes flashing with pride. "That's the way a magician works. Gets the crowd interested in what his left hand is doing, while his right is pullin' a rabbit from his coat-tails."

HAWN PRESSED his ear close to the dial. His long fingers worked skillfully. Two clicks sounded. The bank robber chuckled, stood up, and swung open the vault door. The Kid jumped forward and closed it.

"Yuh got me wrong, Eagle," he said. "Yo're not packin' anything away from this job. Yo're comin' with me. The Horde wants to meet yuh. There's a little gent in our bunch who hankers to flip cards with yuh. Little Dandy McLain is sure interested in that lucky deck yuh always tote."

Hawn eyed the Kid sharply. For a flash he dropped his attitude. Then he grinned. "Oh, I see. A friendly little game. I should think he'd be afraid of my cards. Most sharps figure they're marked." He gazed at the Kid's leveled gun, frowned, then shrugged.

"You're not in a sporting mood tonight, Kid. But you did me a neat favor this afternoon—and I'm not forgetting. You think I should leave this *dinero* for the poor muckers up on the dam. All right. They'll only squander it, but I'm willing to overlook human frailty for once. Let's go, pard."

Hawn cast a longing look at the vault, and then went ahead of the Kid. They reached the street without being seen, and hurried into the darkness of an alley.

His gun still leveled, the Kid escorted Hawn into the back room of the Broken Spur. The owl-hooters jumped at the sight of the bank robber. The Kid quickly explained.

"By coots, Eagle!" exclaimed Peel Rogers, his Adam's apple bobbing. "Yo're the fust millionaire I've ever seen that wasn't posin' as an upstandin' citizen."

"A little high on your figures, pard," said Hawn, bowing to the grizzled cook. "I've got to open about five more vaults before I get in that class. But I'm sure gratified with the reception you've given me."

The bank robber grew serious. "Gents, I've got a confession to make. This game's getting too tough to play solo. It isn't the law, you understand. I can handle the star Johnnies. They mess me up a bit, but they don't get results. Morales is different. Morales—" Terror suddenly shone in his eyes. "Gents, I need protection. I want to join the Horde."

Hawn's gaze swept the group. He saw nothing but cold poker eyes. He nodded. "I understand. You don't take in any scut. Um-m. That's why I tried to rob the bank tonight. I wanted to show you that I'm not exactly a jughead.

"I wanted to show you that I'd go through with a proposition—even when I'm afraid. And I fear Morales. I fear him more than any living thing." Hawn made a gesture of appeal. "I'm willing to do anything to prove my worth. I earnestly beg you to consider my application. I need the Horde."

His request met with silence. Men stared at the table. Men drummed the board, but they didn't answer Hawn. For once this gent was awkward, abashed. He started to speak, then broke off, shaking his head.

Outside sounded the rattle of wheels and the beat of hoofs. In the saloon boot heels thudded, spurs jingled. The Kid grew uneasy.

"By dogies, Hawn," said the explosive Peel Rogers, "the Horde oughta be proud to have yuh join up! What do yuh ring-tailed baboons say? Is Hawn in the Horde, or ain't he?"

"The Horde!" came a shout from the corridor. "The Horde's got Hawn. They're in the back room. Surround the place, men!"

The Kid went for his gun. Some one had been eavesdropping. The man's cry started a wild scramble in the barroom. Men were shouting, running from the building. A shot rang out. Citizens in the street were blaring for reenforcements. Deadline had been pushed too far. The town was ready to fight.

The Hordemen leaped up, edging away from the window. Their eyes slitted; their faces grew harsh. Peel Rogers knocked over a chair and bounded for the door, gripping his Colt and shouting for the others to follow. The Kid blocked his way, shoved him back.

"We don't want any ruckus," he said sharply. "Get to yore broncs, men. Fog for the old Montero adobe. We'll hole up there. I'm afraid something's happened to Terry. It ain't her style to stick at home when Deadline's in trouble. We best stay in town until we find out for sure. Hawn, get between Giant and Nate."

THE CORRIDOR was clear when the Kid opened the door. The Hordemen eased out the back way, where their mounts were ground anchored in the alley. Citizens were swarming in front of the Broken Spur, but none of them ventured into the darkness.

The Montero adobe, long abandoned, stood about a half mile from town. While the Horde rode there, the Kid went to Terry's home. He grew clammy with dread as he reined Star to a halt before the dark house. Dismounting, he ran up the steps and hammered on the door. A dog scooted around from the backyard and barked at him, but no sign of life showed in the house. The Kid suddenly went weak. Terry was gone. He pictured her lying dead somewhere.

"Terry! Terry!" he cried frantically. He rapped on the windows, banged on the back door. Cold sweat studded his forehead. Terrible thoughts plagued him. His heart thumped. He raged at himself for not hunting for Terry sooner.

A man next door appeared on the porch. "What's all the fuss about, stranger?" he asked.

"Terry," the Kid said tensely. "Have you seen Terry Reynolds?"

The man shook his head. "She visited my wife about three hours ago. Said she was going to round up a posse to herd the Morales gang off to the calaboose. Mebbe she's up at the dam."

The Kid's heart raced with hope. It crushed him to think that Terry had been hurt or killed, and he grabbed eagerly for any idea suggesting she might be safe. Thanking the man, he sprinted for his mount. In the saddle, he gave Star an unaccustomed dig of the spurs, sending the steel-dust at a breeze-burning pace across the flats.

The stallion never slackened speed until he reached Lobo River, which had dwindled again to a shallow stream. Star splashed through the water and plunged up the hill through the chaparral at a high lope. The dam was a hive swarming with men.

Hawn had dynamited a jagged hole in the gigantic concrete bulwark. Already the flood had ceased, for the water level had reached the bottom of the fissure. Scores of men were wielding singlejacks and mixing concrete. Strings of lanterns lighted the dam. The Kid saw that Hawn hadn't done as much harm as he had imagined.

Through the milling crowd, the Kid searched for Terry, for a fluffy-haired girl with a star on her blouse. He spoke to dozens of men. The Kid's eyes deadened as each one shook his head. Terry hadn't been at the dam. With shoulders drooping, the Kid rode down the slope, heading for the Montero adobe. His heart seemed as heavy as a millstone. He felt like a withered old man.

A couple of owl-hooters rode around the crumbling structure. They spotted the Kid, and raised their guns in challenge. As he neared the adobe, the Kid heard loud talking from within. The voice of Giant Anderson rose stridently.

"Let me handle him, Dandy," the big fellow boomed. "I'll give the dirty, struttin' skulker his deservings. I'll bust his spine across my knee. I'll tie him in a knot an' throw him to the wolves."

The Kid snapped out of his slump. His eyes flashed. Star responded to a touch of the spurs with a plunge. The guards cracked out a command for him to stop. The Kid shouted to them, streaked by. Then he was tugging the steel-dust to a sliding halt and springing from the saddle. He rushed inside to see Giant's shoulder-of-mutton paw reaching out for the gullet of Pete Quill.

"Stop!" the Kid yelled. "What's the trouble, Giant?"

"Trouble?" snorted Peel Rogers, before the big fellow could speak. "This hydrophoby skunk is foulin' the atmosphere, by coots. Giant's goin' to kill him, so decent men can breathe clean air. The sidewinder says Morales has Terry a prisoner. Says we have to give up Hawn—or Terry goes below the Line!"

The Kid shrieked. Never in his life had he let himself go so completely. His eyes blazed like a madman's. Vicious snarls came from his throat. His face turned death-gray beneath its bronze. Then the color mounted. His lips curled back. His face became as savage as a wolf's.

He lunged at Pete Quill. He drove Quill against the adobe wall. Steel-spring hands closed around the man's neck. Powerful fingers tore at the windpipe. The Kid would have clawed a hole in Quill's throat, would have killed the man with his bare hands—but little Dandy stepped in.

"Back up, son," the gambler said calmly. "Yo're buckin' a royal flush with a pair of deuces."

THE KID did back up, but he almost screamed at Dandy. "Didn't yuh hear? Terry goes below the Line if— Below the Line, Dandy! Don't yuh know what that means?"

"Yes, son. Too well. Too well." Dandy put his arm over the Kid's trembling shoulders. "Hell is paradise compared to what happens to girls when they go below the Line. But we've got to handle this matter sensibly."

Pete Quill had recovered from fright. He rubbed his neck tenderly. "Yeah," he sneered. "Yuh got to be sensible. Kill me, an' yore dainty little peach blossom goes below the Line. Morales means business. I take back Hawn tonight or—"

The Kid regained control, but he was still shaking. He saw that Morales must have captured Terry when the girl had started out to organize a posse. The whole town knew that the Horde had caught Hawn. The word had traveled to Morales, who had sent Quill back.

"What can we do?" the Kid murmured. "We can't turn Hawn over to Morales, an' we have to get Terry."

Hawn was slumped in a rickety chair. He had gone white. He had gnawed at his lacerated lips until they were bleeding. His fingernails pierced the flesh in the palms of his hands. His eyes were feverish. Often he started from his chair only to drop back again. His face was haggard. Perspiration drenched him.

Dandy had no plan. The others were silent, thinking. Quill leered at them, and swaggered about the room. Every time Giant looked at the man, he shuddered with rage.

"Mebbe if I went along with Quill an' posed as Hawn—" began the Kid. His voice was broken. His features had aged.

Quill guffawed. "Why don't yuh try it, Kid? Mebbe Morales will take yuh below the Line, so yuh can see what happens to gals that are sent south. Come along. Morales kin get Hawn later."

The ex-deputy strutted up and down, flaunting his contempt. The owl-hooters had become very, very still. But cold ferocity masked every face.

None of them looked at Hawn. The thought of turning him over to Quill hadn't entered their heads. They had to get the girl, yet they couldn't send Hawn to fiendish torture and slow, agonizing death.

"Might be a good idea for the bunch of us to go after Morales," suggested Nate Willstock, the wintry-eyed one. "Mebbe we can surprise him, find the girl before Morales can get away with her. I don't think he'd kill her. She's worth money to him alive."

"Sure, sure," jeered Quill, "that's the idea. Only thing wrong is that Morales thought of it first. He's sorta expectin' an attack. He says that Terry Reynolds dies the second guns begin to talk."

Hawn leaped up, tense, and white, and drawn. He raised his hands. "This has gone far enough!" he exclaimed shrilly. "Quill, come on. I'm ready. I don't care what Morales does to me. Let him feed me to the ants, burn me—anything. A man can stand so much; then he passes out. I can take physical torture better than what I'm going through now. I wouldn't want to live, knowing that I'd been the cause of a girl going—below the Line. I'm ready, Quill."

There was a wild light in Hawn's eyes. But his body had relaxed. No longer did his nails dig into his hands. No longer did he gnaw at his lips. He had reached the state of mind of one who has thrown away all hope.

"Eagle," cried the Kid, "yuh can't do this! Yuh can't, man! Lord in heaven, yo're insane. Morales won't stop at anything.

He branded yuh once, Eagle. Yuh said that the next time, yuh was through. Yuh said that, Eagle. An' yuh know it's true. It's suicide. Yo're insane."

Hawn shook his head slowly, and there was a smile on his torn lips. "No, Kid, *amigo*," he said quietly. "Not insane. Not any more. I *was* crazy. But now I'm seeing things right. Come on, Quill."

Even Quill was shaken now. He stared in awe at Hawn. The bank robber grabbed the ex-deputy by the arm and shoved him out the open door. The Hordemen stood frozen, spellbound. Suddenly the Kid sprang toward Hawn, to stop him. Dandy McLain clutched the Kid's arm.

"No, son," he spoke softly. "Let him go. It's the only way. We all have to die, Hawn's goin' sooner than the others, that's all." Dandy called to the sentries. "Let 'em through, men."

The Kid fell into a chair, brushed a hand wearily across his face. A great sob escaped him. He looked so tired.

PRESENTLY HOOFS were drumming the alkali. Quill and his prisoner were heading toward the southwest. The Hordemen shook themselves from a spell. Men swore. Men exclaimed in awe at this stripling who was giving up everything for a girl who was his enemy.

"God," spoke the Giant softly, "there goes a man. A man."

"He had everything to live for," muttered Nate Willstock. "Looks, health, money—an' he loved life."

"By coots an' by dogies!" yelled Peel Rogers. "It's a rotten trick, lettin' that swell gazabo ride into hell. I'm fer follerin' them, an' shootin' that Morales pack so full o' lead that the buzzards will bust their beaks peckin' at thar carcasses. Come on!"

"No," exclaimed the Kid, jumping up. "Yuh stay here—an' the rest o' yuh. I'm goin', see? I'm goin'. I'll give myself up. At least, I'll be near Terry. At least, I can save her from being shipped below the Line, even if—if I have to shoot—"

Before any of them could respond, the Kid flung out the

door. He mounted Star and rode away without looking back. An expert at reading signs, he had no difficulty following the tracks of the other mounts. He sent the stallion at an easy pace, because he didn't want to catch up.

Heading up the first slope, he became aware that some one was riding madly on his trail. He turned. The moonlight gleamed on the little figure of Dandy McLain, bent low over his bronc's neck. A pang went through the Kid. He might have expected this of Dandy. But the little gambler would have to turn back. This was a one-man job. The Kid was frowning when the owl-hooter reined up beside him.

"I figured two heads would have more ideas than one," said Dandy. "We're takin' a long chance, headin' into Morales' hideout; but mebbe we can stack the deck to draw winnin' cards. Let's drift, son."

"Dandy, yuh oughta go back," spoke the Kid tensely. "I'm not returnin'—unless Terry is with me. The Horde needs yuh, Dandy. Yuh've got to carry on. Yuh've got to hold the men together. Go back, Dandy. I'm ridin' in solo."

"Yeah?" grunted the gambler. "As long as I'm breathin', yo're not goin' alone. I'll turn back if yuh do. But I'm stickin' with yuh, son. Mebbe Morales will let Terry go."

The Kid shook his head. "Yuh know better than to say that of Morales. Even if he did, he'd still have Hawn. I'm the cause of Hawn gettin' into this mess. Either I get him out, or I go down tryin'."

They rode on in silence. Anxiety numbed the Kid. Fear for Terry dwarfed the danger that lay ahead. Dandy was moody. Often he gazed at his smooth hands, wiggling his slender fingers and making gestures as though he were dealing cards. The Kid gritted his teeth. He understood. Dandy believed he had played his last game.

The trail took them through thick stands of timber, through a tumbled land slashed by many gulches. They rode slowly, expecting at any moment to hear a shot. An hour had passed.

They pushed out of a draw onto a level, brush-grown straight-away.

Ahead rose two jagged, bald chimney buttes, marking the entrance to a narrow defile. Dandy stared at the gap, swallowed hard. He whistled very softly. His hand started for his gun. The Kid grabbed his wrist.

"Want to get picked off by a sniper?" he growled. "If the hideout is yonder, sentries are—"

Something shrieked overhead, followed by the staccato crack of a high-powered rifle. Midway up a rock-studded butte, powder smoke puffed out. Long barrels glinted in the moon-light. Rifles began a harsh clatter, and steel-jacketed bullets screamed around the two. They reined to a halt, raised their hands.

Muscles bulged on the Kid's jaw. He stiffened. His eyes were flinty. Low snarls escaped him. It was hard to leave his gun holstered. Five sombreroed spics, shrieking like madmen, swooped through the defile. Flame stabbed from their pound-ing sixes. They surrounded Dandy and the Kid, took their guns, and herded them into the *bandido* hideout.

6

VALLEY OF DEATH

BEYOND THE gap lay a small valley locked in by sheer, rocky walls. The defile provided the only entrance. In the valley were the remains of an ancient civilization—crumbling heaps that once had been mud huts, remnants of crude agri-cultural implements, and several small stone houses which had weathered the years.

Toward one of them, the spic prodded the prisoners. Strewn about the ground were bits of broken pottery. The Kid stepped among skeletons that crumbled into dust under his weight. He saw a large flat stone, inscribed with many weird designs. Probably a sacrificial stone used in ancient ceremonies. Near it lay the head of a bronze idol, crusted with green corrosion. The Kid realized that centuries ago this valley had sheltered an Aztec settlement.

The half-breeds shoved the two into a lighted stone house where Blade Morales sat behind a rough-hewn table. At the sight of the Kid, the *bandido* leaped up. His hand flashed for his gun, but he didn't raise it. He chuckled, and his tiny eyes glittered.

"The gun, eet ees too queeck, *señor,*" he purred. "For you, who tell me een the Broken Spur what I should do, I have sometheeng much better, sometheeng that weel mak' you squeal, *amigo.* I have beeg red ants!"

Pete Quill swaggered into the room. He blinked and gasped at the sight of the prisoners. Then a cruel, gloating smile curled his lips. "Why, howdy, Kid Calvert. How yuh stackin' up these days?"

The name gave Morales a start. His wicked little eyes widened. He stared at the Kid, his mouth agape. Then awe changed to anger, and anger was replaced by amusement. He bowed low before the owl-hooter.

"Keed Calvert! The gr-r-reat Keed Calvert. Eet ees a pleasure to know you. Ver-ry much do I admire you. Today you fool the gran' Morales! *Si!* The hombre who fool Morales ees wan smart *caballero.* Tonight, Keed, you are my guest. Tomorrow—" The peon shrugged. "Tomorrow, mebbeso you go below the Line weeth *Señorita* Terry."

Snarling, the Kid lunged for the squat, leering spic. His fist lashed out, but Morales swayed back, and four of his henchmen piled on the Kid, hurling him against the wall. The *bandido* chuckled, motioning for his hirelings to take the prisoners away.

The spics led the Hordemen to another stone house. Inside, the Kid confronted Eagle Hawn and Terry. He uttered a glad cry and rushed toward the girl, who shrank from him.

"Don't come near me!" she cried. "You—you brute. How could you be so cruel? How could you turn Hawn over to Quill? You knew what Morales would do, yet you—"

"Miss Terry!" exclaimed Hawn. "Don't say that. It isn't true. A finer gent than Kid Calvert never breathed. He tried to hold me back. But I wouldn't stay. I couldn't, knowing that Morales might send you—"

The bank robber stopped suddenly as the girl shuddered. She knew where Morales planned to take her. The Kid ignored her accusation. She was under a great strain. The hate that Deadline had for the Horde, and the evil things said about the Kid, couldn't help but influence Terry. She only caught glimpses of his true character.

"I'm sorry," the girl said, touching her hand to the Kid's arm. "I'm unstrung. I've been pleading with Hawn to tell Morales where his cache is hidden. If Morales gets the treasure, he'll let us go. I can get a posse together, and catch his men before they can get below the border."

Hawn shook his head. "That's a vow I made that I'll never break. I risked my life a hundred times to build up my stake. It's mine and I'm keepin' it."

The Kid was still anxious about Terry. "Did Morales—hurt yuh any?" he asked, his eyes glinting.

The girl shook her head. "He's all that is bad. He might kill me. He would send me—away. But he is awed by a white woman. He broke the jaw of a man who tried to put his arm around me."

The Kid nodded grimly.

"What are we goin' to do?" asked Dandy McLain. "We're not locked in here. We can roam around. Mebbe I can sneak up on one of them Mexican jumpin' beans an' get his hogleg."

"You won't be able to sneak up on them," said Hawn. "I tried it. We've got to work out a better scheme. Maybe when Morales starts working on me, you three can make a getaway."

The Kid growled at that suggestion. There were loud voices

outside, the heavy clump of footsteps. The door opened and Morales strutted in. Behind him strode two spics, carrying a couple of roast chickens, wine bottles, and platters of steaming food. Those platters were of silver—loot obviously from some big rancho.

"Ha!" laughed the peon, pulling a leg from a chicken and tearing the meat from the bone. "Morales, he breeng wan beeg feast for hees *amigos.* See? I, the gran' *caballero,* eat the cheecken. Be not afraid, my *compadres.* There ees no poison een thees chuck."

The food was set on the table, wine bottles opened, and the prisoners invited to dig in. They were hungry, and the chicken was savory and browned to a turn. Dandy was the first to carve off a big slice. The others followed suit. Morales chuckled in childish glee as his captives devoured the feast. He was under the spell of another whim. There was no doubt that at the moment he looked upon them as his friends.

When they had finished eating, Morales clapped his hands with a flourishing gesture, and spics entered to clear the table. One of them brought in a box of poker chips. Morales was chuckling like a witless child.

"Now we play the game," he said. "I show you what I am. I show you that I am not only the most gran' *caballero* in all the worl', but the bes' cardman in the worl', too. *Señor* Hawn, I hear much about your lucky cards. I hear you nevaire lose. No—no, not ontil you meet the gr-r-reat Morales. *Si? Señor* Hawn, the cards. *Señor* Dandy McLain, they say you are ver-ry clevaire. Nobody can beat you, they say. But have you play' Morales? No, *señor.*"

EAGLE HAWN had a strange look in his eyes as he brought forth his deck of soiled cards, with the queer designs on the back.

Morales motioned for them to sit down. "*Amigos,* you have won thousands. *Si.* But tonight you play for millions. Ever' cheep, she count for wan million peso. We play for ver-ry high stakes, but we do not put oop *dinero*, 'cause eef you have *dinero*, I take eet, anyway."

Hawn shuffled the cards. Morales eyed him closely, and made the cut. The cards were dealt. The men were silent. Dandy held his cards close to his flowery vest, his eyes blank, his face as inscrutable as a Chinaman's. The betting was high and the play brisk. Hawn raked in the chips on a filled straight against three jacks held by Dandy and two pairs in Morales' hand. The *bandido* muttered Spanish oaths.

The Kid's eyes were on the game, but he was racking his head for an idea. How could he trick this mad spic? It would be foolish to slug the peon, to snatch for his gun. Morales had guards outside. The Kid had to think always of the girl.

At the moment Terry had forgotten her danger. She had picked up a fragment of pottery, and was studying its strange carvings.

"A tribute to Quetzalcoatl, the Aztec sun god," she said, showing the inscription to the Kid. "What a rich find this valley would be for a museum."

"You savvy this Aztec hen scratchin'?" the Kid asked.

"Yes," answered the girl. "I studied it in school, an'—"

Her words were lost in a roar from Morales. The cards had favored Hawn again. His pile of chips was mounting. The spic had the smallest stack of the three. Although no money was at stake, Morales was angered at losing. His eyes watched every move that Dandy made as he dealt; but keener eyes than Morales' had failed to catch the little gambler in the act of second-dealing. He was doing that now.

Suddenly the Kid got the idea for which he had been groping. Standing in back of Morales, he got Dandy's eyes, and silently formed the word "win" on his lips. At the same time he pointed to Morales. Dandy understood. The Kid got the same message to Hawn.

The Kid spoke to the spic. "Any chance of steppin' outside for a breath of air, Morales?"

"Go ahead," muttered the disgruntled *bandido.* "Try to escape, *amigo,* and see what happens. Come on, *señores,* we play for beeg stakes now. I open the pot weeth the million pesos—so. Now I show you the real stuff, by golly."

Terry started out with the Kid, who motioned her to stay. The guards eyed him suspiciously, but they didn't stop him. The Kid casually wandered over to a rock house where he knew Pete Quill had his quarters. He knocked on the door.

Quill opened it. "What do yuh want?" he demanded belligerently.

"Nothing, pard," said the Kid sarcastically. "I jest dropped around to give yuh the hoss laugh. Yuh seemed to have got some chuckles out of me. Now it's my turn."

"Yeah?" growled Quill. "What are yuh talkin' about? Not tryin' to get friendly, are yuh? I can shoot yuh down, an' tell Morales I caught yuh tryin' to escape."

"Sure, sure," said the Kid easily. "But yuh won't. Morales isn't any *amigo* of yores, Quill. Yuh figured to get a nice whack out of Hawn's cache, didn't yuh? Well, Morales has sold yuh out. He's hookin' up with Hawn. He's over in yonder house now, actin' like he's jest met a long-lost brother. I wouldn't be surprised if you were buzzard bait, come mornin'. Who's the jughead now, Quill?"

Quill scowled at the Kid and chewed on his pipe. "Tryin' to hooraw me?"

"Hoorawin' yuh, am I?" gritted the Kid. "Crow-hop over to that house an' see for yoreself."

Quill nodded. He grabbed his hat and strode alongside the Kid, who fell a little behind when they neared the house. He was only playing a long chance. Then his heart pounded exultantly. Morales was guffawing. Through the slats secured over the paneless windows, he saw the spic slapping Hawn on the back.

"Ha, *amigo,* you are *bueno caballero,*" yelled the boisterous *bandido.* "You are the bes' frien' I got. *Si!* But you cannot beat old Morales weeth the cards."

"Havin' a friendly little game between discussions," the Kid whispered insinuatingly. "Yo're through, Quill. Yuh were jest a tool for Morales. He used yuh, an' now he'll toss yuh aside. Now if I was in yore shoes, I'd be havin' a little discussion, too." The Kid's eyes shifted to another rock house, where through the window, he saw several spics around a table. "So long, Quill." The Kid's voice was mocking.

He entered the house, wondering if he had planted the seeds of hate deep enough. Morales was stacking up the chips and laughing at Hawn. The *bandido* was feeling very expansive. The girl looked a question at the Kid. Hawn and Dandy showed curiosity, too; but Morales' only interest now was in winning hands.

The Kid stood against the rear wall, watching the window. Morales hauled in the chips again and again. The great idiotic grin never left his face. Often he guffawed. Often he slapped Hawn on the back, ruffled Dandy's hair; begged Terry to have a sip of wine. His booming voice filled the room.

Suddenly the Kid grew tense. Men were standing before the window, out of the circle of light. The Kid recognized the beefy face of Pete Quill, saw the sombreros behind him. While Quill watched, Morales scooped up another pile of chips. The *bandido* was drunk with success. He reached over and hugged Hawn, hugged the man he later intended to torture.

QUILL DISAPPEARED. The Kid's pulses hammered. What would be the result of his trick? With his eyes he indicated to Hawn and Dandy that they could play to win. Soon Morales was swearing again. And it was Hawn who won all the pots. The spic's stack of chips became smaller and smaller.

Suddenly Morales' manner changed. He gathered up the cards and shoved the pack in his pocket. He kicked back his chair, knocked over the table, and slammed a wine bottle against the wall.

"*Caramba!*" he snarled. "You cheat, you dam' greengo peeg. I tak' these cards. I weel study them and learn how you ween weeth them, by golly."

The spic clumped from the house. He hadn't gone more than twenty yards when a gun blast shattered the night's stillness. Morales uttered a howl. The Kid peered out the window. The spic was sprinting for shelter, his guns roaring. Three of his henchmen were with him. Suddenly one dropped.

"He's doing it!" exclaimed the Kid. "Quill has turned against Morales. Come on gents. One man's down already. There goes another. We can get guns."

The Kid didn't need to explain. Hawn leaped ahead of the Kid, plunged out the door. The shooting was centered around two buildings about a hundred yards away. Less than half that distance lay two spic bodies.

Morales was thundering orders. Suddenly shots roared from the mouth of the defile. The Kid was outside now, racing behind Hawn. He heard an agonized scream, saw one of the sentries hurtle from a chimney butte.

Shouts sounded from outside the valley. The Horde had arrived, was centered there, fighting to get through. The Kid didn't think the owl-hooters could make it. A couple of men hidden on those buttes could hold off an army. It was up to the Kid, and Dandy, and Hawn.

The little gambler was speeding along close behind. The girl had left the house. A chill went through the Kid. He turned and motioned for her to go back.

"Stick to shelter, Terry. Stick to shelter."

The girl pointed to her star and kept on running.

Hawn had reached the dead spics. He grabbed a gun. A man darted from a tree a few yards from the bank robber. The Kid yelled a warning to Hawn. The safecracker threw himself to the ground, behind one of the corpses.

The Kid zigzagged toward a tree. But he knew he could never make it. Pete Quill was swinging a gun on him. The Kid had warned Hawn against the ex-deputy, and the cry had caused Quill to shift his aim. The beef-face's gun snarled, but it snarled a split-second after hell spouted from Hawn's gun. A bullet plucked at the Kid's shirt.

That slug was from Quill's gun. But the lead from Hawn's Colt got the killer in the pit of the stomach. The gun slipped from Quill's nerveless fingers. He fought madly for life. He reeled, tried to grab the falling gun, and sprawled headlong. Pete Quill was dead.

"There goes Morales!" yelled Hawn. "He's mine—that jasper."

Morales was astride his bronc, heading up the valley, where sheer walls reached to the clouds on three sides. The firing had lessened, for the spics had been fighting viciously among themselves, and many of them were dead or out of commission. Quill had organized his faction well, for the sombreroed men were still pouring lead at each other.

Dandy McLain had grabbed two Colts, and they were bucking in his hands. The little gambler uttered a yelp as a bullet nicked him. He went down on one knee, rocketing lead at the kill-crazy peon who was trying to bring him down. Another slug caught him in the side, and the little fellow slumped.

"Dandy! Dandy! Are yuh bad hurt?" cried the Kid, snatching up Quill's gun and blasting away at the spic. The first shot tore through the gunhog's chest. The Kid raced toward Dandy. He felt a sting along his neck. The spic was sagging, losing strength fast, but he still had his six leveled at the Kid.

Again flame slashed from the peon's Colt, but the hand was numbing and the bullet plowed into the dirt at the Kid's feet. The owl-hooter didn't fire, because the man was dying on his feet. Suddenly the peon's body lurched, and another evil career was over as the hulking figure pitched to the ground.

"I'm all right, son," gasped Dandy, trying to struggle erect. The best he could do was to reach his knees. His side was drenched with crimson. He was in pain, but he waved the Kid away.

Suddenly Terry screamed. The Kid whirled. She was close to Morales' house, struggling with a massive spic. The Kid ground his teeth, charged after the peon. The gunhog fired twice, but each time the girl struck his arm, spoiling his aim. Then the hammer clicked on an empty shell.

The Kid raced in. A blade flashed. The steel whipped down. The Kid felt the tip slice his shoulder. He jerked to the side. Fear turned the spic into a maniac. The knife raised. Again it descended—straight for the girl's trembling heart.

THE KID uttered a frantic cry. With all his might, he brought the gun barrel down on the spic's head. There was a sickening crack. The body collapsed. The girl sagged against the wall.

"Are yuh hurt, Terry dear!" cried the Kid fearfully, grasping her in his arms. She clung to him, this girl who had sworn to exterminate the Horde, and the Kid kissed her. Hungrily his lips pressed against hers. She gasped from the pressure of his embrace.

"Oh, Stan dear!" she murmured, using the name that came to her lips only when love swept away all the complexities of their lives. "If we could only have peace. If we could only go away—"

A shot smashed out ahead. Some one screamed. The Kid broke from the girl's embrace. Hawn was yelling in agony. Morales was a quarter mile up the valley. Hawn had been in close pursuit. But now he swayed in the saddle. Morales fired again, guffawed as the bank robber hurtled into the bushes.

The Kid ran to where a saddle horse was standing, a dead spic still clutching the bridle reins. A sudden idea had occurred to the owl-hooter. He had puzzled why Hawn had taken after Morales—Hawn who had such fear of the *bandido*. Now he knew. And he also knew that he was on the verge of discovering a great secret.

Forking the mustang, the Kid headed up the valley at breakneck speed. He couldn't stop for Hawn now. Too much depended on catching Morales. Suddenly he saw why the killer had ridden this way. The spic had dismounted, and he was muscling himself up a rope that was looped around a jagged outjutting of rock on the crest of the wall. The *bandido* was hauling the rope up after him.

"Come down, Morales, or I'll pour lead into yuh!" yelled the Kid, firing close to the spic's head.

The *bandido* held a gun between his teeth. Clutching the rope with one hand, he grasped the Colt and blazed away. A bullet struck a boulder, chipping the rock. A granite splinter caught the Kid on the forehead, knocked him flat.

He fought mightily to keep his senses. He had to get Morales. Maybe Hawn was dead. And the only other man who had the secret of the bank robber's cache was the spic.

His head whirling, his eyes blinded with pain, the Kid struggled to his knees. Morales fired again, hitting rock that showered the Kid with sharp fragments. The Kid raised a feeble hand, got an unsteady aim, and cut loose. Before the last explosion had ceased echoing, he was sprawled out again, unconscious.

He did not know how long he had been relieved of his senses. When he came to, dawn was graying the eastern sky. He was surrounded by men. He looked up at familiar faces. The Horde had got through the pass. Giant Anderson was bending over him, sloshing water on his face.

"Morales," murmured the Kid. "Get Morales!"

"He's got, by coots!" exclaimed Peel Rogers. "Yuh put three slugs in the critter, Kid. He musta fell nigh onto a hundred feet. He'll be orderin' his chilli con carne in hell after this."

Terry had stepped forward, and was kneeling beside him.

"The cards, girl," he spoke in a whisper. "In Morales' back pocket. Yuh can read that Aztec stuff. See what's on the back of those cards. Hawn wanted them powerful bad. He—"

Nature rebelled again. He regained consciousness once more

to look up into Terry's eyes. The Horde was standing away, out of earshot.

"I have deciphered most of the figures on the back of Hawn's cards," said the girl. "I'm not sure that I interpreted all the symbols correctly, but a free translation goes something like this: 'At the headwaters of the Wolf, face the newborn day, and walk thirty strides to the lair of the cougar, and therein find the eagle's nest.'"

"Sure, that's it!" said the Kid exultantly. "'Headwaters of the Wolf.' That means the source of the Lobo River, about twenty-thirty miles from here. The newborn day starts in the east, doesn't it? Thirty strides east to a cougar's den, an' there yuh'll find an eagle's nest. Golden eagles, Terry! Hawn's cache! Doggone, he had the directions to his cache in plain sight on the backs of those cards, an' nobody caught on. How the heck did he get cards like that?"

"Probably made the drawing himself," suggested Terry. "Had a plate made, and the special deck printed just for himself."

Down the valley a short distance came the wails of a man in the throes of delirium. Eagle Hawn. And he was babbling about his lucky cards.

"Go, Terry," spoke the Kid. "Ride like the wind. Get out of here quick. Get a bunch of reliable men an' go for the gold. There are a lot of folks needin' that *dinero*. Hurry. Hawn is liable to give away the secret. The Hordemen are swell gents, but they're human. The chance for sudden wealth is apt to turn any man's head, so run. Get away, because I'm too weak to help if one of the bunch goes hog-crazy with greed. They're bitter men, Terry. Ride, girl! Go!"

"I must take Hawn back," the girl said. "He is my prisoner."

The Kid shook his head. "No, Terry. Hawn had proved himself. He's one of the bunch now. He rides with Calvert's Horde."

Deep hurt was expressed in the girl's eyes. "And you, Kid Calvert, you're of the hated Horde—you who can be so kind. You're a bandit. You mock the law. Some day you will be my prisoner. But now—I can't forget what you have done." She stopped, stifled a sob. "Oh, why, why must there be so much bad in a person who can be so good?"

Tears welled in her eyes. She swung around, ran for her horse, and soon the hoofbeats dwindled into the murmur of the wilderness. Though the Horde was gathered here, crushing loneliness pressed down on the Kid. Terry was gone.

Hawn's delirium broke out anew. Little did the man know that in worldly goods, he was as poor now as the poorest peon. And little did he know that he had won the proudest honor of the owl-hoot. He was a member of the Horde—hell's recruit.

SEÑORITA DEATH

*Wealthy men disappeared from the Rio Casa—vanished
like smoke in the wind. Yet people flocked to the* cantina.
*For the darkly beautiful Dolores sang there. She sang of
Spanish love in old Castile. And men forgot their missing
neighbors. That is, all but one. That one was Kid Calvert
of the gunhawk Horde. But even Kid Calvert found a
hot-lead barrier shielding the secret of* Señorita Death.

S HE WAS exquisite. Men gasped at the sight of her. Never had the *Rio Casa* seen such a girl. The *cantina* had known a legion of brassy-voiced percentage dames. From nowhere an endless line of them drifted here one by one, shook down a few greenhorns, vanished. But *she* was a stranger to the shallow, mouthy tribe.

When she appeared, men doffed their Stetsons. Men forgot their drinks, stared open mouthed, unpuffed cigarettes glued to lower lips.

Now she was singing. The deep, mellow tones rolled out with the rich timbre of mission bells. She was a vision of old Castile. Black lace sheathed her slender form. From the jewel-studded comb in her raven-black hair, a mantilla draped over her lovely shoulders.

She sang a lilting pæan of Spanish love. The spic orchestra played like inspired music masters. In the gambling annex, the slap of cards, the rattle of dice, the click of the roulette, stopped on the first note. The scuffling and crow-hopping ceased in the dance hall. Men and ladies tiptoed into the barroom, stood awed.

Not her voice alone inspired the *cantina* crowd to silence, though she sang like a meadow lark. Nor did her beauty in itself make swaggering, blustering gents see themselves as two-bit slouches, though she was as beautiful as a budding rose.

It was an indefinable quality that awed men. She seemed

Old Jake staggered in,
dying on his feet.

like one born for homage. She was an aristocrat. Descended probably from a proud line of dons. She had the grace, the delicacy, the cultured air that are the heritage of the noble.

Her attitude was friendly. Yet men stayed their distance. Even the orey-eyed ones attempted no advances. Far away a gun roared. In the space of one melodious measure, three shots blasted. Before the girl had begun, Colts had rattled in the distance. Men had snapped alert, had gazed toward the west. Now they ignored the gun talk, ears attuned only for the sweet-

ness of her voice, eyes seeing nothing save a dazzling dream in Spanish lace.

One gent wondered. At a wall table, he sat stiffly in a chair. He was as nervous as a cat. His eyes never shifted from the girl. Her voice thrilled him. But those shots made him sweat with dread.

Guns pounded savagely. In the western hills, men were fighting. The gent caught a faint *clop-clop* of hoofs. Then sudden silence that turned him slate-gray beneath his bronze. His finger traced a J on the beer-slopped table.

J stood for Jake.

"Kid" Calvert—Calvert of the Horde—saw in his mind a battle-scarred veteran of the owl-hoot, preening walrus mustaches and swaggering up and down the barroom, flashing gold and acting like a locoed jughead. That was Jake Ranshaw, Hordeman, as friends of the owl-hoot clan had last seen him, here in the *Rio Casa*. Four men had disappeared in San Pablo.

Jake had been sent down to investigate. And now he, too, was missing.

What had happened to Jake? The old veteran wasn't a trouble hunter, though he managed to get into plenty of tangles. He was a hellion behind a brace of bucking Colts.

The song ended. There was a span of silence—an audience's highest tribute. Then deafening applause. But no whistling, no tossing of coins, no drinks rushed to the girl. She flashed a grateful smile that made men gulp.

She started from the floor. The spic orchestra leader raised beseeching hands. The mob took up the plea with loud clapping. The girl hesitated, caught her lower lip between glistening teeth, nodded.

Her next song was sad, low, pitched in a minor key. The mood carried to the man-pack.

The song plunged the Kid in gloom. A deck of cards lay on a nearby table, the ace of spades upturned. His broad shoulders drooped. His handsome face darkened. Then his spine stiffened. A shot ripped the night. The Kid caressed his holster, clamped his jaws.

He looked at the girl, and wondered about her. Her name was Dolores Estrada. She traveled with a brother-in-law, a dude with a whining voice and eyes too close together. He was a salesman for a land-promotion outfit. A free spender who always toted a fat purse. Why did he let this glorious girl work here? Dolores Estrada belonged on a *hacienda*.

The Kid gazed long at her eyes. Big, luminous—tragic. She had the face of the Madonna, the smile of a saint. Yet she was baiting an old codger with that smile, spellbinding him with that face, all but deranging him with those eyes.

And Colonel Gaylord Pride had a past that was graced with glamorous women. The Kid had talked with the old blade. Pride had a fortune—and not many years left in which to spend it. That was what narrowed the Kid's eyes.

Was this lovely girl, this vision out of a *marijuana* dream, tawdry and designing beneath her gorgeous exterior? Was she playing for easy stakes? One of the all-take and no-give brigade?

Gun racket broke out anew, louder, closer. A picture of Jake Ranshaw came up again. The Kid started from his chair. Maybe the Horde was in that clash. He stopped in a crouch, tensing. His jaw set; his eyes slitted.

The cold ring of a gun muzzle jabbed the small of his back. The Kid caught a fragrance that sent a chill through him.

"Sit down!" came a low, crisp command. "We're not spoiling the *señorita's* song. You're my prisoner, Kid Calvert."

THE KID didn't sit down. Behind that gun stood Terry Reynolds, sheriff of Washakie County. He leaped away, knocking over the table. The crash startled Dolores Estrada. She faltered, stopped. A musician flatted a note. The crowd snapped out of its spell, swung around.

Before the Kid sprang, Terry had grabbed his gun. When he spun to face her, he saw his own Colt gripped in her little hand. His lips pressed tightly. His paw closed over an empty holster.

She advanced, guns leveled, eyes steady. They were beautiful eyes, wide and clear and as dark as midnight. But now they glistened with anger. She was a wisp of loveliness, with a peach-blossom tint to her cheeks and curly hair that looked like gleaming gold. But there was nothing lovely in the guns spiking from her hands nor in the star that glittered on her blouse.

The Kid felt a gnawing in the pit of his stomach. He should have been watching. He might have known that Terry would be in town. It was her job to find out about those missing men. Three of them were wealthy. The fourth was Dan Lester, the local deputy.

And she hated the Horde, vowed to rid the country of that band of untamed, fate-badgered long-riders. The Kid's father—old "Gunner" Calvert—had gathered this wild bunch. The Gunner was gone—killed in the same battle that had taken Terry's father, the old sheriff of Washakie County.

The girl was carrying on, fighting for the principles for which her father had died. The Kid led the Horde in a ceaseless war against injustice. His grim, gunswift band performed work that could be accomplished only by a clan that answered to no law save that of human mercy.

Terry's eyes flashed. "I thought I'd find you here, Kid Calvert," she said coldly. "Four men missing—and not a trace. Clever work. I suppose the Horde knows nothing about them. I know you'll swear up and down you're innocent. But wait until Deputy Root gets here. He has ways of making you talk."

The girl spoke with conviction and determination, but her mouth quivered and mist clouded her eyes. If the Kid had stopped to think, he would have realized that it was duty, and principle, and misunderstanding which caused her harsh attitude. He would have realized that beneath this antagonism love was hidden. But the Kid had a hair-trigger mind. He was sensitive, quick to resent. He blurted:

"There yuh go again!" He gave his hat a savage yank. "Terry, why in heck don't yuh give me the benefit of the doubt for a change? Before yuh start hangin' every robbery an' killin' on me, why don't yuh dig out a few facts? Yuh know blamed well yuh've never pinned anything on me yet. I'm outside the law. Yeah. But I do my dangedest to help folks who deserve a boost. I'm not sayin' how much good I do. I jest try my best. Yet to listen to yuh, a jasper would figure I was the dirtiest sidewinder in seven states."

Shots sounded close to town now. Hoofs pounded furiously. Men were shouting, cursing. A honkatonk dame screamed and raced through a rear door. Others followed. But Dolores Estrada stood staring.

Uncertainty showed on Terry's face. The Kid's eyes burned into hers. There was a catch to her breath. Unconsciously she swayed toward him. The anger went out of the Kid's face. He stepped close.

"Terry—"

The girl backed away, grew taut. Again her eyes blazed. From her small hands, the two guns spiked wickedly. "Don't move!" she commanded harshly. "Those are probably your hellions riding in. They won't get you, Kid Calvert. Not alive. I'll shoot— and my first bullet drops you. Turn around. I'll get you out the back way."

Some of the patrons were crab-walking toward the exits. A few stayed where they were, puzzled, uncertain.

"Gawd!" muttered a slack-jawed man. "The Horde's in town. I'm slopin'. I ain't hankerin' to move up to boot-hill."

"Lady, ef thet's Calvert—plug him pronto. He's walkin' death. Knows more tricks than a fancy roper."

"Bet he drygulched the deputy," added another. "An' them missin' gents— Pile my chips on the spot thet says the Horde's holdin' 'em for *muy dinero*. That Thayne jigger is wuth a million, I hear. Them fat dudes Grovont an' Ralston wasn't exactly beggin' fer handouts."

A rumble of talk filled the *Rio Casa*. Hoofs drummed on the main street now. Guns barked. A horse squealed; a man howled. The Kid licked his lips, eyed the door.

The men in the *cantina* stayed there because they were afraid to show yellow. But they were showing fright. The Kid turned around. Terry ordered him to walk swiftly to the back door. She pressed the guns against his shoulder blades.

A neckless, stubble-jawed oaf with lumps of muscle on his shoulders and piggish eyes set in a bullet head, blocked the Kid's path, leering at him. The Kid knew the breed—a tinhorn badman.

"Come on, men! We're goin' to lynch Calvert!"

The Kid's lips curled. "Out of the way!" he snarled.

His right fist whipped up, planting a deadly clout on the point of that underslung jaw. The tough stiffened, reeled back against the crowd. He was unarmed—a brawler, not a gunman. And the Kid had taken all the brawl out of him. But anger swept through the mob.

"Lynch him!"

"Swing him from the rafters!"

The girl turned her guns on the pack. "Back! The first man to put his hands on Kid Calvert stops lead. You—in the checkered shirt, leave that gun in—"

Behind them a window went down in a clatter of splintering glass. A shrieking bullet shattered the bar mirror. The main street was in an uproar. Spanish oaths shrilled above the pound of guns.

Lead thudded into the outer walls of the *cantina*. Hoofs thumped and grated on the hard-packed ground. Horses squealed, snorted. Men screamed.

From the south end of town broke out another thunderous volley of slashing gunfire. A band of horsemen was heading in. Above the wild yells sounded a deep-throated roar. The Kid gave an exultant cry. He recognized the voice of "Giant" Anderson. The Horde was on the way. The girl's glance darted frantically over the crowd. She was bewildered. Outside, hell was popping. In the *cantina* men had threatened a lynching. And the Horde was swooping in. For a moment panic bested her. Her guns wobbled in trembling hands. Then they steadied.

"Make way!" she cried. "Calvert is the law's prisoner. He'll get a fair trial. I'm drilling the first man who throws down on him."

Suddenly the mob choked into silence. Eyes grew wild, fixed in horror on the entrance. The batwing doors were swinging. Bullets ripped through the panels.

Old Jake staggered in, blood drenched, holding a bulky, crimson-smeared envelope in his left hand. His right gripped a smoking .45. Old Jake Ranshaw's eyes were glazing. He was dying on his feet.

THE KID uttered a wail of anguish. "Jake! Jake!" he cried. "Down, man! I'm comin', pard! Me—the Kid."

In the street orange-red flame stabbed the darkness. Horsemen were milling before the *cantina*. The peak of a sombrero showed over the riddled batwings. A six in a brown fist spouted hell. Jake stiffened, half spun, groaned.

The man who had shouted "Lynch him!" clawed for his gun. The Colt cleared the leather, the muzzle swinging toward the Kid's head. Jake's gun flamed, bucked in his hand. The puncher's .45 flipped through the air. The gent shrieked, clutching madly at his blood-spurting wrist.

Jake stumbled toward the Kid. Calvert's right swept up. He yanked his gun from Terry's hand. Scarcely had it left her grasp when fire burst from the black bore.

The spic shooting at Jake let out a howl. His gun went spinning over the bar. He clutched at a door. His weight tore it from the hinges. He sprawled headlong, dead before he landed.

Jake Ranshaw thrust out the bulky envelope. The Kid grabbed it, tried to catch the old owl-hooter. Jake struggled to speak. Crimson bubbled from his mouth. He managed a shake of his head. His red-splashed lips parted in a grin.

"Jake—Jake, pard!" The Kid leaped, caught the old fellow. Jake sagged in his arms, raised his Colt and rocketed a final blast of hell into the street—a gunslick until the last.

Then he died grinning, clutching a smoking six, his boots on, the lights glaring—died gloriously in the arms of a boy he idolized, while guns roared and a kill-crazy pack closed in.

The Kid shuddered. Gently he lowered the body of his friend to the floor, while bullets screamed above him. He triggered another slug outside, saw a saddle suddenly go empty. Then he raced back to Terry, shouting a command to the *cantina* patrons:

"Behind tables, men. Give them spiggoties hell!" He pointed at Dolores Estrada, standing by the musician's platform, frozen with fear. "Out the back way, girl. Jump!"

The gorgeous *señorita* jumped. The Kid grabbed Terry. She was always accusing him, always misunderstanding. But when a showdown came, she was the most important person in the world to him. He drew her close, swung her over the bar.

"Out of sight, Terry. An' stay there."

A bullet nicked the Kid's shoulder as he spun from the bar. He crammed the envelope in his boot. A man dropped—the bullet-head who had called for a lynching. He curled up on the floor, pleading for help and clutching his side.

The Kid dragged him behind an upturned table. Bounding across the room, he hurled himself through a shattered window into the alley. Riders were fleeing. The Horde was thundering down.

A spic swung his spur-punished cayuse up the alley. He spotted the Kid, mouthed a profane cry. In mid-air the Kid swung his gun. But the man had the drop. His trigger finger jerked.

No fire blasted. The hammer clicked on an empty shell. The Kid dived behind a pile of adobe bricks. Another sombreroed rider reining into the alley saw the Kid disappear. The spic yelled for the man with the empty gun to dig in the spurs.

"Stay where you are!" cracked out the Kid in Spanish. "Try to escape, and I will shoot."

The Kid wanted this gunhog alive. Wanted him to clear up the mystery of the attack on old Jake. And he might know about those missing men. The spic trembled. He called to heaven, blubbering like a man craving *marijuana*.

The gent at the alley's mouth rapped out a savage oath. A gun roared. Powder flame lanced the darkness. The blubbering ceased, and a frantic, squealing cayuse scooted up the alley with an empty saddle.

The Kid growled an oath. The spic's *compadre* had silenced a waggling tongue. That meant these gunhogs knew something that would interest gringo ears. The Kid's gun spiked above the adobe bricks. He'd cut this gunhog out of his kak and pack him off to the hills where the gent would talk—plenty.

The spic saw the Kid as he raised up. The gun blazed, the slug plowing into the bricks and showering the Kid with dirt. Again the man in the sombrero fired. But his pony was whirling and the bullet cleaved the air harmlessly.

Savagely Calvert's six cut loose. The spic yelled and clutched at his left side. Then the mount carried him out of sight. Down the alley raced the Kid. The spic's horse was rearing and fighting the bit when the Kid hit the street. The gunhog wasn't more than thirty feet away, but his back was turned.

Shooting a man in the back wasn't in the Kid's bag of tricks. He shifted the Colt to his left hand and grabbed a stone. He slung it at the Mex, catching him on the back of the head. The sombrero went sailing.

The spic slumped. The Kid came on. Suddenly the rider snapped erect, swaying groggily. He fired over his shoulder. The Kid felt a burning stab cut his shoulder—the same one that had been creased before.

He staggered drunkenly, trying to control his reeling senses, trying to raise his gun. But his knees buckled, and he pitched into the dust.

T H E   S U N was shining when the Kid got back his senses. He lay in a straw-padded piñon-pole bunk. His shoulder was bandaged, and he could hardly move his left arm. Outside, squirrels chattered in the pines. The odor of bacon and coffee swept in on the cool morning breeze.

A half-pint gent wearing a flowery vest strode into the cabin. He was "Dandy" McLain, gambler, driven onto the lawless trails by a frame-up that had turned him into gallows bait.

"Glad yo're with us ag'in, son," he said, smiling. "For a spell we was afraid of blood poisonin' an' lockjaw. But I reckon ol' Peel's corrosive sublimate fixed yuh up. Yore shoulder drawed two bullet creases in that San Pablo deal."

Dandy McLain put a smooth, slender hand on the Kid's hot forehead. That hand had tricked the wiliest tinhorns in the gambling fraternity. When men held their cards close to their vests and eyed other men's chips greedily, Dandy was a cheat, a wolfish, cold-eyed trickster. But he cheated in the cause of humanity, using his winnings to allay the sufferings of the needy and friendless.

"Dandy—is—is—Jake—"

The little gambler nodded and bowed his head. "Seventeen bullet holes, son," he spoke bitterly. "Don't see how he lived as long as he did. Soon as yo're up, we're buryin' Jake."

The Kid closed his eyes. Grief overwhelmed him. Yet there was no cause to regret. Old Jake had lived, and he had gone out as he'd wanted—in a blaze of burning powder, with Colts blaring a gunhawk's requiem.

"We left 'bout six-seven spics back there," said the gambler. "Reckon Jake settled for most o' them. I'm shore puzzled what got him in that jackpot o' hell."

"I've got a hunch workin'," said the Kid.

"Yuh mean—he learned something about them missin' gents?"

The Kid nodded. "Hand me that fat envelope on the table. Jake gave it to me before he dropped."

The envelope was made of parchment, sealed with wax that bore the imprint of a crest. On the parchment was writing, but so smeared with crimson that the Kid could make out only three letters: C-a-r.

"Tear it open," suggested Dandy.

The Kid shook his head. "Nope. Yuh wouldn't want any stranger pokin' into yore business. This thing's probably doggone personal—an' damned important to somebody. If I open it, some of the papers might get lost. I'm goin' to find out what C-a-r stands for, who owns the packet. Then mebbe I'll have a plumb good reason to break the seal."

A grizzled veteran clumped into the cabin carrying a steaming bowl. For once "Peel" Rogers, the cook, wasn't full of bluster. There was a worn look on his seamed face, a killer's light in his eyes.

"Here yuh are, son," he said huskily. "Wrap yoreself around this rabbit stew." His cowhorn mustache waggled. "It—it was Jake's favorite dish."

The chuck took some of the weakness out of the Kid. Later

he got up. In the center of three towering pines, Giant Anderson and "Grama" Sinton were digging a grave. They were somber, silent.

Giant weighed two hundred and forty pounds, all of it fighting strength. At every swing of the shovel, his tremendous, supple muscles bunched. Giant could break an ordinary man's back across his knee, like a boy breaks kindling wood.

Grama Sinton was talking to himself. A bad sign for one of Grama's high-strung nature. He'd have to be watched. He'd take deadly chances to avenge Jake's death.

The Kid beckoned to "Eagle" Hawn, and the slim, handsome man left his work. Safecracker, forger—craftsman, Hawn had magic in his hands. He had been carving a large crucifix to mark Jake's grave.

"Eagle, after the—burial," said the Kid, "I'd like yuh to go into San Pablo. Nobody there, except Terry, will know yo're in the Horde. Get some fancy duds an' make yoreself look like ready *dinero*. Get acquainted with Manuel Estrada. He's workin' for an outfit called the Washakie Land Company. Tell him yo're in the market for a ranch—an' then keep yore eyes peeled."

Eagle nodded. "Estrada, eh? I don't like anything about that spic. Looked to me like a hairpin who'd rob his grandmother." Hawn's body jerked. His eyes went wild. "Say— Say! Do you— think he had anything to do with Jake's death?"

The Kid touched his damaged shoulder. His eyes slitted. "I dunno. I've got hunches workin'. He flashes too much coin for a common land salesman. An' no jasper who'd let his sister-in-law work in that *cantina* rates higher than a snake with me."

DANDY BECKONED to the Kid, and the Horde gathered around the open grave. Sudden death was coming to them all, yet it was a grief-stricken bunch that gazed upon Jake Ranshaw's corpse. The veteran was making his exit in his holiday finery. His hair was slicked, his boots shined. Jake had asked to be buried with his guns. His cartridge belt had been strapped on; his Colts shoved in the holsters.

Most of the Hordemen turned away when the lid was put on the box. The rough-hewn coffin was lowered with lariats. The men stood with Stetsons off and heads bowed. They weren't a praying bunch, but their long silence was a gesture of reverence.

"Good-by, Jake," muttered Giant. "I don't know where yo're headin', but I shore hope it's for open range country."

The Kid wanted to say something, but his throat had tightened. Nate Willstock, the bleak-faced, wintry-eyed one, stood rubbing his gun butt. Grama Sinton's features were drawn, haggard. Even Dandy McLain's poker mask had vanished. But none of them was so deeply affected as Peel Rogers. He was in a daze. When Dandy motioned for the men to shovel in the dirt, the old cook shuddered. He shuffled away, shoulders sagging.

The grave was filled. Eagle thrust the crucifix in the ground, and the gathering broke up. The men were subdued, dispirited. Hawn saddled up and headed for San Pablo. The Kid sat outside the bunkhouse. He wanted to fog the vengeance trail. But it would be sure death to try anything while his arm was crippled.

He sent Giant Anderson and Nate Willstock into San Pablo to look around. He ordered the rest to stick around camp. Let the Horde get into town, brooding over Jake's death, and anything could happen. Sorrow had tamed them. But hate smoldered in their hearts. If they found Jake's killers—it wouldn't matter where—hell would bust loose.

Toward dusk old Peel staggered into camp, blind drunk. He wasn't whooping or blustering. That meant Peel was dangerous. He went to the cook house, buckled on a cartridge belt and a brace of .45s. He said nothing and started to saddle up. Dandy and the Kid nodded at each other.

They steered Peel into the bunkhouse. The Kid poured the old cook a stiff drink, and Dandy slipped some knockout drops in the glass. Peel tossed off the whisky and started for the door. He slumped to the floor. They put him in a bunk and left him snoring. Those knockout drops saved somebody's life. For in his grief-crazed drunken condition, old Peel, usually harmless, would have killed before the night was over.

For three days the Kid grumbled around camp. The third day, after sundown, Eagle Hawn rode into the hideout.

"Your man is up to something," he told the Kid. He pulled out a wanted bulletin, offering a five-thousand-dollar reward for the capture of Eagle Hawn, and listing Eagle's accomplishments as a safecracker and forger. "I told Estrada that I wanted to buy a ranch, and he didn't show a hell of a lot of interest at first. But when we met again, he treated me like a rich uncle. He spread this out. Said he got it out of the post office."

"A shake-down, huh?" growled the Kid.

Hawn shook his head. "I thought so. But he said he had a little proposition that would net me five times the bounty on my head. Said he'd have a penmanship job for me soon. Wants me to forge some sort of a document. So I'm to keep in touch with the buzzard until he's ready."

The Kid's eyes narrowed thoughtfully. "Uh huh. I'm beginnin' to savvy. I'm beginnin' to savvy a whole lot o' things. Of course, yuh said yuh'd play in with him."

"You know the answer to that," said Hawn, grinning. "Me pass up a chance to give a rat like Estrada a trimming?"

"He tell yuh what he wanted forged?" asked the Kid.

"His kind doesn't show his hand until the play is called," said Hawn.

The Kid's face set. "Maybe that play's goin' to be called sooner than Estrada thinks."

"I learned something else," said Hawn. "That old Kentuckian who's been in town— You know—the frisky grandpa who thinks he's a heller with the women. Gaylord Pride. Calls himself a colonel, and has plenty of golden eagles rubbing against each other. Well, Colonel Pride's disappeared. Vanished completely. Not a trace."

THE KID whistled softly. "That tallies up with my hunch. Too damn bad. Looks like a swell kid. Has talent, beauty, youth."

"What in hell you talking about?" demanded Hawn. "Colonel Pride wouldn't win a beauty prize against a line of Siwash squaws."

But the Kid wasn't talking about Colonel Pride. After Hawn left, the Kid saddled up Star, his swift steel-dust stallion, and rode into San Pablo. He ground-hitched Star in an alley back of the *Rio Casa* and entered the *cantina.*

His left arm was working freely now. His gun rested in a greased holster, and when he shoved through the swing-doors into the barroom, he was ready to take care of himself.

His eyes swiveled about the room. Terry wasn't here. Neither was the man Root, her deputy. Gents recognized the Kid, nodded respectfully. The men of San Pablo had changed their ideas of Kid Calvert after that ruckus.

Dolores Estrada was singing again. The bruiser, who had called for a hanging, strode up to the Kid. The big gent was sheepish and awed. His arm rested in a sling. He held his body stiff. The Kid remembered that he had got a slug in the side.

"Calvert, I wanna thank yuh fer savin' my life," the man mumbled. "I shore tabbed yuh wrong. Yo're plenty man. Me—I'm a slob, an' I know it now. Say, would yuh—shake?"

The Kid grinned. "Why not?"

"So you are Keed Calvert?" spoke a sleek Mexican standing at the bar. A faint sneer tainted his manner. He wore a shirt of pleated silk, a snug velveteen jacket and tight-fitting, bell-bottomed trousers. His flat-crowned, stiff-brimmed hat was canted rakishly. The Kid would have preferred the stench of a saddle blanket to the sickening perfume that the Mex flash used.

"An' yo're Manuel Estrada," said the Kid coldly. "Yuh belong to a breed I don't like to rub shoulders with." He nodded toward the girl Dolores. "Her brother-in-law, eh? Lettin' yore own kin work in a hell-hole? She belongs here like one of these percent-age dames belongs in a convent."

Manuel Estrada showed his teeth in a leer. "Your manner ees ver-ry insulting, but I weel not get angry."

Gents guffawed.

"Go ahead, *caballero*," urged a puncher, "get proddy with Calvert. We'll plant yuh in boot-hill, an' then we won't have to whiff any more of that foo foo water you dash over yoreself."

The Kid frowned. He wanted no trouble.

"I am *Señorita* Dolores' business manager," said Manuel. "She ees beautiful, *si?* She have gr-reat talent, *amigo*. But she know nothing of the worl'. She is lak the hot-house flower, *si?* Soon I tak' her east for the stage career. But first I want her to know that life, she ees nothing lak *Hacienda* Estrada in Mexico. *Sabe?*"

The Kid eyed Estrada sharply, then nodded. "Some sense to that, all right. I reckon I talked outa turn. Sorry."

The Mexican smirked. "There ees no offense, *Señor* Calvert. True eet ees that a *muchacha* of Dolores' high station do not belong among thees—thees rabble. I am glad you mak' the question. I have explain', and now ever'body weel know. Since my brother, he ees kill', I have been the *señorita's* guardian. *Amigo*, have a dreenk."

The Kid called for a small beer. A puncher to the left of Estrada jostled the Mexican, who jumped away, wincing. The spic's face twisted with pain. He touched his side tenderly. In the bar mirror, the Kid saw the look of pain. He saw, too, the hard, piercing glance that the spic shot him. Then Estrada laughed.

"My side ees ver-ry sore," he said. "Yesterday a *caballo* give me wan swift keeck."

THE KID knew Estrada was lying. He raised his glass. "Here's hopin' yore sister-in-law gets booked solid fifty-two weeks a year when she starts her stage career."

The snake-eyed *caballero* bowed. *"Muchas gracias, señor."*

The Kid took a sip of his beer, and then pulled out a bandana from his back pocket to dry his lips. Something fell to the floor. Swiftly the spic picked it up. He handed it to the Kid. The sealed parchment envelope. Calvert nodded his thanks, thrust the envelope in his pocket.

He'd seen Estrada's eyelids flutter, the corners of the mouth twitch.

Dolores Estrada had finished an encore and gone upstairs to her dressing room. The Kid broke away from the mob and strode through the swing-doors onto the plank sidewalk. He cast a side glance through the window. Manuel Estrada was pouring another drink, spilling the liquor.

The Kid sauntered down the walk, then ducked into the darkness of an alley and cut around to the back of a door-flanked hallway. The dressing rooms of the honkatonk girls. Light pierced the keyholes of some. But voices sounded within. He knocked on a door and a raspy woman's voice told him to come in. He hurried on.

He rapped on another. A frowsy, over-rouged dame poked her bleached head out. Two doors down, he knocked again. A musical voice responded. The Kid's pulse quickened.

The door opened slightly to his second knock. He gasped at the loveliness of Dolores Estrada. A close-up showed her flaw-less beauty. She started at the sight of the Kid.

"I've got to see you, Miss Estrada. It—it's about yore broth-er-in-law. Please let me in. There are too many ears around here."

The girl paled. Alarm showed on her exquisite face. She hesitated, searched his eyes, then nodded for him to enter. The Kid felt himself getting dizzy. He was no veteran at facing beautiful girls.

She closed the door and came close to him, her eyes wide with concern. "Manuel is not in—trouble?" she asked fearfully.

The *señorita's* beauty awed him, but he hadn't forgotten those missing men. He pictured them lying in gulches, bones picked clean by buzzards. His eyes grew flinty. He saw no indication on her face that her character was less beautiful than her appearance. But he had known other Madonna-faced women whose souls were shriveled by greed and treachery.

"Maybe yore brother-in-law is in a tough spot," said the Kid. "I'm not goin' to mince words, *Señorita* Estrada. I'm here to get hard facts. A lot depends on yuh. Maybe Manuel is in the shadow of a gallows."

T H E   G I R L   shrank back, her eyes filling with horror. "No!" she cried. "Not Manuel! He's weak. *Si.* But he wouldn't—he couldn't—do anything that—" She broke off and her slender form quivered.

The Kid's resolve wobbled. Her tears almost dissolved his determination. He hoped he was all wrong. Then he steeled himself against those tragic eyes.

"Yuh were playin' up to Colonel Pride the other night," he said. "Why?"

That startled her. "You—you saw?" she faltered. She paused, looked away. "That was cheap—cheap. I despised myself for doing it. I hoped later that one of those bullets would hit me. It was only for the memory of my dead husband that I did it—for my beloved Don Carlos. He worked so hard to keep Manuel straight, to help him live a worthy life.

"And Manuel is trying, *Señor* Calvert. He is living honorably. He is engaged in a legitimate business. He is building for the future, and that is why I smiled at Colonel Pride. I know I acted like a tawdry dance-hall woman. I had no interest in Colonel Pride but to help Manuel."

The Kid shook his head. "*Señorita,* yo're shore talkin' riddles now. I'm no hand at guessin' games. What's makin' eyes at an old gink got to do with sellin' land?"

The girl seemed eager to explain. Six months before, her husband, Don Carlos Estrada, had been killed on his *hacienda.* Manuel Estrada, the don's half-brother, had always been a scapegrace. Don Carlos had settled his gambling debts, had often saved him from imprisonment. And now, the girl felt, without her steadying influence, Manuel would ruin his life completely.

"Since he got the sales job with the Washakie Land Company," she said, "he's showed that he can become a good citizen. That's why I'm working here to help him get his commissions. I learned that Colonel Pride is looking for a place to raise horses. I got acquainted with him. That gave me the chance to talk about Manuel and about Peaceful Ranch."

"Peaceful Ranch?" the Kid asked.

"Yes. Don't you know about it? It's a beautiful ranch in the hills about fifteen miles west of San Pablo. *Señor* Ragle is Manuel's boss. The Washakie Land Company invites prospects out there for a vacation. Manuel says it's to break down sales resistance. I make the contacts here at the *Rio Casa*. Manuel does the rest."

The Kid was silent, forehead creased thoughtfully. "Listens good," he said finally. "The only hitch, *señorita*, is that three wealthy men have disappeared. No trace of Deputy Lester, either. An' now Colonel Gaylord Pride ain't accounted for. It looks like this Washakie Land Company uses a little bushwhackin' to break down sales resistance."

The girl looked at the Kid puzzledly. Then the significance dawned on her. She uttered a cry of protest, clutched at his arm.

"No! No! You are wrong. Colonel Pride ees at Peaceful Ranch now." Emotional turmoil made her accent pronounced. "Those others—they have gone away. *Señor* Calvert, do not say such a theeng. Manuel ees but a naughty child. He does bad theengs, but they are small bad theengs. Maybe he cheat at cards, *si*. Maybe he get drunk. But—but—" She shuddered. "Manuel wouldn't—kill. He ees kind, ver-ry kind. You are wrong, *señor*. Colonel Pride ees at Peaceful Ranch. I know."

The Kid's face hardened. He wondered how much of her outburst was acting. He was beginning to connect up scattered facts. He wanted to draw her out.

"I hope so, *señorita*," he said. "I hope Pride is at Peaceful Ranch. Because if he isn't, it means the rope for Manuel, an'—an'—"

She came forward and slid her hands over the Kid's broad shoulders. The Kid started to retreat, but her fingers gently caressing his cheek, glided to the back of his neck and drew him close. His jaw set tightly. He wanted to tell her that his name wasn't Gaylord Pride.

Tears welled in her luminous eyes. His expression soured. Her mouth drew down at the corners like a hurt child's. He looked at her coldly. He was irritated. She was the most beautiful girl he'd ever seen. But he was a one-woman gent, and Terry claimed his sole interest. Certainly he knew nothing of the subtleties of a woman's mind, but it took no insight to understand her obvious tactics.

Whether she was mixed up in treachery or whether it was loyalty to Manuel Estrada that made her use these tactics, the Kid couldn't decide. She either knew or believed that her brother-in-law was up to something crooked.

She was making a play for the Kid to bring him over to their side. But she was wasting her time. His mouth tightened against his teeth. She took him for a prime fool, and that made him sore.

Her arms were around him. Her fragrant hair brushed his cheek. She was looking into his eyes, smiling through her tears. Trying to hypnotize him. His lips curled a little. He started to speak, started to push her away.

The doorknob rattled. A sudden draft swept through the room. The Kid turned, stiffened. Rage surged through him. It was all he could do to keep from flinging this woman from him.

In the doorway, clutching a leveled Colt, stood Terry Reynolds. And Kid Calvert, with thoughts far from romantic, was holding the gorgeous *Señorita* Dolores in his arms.

TERRY STARED at the Kid, a hard little smile playing

on her mouth. She advanced slowly, her burning eyes boring into the Kid's.

The sight of that gun, and the look in Terry's eyes, frightened the *señorita*. She clung to the Kid. Terry circled around them, the Colt clutched so tightly that her knuckles showed white. The smile died. Her eyes fixed steadily on the Kid.

He broke away from the singer, faced Terry. His face was flushed. "Stop starin' at me like that," he said. "I know what yo're thinkin'. Well, yo're wrong. Savvy? Things aren't always the way they look."

"Oh, don't try to talk your way out of it," she replied coldly. "I'm sick of explanations. Anyway, what does it matter?"

"Huh!" grunted the Kid. "Matter? It matters plenty to me. Terry, yuh never miss a chance to slug at me. I've certainly come more than halfway every time. But the whole distance is too far."

"We'll end it here," she retorted.

"End it?" blurted the Kid. "That's it, huh? That's the way yuh feel about it? All right. That suits me. That suits me to a T. I always figured you was the swellest girl— I'm through talkin'."

Señorita Estrada clutched the Kid's arm. He yanked away, ignored her. "I'm goin'," he muttered. "Put that gun up. If it goes off, the noise'll make yuh jump out of yore boots."

Dolores Estrada uttered a terrified cry. The Kid glared at her. He stiffened. He saw horror in the *señorita's* eyes. She was staring past him, staring as though transfixed. Some one else was in the room. The Kid whirled, going for his gun.

He didn't draw. In the doorway stood a leering, pockmarked spic, holding a long-barreled Colt. The Kid ducked to the side, fell into a fighting crouch, snarling. The Mex laughed. He thumbed back the gun hammer, shifting the muzzle to Terry.

"Come on, gringo," sneered the spic gunhog. "Draw your shooting iron, and I weel cut down the leetle *muchacha*. Sabe? *Señorita* Sheriff," he spoke to Terry, "drop your gun, or mus' I bend thees gun barrel on your so beautiful head?" In Mexican-

Spanish, he cracked out an order for Dolores Estrada to get out. She hesitated, frozen with fear.

Terry Reynolds dropped her gun. The spic snatched it from the floor, stuck it in his belt. He relieved the Kid of his Colt. Herding him and Terry against the far wall, he clutched the *señorita* by the arm and roughly shoved her out the door. This gave the Kid a chance. He sprang, his fists swinging. His foot struck a squeaky board. The spic spun around and dodged.

Before the *bandido* could bring his gun up, the Kid slammed in a bruising right that connected with the Mex's ear and drove him crashing into the wall. He sagged there, groggy, eyes glazed. Lunging in with fists cocked for destruction, the Kid measured for a knockout punch, while his left hand streaked toward the skulker's lowered six-gun.

The Mex staggered away. He whipped out the six from his gun belt and leveled it at Terry. The gun in the other hand raised overhead.

"Gringo—the *muchacha*, she die first."

The Kid checked himself. His eyes shifted to Terry, standing against the wall, her hands clenched, her face pale.

Something flashed overhead. Too late he dodged. The spic's gun barrel descended. The Kid bobbed down in time to save himself from the full force of the blow. He missed getting a fractured skull, but the impact drove him into unconsciousness.

HE OPENED his eyes. Terry was bending over him, bathing his injured head. The spic had gone. His head felt as though a blacksmith were swinging a sledge on it. But his pain was nothing to his delight at seeing Terry so anxious and worried.

"You *do* care!" he blurted.

She started at the sound of his voice. Her face brightened. She uttered a happy little cry, and then her forehead creased.

She groped for words. Her pretty mouth drew taut. "I wouldn't even let a sick calf suffer, if I could help it."

"Yeah?" the Kid flared. "All right. Have it that way then."

The girl tossed her head. "I had to bring you to," she said coldly. "You're my prisoner. I couldn't drag you off to jail. And I couldn't call for help. Too much risk of a lynching. I wouldn't want even you to have that end."

The Kid jumped up. "Even me, huh?" he exploded. "I shore like the way yuh put it." He felt in his back pocket, found only his bandana there. "That dirty skunk robbed me!"

The girl nodded. "He took a large envelope—"

A swift glance showed the Kid that Terry wasn't armed. He looked at the girl. No use trying to reason with her. A single-track mind. And he'd had his fill of giving in to her. Let her think he made love to every dame he met. He was on the trail of something important now. He had no time to waste.

"Well, good-by, lady," he spoke in a sulking manner. "The only time yuh'll see me after this is in a cloud of dust."

He bounded from the room. Terry's protest was lost in the thud of his running feet. He sped down the back stairs and into the alley where he sprang astride the ground-hitched steel-dust. Reining the alert stallion, he headed in the direction of the Horde's hideout.

He made up his mind that he'd never see Terry again. But somehow that idea didn't exactly exhilarate him. She sure gave him a rough deal of it, but he had to admit that there was only one Terry. And she was as spunky as all get-out.

Star lengthened out to a gigantic stride. Soon San Pablo became a blur of light far behind. The swift mount worked up a brushy slope to a hogback, raced along it a mile or so, and then dipped into a broad basin overgrown with junipers and wind-gnarled cedars.

The Kid was tense, eager. He had learned enough to know that Manuel Estrada had some connection with the death of Jake Ranshaw. About the girl Dolores, he wasn't so sure.

The Horde's holding up grounds were atop a ridge that looked out toward the San Pablo flats. Riding over the rim, he called out: "Saddle up, gents. We're ridin'."

Nothing more was necessary. Men poured from the cabins, heading for their horses. A light in the cook house showed old Peel dropping a dish towel and buckling on his gun belt. Dandy McLain ran to the Kid.

"Is Eagle Hawn back?" the Kid asked.

The gambler shook his head. Alarm clouded his face. "What's happened? Has Eagle disappeared—like old Jake did? Lawdy, son, if the Horde loses anyone else, we won't be able to hold the men."

"Reckon Eagle's okay," said the Kid. "But some gents in the hills across the flats are liable not to be—afore the night's over."

The men rode up to the Kid, Grama Sinton leading Dandy's mount.

"Mournful," the Kid spoke to one of his lobos, "that bullet hole in yore leg calls for rest. I want yuh to stick around camp. If Eagle drifts in, tell him we've hit for Peaceful Ranch. West o' San Pablo. Any wood-chopper or trapper will put him on the right trail."

Mournful mumbled in his beard. Hordemen didn't enjoy being on the inactive list.

AND THEN the owl-hooters were riding. They swept along in a wide circle, keeping always to the hills. The Kid and Dandy and old Peel headed the swooping band. All the way, the cook said not a word. Men who had tabbed him as a harmless old duffer would have altered their opinions now. His face was wolfish; lips drawn back in a fixed snarl.

For two hours they held a terrific pace. Reaching the hills west of San Pablo, the Kid rode up alone to a wood-chopper's shack. He learned the way to Peaceful Ranch.

Soon they reached a timbered ridge that looked down onto a green, water-fed valley and white-washed buildings. The Kid experienced doubt, misgivings. Peaceful Ranch didn't belie its name.

Then he saw a man ride out of the trees a quarter mile from him, heading for the ranch. The gent had spotted them. An ordinary stock ranch might have a guard posted for rustlers. But this rider, streaking hell-bent down the valley, reassured the Kid.

The Horde dropped into the valley. Slowly they rode, eyes swiveling, guns loosened and hands ready. The Kid expected an ambush. They passed grazing cattle, prime stock. A deer fled from the brush. A coyote yapped behind them.

The buildings had been dark when the owl-hooters had viewed them from the ridge. Now a light gleamed from a window of the ranch-house. But the rest of the spread seemed asleep. Horses crunched hay in the corrals. The windmills creaked. A duck floated placidly on a pond.

The owl-hooters reined to a halt in the ranch yard. Back of a corral they dismounted, ground anchored their horses. The men strode toward the ranch-house, which was surrounded by huge, spreading oaks. The Kid saw some one peering at them from the second-story window. Then the evil-looking face disappeared.

The Kid went ahead of his men and knocked on the front door. He felt uneasy. His back was guarded, but he expected snipers' bullets from the sides. A rangy, hard-muscled man opened the door. He was well groomed; looked smooth, capable.

"I reckon yo're Ragle, the ramrod on this here spread," said the Kid. "A wood-chopper up yonder described yuh to me. My name's Calvert. I hate to bust in on yuh, but we're runnin' down a little trouble. I'd like to ask yuh a few questions, Mr. Ragle."

"Sure," said Ragle, "sure, come in. Bring your crowd. I'll be glad to help you any way I can. Heard a lot about you, Calvert."

The Hordemen entered the ranch-house. Ragle was smiling, affable. Too much so. The Kid couldn't detect a trace of annoyance on the man's face. That was bad—bad. Ragle was sure of himself.

"What's bothering you, Calvert?" Ragle asked, motioning the owl-hooters to be seated. No one accepted. They ranged along the walls, away from the windows, their eyes on the doors.

"This ranch is the headquarters for the Washakie Land Company, isn't it?" asked the Kid. "Yore idea is to get wealthy men out here, show 'em a good time, an' try to sell 'em a ranch like this. Haven't you a salesman named Manuel Estrada, an' isn't his sister-in-law the lure that gets him the contacts?"

Ragle rose from his chair, thoughtfully puffing on a big cigar. "Yes to all those questions, Calvert. I see what you're aiming at, and I'm eager to help you. Men have vanished from San Pablo, and the Washakie Land Company is under suspicion, isn't that it?"

The Kid nodded. "Four wealthy men have disappeared—Thayne, Grovont, Ralston, and now Colonel Pride. Weren't they all prospective customers of the Washakie Land Company?"

"Yes—yes, they were," answered Ragle. "The first three you mentioned were our guests here. But I assure you, Calvert, they disappeared *after* they'd left Peaceful Ranch. Colonel Pride never arrived here."

Ragle raised his hands helplessly. "You see what I'm up against? I'm facing ruin. I need your help, Calvert—you and the Horde. Get me out of this mess, and I'll pay you handsomely. I'll lose a fortune if—"

Ragle shook his head and stared at the floor. Then he walked slowly to an open window and flicked ashes outside. He returned to his chair, but didn't sit down.

"Men, it's worth fifty thousand dollars to me to clear the name of my organization."

"That's piker *dinero*," said Danny McLain, who more than once had staked fifty thousand dollars on a single flip of a card.

"All right," said Ragle, "I'll double the ante. And while you're thinking about it, suppose I rout out my cook. I insist that you men join me in a little lunch. After a hard ride, I'm sure you'd enjoy a few drinks."

Ragle nodded and left the room, closing the door. Old Peel started after him, muttering savagely. The latch clicked. The Kid grabbed Peel's arm, swung him back against the wall.

"Down, yuh fool! That's a—"

OUTSIDE, A gun blasted. The lamp jerked from the table, crashing to the floor. The owl-hooters flattened out. Lead rained into the darkened room. The attack was coming from two sides. The door and windows were raked with slugs. The Kid raised a chair, and instantly snarling lead ripped it into splinters.

That flick of Ragle's cigar ash had been the signal. The Kid had suspected that, but he couldn't have got to the man without exposing himself before one of the windows. And now from outside came the voice of Ragle.

"You scuts know too much for your health."

The Kid snaked across to a window, raised up and fired at Ragle. A howl came from the ranch boss. His fuming and cursing prodded his gunhogs into a hell-roaring attack. A bullet nicked the heel of the Kid's boot. The skulkers firing through the door were sweeping the floor with lead.

The Hordemen were fighting savagely. Nate Willstock had brought down two of the attackers. He was crimson smeared from a flesh groove on the cheek, another along the neck, and a third crease across his arm. His eyes glinted through the swirling smoke. The Kid marveled at the speed with which Willstock jammed fresh loads into his gun.

That brought up another danger. They had a limited supply of lead, and they were using it up fast. Peel yelped. The Kid saw him clutch at his thigh. But Peel's gun didn't get a chance to cool. He twisted a bandana above his wound, and then his Colt was bucking again.

Suddenly a flaming arrow streaked through a window, digging into the wall. Then another whizzed through—and a third. An old Indian trick. Already the room was ablaze. Above them windows clattered as burning missiles crashed through them.

The Kid ground his teeth. That was it. Ragle and his hirelings were through with Peaceful Ranch. They had made their haul;

would split up or move on. And they wanted to leave the Horde behind as charred skeletons.

"By coots an' by dogies," exclaimed Peel grimly, "I hope I don't get broiled until I cut me down another one of them skunks."

Soon the ranch-house would be a roaring inferno. The Horde was close to the end. The air was stifling. The Kid felt his senses reel with every breath. The sweat poured out, drying instantly. He thought that his skin would crack open.

His lungs pained. They felt as though he were inhaling embers. His eyes smarted. He gazed at his men. Not a one was showing the white feather. And they were fighting like madmen—not to get out, but to bring down as many of their foes as possible before they died.

Dandy wormed over to the Kid. "Well, son, yuh know what this means. I hate to see a younker like you—" He broke off as a rafter crashed down within a foot of his head. "I'm headin' out for air, son, an' pickin' me off a coupla spics afore I cash in."

The Kid grabbed the gambler's arm. "No! Stay here, Dandy. I've got a scheme. Giant!" The big fellow crawled across the floor. "Giant, bust down that door over there."

"It won't work, son!" exclaimed Dandy. "The house is surrounded."

"But we're goin' upstairs," said the Kid, "an'—"

"I gotcha, son!" yelled Dandy. "Come on, Giant. Get to it!"

Giant's foot broke the lock and nearly rammed the door off its hinges. While the Kid and Nate Willstock and Dandy answered the attack in the front room, the others crept upstairs. The three followed. The lull in the gunfire brought a shout from the attackers.

"They're through! The fire's got 'em!"

While the gunhogs were congratulating themselves, the Horde was crawling through a skylight onto the roof. Limbs of the broad oaks were hanging over the roof. The owl-hooters climbed into the trees.

Down below, the ceiling in the front room crashed. The gunsters surrounding the house guffawed, closed in. Then an owl-hoot came from one of the oaks. A signal from the Kid. The Hordemen began to descend. Peering through the foliage, the Kid saw fifteen or more men. Kneeling on a limb, he cracked out:

"Yo're covered, men. Drop those guns."

A roar came from Ragle, already creased by the Kid, and the gunhogs opened up. A deadly fusillade poured from the trees. Five spics dropped. The others began streaking for the outbuildings and the timber beyond.

The Hordemen lowered to the ground and tore after them. The Kid saw the rangy Ragle sprinting for the pine woods to the east. He took after the ranch boss, thudding shots close to him. The Kid wasn't a back-shooter. But he had to get this man somehow.

If Ragle reached the pines, he could bring the Kid down from cover. And if Calvert did get to shelter, he wouldn't have much chance of catching the killer. The Kid kept shouting for Ragle to halt. While the Kid was reloading, the rangy man fired over his shoulder. The bullet plowed the dirt at the Kid's feet. He rocketed a shot at Ragle. That drove the gunster into swift flight again.

The Kid was gaining fast. Ragle was crying for help. But from the yells around the blazing ranch-house, it was evident that his hirelings were occupied with their own problems. Ragle was growing too near the woods to suit the Kid. And the Kid wasn't a back-shooter.

Suddenly the Kid yelled, stopped firing. "I—I'm shot!"

HE THREW himself headlong. Ragle spun around, triggered lead. His aim was high, the bullet burning through space where the Kid had been. The flame from Ragle's .45 was still streaking, when the Kid fired. It was a center shot. Ragle folded up without a sound. When the Kid reached him, the man was dead.

Something was moving in the brush ahead. The Kid darted behind a tree. Back of him came the shouts of gunhogs and Hordemen in a deadly trade of hot lead. Sixes rattled harshly. Men shrieked. The Kid bobbed up behind another tree. Then he gave a start.

Moonlight shone on a man pawing the dirt. He was moaning in dying agony. From his back protruded the hilt of a knife. The Kid ran forward. The man was the spic who had gunwhipped him back at the *Rio Casa.*

"Queeck—*señor,*" gasped the spigotty, "I die. Een my pocket, get—my—"

The Kid knelt down. Pulling out the knife, he knew, would only add to the man's torture and hasten the end. He rustled the spic's pockets, brought forth a small crucifix. The man's eyes gleamed brightly. That was what he wanted. It was a strange paradox—a man who lived violently, viciously, clinging to his religion.

At the spic's plea, the Kid lifted him to a kneeling position, doffed his Stetson while the Mex clung to his crucifix and muttered prayers. Peace came over the wicked face. He asked to be lowered again.

"Manuel—knife—me," he gasped painfully. "Manuel Estrada. I lock heem—and—the *señorita* een the adobe near—the—tool-shed. Then—he throw knife through—window—"

Slowly the spic choked out the words. Estrada had asked him to lock himself and Dolores in the adobe, to make it appear that he was a dupe of Ragle. Estrada meant to pose as an honest salesman. Instead, he had been Ragle's executioner, had done away with all the missing men, had been the one to start the chase of Jake Ranshaw.

Jake had been enticed to the ranch by Dolores, had stolen a will which had been in Estrada's possession. Ragle and Estrada killed their prospects after they robbed them—to prevent the victims from bringing them into court. The spic—Ramon he called himself—gave the Kid the direction to the pit where the bodies had been thrown. Always the murders had been committed miles from Peaceful Ranch.

"But the *muchacha* Dolores—she—is—innocent of the murders," gasped Ramon. "*Señor,* get that—weel. Eet belongs to Dolores—the *Hacienda* Estrada."

Suddenly blood gushed from Ramon's mouth. His eyelids fluttered. He held the crucifix to his chest, and as death overtook him, he was muttering another prayer.

The Kid saw some one sneaking through the woods toward the ranch buildings. He crept toward the man until he was close behind.

"Stick 'em up!" he rasped.

The man whirled, laughed. "Kid, it's Hawn. Say, I was worrying that you'd been killed. I just got here. Heard the shooting, and came this way to get the lay before I showed myself."

The firing had ceased. The ranch-house was just a smoldering ruin. The Kid heard loud voices coming from the front of an adobe on the other side of the burned-down house. He gasped. One of the voices belonged to Terry Reynolds. And he heard the deep basso of Deputy Root.

The Kid realized that Terry must have been listening at the door before she had entered Dolores Estrada's room, had heard the mention of Peaceful Ranch.

A half-pint man came around the corner of charred mass that had been a house. Dandy McLain. The little gambler spotted the Kid, hurried forward.

"Lawdy, I'm glad to see yuh, son," Dandy said. "I thought one of them skunks had got yuh. Say, we got a problem. Terry's here. She found Dolores Estrada and that wuthless brother-in-law locked in an adobe. That Manuel jasper claims he thought he'd been workin' for Ragle on a legitimate proposition. We say different. Dolores has pleaded for the rat. An' now Terry's promised him safe escort into Mexico."

The Kid felt his flesh creep. Manuel Estrada, the most treacherous of them all, was going free. The Kid was sure he was a murderer. Manuel had been the one who'd shot his *compadre* in the *Rio Casa* alley. The Kid was certain of that, because he had shot that killer in the side, had lammed him on the back of the head with a rock. And Manuel had an injured side and a lump on the back of his head. The Kid had discovered that when he met him in the *cantina*.

"Why, the mangy son killed his own half-brother!" exclaimed Eagle Hawn, pulling a document from his pocket. "This is the will of Don Carlos Estrada, Dolores' dead husband. Don Carlos left everything to his wife. Hell, every other line tells about the don's fear of his no-good half-brother.

"That's why he made out the will—because Manuel had threatened him, and he expected sudden death. You can lay your chips on it, Manuel killed Don Carlos. Manuel gave me the will—to forge one making him the heir of *Hacienda* Estrada and the guardian of Dolores."

The Kid grabbed Eagle's arm. "Would you have much trouble forgin' Don Carlos' handwritin'?"

"Almost as easy as writing my own name," said Eagle.

The Kid led him into a bunkhouse, found a bottle of ink and a pen, and instructed him what to write. Dandy and the Kid stayed in the darkness, when a few minutes later Eagle Hawn rushed up to the group.

THE HORDEMEN, gripping sixes, were facing Terry Reynolds and Deputy Root, a burly, red-faced man, who also were leveling .45s. Behind the girl stood Dolores Estrada and Manuel.

"Gal," old Peel was saying, "I think a heap o' yuh. I shore do. An' I'm askin' yuh reasonable-like—turn Manuel Estrada over to us. He needs killin'. He had something to do with murderin' my pard Jake, an'—"

"If you take *Señor* Estrada," returned the girl, "I won't be alive to see it. The *señor* and the *señorita* have explained. They were tricked. I've promised them safe escort into Mexico, and I'm going through with it."

Eagle Hawn rushed up to Manuel Estrada, waving the will. "Here you are, you low scum. Here's your brother's will. I was willing to forge one in your favor. But I'm not willing to work for a murderer. You killed your brother, mister."

Dolores Estrada sprang forward, took the will. On the first page was a scrawl such as a dying man might write. In Spanish were the words:

I am dying. Manuel has stabbed me.

Eagle had done a clever enough job of forging the line to cause Dolores to faint. Deputy Root grabbed the will. One glance, and his gun was swinging.

But the spic was ahead of him. He wrapped an arm around Terry, wrenched her gun out of her grasp. Then he backed away, using Terry as a shield.

A man streaked out of the darkness. Estrada whirled. But the big fist of Kid Calvert collided with his jaw before he could get his gun into action. Estrada staggered back. His six spouted flame.

The Kid got the girl from his relaxed hold. But before he could swing her behind him, Estrada raised his gun. It lined up with the girl's back. There was a deafening explosion.

It was Peel Rogers' six that had blazed. Estrada's Colt slipped from his grasp. His mouth twisted and his eyes widened with horror and astonishment. Then they deadened, and he slumped down.

"I reckon that tallies it up, Jake," muttered old Peel.

In the darkness the Kid was holding Terry Reynolds close. All his resentment had been swept away by the danger that had threatened the girl. She was weak from shock, and she seemed glad to have the Kid's strong arms about her.

No one saw the kiss, no one but Terry heard the murmur of his voice. But suddenly she wrenched away.

Then she picked up the will, scanned it. Instantly her manner changed. "I suspected this!" she exclaimed. "Hawn, you forged that line. You wanted Estrada dead, so you did this. You killers! And you, Kid Calvert, you're the worst of the lot. You probably planned it all."

The Kid turned his back. The Hordemen were mounting, and he was eager to get away. His face was sad.

"I never want to see that girl again."

"I understand, son," spoke the gambler sympathetically. "But you wanta remember that she's a woman, and there's no accountin' for the way a woman acts."

THE HELL-BORN CLAN

A bullet creased Kid Calvert of the Hunted Horde. That bullet just burned his skin, but it seared deep into his soul. For it had been fired by the girl he loved, Sheriff Terry Reynolds. And that soul scar flung the long-riding Kid into the mystery maw of a renegade's frame-up—a hate-baited trap that needed more than the guts and guns of Kid Calvert and his owl-hoot Horde to break.

I

THE MAVERICK

THEY WERE on the ridge. They were down the ridge. They were streaking madly across the timbered bench-land. Bullets whirred close, searching eagerly, greedy for living flesh. Death crowded them. Death voiced a spiteful promise in every evil whine of a slug.

Out of the line of smoking dust rushed two fleet mounts. Slit-eyed long-riders hunched low in the leather. Behind them thundered a howling pack of reward-hungry possemen, guns clutched in brown fists. Flaming destruction spouted out of those Colts. And every wicked little slug, burning its path of ruination, seared hate into the heart of "Kid" Calvert.

The roaring, kill-crazy man-pack was nothing new. Time out of mind had his horse Star unleashed phantom speed to run the wind out of posse mounts. Always it had been a game. Always a thrill and a laugh—that business of choking lawmen with the dust of their escape. But now it was no game. No game at all. For the girl the Kid had loved, the girl who had touched his life with beauty and magnificence, headed that posse.

"She's throwin' down on us!" flared the Kid. "Terry's tryin' to empty our saddles!"

"Dandy" McLain, cold-decking cardman, allowed a tolerant smile to split his poker mask. "She's the sheriff, son." He had to yell. "She can't flip duty into the discard jest because we've helped her now an' then. She sees—"

The Kid began to mutter.

"Don't yuh savvy?" yelled Dandy. "She sees us only as Horde-men. Her dad got killed fightin' us."

The Kid's face tightened. "Yeah! An' what happened to my dad? Huh! What happened to Gunner Calvert?"

"I know. I know," came back the flowery-vested little gambler. "He went down, too. But he was outside the law, son. He was a Hordeman. An' we're wanted, son—wanted bad."

The heavy jaw of the Kid jutted like a chunk of granite. Granite was wedging into his soul. Every blast of those bucking law guns added to his bitterness. Anger surged up in his lean-muscled body. He didn't want to be that way. The law was driving him to it.

The law would never understand. The Horde—Calvert's Horde—had always fought for a justice far higher than the unwieldy statutes of legislation. Old "Gunner" Calvert had gathered a clan of embittered, fate-badgered men, driven onto the death's-end trails by crooked law, to champion the cause of

the underdog. After lawman's lead had finished the old Gunner, the Kid—his son—had carried on.

The owl-hooters, forsaken men, forever hated and reviled, found solace in their unceasing war against oppression, found peace in the battle for the weak and downtrodden.

"I don't ask fer thanks," yelled the Kid. "But I don't want to be shot fer helpin' folks. We didn't have to fog for the Hatchet outfit. It's no *dinero* outa our jeans if them Brazito rustlers run off all their stock an' snipe every puncher on the spread."

"That talk'll make yore ol' man turn over in his grave," shot back half-pint Dandy.

Terry Reynolds, girl sheriff of Washakie County, and her posse had surprised the owl-hooters near the great Hatchet

Terry was leveling
a Colt at the Kid.

Rancho. This huge cattle domain spread over the vast Gallinas land grant. For generations stock—first longhorns and then Herefords—had fattened under the Gallinas brand. But the rancho was collapsing now, falling before the ravages of the swift-striking Brazito *bandido*.

The Kid glanced back. His slitted gray eyes were shot with savage flames. The girl was coming on. The girl was spurring her pony to its utmost speed. Her beauty was lost in the anger that blinded the Kid to reason. He saw nothing of the rich golden hair framing the delicate contour of an oval face. He saw only the star on her blouse, the long-barreled Colt clutched in a small fist. That gun was smoking.

She called something to him, but he caught nothing save the intensity of her tone. He swung front, urged Star into another breakneck spurt. The stallion lengthened out to a rhythmic stride. Beneath the grain-fed sheen of his steel-dust coat, sinewy bunches of power crawled and rippled. Every fiber of that big-barreled stallion strained to take the Kid away from whining death.

"We'll show 'em, Dandy!" yelled the Kid. "Don't let that buckskin doze off."

"Buck's with us!" called Dandy. "He's got his mind on the oats he'll get at the end o' this ride. I'm trailin' close."

A great jasper, Dandy McLain. He could fleece a tinhorn like a spic herder sheared a sheep. Face-down cards were no more a mystery to him than a primer to a schoolmarm.

A bullet ventilated his dove-gray Stetson. His jaws clamped. The cords in his neck bulged. Iron-band sinews tightened at the thought of the girl trying to pick him out of the saddle. Those whooping general-store loafers, saloon bums, and chuck-line riders didn't matter. But the girl—

TWIGS AND branches whipped raw the Kid's scarred, bronzed face. He raised his head. He noted that the slugs were whining higher. His lips thinned against glistening teeth in a mirthless smile. They were outdistancing the posse.

The frenzied squeal of a horse shrilled out. A posse mount had snagged a hoof in a rabbit hole. The Kid twisted and saw the rider catapulting through swishing pine foliage and coming up short against wind-gnarled scrub cedars. Swerving away from the fallen mount, horses collided. The stride was broken, the pace slackened. The Kid sent up an exultant shout.

Dipping into a sandy, broomweed draw, the owl-hooters dropped into a gully and sent their mounts splashing across a creek. They took a spruce-grown slope at a full gallop, and got a ridge behind them before the posse rode off the benchland.

The Hordemen hit broken country. Star and the buckskin had fought their first saddles in owl-hoot territory. The rough going was routine work. Behind them, hoofbeats gradually dwindled into a muffled drumming that soon merged with the murmuring of the wilderness.

Atop a rock-ribbed hogback, they drew rein to give the mounts a blow. The Kid rolled a quirley, and then inspected the bullet vents in his Stetson.

"They'll make yore hat cooler fer the hot months," said Dandy.

The Kid smiled grimly. He was through. He'd always accepted wrongs and humiliations as part of the price he had to pay for his owl-hoot heritage. But he'd reached the breaking point.

He drew furiously on the quirley.

"Feelin' a bit rocky, huh?" said Dandy.

"Jest thinkin', that's all," said the Kid. "Jest wonderin' what come first. Reckon I'll cut down the assets of the Cattlemen's Bank. When the first-o'-the-month payrolls come in, I'll save the cashier a lot o' bookkeepin'. Foraker, the lawyer, oughta be sure-fire fer a fat ransom. The claims up Beaver Creek way are yieldin' five-ten bucks a pan. Them prospectors are better off busted. I'll—"

Dandy glared at the Kid. "What the hell are yuh spoutin'? Foraker—yes. Thet *dinero*-bloated shyster is due fer a strippin'. But the Horde doesn't tinker with payrolls. Yuh know thet."

"Yeah—yeah, I know," said the Kid. "Let's see. That spic *cantina* boss in San Cayaco will take all the wet stock I run across fer twenty bucks a head."

"Damn yore heart, Kid Calvert!" yelled Dandy. "Yo're havin' no truck with thet San Cayaco frijole! Once yuh threatened to yank the gullet outa thet low-livin' murderer o' peons. Yuh've gone plumb loco. Yo're forgettin' the code."

That code was the backbone of the Horde. As harsh as fate had been to the Calvert owl-hooters. The Horde's code was more rigid than penitentiary rules, more demanding than a monk's vows. It had to be. Those desperate, hope-shattered men bordered the line that separated gents who killed in the cause of justice from killers who took life wantonly.

At any time something was apt to snap in a hate-maddened brain, and one of the Hordemen would cross the line. The clan had held together because of the principles of justice which dictated their acts, which dedicated them to the cause of charity and mercy.

"I'm goin' to live up to the lobo brand that men have slapped on me," growled the Kid.

Dandy laughed. "Oh, yo're all right. Yo're jest sweatin' a bit because Terry took a couple o' pops at yuh. She gives yuh a bum deal. She's always tryin' to copper yore bets."

"Yuh hoppin' right!" snapped the Kid.

Dandy fingered the golden rowel hanging from a chain of nuggets that stretched across his fancy vest. "Terry's a hundred per cent fer the law. She ain't happy wearin' a star. She took her dad's job because she's big an' fine all through. She puts her principles first. Got a lot o' sand, thet gal. Too much fer a little person."

The Kid glowered at Dandy. "Go ahead. Yo're gettin' plumb unpopular with me. Toot the horn fer her."

"I'll always toot the horn fer Terry," said Dandy calmly. "Yuh ever hear about a thing called tolerance?"

"Huh!" snapped the Kid. "Go ask her that. I'll bet my saddle she thinks we throwed in with Brazito."

"I only bet to win," came back Dandy. "Why shouldn't she think thet? Brazito isn't a tinhorn. He's roddin' about the wildest bunch north o' the Line."

THE FAINT drum of hoofs reached them. The Kid's face grew sullen. He gnawed at his lip and rubbed the butt of his Colt. He heard a distance-muffled shout. Another yell drifted down the wind, louder. The posse was trailing sign at a high lope.

"Them buzzards are shore honin' to collect on our heads," said Dandy. "We'll hit thet stream yonder an' slope fer the hideout."

They reined onto a deer path. The Kid's face was dark. He was making grim resolutions. A gent had to be hard. He had been soft clay, yielding. He was flint now. Within a hundred-mile circle were a thousand men who'd shoot him in the back. Back-shoot him and strut to the mob's acclaim—if they had reason to believe they could escape the Horde's vengeance.

Suddenly the Kid halted Star. "What's that?"

He heard a faint cry, thin, mournful.

"Cougar," said Dandy. "Far off."

A touch of the spurs sent Star on. Again that cry, weak and pitiful. The steel-dust reached the floor of the valley. Through the spruce and pines loomed a weather-warped, tumble-down log cabin. It had long been deserted, long abandoned to prowling wolves and panthers. But that broken wail didn't come from any creature of the wild.

"Come on!" yelled the Kid. Star pushed through the tangle of undergrowth. A crimson path led from the closed door of the cabin. The Kid leaped from the saddle. Trail-trained eyes quickly cut sign.

He saw the imprints of unshod hoofs, the tracks of a cougar. Shreds of a print cloth clung to thorny brush splashed with blood. A trail of broken twigs and trampled grass showed where the beast had dragged its victim. The sign bore out that the tragedy had happened days ago. That person was beyond help. But inside some one needed attention.

"Thet brute was damned starved to attack a human," said Dandy. He picked up a scrap of cloth. "Piece of a dress. Homespun. Stuff a peon woman wears."

The Kid put his shoulder to the door.

"Look out," warned Dandy. "Might be a trap."

"Might be," said the Kid, shoving the door open. A rat's nest stood in the center of the gnawed, splintered floor.

In a piñon-pole bunk matted with weather-stained straw something squirmed under a bright Navajo blanket. The cries broke out again.

"I'll be damned!" exclaimed the Kid.

"Don't use yore hands," advised Dandy. "This might be jest a clever trap. Can't tell what folks will do, when their favorite literature is reward bulletins."

The Kid pulled away the gaudy blanket. Beneath it lay a squirming little bundle of squalling, olive-skinned humanity. He had black eyes and straight, crow-colored hair, but he wasn't a *mestizo*. His clean features suggested either Spanish or Aztec blood. He wasn't much more than a year old.

Hunger pinched his tiny face. Tears had swelled and reddened his eyes. The tongue was puffed from thirst. The tot's long dress, soiled and torn, was of expensive embroidered silk, lace fringed. A jeweled cross and a locket hung from a golden chain around the little neck. The Kid noted the diamond-set ring on a tiny finger, and around the wrist a golden band.

"Poor little shaver," muttered the Kid, gathering the babe in his arms.

"Might be sick," said Dandy. "Might have something yuh can catch."

"Get the canteen," ordered the Kid. "A long drought's goin' to stop pronto."

Dandy went out and returned with the water. "I got a feelin' thet posse is goin' to be spendin' reward money soon."

The Kid scowled. "This feller ain't far from cashin' in. Purty young to be goin' out with his boots on."

He sent Dandy to follow the path of the cougar. He trickled water down the waif's parched throat. The little fellow gulped the drops, stopped crying. From his saddlebags, the Kid got an apple, a strip of jerked venison. He squashed the apple in steel-muscled fingers, fed the babe some of the juicy pulp. Not much, though. He'd heard talk of such things as colic. Or maybe it was croup. Moistening the jerky, he let the tot suck the goodness out of it.

Those hoofbeats were distinct now. Lumps bulged on the Kid's jaw. He began thinking about lynch mobs. Dandy returned, his face drawn, somber.

"I covered up the remains," he spoke in a low, husky tone. "A little ol' squaw woman. Didn't have no more defense against thet cat than a lamb. Dead two days, mebbe longer."

"Good thing she got the door closed," muttered the Kid.

The baby was feeling better. He began to gurgle and babble. He clutched at Dandy's golden rowel, looked up gratefully, and murmured: "Goo-oo."

The gambler's eyes lost their bleakness. "I'll be a thumb-handed tinhorn. The little waddler thinks I'm all right."

Dandy pulled out his pack of cards and riffled them. The infant found that very amusing; but there was no time to entertain, with a wild-eyed pack of reward hunters crowding them. The hoofbeats had grown ominously loud.

"We've got to make tracks!" exclaimed the Kid.

ALREADY THE posse was thundering up the last hogback they had ridden down. The Kid bundled up the babe. His face hardened. A gun blasted. These hellions had grown as savage as wolves pulling down a beef critter. The little Mex wrapped tiny arms around the Kid's corded neck and drooled against his leathery cheek.

A sheepish grin played on the Kid's mouth. Warmth stole into his heart. A thrill went through him that he had never experienced before. He wondered if old Gunner Calvert had felt this way once. This was something new for the Kid—and he liked it.

"Best let me handle the little Mike," suggested Dandy. "There's tricks to baby-totin' thet yuh've never heard of. Yuh got to have the knack. See how he took to me?"

The Kid eyed Dandy, stirruped astride Star. The stallion got the spurs, lunged. A stiff wind shrieked down from the east. They lined out northward. They streaked for the next ridgetop. They rode like hell.

Dread clawed at the Kid. The posse was too close. The posse would be plunging over the rim of that last crest. Those glittering-eyed stepsons of law and order, those greedy bounty hunters, would loose a lead hurricane.

Weaving around storm-blasted cedars and scrub oak, Star churned up the ground to reach the top. He hauled himself over an outcropping of basalt onto a sawtoothed ridge. The posse was cresting the hogback.

The girl was shouting something to her men. The din drowned out her words. A thunderous roll of smashing gunfire rattled from bouncing Colts. Bullets flattened against the basalt. Rock splinters showered up. Bounty hunters were screeching like drunken Comanches.

The Kid hugged the little maverick. His body would shield the baby. Though he expected some kill-crazy posseman to spill him out of the saddle, the Kid's dying thought would be to fall so the little one wouldn't get hurt.

The Kid glanced back. He saw the glint of Terry's star, saw the bobbing head of curly golden hair. His heart leaped into his throat. An agonizing "lost" feeling burned through his vitals. The girl was leveling a Colt at him.

"You can't make it, Kid Calvert!" she yelled. "Haul in! You're the law's prisoner. I'm taking you back."

Flame stabbed from the gun that suddenly bucked in her hand. The Kid heard an angry whir, felt a sharp sting along the right side of his neck. A shudder racked his rock-hard frame. She had shot him. Terry had grooved him, had tried to dump him out of the saddle.

He hunkered down in the leather, his face working. His muscles knotted up in cramped bunches. His tongue cleaved to the roof of his mouth. His head whirled. He felt that his heart pumped molten lead. Never had life seemed so bleak. Never had the Kid felt so forsaken. Terry had shot him. Shot him....

Star got the spurs again. Star wasn't used to the spurs. But he seemed to understand. This was a special occasion.

Guns roared viciously. The baby began pulling at the Kid's nose. The baby said a great many things that only he could understand. But it was all great fun. That was certain. The bouncing stallion rocked like a cradle. It was indeed very pleasant.

He got a grip of the Kid's hair, gave a yank. The Kid's head bobbed.

A whining bullet pulled at the pinched peak of his Stetson. The Kid whistled, gulped. "Thanks, old son!" he exclaimed, hugging the little mite.

He heard a yelp from Dandy that ended in a curse.

"Don't slack down!" Dandy shouted. "I ain't hit. The cayuse stumbled. Near got throwed."

Then the Kid was heading downslope. Dandy trailed. Below, a canyon skirted a frowning bald butte. Through a creek they rode upstream into a slashed country of chimney buttes and deep chasms. For an hour, the Kid held to a hard pace. The babe had gone to sleep in his arms. Dandy kept close. No word was passed. The noise of the posse died out.

"We're rid of them," clipped out the Kid. "But they're not rid of us. Damned bounty hunters. Drygulchers. Hey, Dandy—"

The Kid turned. An anguished cry broke from his lips. Dandy

hadn't talked. Dandy couldn't talk. Because the gambler lay slumped across the mount's withers. Blood splashed the saddle, dyed the buckskin's mane. Dandy showed no sign of life.

2

RENEGADE COURT

A GREAT WEARINESS engulfed the Kid. His shoulders drooped, and something like a sob broke from his throat. Under the bronze of weather-beat, his color had drained to a ghastly ash-gray. He held the little maverick in the cradle of his left arm and slid from the saddle. Grief glazed his eyes. The sun blazed down, but life was black. All life would be like this—pain and misery topped off with the tawdry recompense of death.

He laid the baby gently on the ground, stroked the glistening hair, smiled faintly at the tot's blissful helplessness. Too soon had life bared fangs to the tiny waif. The Kid rushed to Dandy.

The buckskin began cropping a patch of grama grass. The lowered head started the gambler out of the saddle. He slid into the Kid's arms. The Kid uttered a pitiful cry. Mist fogged his eyes. The breath was still in the man. But it came harsh and rasping, every suck and wheeze of it an outrage to bullet-shattered nerves.

Stretching Dandy on the grass, the Kid ripped coat and vest and shirt. The slug had got the cardsharp below the right shoulder blade. An ugly, jagged wound geysered crimson. The bullet had reached him on a slant, missing the spine. But it had burrowed through vital regions.

He washed Dandy's wound, bandaged it crudely, and jolted Dandy out of a coma with a slug of brandy from a flask the gambler carried. The Kid was instantly sorry. Dandy returned to maddening consciousness. He raved like a Mex on a *mari-*

juana jag. A few snatches of intelligence came out of the delirious babbling.

"Save—the—maver—Terry—all—right. A—woman— The li'l' Mex—likes—likes—me."

Nature rebelled again. Dandy needed a doctor, needed one pronto. The ride to camp was out. It wouldn't take much jogging to make the gambler a corpse. The Kid muscled his pard onto the buckskin. His heart trip-hammered with fear that the handling would finish Dandy. He tied him to the saddle. Carrying the waif, he led Star and Buck.

More than a mile of slow going, and wood smoke swept down on the east wind. Up a gully stood a vine-draped cabin, cheery with flowers and clucking hens.

The Kid could have wept. Old Zack Creers lived here, with his wife and boy. Friends who loved the Horde. Townsfolk were hostile to the Calvert wild bunch, because they didn't understand. But the lonely people of the hills looked to the hell-born clan for protection.

The Horde had financed an operation for Zack's wife. Saved old Zack from sad, barren years. The Kid had never called on the homesteader for help. He'd been afraid to. Creers' gratitude was too deep. He was too rashly eager to repay. He'd give his life. The Horde didn't want his life. The Horde wanted to bask in the glow of a man it had made happy.

The Creers woman opened the door. The son ran from a shed. Old Zack crashed through brush, ax poised, rifle ready. No welcome showed on his seamed face. Homesteaders built a defense of hostility that few could break. They had to. Then Zack uttered a happy shout. He recognized the Kid.

That jubilation died instantly. Zack ran forward, face twisting.

"Dandy!" he cried. "They got Dandy! Who, Kid? Tell me who."

The Kid explained. He and Zack packed Dandy into the cabin. The boy carried the baby. And Creers opened the first-aid box, put water to heat. The homesteader got wild-eyed when the Kid told about the baby, about getting shot while carrying the little maverick. The waif was put in a nest of blankets on the cowhide lacings of a pine-pole chair. The Creers boy saddled up and headed townward for a medico.

Creers oiled his carbine, buckled on his sixes, jamming extra cartridges into his pockets. "Who was in that posse, son?" he demanded. "Leave the gal out. Never thought she'd turn out thataway; but women is funny things. Name the gents. They'll get their next chuck outa the fryin' pan o' hell."

Sudden enthusiasms and wild ideas had kept Creers drifting about the West. Honest, labor-bent, perpetually indignant, he needed always the check of a leash. His wife whitened. Her age lines deepened. Her hand shook when she handed the Kid a bandage roll, cut from old shirts boiled sterile.

"Zack, bring in the wood," ordered the old lady. "If you could oil up yore joints like you do them smoke poles, I'd be wantin' you to go trailin' them bounty hunters."

Sullenly old Zack shucked his hardware and trudged out for the wood. The Kid hovered over Dandy. His face was a tight mask of anguish. The fever was rising. Hope was gone. Dandy was going to join old Gunner Calvert. Never again would the little dude gambler sluice gold from greedy tinhorns.

No more second dealing; no more short-card work. The Kid stared with burning eyes at the half-pint card cheat who would die poor, who could have cold-decked his way to a million. Dandy would die poor, because he had cheated for humanity, had used his magic fingers to deal winning cards for the needy and oppressed.

OLD LADY Creers bathed the little Mex, fed him. The Kid paced the floor, smoking quirley after quirley. Hoofs drummed. He bounded to the door. A herd of broomtails raced across the gully. Once horsemen rode along the ridge. The Kid's hand filled. Zack grabbed a sawed-off shot-gun, eyes glowing. The strangers headed on—punchers about their own business.

Then the Creers kid got back with Doc Ringel of Deadline. Bad lungs had brought the medico to Washakie County, with an unconditional death sentence delivered by specialists. The miracle of Western air had granted him a pardon. A man reclaimed from the dead, he knew the meaning of tolerance. To him a wounded bandit was just another hurt, sick man.

"A man's after Terry Reynolds," said the Creers lad.

The Kid was deaf to everything but the medico's verdict. Ringel probed the wound, grew grave. "I'll have to cut."

"Is he through?" The Kid's face went gray.

"Depends on his vitality," said Ringel.

"Save him an' name yore price!" exclaimed the Kid. "I heard talk about Deadline needin' a hospital. Keep Dandy from cashin' in, an' that hospital goes up!"

"I can't make promises, son," said Ringel. "Thanks for the hospital. You gents will get a bill. Now keep to hell out of my way."

But the Kid stayed close until the doctor whirled on him and ordered him out. "Some sort of jamboree is going on in town. Maybe you can do some of your kind of operating there. I'll handle the surgery here."

"It's Terry Reynolds, Kid. She's in trouble," said Zack.

The Kid came to life. "Huh?"

"Terry," said the Creers boy. "She's done something that's got folks down on her. A big mob's in front of her office, an' a jasper's yelling for her to come out an' face the music."

The Kid gulped. A chill went through him.

"Some proddy gent called Terry a low-down she lobo," explained the youngster. "Said she was Brazito's *segundo*."

The Kid mashed a quirley in his fingers. He stared at Dandy under the medico's knife. He leaned over the sleeping baby, tucked in the blanket.

"I heard lynch talk," went on the lad.

The Kid stiffened. He grew more fidgety. He wasn't going

to town. He had to stay with Dandy. Let the folks who'd voted for Terry take care of her. Let the men of the town council give her a hand.

"That Boday hombre was bellerin' he'd bust the door if she didn't come out," added the boy.

"Boday said that, huh?" The Kid hitched his gun belt. Any crowd Boday was in was a no-good crowd. Boday was a town brawler, and he hated Terry, who'd jugged him for six months. He'd promised to rid the county of skirt law.

"If Boday said that, I'm ridin'," muttered the Kid.

Assured by the doctor that he couldn't help here, the Kid turned to the Creers younker. "Pete, yuh know where we hole up. Fog fer camp an' rout out the boys. Tell 'em it's the same spot—the old adobe. I'll be meetin' 'em there."

A last look at Dandy, and the Kid went out and forked Star, heading south. Pete Creers started for the Horde's hideout. The Kid told himself he was riding in to smash Boday. If Terry was in trouble, her bounty-hunting posse could help her. He kept touching the bullet crease on his neck, kept thinking of little Dandy. And he wondered about the waif, too.

The Kid was riding in to settle with a two-bit barroom slugger, but he urged Star to the speed of a posse-goaded flight. The face that loomed up wasn't Boday's. He saw a pretty little oval beneath golden hair. It puzzled him that the girl's face was always before him. Terry had shot him. He ought to hate her. Yet a strange dread assailed him. And Boday, with all his hulking strength, couldn't have aroused that dread.

The brassy sun had turned to a molten ball that tipped the western peaks when the Kid hit the stage route winding into Deadline. The town sprawled nakedly across the flats. Weather-warped buildings flanked the wheel-rutted streets.

The splintery, pitch-seeping plank sidewalks were deserted. Mounts stood tethered at the hitchrack. But the usual scattering of citizens trailing in and out of stores was missing.

A mob bunched up in front of the sheriff's office. Some one

was talking. The Kid couldn't catch his words. Two blocks away, he recognized some of the men in that sullen crowd. Cronies of Boday—tinhorns who preyed on greenhorns and pilgrims. Probably a hundred men stood in that mob.

A thin little smile showed on the Kid's mouth. If he rode into that pack, his life wouldn't be worth a plugged peso. Somebody would produce a rope, and he'd get his last view of the sun, swaying from a cottonwood.

His face hardened. "I'll trump them chuckleheads," he muttered. "I'll have them thinkin' they're all hangin' on the rim o' hell."

HE REINED Star to the north and rode to the crumbling adobe where the Horde often gathered. He shucked his guns, hiding them under the debris of a pack rat's nest. Then he returned to town by a back street, leaving Star ground hitched behind the Broken Spur Saloon. He went down the alley and stood on the saloon's porch.

The door to the sheriff's office was closed. A bull-necked giant stood before the office, holding a watch. He yelled:

"Three minutes!"

Disgust twisted the Kid's mouth. That was Boday's style. He was the sort who'd hooraw a helpless hombre. He liked to bait a tenderfoot. And he'd never miss a chance to prolong the agony. He loved to gloat. Boday ate this sort of thing up—badgering a defenseless person. He was giving the girl sheriff three minutes to open the door. That was the way Boday's thick head worked. He was giving the girl a chance—the big, simple, tender-hearted skunk.

Boday's mob represented only the tough element of Deadline. The Kid felt certain that Terry was guilty of no wrong. Whatever her injustice to the Kid, she was on the level, true to her belief of what was right.

And now she needed help. A bullet wound had put Deputy Root, trusted lawman, out of commission. The Kid knew that members of the town council and many of the stronger citizens of Deadline—men who would have come to her aid—were attending a cattlemen's convention in San Pablo.

The citizens in town now were the shopkeepers, family men who dared not get into trouble that might leave their dependents destitute. And the bounty hunters who'd ridden with Terry were the kind who wouldn't take a risk unless they saw a chance of a clean-up.

Kirpas, the Broken Spur swamper, stood by the batwing doors, leaning on a mop, watching intently. He saw the Kid and sidled over, dragging his mop under his arm, rubbing his hands, fawning.

"Oh, Mr. Calvert, it's awful. I would 'a' tried to stop it if I was a man like you. But I'm a weak, twisted swamper, Mr. Calvert. I'd be just a gnat buzzing around them. But I reckon even you can't do much now, sir."

Kirpas was a sort of professional self-effacer. He traded on humility, got himself a lot of drinks and tips that way. He was the most thorough and consistent envier the Kid had ever known. If Kirpas had been born anything but a human being, he would have been a flea. He was that insignificant and that persistent.

Yet he had dreams and yearnings. Kirpas wanted to be a gunslick, a lightning flash with the Colts, a man who made other men talk low. And beyond all else, he longed to be an owl-hooter riding with the Horde.

Undersized and hungry looking, he was imprisoned in a humped and twisted body. His pinched face was dark, swarthy. He claimed that he was all gringo, but he was accused of having spic blood. Punchers hoorawed him cruelly. He was the kind that women scorned and men shoved aside. The Kid felt a great pity for him—and tried not to show it. He'd always treated Kirpas like a man and an equal.

"What's it all about?" he asked.

"Somebody found a letter from Brazito," said Kirpas. "Brazito thanked Miss Terry for helpin' him rustle the Hatchet beef."

"THAT'S A damn' lie!" blurted the Kid.

"Yes, Mister Calvert, that's what I said. But no one bothers 'bout what I say. I'm just a poor swamper. I'm much too humble to have any real ideas. That's what gents think, Mister Calvert. They think I'm just smart enough to know when a spittoon needs cleanin'."

The Kid stared at the crowd. No one had noticed him yet.

"But I'm rather smart—in a humble way," Kirpas was saying. "I'm shore Miss Terry wouldn't stoop to anything like that. I don't believe it even if they did find twelve thousand pesos in her strongbox—and a list of her cuts from the raids on the Gallinas spread."

"A plant!" growled the Kid.

"Two minutes!" yelled Boday.

"Of course it is," said Kirpas. "A plant. A frame-up." He touched a trembling hand to the Kid's sleeve. "You're goin' to help her, ain't you? You an' me, Mister Calvert. Let me show you that I'm somethin'."

There was a restless stirring in the crowd.

"I got guts," Kirpas chattered on. "You wouldn't think so, would you? Seein' me all the time with a pail an' a mop. Reckon if it came down to it, I couldn't lick my weight in chipmunks. But I'm a good man to clean your cabins. I'm mighty handy. Yes, sir. I'd keep your clothes washed an' patched, an' your boots shined."

The sheriff's office door flung open. Terry Reynolds stood in the oblong, a forlorn little figure in gray whipcord skirt and green blouse. The Kid swallowed hard. She was pretty, dainty, scarcely more than a child. Just a forsaken, framed-up, all-alone little kid facing a hate-inflamed mob.

She wasn't the weeping kind, but her eyes were red. She brushed a golden wisp of hair off her cheek. It was a tired, dazed gesture. As though her head ached like hell. Her arm sagged. The slender shoulders drooped.

The Kid's pulses hammered. He recalled another picture of

Terry—behind a smoking gun, firing at him. He forced a scowl, tried to smirk. But his eyes swiveled over the crowd, slitted, glittering.

Terry's peach-blown complexion was missing. Her face was ashen, drawn. Even a brazen dance-hall dame would have flinched before that man-pack. Terry didn't flinch. Her jaw quivered a bit. She leaned wearily against the door jamb, plenty unhappy, saying nothing.

"Yeah—yuh come out all right," sneered Boday. "Hoppin' right yuh did. We'd 'a' ripped that office into kindlin'. Now get it straight, lady. Pack an' fog. Ride with Brazito. Ride with Calvert's Horde. But be plumb shore yore hoss's hoofs head one way. Out!"

"Thet's tellin' her!" came the yell.

A rumble of approval swept the crowd.

"Yuh ain't wanted," went on Boday. "Skirt law ain't wanted. An' yuh— Why, yuh cheatin', stealin' law jane, yo're worse than—"

"Go ahaid, Boday. Make 'er blister!"

Boday's voice became a roar. "Yo're worse than any knife-flingin' percentage dame. Lucky yuh ain't a man. Damn' lucky. Plenty o' good trees right handy—if yuh was."

"Gone soft, Boday?" came a jeering voice. "Lettin' fluffy hair an' sad eyes bust yore nerve?"

"Lot's of women has got the rope," shouted another. "In England they hang 'em reg'lar. I read thet, so it's so. This law filly is a murderin', no-good—"

3

EMPTY HOLSTERS

THE KID lunged off the saloon porch. The sweat was dripping from him. Savagery masked his face. His flame-shot eyes were wild. He crammed through that mob, battling men out of the way, gouging bellies with elbows, butting, heeling, kneeing. He threw a lumpy-shouldered hulk against a dozen gents, cleared his path.

A sullen-eyed brute blocked his way. The Kid bulled into him. The Kid nearly smashed a knuckle, leveling that hombre. The sun glinted on a gun barrel. The butt was wrapped in the fist of a man behind the Kid. The gun came clubbing down, aimed at his skull. The Kid's fist was chopping at another jaw. His body swerved; his head bobbed. The movement saved him. The gun grazed his shoulder.

The girl stiffened, grasped at her throat, and gave a startled cry. She murmured a name that swung Boday around, clawing for his Colt. The crowd pushed back. The Kid reached an hombre who'd made lynch talk. The gent backed away, turning green around the gills. He raised his hands to guard his face. Then a sudden impulse whipped a paw toward his holster. The Kid got to him. All the power and weight in his body went in the winging left.

There was a crunching sound that made men gasp. The gent collapsed. He didn't move after that. He just lay in the dust, his jaw twisted and blood drooling from his mouth.

"Get him!" yelled Boday. "That's Kid Calvert. There's bounty on the buzzard."

The Kid reached the puncher who knew what they did in England. A sickly grin spread over the gent's twitching lips.

"I was jest talkin', Calvert. I was jest showin' off what I know. Honest—"

The owl-hooter nearly uppercutted the man's head off.

Hombres stared in awe, felt of their own necks. For it looked as though the puncher had a broken neck, the way he sprawled, with his head lopped on one shoulder. But his breathing was normal.

Hands wrapped around gun butts. Men cleared away from the Kid, got out of the line of fire from Boday's gun. The mob leader took a few steps. Murder glinted in his wicked little eyes. Men expected to see the Kid turned into a human sieve.

"Boday," yelled a henchman, "Calvert ain't armed. His holsters are empty."

Boday stopped, suspicious, uncertain. The girl raced to the Kid. She tried to speak, couldn't control her voice. She stood in front of the owl-hooter, a shield against Boday's six. Calvert shoved her aside roughly. Sardonic, inviting trouble, his eyes locked with Boday's. A challenging little smile played on his lips.

"Don't shoot him, Boday," shouted a crony.

"It'd be suicide," warned another. "Don't yuh see it? A trick! Calvert's bait—boot-hill bait."

"By Gawd, yo're right!" yelled a third. "No gent is loco enough to come in like this—unarmed—less'n his gang is ready to cut loose on us."

"Hell, I'm slidin' out," added a discrete one. "Boday, yuh kill Calvert, an' we'll all be singeing our beards down below. The Horde's hidin' somewheres. No doubt about it!"

Boday grimaced and muttered. A gent next to him pushed down his gun arm. Boday didn't argue. The Kid's lip curled.

"Rabbits—the whole lot of yuh!" he rasped. "Ready to beeline fer a hole."

The Kid yanked a gent's neckerchief, knocked the Stetson off another man's head. "Yo're the kind who can talk a great fight over a whisky bottle. Yeah! But when it comes to shoulderin' up agin' a man, yuh want him dead drunk or crippled before yuh begin slammin'."

He grabbed two loafers by the scruff of the neck and cracked their heads together. They reeled around as groggy as day-old calves. The Kid got their Colts, hurled them over the heads of the mob.

Terry started for her office. The Kid savvied. She was going for her gun. He pulled her back. Scores of sixes were in this throng—and they were sheathed. The Kid's empty holsters had the pack guessing. Uncertainty kept them from drawing. But a Colt jutting from a fist was something they'd understand, something that would send hands flashing for gun butts.

"Think I've got my men hidin', huh?" the Kid rasped. "No. No, yuh poor mangy pack o' flea-bitten rabbits. I'm just one lone jasper who's got yuh bluffed right out o' yore boots. No hideout gun, no gang waitin'. Just me."

MEN ON the fringe of the mob edged away, went slinking down alleys. The Kid strode up to Boday.

"Yuh accused Terry Reynolds of workin' with Brazito. Yuh found money an' a letter Brazito sent her. Yuh claim she's a rustler. Runnin' off stock from the Gallinas rancho. Yuh claim she's worse than a below-the-line percentage dame. Um-m. Yuh had a pretty good flow of hot talk for a while there. Now that talk's gonna flow right back."

The Kid knocked the Colt out of Boday's fist. "Hat in hand, mister," he grated. "Tell Miss Reynolds yo're just a big, over-grown lunk who likes to tease girls. Tell her yuh know she was framed, an' that six months in the 'gow would give yuh time to think about manners. Talk fast, Boday."

The big hulk stood there glowering, lobbing his head from side to side, and searching the thinning mob for help. But those saddle tramps, barroom bums, stick whittlers suddenly remem-bered that Providence helps those who help themselves, and they had become vastly concerned with their own welfare.

The Kid's palm lashed out, leaving a scarlet handprint on Boday's face. Rage shuddered through Boday. His beady eyes fixed on the Kid's neck, as though he longed to sink his teeth in the jugular vein. He spluttered and fumed, said nothing intelligible. Hate mounted his slow-motion brain.

"I haven't the guts to apologize, huh?" grated the Kid.

Terry tried to draw him away. Boday's mob was deserting the ranks. Shopkeepers peered through windows, furtive, but all eyes. Kirpas stood on the saloon porch, holding the two guns the Kid had thrown over the mob's head.

Hoofs drummed on the edge of town. Riders heading in. Boday appraised the Kid's slim, wiry build. He tensed his own bulky muscles.

"If yuh didn't have yore outfit of killers hidden," he said, "I—I'd—" His hands made a throttling gesture.

"Apologize!" rapped the Kid. He slammed a left for Boday's mouth, brought blood. Boday went blind crazy. He charged. The crowd was scattering. Men shouted and cursed. The Kid got a glimpse of green-jacketed riders thundering down.

A gun roared. A window crashed. Boday missed a slow-freight swing. His head snapped back under a bone-shattering onslaught. The Kid went into him with hell in his heart and dynamite in his fists. Boday staggered, punch drunken, flailing madly. A flesh-rip over his eye flooded his face with red.

Gunfire rocked the town. A vicious whine close to his head froze the Kid. The mob had vanished. Even the fallen men had been dragged off the street. Boday swung around and headed for the saloon. Kirpas ran to the Kid, lugging a half-dozen six-guns.

"Brazito!" The terror cry swept across the town. "Brazito and his riders!"

Ponies snorted and reared at the hitchracks. An empty buggy went careening down the street, hauled by a squealing runaway horse, red staining a bullet-creased flank. A ground-anchored mount galloped across the road, got front-footed by its trailing reins.

The Kid herded Terry and Kirpas into the sheriff's office. He got another glimpse of Brazito and his kill-crazy pack. No slouching, unwashed border trash in the Brazito band. Those hellions were *caballeros,* sleek and groomed dandies garbed in gaudy finery. Looked like wealthy young dons riding to a *baile.* They'd kill a man with the same courtesy and smiling deference they'd show a *señorita* at a dance.

No one under six feet rode with Brazito. No spic who wooed

dreams with tequila and *marijuana* hired his guns to Brazito. For Brazito regimented his gunslicks like soldiers.

EVERYONE KNEW that Brazito was rustling the Gallinas stock, drygulching the rancho's punchers, bankrupting the richest spread in Washakie County. Brazito worked hard at his banditry. He struck swiftly, boldly. Then his hirelings streaked away.

In the sheriff's office, the Kid bolted the door. The girl was grim faced and cool now. She'd had her baptism of fire. Kirpas was a problem. He gripped a pair of guns. Cartridge belts sagged from his bony hips. Madness gleamed in his eyes. He holstered the guns, slapped the leather as he had seen gunmen do. He fumbled the draw. Snagged the sights on his shirt.

"Easy does it!" he muttered. "Easy does it."

Again and again he practiced the draw. The Kid frowned.

"Yuh stay back an' reload, Kirpas. We haven't any lead to waste."

Kirpas' face darkened. He weighed the guns in his hands, shook his head slowly. "Yes," he muttered. "Yes, you're right. I'm jest half a man, jest Swamps, the humpy little roustabout who sweeps up after real gents."

"Yo're well off an' yuh don't know it," muttered the Kid.

"A jasper ain't well off who wants to be what he ain't," came back Kirpas. "I'd rather be a gunman six months, an' go out sudden with my boots on, than a swamper sixty years, an' jest slowly rot away."

Terry was saying nothing. She pressed against the wall close to a window, six-gun poised. The Kid couldn't see Brazito. Maybe it was the bank this time. The bandits would scoop up all the *dinero* in sight and fog for the hills.

"Hello, theah, Keed Calvert. Sorry to be a beastly bore, old chap. But would you send the *señorita* out? She's one of us, you know. Eet was sporting of you to save her. No need to bother you further, old bean. You can come out, *querida mio*. Eet's quite safe now."

Brazito talking, Hermanas Brazito—as spic as a frijole. The voice sounded from an alley across the street. The Kid couldn't see the arrogant, four-flushing devil. He swung on Terry.

"Well!"

She turned white. She had to moisten her lips before she could speak.

"It—was fine of you to help me," said the girl. "I don't know how to—to thank you, after what I—"

"No call fer thanks," broke in the Kid coldly. "I'd do as much fer any lady in trouble."

TERRY TURNED back to the window. She was breathing hard. She gripped her guns so tightly, her hands trembled; but there was a catch in her voice.

Farther up the street, guns blasted savagely. A lead hurricane buffeted the town. Brazito's raiders were doing their chores. Beside the Kid, Kirpas crouched, every shrunken muscle aquiver. He kept muttering: "I'll get 'em! I'll get 'em!"

"Going to be a bit trying, are you, Keed?" yelled Brazito.

The spic *bandido* had begun his career as houseboy for an English rancher in Chihuahua. That accounted for the Oxford accent that got tangled in with his spic lingo. Just another gent trying to be what he never could be.

"Why don't you bowleg over an' do the *caballero* stuff in person?" shouted the Kid. "Show us how it's done down in the chilli country."

"Right-o!"

"An insult's a compliment to that jasper," growled the Kid.

Guns began to roar, and in the alleys, hell spouted from steel throats. Wicked little stabs of flame lanced the thickening dusk. The Kid crouched down, his lips snarling, one eye slitted, the other eyebrow arched and twitching. Window panes crashed.

The Kid ducked, but splinters ripped his face. He cut loose, and his bucking guns grew hot in his rock-hard hands. Terry's Colts added a harsh note to the savage thunder. The Kid shot a wondering glance at the girl. Kirpas stood back. His eyes gleamed. He trembled. He uttered throaty sounds.

The Kid emptied a gun, tossed it to the swamper, motioned for a loaded one. The job steadied Kirpas. He worked feverishly, his hands all thumbs, but he got fresh loads into the hot six-gun.

"Terry! Terry!" cried Brazito. "Keep to the wall, leetle one. Wouldn't do for you to stop lead, you know. An ear shot away would spoil your charm, wouldn't eet?"

Screams shrilled out from the alleys. The guns in the sheriff's office had scored. Suddenly the Kid rapped out a savage oath. An overturned spring wagon blocked an alley. Powder flame winked around it. The Kid glanced at Terry, his face twisted wryly, all the bitterness gone from his eyes.

Terry was all business, aiming her guns at slashes of fire ripping from the wagon. Twice while the Kid watched, agonized cries rewarded her triggering. But it was a hopeless job, and the Kid knew it. Brazito had the deck stacked for a winning play.

The Kid thought of the Creers younker. A flash of hope lighted his face. He turned his ear to reach beyond the thunder of gunfire. His face darkened. He shook his head.

No help trailing in. He had to go down fighting. He glanced at Terry again. When the end came, he ought to put a bullet through her. That would be better than letting Brazito get her. He had a sudden sensation as though all the blood was sucked out of him. Kill Terry… Kill—Terry. A groan escaped him. He swung back to the window, slammed his guns into action. His face was as harsh as a hunger-crazed wolf's.

4

KIRPAS, GUNHAWK

H E TOSSED an empty gun to Kirpas. The swamper's knees had buckled. He had the face of a corpse. His hands were palsied. He couldn't get the loads into the chambers. He had to put the gun on the floor to reload it.

The Kid gave him a pitying look. Poor little misfit. Wanted to be a gunman the worst way. He was getting his chance. He wouldn't slowly rot for sixty years. And he wouldn't have his six months of hell-roaring glory. He'd get less than sixty minutes of gunsmoke and powder flame, and he'd find that all the glory was in his imagination.

Bandidos shoved the upturned spring wagon through the dust. They'd reached the hoof-pocked middle of the wheel-rutted street. Their lead made the front of the sheriff's office look like the execution wall of a Mex revolutionist.

The Kid had a bullet groove on the arm. Lead had scraped his hands. Sweat rolled into the glass rips on his cheeks. The hot guns blistered his fingers. So far the girl was unharmed. The attack centered on Kid Calvert.

The wagon worked nearer. The gunfire grew more savage. No help came from the citizenry of Deadline. There was a little scattered shooting north of the sheriff's office. Some of Brazito's hirelings keeping the townsfolk in check.

"Come out, old bean!" yelled Brazito from the safety of a dark alley. "You're making a bit of an ass of yourself, Keed. Fancy a cull like you bucking Brazito. I say, let's have done weeth thees arguing. Eet's getting quite boring, I assure you."

"I ain't through until I see yuh skiddin' into hell!" shouted the Kid.

Brazito's laugh was lost in an ear-splitting crash of gunfire. Terry had got a supply of cartridges from her desk. She tossed a box to the Kid. They could hold those kill-crazy spics off for a while. The Kid directed all his shots in a small circle on the advancing spring wagon.

The continual *chop-chop* of his lead pierced the stout board. A howl cut through the roaring. A tall spic straightened above the wagon shield. He clawed at the air, crossed himself. In a spasm of agony, he stretched beseeching hands skyward. Then he pitched across the upturned wagon. His *paisanos* behind the wagon left him there. His body covered the hole the Kid had bullet bored.

The girl wasn't at the window. Terry was down—down!

The Kid uttered a strangled cry. She lay on the floor. A yellow gleam from a full, low-riding moon threw a ghastly glare over the girl. Her face bore the color of death. She didn't stir. Her eyes were closed. There was no sign of breathing.

"Boday!" croaked Kirpas. "I saw Boday—k-killed her."

The Kid shuddered. The blame saddled onto him. He'd gone soft. He'd let Boday get away. He should have torn the gullet out of Boday. He should have twisted the gunhog's head off. Could have done that. Could have done it easily enough. But he'd let him go. Go! And now the girl was down. Dead. Shot by Boday. Murdered by Boday.

"Boday got her!" screamed Kirpas. "You understand? An' he'll get me. Somebody'll get me, anyway. I'm going to die." He made a blood-curdling choking noise.

The spring wagon was getting closer and closer. Brazito taunted the Kid from his alley haven. A bullet-riddled moose-head crashed from its wall mounting behind the Kid. Moonlight shafted through bullet rifts in the lead-pelted wall.

The Kid got to the girl, cradled her head in his arms. A slug shrieking through the window knocked a framed picture of her father from the desk. The flow from a flesh rip on her scalp reddened the girl's golden hair. The Kid uttered an exultant cry. She lived. Terry lived.

Kirpas rose up. Hysteria had got him. "I'm going to die!" he screeched. "But first I'm going to live. Me—Kirpas. Me—Swamps. I'm going to live. I'm a gunman. I've got two guns."

He moved toward the window. "You hear that, Brazito? You hear that, you chilli-eating dude? Wouldn't it be funny if I killed you, Brazito. Mop-pushing Swamps killing Brazito. I've got two guns, Brazito. I'm a gunman. I'm a bullet-throwing hell-gunner. I'm Kirpas!"

The name blared forth in a roar of savage triumph. Kirpas had won to his life's hope. In a fighting crouch, he looked nothing like the self-effacing, humpbacked roustabout of the Broken Spur Saloon. He looked like a little man-devil now, more wicked because of his deformities and wizened figure.

His Colts almost bucked out of his hands, but he kept his trigger finger working. He sprayed the street with lead.

The Kid started for the crock of drinking water in the corner. It jumped like something alive, collapsed in shattered fragments. The Kid ground his teeth. He soaked a bandana in the water dripping down the stand. He cooled Terry's feverish head with it. He didn't know how bad she was hurt. If the bullet had crashed the skull, she was through.

"Maybe it's the best," he muttered. "Mebbe yuh got shot to save me from doin' it, Terry. Because I shore would 'a' finished yuh, before I'd let Brazito take yuh." His throat swelled, throbbed like hell. He couldn't speak.

A ripping sound above sent his glance upward. Moonlight suddenly poured through a hole in the roof. The Kid groped for his guns. One of them lay where Kirpas had been reloading it. He couldn't locate the other. The moonlight glinted on the keen blade of an ax. A gun barrel spiked through the opening.

THE KID snarled. This was the end. A *bandido* had got on the roof with an ax. The guns of the swamper had drowned out the ax's hacking.

"Throw down your gons, leetle wan!" came a gloating voice through the hole. "Or do you want to swallow bullets that go een through the roof of your head?"

Kirpas whirled, shrank back, and threw his guns from him as though they were loathsome things. He fell on his knees and started to pray for mercy. "Please! Please! I—I don't want to die. I'm—afraid!"

"Come out, old chap!" yelled Brazito to the Kid. "Daresay you know you're leecked. Bring the leetle *señorita,* like a good fellow."

"All right, Brazito," said the Kid wearily.

The gunfire had ceased. The *bandidos* guffawed and mouthed ribald taunts. Kirpas got to his feet, looking as wretched as a man on the way to his execution.

The girl was moaning and mumbling in a delirium. The Kid lifted her in his arms. Maybe the sight of her might arouse the townsfolk, goad them into an attack. The Kid turned the knob, kicked open the door. The gun poking through the roof was trained on his head. The *bandidos* still crouched behind the spring wagon. A tribute to the Kid. They knew he was tricky, a man to fear as long as he could move.

Kirpas cowered behind the owl-hooter. The Kid saw no one. But he knew the darkness bristled with guns leveled at him. He grinned a little. They'd get him. But these spics were just borrowing time now. Just postponing their journey to boot-hill a short while. When the Horde struck— The Kid's eyes gleamed. Muscles stood out on his lean, angular jaw. He'd rather fall into a rattler den than be one of those gunhogs when the Horde got him. A hell of a lot rather.

Terry opened her eyes. The Kid gazed down at her. His face was drawn with sadness. Nothing showed in her eyes. No recognition, no intelligence. Just the glaze of pitiful agony. Just the dead look from an overtaxed nature, outraged and pain ravished. His grip of her tightened into an embrace.

Brazito, still hidden, shouted an order to his men. Before any of them responded, a bulky figure sprinted from the darkness. The Kid looked up to see the savage face of Boday leering at him. Boday was a Brazito man. A glinting gun barrel jutted from the big hulk's hairy paw. A metallic laugh broke from his lips. An inhuman laugh. He thumbed back the gun hammer.

"Here's yore ticket to hell, yuh slab-sided hairpin—"

A wild, frenzied roar sounded behind the Kid. Kirpas jumped to the side, hauling a long-barreled Colt from inside his threadbare shirt. The Colt the Kid couldn't find in the office. Kirpas danced in front of the Kid, a glittering-eyed madman with a gun. Boday stared like a dying man. That chattering jumping-jack of a swamper hypnotized him. Transfixed him with amazement.

The *bandido* on the roof could have sent Kirpas somersaulting like a drilled jack rabbit. But he, too stared at the feverish little gink who'd dropped a broom to grip a gun butt.

A shriek pierced from Kirpas. His gun bounced. A jagged line of living fire snaked from his Colt. Boday stiffened. His mouth twisted, then sagged. Instantly his face was a smear of crimson. There was a hole the size of a quarter between his eyes. A greenhorn's wild shot that drilled dead center.

The Kid was throwing himself to the side. Death released Boday's thumb from the gun hammer. The blazing six leaped out of his nerveless fist. Flame pin-wheeled from the spinning Colt. The slug grazed the Kid an inch below the temple. Just a whizzing glance. A skin-split but no damage to the bone.

Yet the shock of it was harsh, draining the strength from his knees. His legs failed him. He went down, managing to swing the girl so she wasn't injured.

5

THE WILD BUNCH

THE STACCATO crack of a high-powered rifle ripped the sudden stillness. A murmur of awe arose from the darkness where Brazito's men were hidden. The *bandido* on the roof had stopped a shrieking, steel-jacketed slug.

He teetered a moment on dying legs, something close to a grin beneath a well-groomed pencil-line mustache. Then he tumbled over the side, landing on his head in front of the sheriff's office.

Then the main street vibrated to the thunder of galloping hoofs. Wild, whooping yells broke out south of town. Riders were racing the wind into Deadline. Guns bristled in that bunched pack that avalanched down the main street.

Startled cries arose from the Brazito men. The spics behind the spring wagon raced for cover. Brazito roared for his gunsters to make a stand. One of them was caught by a bullet from the oncoming riders. The slug got him while he was diving into the darkness. His hurtling body had left the ground, writhing, pulsating with fear. It landed, a deadweight corpse, clothed in gold-worked velveteen finery.

"The Horde! Calvert's Horde!"

More fearsome than the cry of "Brazito!"—that warning of the Horde. Spics raced for their mounts. From the darkness, shots were aimed at the Kid. But he'd crawled behind the spring wagon, turning it as a shield against his own hand. Terry was there, still dazed, but fast recovering.

Kirpas crouched behind the barrier, babbling hysterically and caressing his six-gun. "I'm a gunman," he chattered in an awed tone. "I have sent a man into the everlastin'. Humble little Kirpas. Despised little Swamps. A gunman, a real, lead-slammin' gunman—at last!"

The Kid's heart leaped with exultancy. The Horde was in. The owl-hooters had trumped Brazito. Had walked their horses across the flat, had silently worked close enough to get the lay, before they announced their arrival in a hoof-thudding, gunblasting onslaught. The Creers younker had done his job.

"Giant" Anderson's thunderclap of a voice boomed out. "Stick with it, Kid. We'll gunsmoke them pigs till they're ready to be sliced into slabs o' tender bacon."

"When you call them spics pigs, yo're shore paying 'em a

compliment." That easy drawl was from "Eagle" Hawn, best safecracker between the Milk River and the Pecos.

"Cheerio, Keed," called Brazito. "I fancy if I stay around, I'll get my jacket soiled. *Quién sabe?*"

The raiders split the breeze for distant territory. Some of the Hordemen headed after them, but the Kid called them back.

"We'll take everything in its proper stride," he said. "I've got to get a medico for Terry. Don't know how bad off she is. She's plumb out of her head. God, if she dies—"

"If she dies," said tall, cadaverous, wintry-eyed Nate Willstock, striking a match to look at the girl's wound, "Deadline will become nothing but a spot that got in the way of a cyclone. Nothing but a lot of splintered wood an' charred sticks. The cyclone will be us."

Crooked law had driven Nate Willstock onto the owl-hoot. Law, crooked or honest, would keep him there. For Willstock had broken the statutes a thousand times. Three-four times he'd watched men erect a gallows and test the rope that was to snap him into eternity. Men thought he was sullen and cruel, a merciless man-brute who craved to throttle and maim.

That was all wrong. He had a shell of bitterness. He never smiled except when he was working his guns. He seemed cynical. He had to be hard. But underneath he had a heart as big as a mountain, a heart that got him in a lot of trouble, because it sent him out helping the underdog, no matter what the odds.

"It's a shame, a damn' shame," muttered Giant Anderson. "Town's full o' strong-backed jaspers. But when somebody's in trouble, when they're liable to get their snouts skinned, they're jest a pack o' coyotes huntin' fer a hole."

"I got to get Terry to Doc Ringel," said the Kid. "He's over at the Creers place."

Eagle Hawn shook his head. "He'll be at the camp by now. Peel and Grama and some o' the boys headed for Creers' spread to bring Dandy back."

"He can't be moved," said the Kid. "He's bad hit."

SAVAGERY SPREAD over Giant's face. He carried two hundred and forty pounds of leathery tissue and hickory-tough sinew on his massive ox-bone frame. He could be as gentle as a playful cub, as vicious as a wounded grizzly.

"Who got him?" Giant demanded. "I'll tie the skunk's backbone in a knot."

"Come on! Come on!" growled the Kid, dodging the question. "This is no spot to make talk. Brazito might come back an' snipe us."

"You head back to the camp with Terry," said Eagle Hawn. "I'll ride to the Creers place. If Ringel's there, I'll bring him along, if I have to hogtie him."

The Kid got his steel-dust Star where he'd ground anchored the sleek mount behind the Broken Spur. He carried Terry on the saddle in front of him. He motioned Kirpas to ride with Nate Willstock.

"Me?" exclaimed the wizened swamper. "You're takin' little Kirpas? Poor little Swamps who cleans up after real men? I'm going with the Horde!" Kirpas swallowed hard. He stroked the butt of the gun thrust in the cast-off piece of lariat that served as his belt.

He looked at the hard, scarred, forbidding face of Nate Willstock. He saw the sleek, tapering hands, a pair of the swiftest gunhands in the West. He stared at his own stubby, blunt, callous-thick paws.

"Little Kirpas has thrown away the mop—forever," he muttered. "But I'll clean their cabins. I'll mend their clothes. I'll shine their boots. Every man has to be an apprentice sometime. I'm an apprentice gunman. You hear that, men? At last—I'm something."

"Halter yore tongue an' climb aboard," growled Willstock.

"Wait!" exclaimed Kirpas. "Wait!"

He straightened his creaking little skeleton of a body. He

stiffened his scrawny neck. And he marched down in front of the Broken Spur Saloon. He sent a slug shattering the first window.

"Kirpas of the Horde in town!" he yelled.

He ruined another window.

"Kirpas of the Horde paying his respects!"

He went up closer and shot out a couple of lamps. Men in the barroom headed for the rear exits. Bartenders who had bullied him ducked out of sight. The proprietor exposed himself to start a plea, but Kirpas sent him waddling for cover. He shot down a pyramid of glasses. Then he blew the smoke from the barrel, deliberately thumbed fresh loads into the Colt, and strutted back to Willstock.

"That's chalked up against yuh, Swamps," said Willstock, poker faced. "It comes under the headin' of entertainment expense."

Kirpas looked puzzledly at Willstock. He couldn't tell from the owl-hooter's bleak expression whether he was joshing or serious.

The Hordemen streaked across the broomweed-studded flats. The Kid looked back. He scowled. During the raid, except for the renegades, Deadline had been like a ghost town. Now lights flashed on, doors opened.

"That's people fer yuh," muttered the Kid, holding a wet bandana to Terry's hot forehead. "The first to yelp fer help, the last to give it."

Sheltered in a dip atop a high, timbered ridge, the Horde's hideout was separated from Deadline by several miles of canyon-slashed country. The going was hard and rough and treacherous, even though the owl-hooters held to the old trails stomped by mossy-horned steers.

From a rock ledge on a frowning butte, Clay Sanish kept an eagle-eyed vigil. He hurled down a challenge when they struck the deer trail that wound through the chaparral up to the hideout. The Kid hailed him.

Sanish left his granite perch. "They brought Dandy in," he said through clamped jaws. Gray and tragedy marked, Clay Sanish had been driven onto the owl-hoot after his son had been hanged for a murder he hadn't committed. Sanish had got old and scarred, hunting down the last of those vigilantes. Now he lived only for the flaming seconds when he blasted some honest-posing drygulcher or suicide maker into boot-hill.

"Who did it, Kid?" he asked grimly. "Who drilled Dandy? Put me hep, son. I'm ready to spray around some liquid hell-fire."

THE KID shook his head. Sanish was dynamite with a short fuse. There'd be too many bones left to bleach in the sun if he went on the prod.

Over the brush-grown rim, the Hordemen rode through a heavy stand of timber, and down into the needle-matted basin, where lights gleamed from old wood-choppers' cabins. No splurge here. As humbly as any ragged nester lived these cold-eyed gunslicks.

From running a shell game to promoting a boomtown, the Hordemen were masters of get-rich-quick schemes. They could have pampered themselves with every luxury. They could have indulged in the grandeur of the richest peon-exploiting don. Yet they lived frugally, denying themselves, eating hard chuck, sleeping on straw-covered bunks.

From the law-twisting rich, they took a lot of *dinero*. They fleeced gouging money grubbers. They levied stiff taxes on land grabbers. But the wealth they sluiced from the unworthy, they passed on to the needy.

Dandy McLain had been brought back on a stretcher of rawhide laced to a piñon-pole frame. Anxiety lined the Kid's face. He carried Terry to a cabin and called Doc Ringel.

"McLain's got an even chance," said the medico, answering the fear that showed in the Kid's eyes. "He's in a quiet sleep now. Don't wake him." Ringel nodded for the owl-hooter to get out.

The Kid paced before the door of Terry's cabin. His hands were shaky. He had to get Grama Sinton to roll him a quirley.

"We're ready to fog clean to hell to blast the skunk who plugged Dandy," said Sinton in a mild voice. He spoke with a gentle smile, and his brown eyes were as soft and glowing as a calf's. But there was a lobo deadliness behind his gentle manner. "I'm fer makin' the whole of Deadline eat crow."

Doc Ringel came out. "Flesh crease," he said casually. "Slight concussion. She needs a rest. In a day or so, she'll be up and riding."

A grizzled, turkey-necked, gangle-legged old duffer with pop eyes and a drooping cowhorn mustache heard the verdict. He bowlegged from the cook house, toting a steaming bowl.

"By coots, it's shore nice to have Terry in camp," said Peel Rogers. "I reckon now she'll l'arn we ain't the mangy critters she's been tallyin' us fer."

The Kid's face darkened. His mouth took on a sullen downward curve. Old Peel hadn't been in that wild flight from a mad-dog posse. The Kid relived those soul-shriveling moments. Again he saw the girl fire at him. His lips curled. He ran his fingers over the bullet groove on his neck. All his life he'd carry the scar of her treachery. Old Peel's eyes glowed at the look of savagery on the Kid's face.

"Yeah," said the wrinkled veteran, "we'll get 'em, son. We'll gunsmoke Brazito's bunch o' fancy dudes into pine boxes. I know how yuh feel. Brazito got Terry plugged, an'—"

The Kid walked away, face twisting.

"Hey," said Peel, holding out the bowl, "ain't yuh takin' this sage-hen soup to the gal? She'll be wantin' to see yuh. Wantin' to thank yuh."

The Kid whirled. Touched that raw bullet rip again. "Yeah." His tone was heavy. "Yeah, she'll be wantin' to thank me. But me—I ain't in the mood to hear any gush today." He strode to his cabin, muttering.

Later, he sent a Hordeman for a nurse—Mary Little Fawn,

wife of an Apache trapper. She arrived in camp on a sad-eyed burro. Mary was a grunting old squaw woman, who'd eaten her way out of the fawn class years ago. Her face looked like a dried apple with holes in it. But her gentle hands had been a blessing to scores of sick and injured.

She chased Peel Rogers out of the cook house. She stole Nate Willstock's favorite and foulest pipe. She lumbered around the hideout, puffing great clouds of smoke and bossing everybody. Mary would have fought a famished cougar in defense of a Hordeman. The owl-hooters had saved her man from a hang-rope, and they were her brood.

The girl was up, staying close to her cabin, or walking through the pines with Mary Little Fawn. Often she spoke to the Kid. He wouldn't answer her. He was downright rude. He knew he was rude—and he meant to be.

Dandy McLain heard about it. He sent for the Kid. "What are yuh up on ear about?" he demanded. "I'm the one who got plugged. Quit actin' like an ornery mule. She couldn't help headin' that posse, could she? When yuh sit in a game, play the hand that's dealt to yuh. Take the cards as they fall."

The Kid smirked. He wasn't the smirking kind. That attitude had always been beneath him. But now a vein of ugliness was pulsing through his nature. He was human. He was haunted by the picture of the girl behind a flaming gun.

The Kid stormed out of the cabin.

HE'D DONE a lot of talking about turning into a hell-riding sidewinder. Yet he worried about that little maverick. He worried like hell. Men fogged through the country trying to pick up some clue about the little fellow.

The Kid sent his long-riders below the Line. They learned nothing there. No onc knew about the nameless waif found in that deserted old shack. The Kid didn't want the baby brought to the camp, but he was uneasy about having the little thing at the Creers spread.

He rode to the homestead, and paid old Zack to take his family and the baby to a hideout far from the beaten trails.

"We jest about love the little rascal to death," said Ma Creers. "It hurts to think I'll have to give him up. Can't we have him?"

"Have him as long as he ain't claimed," said the Kid, holding the jabbering little fellow in his arms. "Now, remember, Zack—get out o' here pronto. Hit fer the ol' Stevens' shack. Use the streams an' backtrack plenty. Get yore grub at Beaver Creek."

From the Creers homestead, the Kid rode to the Gallinas spread. This land, sixty miles of grass-rich fertility, had been a grant from the king of Spain to a Gallinas many generations removed. A woman owned the vast domain—Dona Consuelo de Gallinas y Pajarito.

The Kid reined Star into the ranch yard. Three cowpunchers bounded quickly around a corner of the great, thick-walled adobe mansion. No welcome showed in the grim set of their seamed faces. Guns glinted in labor-gnarled hands. Thumbs yanked back gun hammers.

"Up with 'em, hombre!" snapped a weather-beaten veteran.

"To hell with that!" boomed a curly-headed gent. "I'm pluggin' him. He's trespassin', ain't he?"

"Damn' right he is!" rasped the third man, tall, swarthy. "Let him have it! He's fancy lookin'. He's from Brazito. It's written all over him. He's a Brazito man."

Guns leveled. The Kid shouted. A chill crawled his spine. These gents weren't bluffing. Hate glared from their eyes. Thumbs were slacking off from gun hammers.

6

GHOST RANCHO

THE KID grabbed for the sky. "Hold it, yuh chuckle-heads. Ease down them hammers. Buck, yuh doggone old walrus, gunfire makes my ears ring. You know that. Postpone my execution. I just had a stack o' flapjacks, an' they ain't plumb-digested yet."

"Huh!" "Buck" Manvers peered through age-dimmed eyes. "Waal, damn my heart, it's the Kid. It's Calvert. Step down, stranger. Yuh oughta announce yoreself, feller."

"Yuh bet," put in the curly-headed one, whose left arm was bandaged. "Brazito's ridin' us hard. Run off fifty head last night. We're the only jaspers what ain't been killed or scared away. Me an' Joe got plugged."

"An' we're plumb ringy about it," said the swarthy puncher Joe, walking with a limp. "That Brazito lobo set fire to the line camp on the north range. Hell, pard, Curly was goin' to sling lead at yuh."

The Kid dismounted and shook hands. He nodded toward the adobe mansion. "Everybody gone, huh. Last time I was here, yuh had a reg'lar village."

The old-timer kicked at a rock. Buck Manvers had been with the Gallinas spread since his horse-wrangling days. Fifty years at least. In good times he'd ramrodded twenty or thirty punchers who'd handled upwards of twenty-five thousand head. Gringo punchers had worked the stock. But a score of peons and their families had performed the chores. And a bunkhouse had always been filled with pilgrims and chuck-line riders.

"Village is right," said Manvers. "Jest a ghost town now."

"Looks to me like Brazito is bustin' this spread to get the land," said the Kid. "What's happened to the lady? Why doesn't Dona Consuelo come back?"

Old Manvers tugged at his cowhorn mustache. "Something's wrong, Kid—doggone wrong. Yuh know, she hasn't been here since Don Adolfo got sniped."

"Her husband was murdered a year ago, wasn't he?"

The ranch foreman nodded. "Had a nervous breakdown. In a Denver hospital most of the time. I sent word to her. No answer. She wouldn't let the Hatchet down. Not Consuelo.

She—"The lines deepened in his seamed face. "Mebbe—mebbe she's daid!"

The range veteran gazed over the vast expanse that reached through the haze far beyond the purple bulwarks of the sheltering hills.

A wistful smile played on his lips. "I toddled the dona on my knee when she wasn't bigger'n chipmunk. Gentled her fust pony." His eyes widened as he warmed to reminiscence. "Why, fer years the Hatchet brand was my mark, when I had to sign anything legal. I was nighthawkin' here afore Deadline was even a flea-infested Apache village."

The Kid felt some of the wrenching anguish that gripped the sun-dried cowman. The old gentleman told of the great herds that had first seen daylight here, fattened, gone down the long trail.

"Punchers!" exclaimed Manvers. "Why I've had father, son, an' grandson workin' stock on the Hatchet. Scores of the best tophands in the cow country roped thar fust critters on the Gallinas spread."

The Kid felt a stirring within him. Manvers' age-dimmed eyes were seeing ghosts. His two punchers caressed worn holsters, muttering about Brazito.

"Look at them adobes!" yelled Manvers. "Yuh'd think nothin' but bats an' hoot-owls an' saddle tramps ever holed up thar. But yo're wrong—dead wrong. Why, the *bailes* they had in the big house— The music is ringin' in my ears right now." The old gentleman pointed at a balcony. "Up thar—in the south corner—Don Ramon got the *señorita* who became Consuelo's mother to agree to tolerate him. Thuty y'ars ago, come fall roundup."

Manvers choked. "This tobaccy o' yores dries my throat," he said to the dark puncher Joe, shooting a hard glance from under bushy brows.

"What I can't understand, Kid," interrupted Joe, "is whar

Brazito herds the stock. He drives the critters into Sudden River."

"The river flows from under the cliffs of the San Toriba Mountains on the west, doesn't it?" asked the Kid.

"Yeah," said Curly, "an' we've follered the stream east fer miles. No sign atall. The beef go into Sudden River an' they don't come out. It's plumb spooky."

"THUTY Y'ARS ago." Buck was still in his reverie. "I was meanderin' about. I seed the pair o' them. A picture, I tell yuh. The music was floatin' out. Plenty o' laughin' comin' with it. Castinets was clickin'. A *señorita* was singin'—"

The Kid's lips tightened. He gazed into Manvers' burning eyes, glimpsed the chaos of memories that was ripping the veteran's spirit.

The old-timer slowly stoked up his pipe, nodding his head. "Wasn't all laughin' an' waltzin'. Francisco, Don Ramon's brother, was disowned fer marryin' a dance-hall gal. The smallpox got us one y'ar. Took the don's fust-born. An' then came the black-leg. Thar was gunfightin', too. Even in the happiest times. But it was—waal—it was life. Do yuh get me, Kid? Understand?"

"I understand, all right," said the Kid. "I understand plenty."

The leathery old fellow gazed sadly toward the mountains. "The land's here. Allus will be here. But we're gone. The Hatchet brand will be vented. The Gallinas name will be only on yellowed tally books."

Manvers' shoulders sagged. "Yet the streams flow on. The grama is hock-high. The barrier ridges still shelter winter range. Miles of summer grazin' fer the antelope an' deer. But not enough beef left to stock a ten-section spread. Brazito—a dude spic. Jest a dude spic—"

Manvers' creviced face worked, jiggling the drooping mustache comically. But the Kid did not smile. Instead, he gazed at the old puncher, and made a solemn vow. It was a desecration that a swaggering marauder from below the Line should pillage this land.

The Gallinas grant had aided a flourishing community when Brazito's grandparents were ragged peons. Brazito was an upstart—a strutting renegade. He had to go.

"Yuh stickin', Manvers?" the Kid asked gruffly.

"Some day, if yuh see a sun-bleached skeleton on the Hatchet range that measures nigh six foot, look fer a bullet hole in the third rib on the left side. Got that puncture in the beef an' mutton war twenty-one y'ars ago, come brandin' time."

Joe and Curly were staying.

"All right," said the Kid. "Don't be invitin' lead, an' keep guard all the time. When Brazito swings a hungry loop again, send up a signal. Smoke by day; fire at night."

Manvers was trembling like an old prospector who'd made a big strike. "Yuh mean—"

"Yuh've done cut yoreself an ornery string o' raw broncs. As long as the Horde has a crow-hop left, count on it to keep that Brazito herd from roamin' wild on this range. I'll have a lookout posted. Send up yore signal an' help will be a-trailin'."

The punchers whooped it up like cow-pokes primed on redeye. Manvers stood stunned. Like a condemned man who'd got a reprieve after the noose had been adjusted. The Kid crawled his mount and the steel-dust headed out.

He rode back to the Horde's hideout, feeling that balance had been restored. He'd carry on as his father had planned, living and fighting for the principles that had cost old Gunner Calvert his life.

In the swaying top of a skyscraping pine, the Kid posted a lookout. He told the owl-hooters his promise to Buck Manvers. Faces set; eyes grew flinty. The weathered old ramrod of the Gallinas spread was a real jasper. On the Hatchet there'd always been an extra plate of chuck and a warm bunk for a Calvert man. The clan was eager to burn powder in defense of the *hacienda*.

"We best be saddlin' up," suggested Giant Anderson.

The Kid shook his head. "Oil yore Colts, but we'll wait till the signal goes up. That might happen a week from now. Or mebbe in the next five minutes."

"With only three left, Brazito will be foggin' in right pronto," put in Nate Willstock.

"They're bait," admitted the Kid. "If we head in, Brazito will hold off till we leave. But those three will draw the damn' spics."

HEADS NODDED. Eyes glowed at the prospect. The Hordemen were bandits, richer bounty for the reward hunters than the Brazito renegades. In the eyes of the law, the Calvert men were more desperate, more treacherous than the spics. That was because the law judged a man only by the statutes that he broke.

It was not in the law's province to consider that the statutes were broken in the name of a higher justice than book code. But the Brazito pack violated that higher justice, and the Horde vowed to gun those hellions out of existence.

The Kid found Kirpas back of the cabins, practicing the draw. Old Peel Rogers was trying to get the little swamper to flash his hands in a circle. That made the draw a blended movement that didn't stop until the guns leaped up for business.

Kirpas snagged the sights on his gun belt. "I'll never learn," he muttered. "I'm jest a clumsy-pawed little gopher, an' I oughta crawl back into my hole at the Broken Spur. I'm only a half-pint."

"Hell, man," said Peel. "I done swigged some powerful liquid dynamite thet'd been poured into half-pints."

The swamper tried again. The Kid shook his head. Kirpas was all tensed up. He shot his hands straight downward. Made two distinct motions. The pause between those motions was the split-second that meant life or death in a gunfight.

"Yuh gotta smooth it down a lot," the Kid said kindly. "Watch me. I don't claim to be lightnin', but mebbe yuh can get what I mean."

The Kid's hand dissolved in a brown blur that exploded into

red flame. A hole dead center showed in the ace of diamonds tacked to a tree trunk twenty feet away. Peel Rogers nodded.

Kirpas gulped. "Wonderful!" he breathed. "I could never do that. Do you think, Mister Calvert, I could ever be half that good?"

"No handle on my name, old-timer," said the Kid genially.

Kirpas swallowed hard. "I used to dream o' something like this. Of being a Hordeman, respected, feared. Those dreams made me forget the mops an' spittoons an' bullyin' bartenders."

Kirpas had shot Boday, and the Kid had to pay the debt. But the swamper wasn't Horde material. The Kid would allow him to stay around camp a while. The owl-hooters would humor the little man, build up his ego.

Then the Kid would talk Kirpas into homesteading, and stake him to a chance for independence.

Eagle Hawn sauntered over, nodded to Kirpas.

"I don't like that jasper," Eagle Hawn told the Kid later. "He's slimy. Makes me think of something that crawls."

The Kid smiled. "Yeah, I have the same feelin'. But I want to be easy with him. He's a little coot who got cheated at birth. Hell, everybody deserves a decent chance."

The Kid was entering his cabin when Terry touched his arm. He turned. The sight of her took his breath away. The few days rest had restored the delicate tint to her cheeks, the dancing lights to her eyes. The closeness of her made his heart trip-hammer.

He wanted to scowl, but instead he grinned. It was a sheepish grin that kept widening. Not much charm came into the Kid's life, and he succumbed to her loveliness. He felt like a fool, and her look, half amused, half reproachful, made him flush. He raised a hand to that bullet crease.

She groped for words to break the awkward silence. "You have a bad cut on your neck."

The Kid shrugged. "Just a scratch," he muttered. "Yore aim wasn't so good."

The girl gave a start. "My aim? I—I don't understand."

His lips thinned. "You shot me!"

7

THE BARRIER

TERRY'S FACE blanched. She grasped her throat and shrank back, horror in her eyes. The Kid scowled at the ground, and began tracing a finger along the seam of his holster. From behind the cabins where Kirpas practiced the draw came the drone of the swamper's voice.

"I—shot—you!" murmured the girl. She stared at that ugly flesh rip. "No! It's untrue. You are lying, Kid Calvert. You're trying to hurt me. I—I—"

Her outburst broke the spell. The Kid suddenly wanted to hurt her. She deserved to be hurt.

"Mebbe next time yuh'll drill me dead center. Yuh did yore duty, didn't yuh?" Bitterness arose in his tone. "I'm bounty. I'm just a lobo the law's tryin' to exterminate. I admire yore nerve, lady, but I advise yuh to go back with Kirpas an' practice shootin'."

The girl's jaw quivered. Tears glistened in her eyes, and the corners of her mouth pulled down. She clutched the Kid's arm, and instantly he knew that he was lost again. How could anyone hate Terry? It amazed him that a harsh thought of her ever entered his head. He gazed into those hurt-clouded eyes, and felt a throb in his throat.

"I was aiming wide," she faltered. "I ordered my men to do that. It was my duty to bring you in, but I meant to bring you in alive. Oh, you don't understand. You'll never understand. If I had only my own feelings to consider, I—I— But I took an oath. The citizens have put their trust in me—"

"They were trustin' yuh in a funny way back in Deadline."

The two walked along a brush-lined trail away from camp. A doe stared at them with startled eyes, nudged its fawn into flight, and raced away. A bluejay scolded them from its pine-limb perch. Sadness and futility engulfed the Kid, while a strange exultation leaped within him. The rift between them had been spanned, yet a barrier held them from meeting on common ground.

"I feel no bitterness toward Deadline," said Terry. "Brazito planted letters and money in my office. It's rather flattering to know that he wants me out of the way. That mob was his work. You know now that Boday was his underling. And why should the town believe me innocent? Haven't lots of sheriffs used their office as a cover for outlawry? I'm even glad that the people kept out of sight. Brazito would have mowed them down."

She looked up at the Kid and teeth like matched pearls glistened through her smile. The Kid's eyes glowed. Terry didn't hate him. He felt sure of it. And never had they been so close to understanding. He was actually thankful for that bullet crease. And bitterness, which had been withering his spirit, dissolved into rapture that effervesced into maddening happiness.

"Stan, I think I can explain about that shooting," she spoke softly. The Kid felt that he was treading clouds. Stan was the name she had first known him by. Only in those rare moments when they lost their identity of hunter and hunted did she use it.

"It doesn't need explainin'," said the Kid.

"Windage," said the girl. "I'm not a poor shot. You know that. And I was sure of my aim. But I forgot about windage. The wind can swerve a bullet amazingly. And a stiff wind was blowing from the east."

The Kid grasped her hand, and it was lost in his big paw. Their shoulders touched. The fragrance of her golden hair dizzied him. She looked at him and was unable to speak.

They reached the rim of the ridge, and stood gazing across a lush valley where antelope grazed.

He turned to Terry and took her hands. "Yuh heard me talk about love before. I reckon it musta been pretty funny. I reckon yuh had a hard time to keep from laughin'. But it ain't no laughin' matter to me, lovin' a girl whose job is to get me hung. There's probably some danged fancy ways o' tellin' a girl she's the most wonderful person livin'."

THE KID felt the sudden pressure of her hand. And then she pulled away. But the protest in her manner was not shown in her eyes.

"Why do you say that?" she cried. "Whatever you feel; whatever I feel—we're enemies. Nothing can change that."

The Kid laughed. "Now, listen, Terry. Be reasonable. Yuh've met the Calvert men. Yuh've been helped by us. Every ornery son of us would walk into a rattlers' den, if it'd help yuh."

The girl nodded. "I like the men in the Horde. I like them better than most law-abiding folks."

"*Bueno!* Now we're gettin' somewhere. Listen, here's the lay. We're workin' together after this. The Horde's outside the law. We're not cramped by laws made by stuffy, near-sighted old judges. We don't worry about what's on the books. The Horde has a code that lets us do anything that brings happiness to the deservin' an' smashes the skunks."

The Kid's eyes were shining. "Yuh hire deputies, but yo're never shore o' them, are yuh?"

"Most men will take a bribe," admitted Terry. "But I am certain nobody can corrupt Deputy Root. That's why he's laid up with one of Brazito's bullets in his leg."

"Uh huh." The Kid's enthusiasm mounted. "An' the Hordemen are outside the law. If we were out to grab, we wouldn't be livin' like a pack o' sheepherders. Bribery is penny-ante stuff fer gents like Dandy McLain an' Nate Willstock an' the rest. We cheat an' steal. But we do it to spread *dinero* around where it'll ease sufferin'."

The two started along the trail toward camp. Dusk was thickening. Already in the east night was crowding out the day.

"Terry," said the Kid, "I want yuh an' the Horde to work together. Folks are thinkin' yuh throwed in with the Horde. We'll fix you right with Deadline. We'll make it seem yuh was held prisoner here. We'll send down a ransom note. Later, yuh can go back makin' out yuh escaped. An' between us, workin' from both ends, we can smash gents like Brazito."

Some one shouted back in camp. Carried away by his plans, the Kid scarcely heard the outcry.

"Our first job will be to gentle Brazito," went on the Kid. "After that, whenever some critter is disturbin' the range, send word to us. We'll dab a loop on the jasper, flank him down, an' plumb dehorn him."

The girl's eyes were wistful, but she shook her head. "There is so much that is good about you— It hurts me to think that you are outside the law. But you *have* violated the law that I have put above my life."

The Kid frowned. "Yeah," he protested, "but me an' the Horde have done it in the name of right. Believe me, Terry."

"I wish I could—"

MEN WERE shouting back in camp. In the horse pasture, lariats snaked through the air. Giant Anderson was calling the Kid. But the Kid was unheeding. His temper was up. Trying to make Terry see his side was like crashing through a stone wall with his fists—impossible.

"When I pinned on my father's star," the girl was saying, "I realized that my own happiness was the last to consider. I made up my mind that I would be impartial. I would follow out the dictates of the law to the letter. Friendship, love, personal feelings—nothing would come before the law."

"Not even mercy, huh?" growled the Kid.

"You are unfair!" cried the girl.

"Terry Reynolds talkin', folks," the Kid flung back. "The girl who shot that Calvert lunkhead, who would have given his life for her. Why, doggone it, she—she'd hang me if she got the chance."

A sob escaped her. She brushed a weary hand across her face. "Yes," she murmured. "I would. You have killed, Kid Calvert. The law demands your life. Some day I—I'll have to—"

The Kid's face hardened. His eyes burned. "At least, yo're frank," he spoke harshly. He strode away angrily.

"Kid—Kid—please—" The girl called after him. Her voice broke.

The Kid heard Giant calling him, and broke into a run. The Hordemen were gathered before the cabins. Mounts stood saddled, stomping, champing bits. Eagle Hawn was tightening the cinch on the steel-dust Star. At the sight of the Kid, men vaulted into leather.

"Buck sent up his signal, huh?" spoke the Kid. "All right. I hope those gents can stand 'em off till we get there. Couple o' yuh boys'll have to stay. Dandy an' Doc can't go. An' there's Terry an' old Mary."

The Kid eyed them shrewdly. Faces hid behind sullen masks; eyes shifted.

"No volunteers, eh?" laughed the Kid. "We draw lots then."

Grama Sinton and Peel Rogers lost. Grama didn't voice his disappointment, but turkey-necked Peel howled that he'd been framed.

The Horde hit the trail. In camp stayed Dandy and Doc Ringel, with Sinton, Rogers, and Clay Sanish on guard. Some one had roped a horse for Kirpas. He packed two guns, and in his eyes gleamed madness. Before they got over the next ridge, a line-backed dun thundered up the trail into the pack. Terry astride Grama Sinton's pony.

"I thought yuh was against the Horde," snapped the Kid.

"I am," flung back the girl. "But I'm against Brazito, too."

"We're outlaws!" granted the Kid. "We're killers—an' we're goin' to kill!"

"Yes," said the girl. "But you'll do it this time in the name of the law. Men," she shouted, "I'm deputizing every man here. You're working now for Washakie County."

The Kid's scowl brightened into a smile. What a girl. He knew he ought to hate her. He knew he should be granite. But he wasn't granite. He was soft clay that she could mold at will. Admiration warmed him. She had sand.

They didn't spare their mounts. They couldn't spare their mounts. Down on the Hatchet three men were making a stand against a kill-crazy pack that might number a score. They might hold the spics off for hours, yet maybe now they were finished.

The Kid didn't think so. Atop a hill, he saw a splash of fire against the night sky. The flames kept mounting. Somebody was feeding the blaze. The mounts were lathered and foaming when the clan swooped down from the last saw-toothed ridge into the broad valley rolling out to the boundaries of the Gallinas grant.

Pain suddenly pounded in the Kid's throat. The fire had died. Only a star-pierced smudge showed where the signal had flamed up.

"Too late!" muttered the Kid. "Poor old Buck."

8

WAR ON THE HATCHET

THE WORD went down the line that the fight was over, at least, Buck's fight. He was done. It was a certainty he was done. Or Buck would have kept that signal flaring up. The streaking broncs got the spurs. The owl-hoot clan swept across the levels more swiftly than the wind rushing in from the south. And it was a savage pack that kept eyes straight ahead.

During the slow going in the chasm-slashed uplands, Kirpas

had stayed with the wild bunch. He had jiggled around on the saddle and got a shaking up, but the mount, though weakly ridden, had taken the bit and held close. Now the owl-hooters pulled away. They couldn't let the greenhorn set the pace. Farther and farther the little swamper dropped behind, until he was swallowed in the night.

The wind shifted, blowing from the southwest. The Kid uttered an exultant whoop. The rattle of guns reached him.

"Push them crowbaits, men!" he yelled. "Buck's still in it!"

Star lengthened out in a stride that left the rest choking in his dust. The steel dust showed the fleetness of a deer. Crouched low in the saddle, the Kid peered through the gloom. Guns pounded in the Hatchet ranch yard. The Kid grinned and nodded. Stabs of flame slashed out from the roof of the adobe mansion. Answering flashes lanced from the sheds and bunk-houses.

Buck and his men had gained the roof. There they could command respect until their supply of lead gave out.

The Kid felt a tug at his hat. A sharp crack ripped out from the west. A vicious utterance rasped from the Kid's throat. He swung his mount out of stride, sending Star catapulting across an arroyo. A shriek a little ahead of him showed how wise had been that sudden shift. A sniper had fired in front of the Kid, and a screeching, steel-jacketed slug told that Star would have carried the Kid into that rifle fire.

A jerk of the reins brought the steel-dust to a sliding, stiff-legged halt. From the oak-hard knot that was the Kid's fist spiked a Colt. The rifle barked again. The bullet just skinned the back of the cantle. Flame spouted from the Kid's gun.

He triggered at the orange-red streak spurting from a patch of saccaton grass growing higher than the head of a man on horseback. A Spanish oath ripped out. Shod hoofs clinked on the gravelly bed of an arroyo. From the saccaton darted a pony carrying a sombreroed rider. The rifle had gone into the saddle scabbard. A brown paw wrapped around the butt of a long-barreled six. Twisting in the leather, the spic rocketed lead at the Kid.

A wild clamor arose from the ranch headquarters. The attack shifted. The men on the roof got a respite, while lead burned around the Kid. Lead nipped him. Lead whined a promise of swift oblivion. The sniper got the range, and twice he came within a slice of picking the Kid off. Then the renegade's gun clicked empty. That was good. That was plenty damned good.

There was a twist to the Kid's mouth, a hard, fighting twist. He had this chilli bean on the receiving end now. The Kid's gun began to talk.

The spic clawed for his second iron. Half out of the holster leaped that Brazito man's .45. Twice the Kid's Colt snarled. The spic howled. Agony was in that howl—and hate.

The killer clutched a shattered wrist. Knife-pointed rowels raked crimson streaks on the pony's quivering flanks. He yelled to his swarthy cronies. He begged them to blast the Kid into a bullet-sieved carcass. They tried to oblige. They sure tried to do that spic a favor. The Kid kept Star zigzagging like a cutting horse after a steer. That saved him from aimed shots. But wild lead whined close.

MADLY THE spic spurred for a getaway. All the while he snarled curses at the gringo crowding his trail. Even taunted him. The spic's right hand flashed over in a cross-arm draw. But a blood-slippery butt and a bouncing horse made him fumble. The gun went spinning.

The Kid's face was somber. He waved both arms, signaling his men to form a broad fan. Giant answered. Back of the Kid, guns pounded from both sides. The clan was spreading. There'd be no bunched-up target for the Brazito hellions.

A few lengths behind the fleeing spic plunged the relentless steel-dust. The bandit fought to get his rifle clear. He yanked the high-powered weapon from the scabbard. His mount shied from a prairie-dog hole. The violent twist flung the gun out of the killer's hand.

The Kid was close. He took his lariat from the saddle, and shook out a loop. Those hellions in the ranch yard couldn't get him now. Not unless they burned down a crony. Nate Willstock yelled for the Kid to cut back and drop to the shelter of a barranca. From the mansion roof sounded the bull-throated voice of Buck Manvers.

"Haul in, son! They'll git yuh. They're swarmin' all over. We can't cover yuh from here. We can't. We—can't."

"Stan! Stan!" the fear-laden cry of the girl sent a strange sensation through the Kid.

The dude in front of him turned and sneered. He was a handsome brute, save for the mouth shaped in a perpetual leer.

"*Señor*, you who are about to die, I salute."

Up went a stiff hand to the brim of a conchaed sombrero. The Kid could have shot the roof of his head off. But the man had no gun. The Kid couldn't drop a man cold. None of the Horde could.

Then the spic went out of the saddle. He spilled as though a bullet had taken him. Frenzied shouts arose from the Brazito crowd.

"Cheerio, Keed Calvert, old chap. I daresay you've caught the idea, what? We're going to keel you. Eet's a bleeding shame, but you're a bit of a nuisance, you know."

Brazito himself speaking from the darkness. Brazito with his English affectations getting tangled with his border accent. A hurricane of lead stormed at the Kid. But he wasn't in the saddle. He was in air, spinning over and over.

Terry uttered an anguished cry. A mad outburst roared from the Horde. A hungering lobo pack was swooping in, untamed, savage. The Kid was down. That was what the Horde thought. That was what Manvers thought, and Brazito.

"Eet's a beastly shame, and all that—"

"Brazito, yuh mangy cur," screamed Manvers, "yuh murdered the Kid! Step into the moonlight, an' I'll ram lead through thet silly monocle thing in yore eye!"

They thought the Kid was all through. Only the spic sniper knew how wrong they were. The spic had dived into a drift of tumbleweeds piled high against sagebrush. He had dived to make a clear target of the owl-hooter.

But scarcely had he landed than a hurtling body crashed down on him. The Kid savvied the dude's move. A knife flashed from the *bandido's* jacket. He slashed at the Kid's back. The gleaming blade ripped the vest, left a crimson line on the flesh.

The Kid sucked in air. The pain nearly got him. And he had a white man's horror of cold steel, anyway. He grabbed the spic's wrist. His fingers closed in a steel-trap grip. Wrist bones crunched. No time to pause here. The Kid had to get going. This gent out of commission first, and then run down Brazito, before the chief put a long trail behind him.

Already hoofs were drumming away from the ranch yard. The Horde was closing in. That meant a cross-fire, that meant hanging on the rim of hell for the Brazito crowd. The Horde thought the Kid had been shot, and they thundered in to wipe out the *bandidos.* Their savage offense proved a good defense. The Kid glimpsed Giant racing in, operating a pair of sixes. The girl was in it, too.

"Well, dude, yore *amigos* are leavin' yuh behind," grated the Kid. "So yo're nominated as spokesman for the pack." He wrenched the knife out of the smooth, callous-free hand. A gunster's hand. "Yo're goin' to waggle yore tongue, an' tell us all about Brazito."

"*Señor,* Brazito teach hees *paisanos* to have a ver-ry short tongue. Even the gr-reat Calvert greengo weel get no talk that I do not want to geeve."

The Kid rammed his fist into the spic's leer. The *bandido* got a hand free and snatched at the owl-hooter's holstered gun. A short, numbing jolt to the jaw ended that play. The Brazito man lay still, stunned.

The fighting had ceased around the mansion. The marauders had fled. Dragging his captive up, the Kid sent him staggering to the ranch yard. Terry saw him and uttered a glad cry. Buck and his two punchers lowered themselves from the roof. They looked as though they'd been mauled by cougars. Their clothes were splashed with red and their faces smeared from bullet creases. The Hordemen were pounding after the Brazito pack.

FIVE *BANDIDOS* lay dead, and a sixth joined them while Terry knelt to ease his pain. The Kid's prisoner made a lunge for the girl, hand snaking out for her Colt. He would have got the gun if he hadn't lunged into the path of a malletlike fist. A fist like an oak knot. The Kid's fist. A paralyzing smash to the point of the jaw rocked the spic to his heels. A shudder went through the powerful frame. The *bandido's* legs seemed to dissolve.

"Man, man!" exclaimed the puncher Curly. "Thet'd make a buffalo curl up its toes!"

Joe, the dark one, inspected the spread-eagled renegade. *"Amigo,* he's as cold as a percentage dame's heart."

"See if his jaw's busted," said the Kid anxiously.

Curly waggled the spic's chin. "Ain't in good chawin' condition, but I reckon he'll be able to open it wide enough to ladle in soup."

The Kid nodded. "Then he'll be able to talk. *Bueno!*"

Buck Manvers started to tell Terry what an upstanding jasper the Kid was. The owl-hooter cut him short.

"Think Brazito ran off any stock?"

Manvers nodded. "After yuh left, me an' the boys rounded up fifty head, an' shoved 'em into the brandin' corral—"

"Uh huh," broke in the Kid. "Figured Brazito had one o' his dudes watchin' yuh, eh? Just laid out a little bait."

"Thet's right," said Manvers. "With the Horde backin' me, I wanted the showdown pronto. Waal, the stock's gone."

The Kid and Terry headed after the Horde. The trail had ended at Sudden River. Sign showed that the steers had been herded into the stream. The *bandidos* had ridden into the water, too. A tenderfoot could have read sign on that. And all had vanished. As though swallowed by quicksand.

Owl-hooters fogged along the river. A couple of miles to the west Sudden River flowed from under the cliffs of the San Toriba Mountains. A deep pool swirled there, water bubbling from under the granite wall jutting below the surface. For miles the long-riders trailed eastward. No sign. Not one fresh hoof-print. They reached a waterfall tumbling to jagged rocks.

"We musta followed a dead trail that looked hot," said Giant.

They went back to the mansion. The Kid puzzled over the strange disappearance. No herd of stock or fifteen-man gun spread went down that waterfall. On the San Toriba side a strong swimmer might have stroked against the current and under the rocky cliffs. But not men and horses; not fifty spooky beef critters.

He knew that his bunch hadn't followed a dead trail. There was a chance that the renegade pack had traveled downstream and disappeared in a cavern under the overhang of the river bank. He'd find out when he persuaded his spic prisoner to talk. But back at the ranch-house, he found the *bandido* beyond persuasion. The *bandido* had a bullet between the eyes.

"I'm sorry, Kid," said Curly. "I had to do it. The jughead snatched a hogleg when Joe bent over to tie him. Plugged Buck in the arm, an' would 'a' got Joe, if—if—"

THE KID put a hand on Curly's shoulder. "What else could yuh have done? Joe's life is worth a regiment o' skunks like that spiggoty." He managed to hide his disappointment.

He wanted the Hatchet trio to slope for the Horde's hideout. Not Buck. Buck wasn't leaving home range. And the cowhands had thrown in with the old ramrod to the finish.

The Horde, with Terry, lined out for the owl-hoot camp. Playing a sudden hunch, the Kid headed along another trail that brought him to Zack Creers' homestead. The cabin was deserted, but it had been entered, ransacked. Drawers had been emptied. Letters and bills littered the room.

"Mebbe saddle tramps," muttered the Kid. "But probably some gents wanting to find out something. About the baby? Where he was taken? Hm-m-m. Figured they'd find a note, I reckon. Who would want to know? Who—"

The moon was riding low when the Kid reached the hideout. Star climbed the steep deer trail to the ridge. The Kid looked up at the sentinel butte. He scowled. If old Sanish had gone to sleep—

His gaze shifted to the trail. Something caught his eye. He stiffened, gave voice to a moan. In the gleam of the moon, he saw dark stains on the brush. Blood. He glanced up at the vacant ledge, Sanish's perch. His head whirled. He suddenly felt like a feeble old man. He had a hollow sensation in the pit of his stomach. As though dread had burned out his vitals.

He spurred Star over the ridge. The Horde was there, a somber, bleak-eyed clan talking in subdued voices. The men had saddled fresh mounts. The men stood waiting, drawn faces ghastly from torturing anxiety. The girl came from her cabin. Seldom did she give way to tears, but the eyes she turned up to the Kid were moist and glistening.

"Oh, Stan," she cried. "Stan!" She tried to hold back a sob.

Nate Willstock strode up, clutched the Kid's shoulder. "I reckon yuh figured it out?"

The Kid nodded wearily. "All of them?" he murmured. "Everyone?"

"Yes," husked Willstock. "Dandy, Doc, Grama, Peel, Clay, Mary. They're gone. Must 'a' got little Swamps, too. Mebbe they're alive. Mebbe.... The men are breakin', son. They'll comb the depths o' hell fer them Brazito snakes. Yuh can't expect 'em to think o' the code."

"I expect 'em to," muttered the Kid. "There ain't goin' to be no butcherin' of innocents. Not as long as I can hold a gun."

The Kid felt that he was going to drop. He grappled with a rebelling nature. An iron will steadied him against collapse. Even iron cracked under tension. But the Kid couldn't crack. Too much lay at stake. Lives... lives....

Dandy had been sort of a foster father. Dandy in Brazito's hands. The Kid's very soul shuddered at the thought. And Doc Ringel. One burning slug, one slice of a gleaming blade, would cheat the world of his surgical skill.

No one knew just what had happened. Raiders had been here. The little group was gone. The renegades left a clear trail. But the dazed owl-hooters had held back, needing guidance.

Brazito himself hadn't been here. Possibly it wasn't the work of his band. Maybe vigilantes from Deadline had ridden in. The Kid reeled toward his men. He felt a weariness that no rest could relieve.

Suddenly he snapped alert. Men rushed forward. Guns whipped from worn holsters. Savagery mingled with the flash of hope on harsh faces. A horse trotted into the dip. A claybank—Sanish's claybank. And in the saddle swayed the old man. The Kid called out. Clay Sanish didn't answer, but the horse whickered and galloped up. A horror cry broke from the girl. The Kid clutched at the reins to halt the mount.

Clay Sanish was tied in the saddle. His eyes, filmed with death, had a fixed, nerve-racking stare.

From the old man's back jutted the hilt of a knife, and stuck to that knife was a scrap of paper with the scrawled name—Brazito.

9

DEATH VALLEY

NO WORD was uttered. Not a man in the clan could have found expression for the turmoil within. The Kid led the girl away. He went back, and the Hordemen carried the body into a bunkhouse, covering the broken old form with a blanket.

Hats off, they stood with bowed heads. They gave mute

tribute to a man they had respected, admired, understood. Grief lined every face. Nate Willstock was the first to move toward the door. Outside, something happened to the men.

Faces hardened. Fever burned in slitted eyes. Savagery twisted scarred features. The killer urge was mounting. Principles, reason, were falling before the promptings of vengeance that throbbed in embittered hearts.

Men bounded for their mounts. The Kid shouted a protest. He was ignored. But he had to stop them. If these hate-maddened men avalanched down on the lowlands, anything in their path would fall. Not campaigners for justice then, but ruthless murderers.

The Kid swung before the mounted clan. Giant reined his stallion, to keep from running the Kid down. The others tugged to a halt. They stared at the young one, bewildered. For the Kid had ice in his heart now, and a wintry coldness in his eyes. His fists wrapped around shiny butts, and naked steel leveled from man to man.

"I'm roddin' this spread!" grated the Kid. "Go over the rim, any gent who figures his idea is good. I'll help yuh down the slope with a slug in yore frame."

The Kid wasn't bluffing. Bluffing wouldn't work with this crowd. He laid it to them hard. He flayed them, called them a flock of sheep in wolves' clothing. As brainless as a Comanche half drowned in fire water. His scorching tirade held them. He told them where they were short. He used names, and he named facts. Then he eased up. He pleaded, and finally he appealed to reason.

"Trailin' them skunks is a job fer two hombres—me an' Eagle," said the Kid. "We'll track 'em. They'll nab us. Then mebbe we can do something for Dandy an' the bunch. Mebbe not. If we all fog down, it'll mean shore death fer 'em. Give us twenty-four hours. Then come on."

They finally agreed, though each man wanted to go with the Kid. But Eagle Hawn had been picked, and the two headed out. They trailed sign at a high lope. The route took them out of the hills, across a broad valley, and into the lower slopes of the San Toribas. Someone followed them. A Hordeman? Kirpas? Creers?

They stopped at a seep spring to rest their mounts. The rider caught up. The Kid frowned at Terry.

"Go back, girl!" he shouted. "Yuh've gone plumb loco. We're ridin' into a trap. We know it. But those devils— Terry, get some sense in yore chucklehead."

The spunky little jaw jutted out. "I have to go, Kid. I'm the sheriff."

The Kid grumbled a lot, but he knew the futility of bucking her stubbornness. They went on. And in the first flush of the gleaming dawn, they reached Sudden River.

"What in thunderation—" exclaimed Eagle Hawn.

The Kid nodded. "That's it. That's the way they've been doing it. I should have known. A dam. Of course."

No water flowed in Sudden River.

The Kid swung toward the cliffs. Where the stream had flowed from under the rock wall, now gaped the black mouth of a tunnel. He stiffened, licked dry lips. Out of the cavern loomed a group of horsemen. Mounts splashed through a shallow pool that recently had been over a man's head.

The riders were garbed in the gaudy trappings of the Mexican dandy. On high-crowned sombreros, silver trimmings flashed in the rising sun. Silk shirts covered wedge-shaped torsos, tightly fitted with jackets of brilliant green and fancy cut. Bell-mouthed trousers of black velveteen flared out over highly polished boots.

"Nice of the boys to meet us so early," said Eagle Hawn with a wry smile. "An' wearing their dancing pants, too."

"Do what you think is right, Kid," said the girl in a tense voice. "I'm with you all the way in this. And don't worry about me."

THE KID shot her a grateful glance. He smiled thinly. Do what was right? He didn't have much choice. He saw a flash high above. Long rifles up there on the cliffs, jutting from crevices in jagged parapets. It looked as though the party was going to proceed just as Brazito wished.

A sleek, swarthy gent on a midnight horse headed the band from the tunnel. Brazito himself—tall, slender, broad of shoulders, with cougarish strength showing in every movement. The early sun caught the sheen of his black pantalones. His green jacket glittered with spangled designs. He swooped his tasseled sombrero from his black head and bowed.

"Handsome devil," said Eagle. "What's that glittering in his eye?"

"A monocle," said the Kid. "He used to be chore boy for an English rancher. Now he spouts high-falootin' lingo an' sticks that glass in his eye, an' thinks he's a gentleman."

Brazito reined up beside the Kid. A leering smile showed glistening teeth beneath a pencil-line mustache. "Welcome to my humble estate, and all that sort of rot. Won't you come een? Want you to see my hideout. Snug leetle place."

The *bandido* bowed to Terry. "Ah, *señorita*, you are so beautiful thees morning. Your veesit ees a gr-reat honor, *si*."

Spics relieved the trio of their guns. Brazito looked up at the cliffs and waved a hand. The rifles vanished. The sun shining in his eyes made him squint. He dropped the monocle, but managed to catch it.

"You're a greenhorn at wrapping your eye around that thing, fancy pants," said Eagle Hawn. "You need more practice."

Brazito adjusted the monocle and scowled. Again it dropped into his hand.

"Where's Dandy?" demanded the Kid. "Where's Sinton an' Rogers? An' all the rest. Where are they?"

"They are well, *Señor* Keed," said the *bandido*. "We took gr-reat care weeth the leetle Dandy, you know. I daresay he ees none the worse for the trip. We'll go een now. The *jefe* ees expecting you."

"The *jefe?*" said the Kid. "That's it, huh? Yo're not the big gun."

Brazito shrugged. "Quite right. I'm not." He shrugged again. "But what the future holds— *Quién sabe?*"

GOING THROUGH the tunnel into the walled-in valley, the Kid learned that Clay Sanish had made a grab for a spic's gun after he'd been disarmed, and a Brazito underling plunged a blade into his back.

"The *jefe* thought eet would be good bait to send heem back," explained Brazito. "And eet was a ripping success, was eet not?"

The Kid put down the urge to wrap his hands around the *bandido's* throat.

They rode out of the cavern into a broad, sun-splashed valley that was green with bunch grass and grama. Aspens and cottonwoods trailed the banks of the stream. A hundred yards ahead stood the dam of sacked sand, crushed rock, and clay.

Brazito shouted an order to a peon. The *paisano* cracked a whip over a donkey harnessed to a treadmill. The donkey began plodding in a circle, winding up the two-inch rope that raised the floodgate. Water gushed along the streambed, and in a few seconds the tunnel was filled.

"Ver-ry simple, ees eet not?" smirked Brazito.

This dam accounted for the vanishing of the cattle from the Gallinas spread. In the distance the Kid saw hundreds of bald-faced Herefords. The cattle were fattening, for there was no short range here. And every beef critter bore the Hatchet brand.

"Manvers weel be quite pleased, I daresay," mimicked the Kid, "when he sees that hees cattle ees gettin' een prime condition for shippin'. Sporting of you, Brazito, an' all that sort o' rot."

The spic's face grew savage. Then a gloating, killer's glint shone in his cruel eyes, and he forced a smile. "Manvers weel nevaire see thees stock again."

"Yeah," broke in Eagle Hawn. "The Horde'll have something to say about that, fancy pants."

Brazito glowered, and the eyeglass fell again. His hand flashed up, caught up the monocle. "Ah, yes, the Horde. Eet weel come een, of a certainty. And the *jefe*, he has been jolly well annoyed weeth the Horde." Brazito's eyes glowed.

"Wup! Look out, fancy pants," said Hawn. "There goes the monocle. Better let me have it. I always wanted to be a dude."

The Kid grew very somber. He knew what this *jefe* was planning, this gent rodding the gun spread with Brazito as his *segundo*. The big boss was working to finish the Horde, to remove the threat that the Horde would always be to his power.

In a clearing on the edge of a spruce grove stood a cluster of white-washed adobes. The buildings were squat, sturdy, built for permanence. If Brazito and his *jefe* got control of the Gallinas grant, they would be able to extend their rustling activities for hundreds of miles. In this fertile valley, trail gaunt cattle could be fattened, the brands blotted—and even a veteran cowhand like Buck wouldn't be able to recognize his stock.

Brazito drew rein before a large adobe. "We go een here. The *jefe* wants a bit of a talk weeth you."

Flanked by six-foot *bandidos*, the trio were ushered into a bare room where a spic with a rifle on his shoulder paced before a door. Brazito knocked. A surly voice responded. The guard opened the door, and Brazito bowed to his captives.

"Walk right in, *amigos*," he said. "Allow me to introduce the wan who weel say whether you live or die. *Señores* and the so beautiful *señorita*, you are now een the presence of Don Bartoleme de Gallinas y Pajarito. Don Bartoleme weel geeve audience to hees guests."

The three stepped into the room. They stopped short. They stopped as though they'd suddenly confronted leveled guns. The girl gasped. Breath went through the Kid's teeth in a hiss. Hawn lunged toward the man behind the table. Two spic six-footers hurled him back against the wall.

"Why, you—" The Kid stopped. He gave the *jefe* a look of loathing that he would have given a crawling thing.

"It can't be!" faltered Terry. "No! Not—him! Not—"

Don Bartoleme laughed. There was venom in the laugh, gloating triumph. "It's true, though. I'm—"

"Kirpas!" rasped the Kid.

"YES—KIRPAS!" PURRED the wizened little man who had been the whining swamper of the Broken Spur Saloon. "That is I played the rôle of Kirpas for over a year. It was interesting. I was constantly amused by the way I was patronized, abused, ridiculed, pitied. But that phase of my life is over."

Kirpas was still the wizened, pinch-faced, humpbacked man of his swamper days, but he was no longer self-effacing. His voice was sharp, sinister, and he had an air of brutal authority. Even his clothes helped to mark the evil change. In contrast to the gaudy flash of his six-foot hirelings, he wore somber, funeral black.

He strode around the table and studied the Kid contemptuously. He rubbed his hands and made mock gestures of humility. "I'm a weak, twisted swamper, Mister Calvert. I'm much too humble to have any real ideas."

He'd taken on that whining tone again. "Gents think I'm just smart enough to know when a spittoon needs cleanin'. But I'm smart, Mister Calvert—in a humble way." Kirpas, now Don Bartoleme, threw back his misshapen head and guffawed. He mouthed an oath. "How I took you in!"

Terry's eyes were jets of flame. "Yes—you took him in, because Kid Calvert saw you as a twisted, deformed person without a friend. You're not just twisted in body, Kirpas. Your mind is all gnarled up. You're crazy. You're a madman."

And there was an insane light in his eyes. "You're right," he rasped. "I'm a madman. I'm crazy to get the power that is rightfully mine. And I've got it." He held his bony hand out palm up and made a fist. "I'm a Gallinas. I've got the royal blood of

Spain in my veins. Yes. And I've come back to claim my heritage."

Kirpas stalked up and down. He told of his father, Francisco Gallinas, driven from the *hacienda* forty years before, because he had married a dance-hall woman. The father had raised the boy on hate. Thirty years had passed since the death of the outcast Gallinas in a street brawl in Montana.

"It took me years to build my plan. But it's been worth the humiliations. What happened to Adolpho? Yes, what happened? I killed him. He was a Gallinas, but not the main branch. He had no right to the Hatchet. I have. I am the rightful heir. And no woman is going to get it. Not my dearly beloved cousin Consuelo." Kirpas' tone was heavy with malice. "You haven't seen her, have you? No. Because she's here. And she's never going out!"

"Yuh wrigglin' little sidewinder," grated the Kid, "I'll tear you in two if you hurt Dona Consuelo."

"Oh, you will!" snarled Kirpas. "Brazito, Mister Calvert will tear me in two."

"A bit optimistic, eh, what, Don Bartoleme?"

It pleased Kirpas' vanity to tell how he'd tricked them. It hadn't just happened, that time Brazito swooped down when the Kid was fighting Boday. Kirpas had sent for his men. Over a month ago, he had shot Deputy Root.

He had planted one of his underlings in the posse of bounty hunters that had ridden with Terry. The renegade had shot Dandy McLain. Kirpas had killed Boday, not for the Kid's sake, but because Boday had failed to get rid of Terry.

"An' now, yuh mangy little chipmunk, what are yuh goin' to do with us?" demanded the Kid.

Kirpas chuckled. "Brazito, he asks what am I going to do with them?"

The guards joined in the laughter.

"Ask 'em another, Kid," said Eagle Hawn. "They find your questions very entertaining."

"I'll tell you what I'm going to do," chuckled Kirpas. "I'm going to make you and all the Horde into swampers. Yes. You're going to clean spittoons. You're going to clear up the leavings of my men."

The owl-hooters laughed.

"Yuh got the makings of a medicine-show comedian, Kirpas," said the Kid. "But yuh oughta lay off the *marijuana*. It's softenin' yore brain."

KIRPAS' FACE hardened. "You and your pack interfered with my plans. And you're going to humble yourselves. I've studied you Hordemen for a year. I learned that you are idealistic fools who'd never work for me. Then you started to mess up my business. And now you're going to be my menials. Or you're going to die."

The Kid yawned.

"Yeah," said Eagle Hawn, "hot air sure makes a jasper drowsy."

Kirpas glowered. He motioned to Brazito, and started out ahead. "Bring them along. They'll learn to respect Don Bartoleme."

Eagle Hawn winked at the Kid and nodded toward Kirpas, who was stepping out the door. A couple of spics stood behind the owl-hooters, prodding them with six-guns. Kirpas was talking to his *segundo*.

"Swamps!" yelled Hawn.

Kirpas swung around. The name had an amazing effect. No longer was he the arrogant master of this killers' hideout. Mentally he was in the Broken Spur again. His shoulders drooped and his mouth fell agape. He took on the cringing manner that had been so familiar to the patrons of the saloon.

"Yes, sir," he cried out in a whining voice. "I'm comin'—"

He actually took a couple of shuffling steps. Then he caught himself, realized with mounting rage and horror what he had done. Even Brazito and the guards had to turn to hide their amusement. Kirpas' face was purpling. He was not far from a stroke.

"See?" said the Kid. "You rig yourself out in fancy duds. You strut an' make big medicine about what yo're goin' to do—but when yore right name is called, yuh come slinkin' along like a cur. Yuh can call yoreself Don Bartoleme de Gallinas y Parjarito—"

"And you can talk about the royal blood in your dried-up veins," added Eagle Hawn.

"But yo're still Swamps!" both of them said at once.

The guards leaped from behind the owl-hooters, out of the line of fire from Kirpas' gun. Terry voiced a little cry of terror. She saw the *jefe's* hand start for his holster. She sprang in front of the Kid, but Brazito swung her back. Eagle Hawn swallowed hard and hunched his shoulders.

This was the end. The Kid knew it. He read the death sentence in Kirpas' glittering eyes. But what was happening to Kirpas? It seemed that the fires of rage were consuming his wasted body. It was an effort for him to get air. He staggered against the wall. They had flayed his ego with contempt, and his burning hate was all but killing him.

A guard brought a canteen of water, held it to his chief's quivering lips. Kirpas regained enough control to stand without support. For a while he was nothing more than a sick man, verging on apoplexy. Veins like whipcords bulged on his forehead. The Kid could see the pulse beating in the little man's neck. Death wasn't far distant for Kirpas. But it loomed closer for the Kid and Eagle Hawn.

Kirpas stood before the owl-hooters whose scorn had robbed him of triumph. "Lucky I got dizzy then. I would have drilled you. Glad I didn't. You wouldn't have suffered. And you're going to suffer. You're going to die a hundred deaths. Today and all night you'll have to think. To think, my brave ones. Do you understand? Then at dawn, gentlemen—at sunrise—"

A chill crawled the Kid's back. His heart trip-hammered,

but his lips tightened grimly against set teeth. Eagle Hawn was breathing heavily. But they hid inner turmoil behind poker masks.

"Say it!" grated the Kid.

"At sunrise," purred Kirpas, "the firing squad!"

10

BRAZITO'S MONOCLE

T HE GIRL moaned. She threw herself at Kirpas, her hand streaking for his gun. Before Brazito could grab her, the Kid had her in his arms. He held her trembling little form in a tight embrace.

"Easy, Terry," he muttered, and his lips brushed her cheek. "Chin up. We're alive yet. An' we intend to see plenty more sunrise. I'll figure something out. You trust me, Terry."

The girl clung to him for a moment, and then they broke the embrace before Brazito could part them. Kirpas rubbed his hands and gloated. His eyes gleamed at the anguish on Terry's face, the anxiety on the Kid's. He chuckled.

"Take them out, Brazito. I'm jest half a man, jest Swamps, the humpy little roustabout who sweeps up after real gents." He guffawed. "Pardon me, gentlemen, if I indulge in a little childish glee. I truly believe that if I had gone on the stage, I would have been a great actor."

Two spics took Terry to an adobe with barred windows. The building stood at the far end of a lane running between two rows of houses. The Kid saw her thrust inside. He took a deep breath. Warmth thawed into the chill of his dread. She was such a splendid little person. No hysterics, no tears or screaming. There'd never lived a person with more courage.

He wished he'd been harder with her on the trail. He wished he had left her bound in some deserted cabin, or with homesteaders who would have held her prisoner. But Terry had had her way, and now the Kid upbraided himself for yielding to her stubbornness.

Across from Terry's prison sounded the explosive voice of Peel Rogers. The Kid's face brightened. Grama Sinton yelled out. Knowing that they were alive helped. He felt better. He had a problem—getting his friends out of a death trap. His mind swarmed with ideas.

Spics shoved the two into a bare cell. Eagle Hawn sat on the floor and rolled a quirley. He rolled it slowly, holding his hands up to show how steady they were. He wiggled his long, tapering fingers. "Babies," he spoke to them, "you've got me into some of the biggest safes in this country. We've been good pards—but I reckon we're not going to whirl any more dials."

"Get that crazy idea outa yore head!" exclaimed the Kid. "We're not goin' to give them spics any target practice."

"Nice sentiment," drawled Hawn. "Tell me your plan."

But the Kid didn't have even a glimmer of a plan. The two of them went to work, and they discarded ideas by the score, because they were suicidal. They could die with a lot less effort. When a spic brought them chuck, they tried to snag his guns, but a cry from the *bandido* brought his cronies swarming in, and they gave the two a slugging and took away their grub.

"Looked like tasteless chuck, anyway," muttered the Kid, nursing a knuckle he'd bruised on a spic's jaw.

"I needed the exercise," said Eagle Hawn, holding a bandana to a flesh split on his cheek. "Was getting a bit cramped up."

Night came, and they were still racking their heads for the right idea. Both of them maintained a flippant attitude, but their faces showed the strain.

"We need shut-eye," said the Kid. "Pile that straw in the corner, Eagle, an' pound yore ear. An' I mean sleep. We're not goin' to die. Settle yore mind on that. There's some way of outsmarting those skunks—an' we'll find it."

They sprawled out, and they slept. They could thank their

owl-hoot training for that. Twice the Kid awakened when the guards changed. The third time, he jumped to his feet. A key rattled in the lock. Eight men stood in squad formation outside. Brazito was there, and Kirpas, eager eyed. In the east dawn was breaking.

The Kid's heart thumped. He had a sudden panicky feeling that clawed at his vitals. Then anger surged up at the sight of Kirpas. The Kid got a grip on himself. He couldn't let that shriveled-up specimen of animal life finish him. There was some way of tricking Kirpas.

"Nice an' easy, pard," whispered the Kid to Eagle, who looked ready to charge into those killers. "I've got an idea."

He didn't have an idea, not even the hint of one. But he had to steady Eagle. An attack now would bring a hurricane of steel slugs.

Kirpas jeered at them. Brazito exhibited mock sympathy. The prisoners were marched to a formation of rocks a short way from the adobes. Slowly the sun climbed above the eastern peaks. On the cliffs over Sudden River a lone sentinel stood guard. With the stream closing the entrance to the valley, that spic could stand off an army.

The owl-hooters were forced against the rocks. A mad swirl of pictures spun through the Kid's mind. He glanced at the sun. The Horde would be on the way. But the Calvert men would never get in. Not unless they got help from those in the valley.

The Kid gnawed at his lip until crimson trickled down his chin. Kirpas laughed. The spics stood in line, waiting for the order.

"Have my recent benefactors any last words?" asked Kirpas.

Eagle Hawn's face had a greenish tinge. Hope had fled from his eyes. He pressed his hands against his sides so no one could see that they shook. But defiance hadn't left him, nor contempt for Kirpas.

"Sure, Swamps, when you start your morning chores, sweep

the cobwebs out of our house. You've been neglecting your broom lately."

A VEIN throbbed in Kirpas' forehead, but he leered. "All right, my brave infants. You've had your say. Get ready, men."

A wild light leaped into the Kid's eyes. That was it. Kirpas had given the word. The Kid should have thought of it before. But his mind had been so filled with other things that he hadn't seen the significance. Maybe he was taking a shot in the dark. But he had nothing more to lose. He yelled for Kirpas to stop his men.

"I'm askin' yuh to hold fire just a few seconds!" he ripped out. "That's all. Then fire. Then blow our heads off. I'll die. Shore! But there'll be a secret locked in my corpse.

"How long ago did yore old man get plugged? Thirty years. Yeah. For more than thirty years, yuh've been plannin', plannin'. For all that time yuh've been the shadow over the Gallinas spread. If yuh kill me, there'll be a shadow over yuh. Kirpas, I found the son of Consuelo Gallinas. The rightful heir to the Hatchet is in safe hands."

Kirpas motioned for his men to lower their rifles. Fury twisted his pinched little face. Murderous hatred burned in his eyes, but the Kid knew that his shot had struck home. That little baby in the care of the Creers *was* the son of Consuelo Gallinas.

"Kill me, Kirpas," grated the Kid, "an' yuh'll never learn the whereabouts of that boy." If it were left for the Kid to tell, Kirpas would never learn, anyway—no matter what torture he put him to. "That boy will be raised as you were raised—to strike vengeance. That boy will live to destroy yuh, Kirpas."

The swamper who had become a king stared at the Kid for a long while. Then he snarled: "Take them back to their cells. I thought you had something to do with Ramon's disappearance, Calvert. I knew he'd been left with the Creers. But they had sloped when I got to their place. Uh huh. So Ramon Gallinas will live to destroy me! Not unless you die—"

"The Horde!" The cry in Spanish shrilled down from the cliffs.

The sentinel sent out a call for help. His rifle barked. Outside the valley, guns blasted in a thunderous roll. Kirpas' eyes glittered. Spics were running from the adobes. The Kid's heart sank. The Horde would be wiped out. The Horde didn't have a chance unless—

Kirpas ordered two men to take the prisoners back. "Now we will welcome Calvert's Horde to our happy valley. It is as I hoped for. To the cliffs, every man of you. Kid Calvert, I'll attend to you later."

The Kid's eyes locked with Eagle's in a look of understanding. The *bandidos* headed on a run for the valley's wall. The guards prodded the owl-hooters along with their rifles. They went without protest. Again their eyes locked, and Eagle gave a slight nod of understanding.

They rounded a corner of an adobe. Suddenly the Kid sidestepped, leaped backwards. He caught the *bandido's* rifle barrel under his arm, wrenched violently. The spic cracked out oaths. The weapon went spinning, and the *bandido* grabbed for a knife. But the blade never got out of its sheath.

The Kid whirled, delivering a right to the solar plexus that made the half-breed jackknife into the path of a bone-shattering left hook. The second punch relieved the renegade of his senses.

Eagle had done the same trick. His man brandished a knife. The Kid belted the spic on the elbow, sent the steel sliver flying. Eagle darted in, planted two well-timed hooks on the chin, and that man was out of commission.

They used bandanas to tie the spics. The Kid took a ring of keys from one of them. Grabbing their rifles and bandoliers, they raced back to the rock where they had stood for their execution. *Bandidos* were swarming up the cliff's wall. Eagle Hawn knelt and fired at the sentinel. The third shot sent the spic hurtling over the parapets to the range below. An exultant shout went up from outside.

Eagle began peppering the wall with steel-jacketed bullets. But the Kid's fire was directed elsewhere. The Kid aimed at the rope that held up the dam's floodgate. Slug after slug he triggered at the rope. At the distance he missed often. But he kept up that hail of bullets. And then the last strand parted. The weighted floodgate came down with a bang. Cries of alarm sounded from the cliffs.

Kirpas and Brazito were bellowing orders. Spics slid down the wall, rushed toward the river bank. Already the tunnel was empty of water.

"Wham hell outa them, Eagle!" yelled the Kid.

Hoofs splashed through the dwindling stream. A huge man on a powerful stallion plunged from the cavern. Giant Anderson, operating a pair of sixes, and picking *bandidos* off the valley's wall. And there was Nate Willstock. Among the Hordemen pouring through the tunnel dashed old man Creers. Buck Manvers rode with Curly and Joe flanking him.

The Kid raced for the adobes. He found the building where Dandy and the rest were prisoners. He had the guard's keys, and one of them fitted the lock. The cook and Grama Sinton bounded out to help entertain.

Yelling a greeting to Dandy, the Kid sprinted across the street where Terry, Mary Little Fawn, and Consuelo Gallinas were locked up.

D O N A C O N S U E L O was a beautiful woman, dark and regal. She wrung the Kid's hand. "*Señor,* is my baby—"

"Full of mischief an' gettin' fat," the Kid reassured her. "The Creers have the little fellow."

"And poor Berta is dead," said the dona softly. "She was the nurse. Terry has told me what happened. A cougar—" She paused. Her eyes misted. "We were driving to the *hacienda* when that Bartoleme attacked us. *Señor,* it was horrible. Bartoleme killed my majordomo. But Berta fled with my Ramon."

"Well, yuh have nothing more to worry about, Dona Consuelo," said the Kid. "Yore cattle are here. Old Buck Manvers has a lot of years left, and he'll build up the Hatchet again. Yore troubles are over."

"Sure of that, are you?"

The Kid whirled. In the doorway stood Hermanas Brazito, leaning easily against the jamb. His gun was holstered, but he had a split-second draw. The monocle still glittered in his right eye.

"I'm on my way out," said Brazito. "There ees another tunnel, you know. Too small for a horse. Sorry to be such a beastly boor, but I'll need a couple of hostages. You—*Señorita* Terry. And the dona—"

The Kid choked back an oath. Eyes blazing, he advanced slowly.

"Wouldn't be too rash, Keed," said Brazito. "I'm quite the master here. Eef the medico comes from the other house, I'll keel him. Then you."

And still the Kid advanced. He was playing a deadly game. Brazito leered. His hand moved slowly toward his gun.

"I'm goin' to kill yuh, Brazito!" rasped the Kid. "I'm goin'—to—kill—you!"

"So!" Brazito glowered.

The Kid lunged in. He smashed in a paralyzing overhand right. His left grabbed for Brazito's gunhand. But there was no need. The one smash had done the work. Brazito was down. His monocle had betrayed him. For when the *bandido* glowered, his monocle always fell. And when it fell, his hand instinctively flashed up to catch it. That move proved enough to give the Kid time to belt in a haymaker.

Down the valley gunfire had ceased. The war was over, and the Horde brought in half of Brazito's men as prisoners. But not Kirpas. Kirpas was dead. Though no bullet had struck him. Doc Ringel's professional eye determined the cause at a glance. Apoplexy.

Terry had Brazito and a lot of *bandidos* to take back to Deadline. Old Creers brought happy news of little Ramon Gallinas to the dona. And the Horde got a new member—Doc Ringel.

The Kid managed to get Terry alone for a few moments.

"Well, yuh've ridden with the Horde. Yuh've lived at our camp. You've seen us work. Now haven't yuh got a different attitude toward us?"

She shook her head. "You—were—wonderful," she murmured. "But—but you're still outlaws. I can never change my attitude. I wish I could, Kid!"

"You're the most unreasonable person in the world!"

"I've been brought up on law and order," said the girl softly. "You know my stand. Nothing comes before duty. Some day, Kid Calvert, I'm going to bring you in. You and the Horde. Like I'm bringing in Brazito. That's my duty. But I can't fulfill my duty now."

She threw her arms around him, pinioning his arms to his sides, kissed him. Then she broke away and ran.

The Kid stared, stunned and speechless. Besides the certainty of death, he was sure of only one other thing—that there was no understanding a woman.